A Broken Gears Tale

Falcon's Favor

Dana Fraedrich

Other titles by Dana Fraedrich:

SKATEBOARDS, MAGIC, AND SHAMROCKS
Skateboards, Magic, and Shamrocks ~ Summer 2012
Heroes, Legends, and Villains ~ Autumn 2015

BROKEN GEARS
Out of the Shadows (Lenore's storyline 1) ~ Autumn 2016
Into the Fire (Lenore's storyline 2) ~ Autumn 2017
Raven's Cry (standalone prequel) ~ Spring 2018
Across the Ice (Lenore's storyline 3) ~ Autumn 2019
Falcon's Favor (standalone queer cozy mystery romance) ~ Autumn 2022
Death Cults and Taxes (short story collection) ~ Autumn 2023

This book is a work of fiction. Any references to historical events, real people, or real locales are used fictitiously. Other names, characters, places, and incidents are the product of the author's imagination, and any resemblance to actual events or locales or persons, living or dead, is entirely coincidental.

Copyright 2022 Dana Fraedrich

All rights reserved

No part of this publication may be reproduced, distributed, or transmitted in any form or by any means, including photocopying, recording, or other electronic or mechanical methods, without the prior written permission of the publisher, except as permitted by U.S. copyright law. For permission requests, contact Dana via her Contact form at www.wordsbydana.com/contact.

Book cover by Dana Fraedrich

Chapter heading art by Dana Fraedrich

Cover and chapter heading art digital scrapbook pieces courtesy Doudou's Design

Maps by Hannah Pickering and Heather Boyajian

First edition 2022

ISBN-13: 979-8-218-02668-4

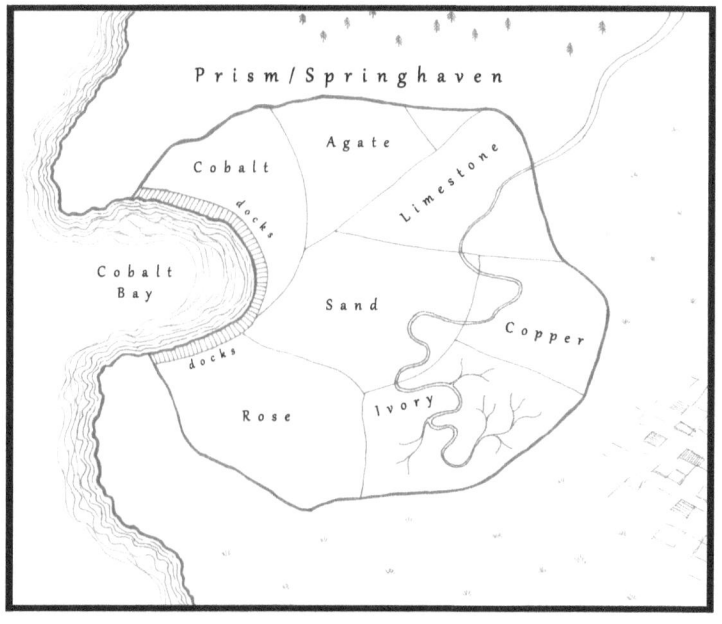

Falcon's Favor

Contents

Chapter 1 ~ 8

Chapter 2 ~ 21

Chapter 3 ~ 31

Chapter 4 ~ 40

Chapter 5 ~ 52

Chapter 6 ~ 64

Chapter 7 ~ 78

Chapter 8 ~ 89

Chapter 9 ~ 97

Chapter 10 ~ 108

Chapter 11 ~ 119

Chapter 12 ~ 128

Chapter 13 ~ 138

Chapter 14 ~ 146

Chapter 15 ~ 157

Chapter 16 ~ 170

Chapter 17 ~ 179

Chapter 18 ~ 183

Chapter 19 ~ 192

Dana Fraedrich

Chapter 20 ~ 198

Chapter 21 ~ 206

Chapter 22 ~ 215

Chapter 23 ~ 222

Chapter 24 ~ 235

Chapter 25 ~ 244

An Excerpt from *Out of the Shadows* ~ 251

Acknowledgements ~ 255

About the Author ~ 258

~Chapter 1~

The flat was... well, it wasn't *that* bad, right?

Falcon looked around the parlor, *his* new parlor. Though "new" by any measure other than it being his—well, partially his—would be laughable.

"It has Old World charm," Beatrice had said of the place.

Literally, Falcon thought to himself now.

Beatrice had been the one to find this "hidden treasure," for him at a bargain monthly rate. Being the daughter of a well-to-do politician came with gaggles of connections, which had come in rather handy given Falcon's sudden limit in resources. He was forever impressed by but could never understand how the socialite bore traversing the complex web of favors and politics with the grace she did.

Like the entire row of houses all along this street, and the next, and the next, the building he stood in now had been constructed just over a century ago after the cataclysmic War of Light, and in short order no less. So much in the city of Springhaven had been destroyed then, and these row homes had been a quick fix for much-needed housing. Walls covered in stained, peeling wallpaper tried to liven up the old place, while windows with ratty wooden frames and thin glass radiated cold against the warmth of the room.

A brick fireplace sat inside the back wall, squashed beneath the stairway to the second level and giving off some fantastic heat against the early spring chill pressing in from the outside. Falcon could see through the back of it to the kitchen on the other side of the wall. A hook for hanging cookware and other fireplace accouterments peeked through the sooty opening.

Mismatched furniture gathered around this side of the fireplace—a long sofa, a battered wingback chair, and what looked like a trio of dining chairs from different sets. These had been provided by his new roommate. Falcon had yet to meet the chap, however, as beggars—thankfully not literally—couldn't be choosers. The scuffs all over the timeworn wooden floor made it look as if this set or previous furniture had often taken lively turns about the room. Petrolsene sconces dotted the wall at intervals, though the wan but persistent sunlight coming in through the grimy windows was filling in for them at the moment. Falcon didn't need to know much about architecture to guess that every other row home along this road shared the exact same floor plan.

Falcon was grateful for the warmth of the fireplace, as the cold made his service injuries ache—injuries that made him feel much older than his nineteen years. Those same injuries were the reason he was currently leaning on a telescoping cane, one he was still getting used to. The handle probably needed some adjustment, but the last few weeks, full of moving preparations as they'd been, hadn't left much time for such things.

Falcon ventured further inside the house and leaned through the open doorway that led into the small… could it even be called a corridor? Whatever its proper name, he looked around the space which served as both a corridor and landing for the stairs, neatly tucked between the door to the sitting room and the kitchen door.

Gazing up the harrowingly steep and narrow staircase to the second floor where the bedrooms must surely be, Falcon grimaced. *Not sure how the movers will get my bed and things through there.*

A knock at the front door made him turn. He felt his cheeks flush with embarrassment as he once again took in the motley crew of furniture and tatty decor, and he hurried to stand up straight on his own power rather than leaning so heavily on the cane. For which his body rewarded him with a gentle warning twinge.

"Hello," trilled Beatrice Holmes' voice as she pushed open the front door with nothing more than a finger's touch.

Seeing how easily she pushed open the door, Falcon wondered if he'd failed to close it or if it had been contrary when he wasn't looking. In either case, he took control now and ensured it was shut before taking Beatrice's proffered hand in greeting.

"I trust you found the little gem of a place all right?" she asked.

Beatrice began to stroll about the room with the same poise and charm as if entering a garden party thrown in her honor, and nothing in her manner showed any disagreement with their rough surroundings. Though her burgundy satin visiting dress, with its ruffles and bustle and ruching and all, couldn't help but make every inch of the flat seem even more tired and washed out.

Nevertheless, Beatrice's composure put Falcon at ease, and he returned to leaning on his cane. At that, he heard his grandfather's voice in his head, remonstrating: "Don't slouch. It makes you look soft." Falcon banished the thought. Given that he was no longer on speaking terms with his grandfather—both a blessing and a curse—he didn't appreciate the reminder, thank you very much. Even so, he stood up straight again. They were familiar with one another, true, but Beatrice was still a lady.

She carried on with her perusal of the flat. "Rather quaint, being tucked away back here, isn't it? It's a sweet little hideaway, which I imagine will serve you well given your newfound celebrity."

Falcon swallowed down no less than three different responses, failing to decide on one. By "tucked away," Beatrice had referred to the fact that this particular set of joined-up homes were down a side street—barely more than an alley, really—which came off a forked road, which was, thankfully, attached to a main thoroughfare.

"Quaint," of course, also referred to the size of the place, which was a mere splinter compared to the family manor in which he'd, until very recently, lived his entire life. That manor, as with so many homes like it, was located in Springhaven's Rose district. This "little gem" was in the Cobalt quarter, which was, well… Cobalt played by its own rules. It was different things to different people, sometimes changing for the same person within a single day. On the way here, Falcon had seen a large, grimy steamworks repair shop next door to a tiny, shiny, high-end watchmaker's and a bustling cafe next to that with people from all walks of life seeping in through and spilling out the entryway as they came and went.

And finally, "newfound celebrity" was about the fact that he was the Enforcers' new poster boy for their recently-formed emergency response unit—literally; his image graced posters all over the city. The detachment had been created partly in response to the fact that, previously, Springhaven had no unified team trained and available to deploy in the case of crises. But also as an attempt to clean up the Enforcer order's public image, which to many was not much better than a gang of thugs who happened to be on the right side of the law.

It had been a little over a month since the harrowing raid on Springhaven's catacombs, during which Falcon had assisted the city's so-called peacekeeping order with taking down a strange syndicate of criminals called the Reaper's Collective. Operative word being "assisted," though the fact that he'd had to take leadership of the operation when his C.O. had gone down—not dead, thankfully, just injured—had rather propelled Falcon to career stardom. Which had then turned awkward when he'd publicly defamed his grandfather, who'd been a well-respected Second in said order—a high rank indeed—but who had grossly abused his power for years.

That brought Falcon back to today, to his new flat. His family was… disappointed wasn't the right word, but these last few weeks since the scandalous revelation had been tense. He could have gone to live at the Enforcer barracks, but ratting out a brother in arms made that an even less welcoming place than his family's manor. At least his parents still liked him enough to pay for movers. The thought made Falcon's cheeks go from hot to cold. Beatrice knew this place was the only one he could afford on both such short notice and his civil servant salary, so he wasn't quite as embarrassed with her as he might have been with someone else. But the thought of movers seeing this place, of them bringing his grand furnishings in here… it made him want to catch them in the street and send them back from whence they came. And he absolutely refused to think of his family coming to visit. In fact, he'd told them not to. At least not until he'd settled in, he'd said. Not that his parents nor either of his sisters, both of whom were younger, had volunteered to come round for tea.

A long silence had passed while Falcon was lost in thought, and Beatrice gave the appearance of not having noticed as she sedately took in their surroundings. She went on. "I admit, it's a bit of a fixer upper, but I'm sure you and Keene will spruce it up in no time."

Ah, yes, the mysterious roommate known only as Keene. All

Falcon knew was that Keene was about his age and, as Beatrice had put it, "In need of new lodgings as soon as possible."

"Having you here already does half the sprucing job for us," came a smooth response from the corridor.

Falcon turned toward the voice, and the sight of the young man leaning against the doorframe made him freeze.

The man was, in a word, radiant. Thick black hair more than a touch longer than current fashion dictated brushed around his shoulders in loose waves. It was the perfect accent to his warm medium brown skin, which peeked scandalously through his shirt, a button or two of which he'd apparently forgotten to button. His dark eyes glittered from a kind, open face, made kinder by the pearly white smile he flashed at Beatrice. The smile was what caught Falcon's gaze for longer than anything else. It was not the ambitious smile of a man who'd decided—foolishly—that he was a match for Beatrice. Nor was it the insincere bearing of teeth Falcon saw so often among the Enforcer order, which was full of backbiting and vitriol. No, this man smiled at Beatrice with pure, unadulterated joy.

Falcon's Enforcer training kicked in then, always on the lookout for trouble. Not that he was worried about Beatrice in particular; he'd seen her decimate powerful men with naught but a single word. But he shouldn't risk underestimating this newcomer. Then again, was he new? No, he'd come from further inside the house. He must have gotten here before Falcon even, so why hadn't he come out before? Was that suspicious? To be fair, Falcon hadn't been here more than a few minutes.

The man certainly didn't appear threatening. His movements were easy and relaxed, fluid like a stream, as he walked fully into the room.

"Keene!" Beatrice sang upon seeing the man.

When they met, they took one another by the arms, grasping each other at the elbows, and popped kisses into the air on either side of the others' face. Falcon suddenly wondered if the man— Keene, apparently—was one of Beatrice's paramours.

"I knew you'd arranged for your furniture to be here, but I didn't think you were coming until tomorrow," Beatrice said in surprise. That was a rare sight indeed; she was almost always a step ahead of everyone else.

Keene gave a nonchalant shrug, as if moving house for him was as easy as changing waistcoats. "My old roommate didn't mind if I left ahead of schedule, so I did."

Blazes, Falcon envied the way he moved. Falcon knew enough of society to know he himself was fairly attractive as such things went. He was tall, taller than Keene anyway, and had his own handsome mane of hair, though it was much shorter than Keene's, always budging against Enforcer regulations, which allowed no more than two inches of length. Falcon's hair was a rather drab walnut color, however, and liked to piece itself into straight, spiny factions, despite his best efforts to tame it. His own skin, which, before last year, had always carried a healthy wheat hue about it, looked sallow now. That, along with his uncertain mobility, was thanks to some misadventures from last year, which included but was not limited to having been blasted into a tree during an attack on the Enforcer headquarters, the Halls of Justice, by the Reaper's Collective. Falcon had subsequently spent some time in a coma and had since then fought an uphill battle to regain his previous vigor. He suddenly wanted to hide the cane he leaned on, to prevent this lithe, beautiful man from seeing his greatest flaws. The saving grace in this shadow of his former self Falcon had become was his eyes—such a bright light brown they were nearly golden.

Something in Keene's previous statement raised a flag in Falcon's brain. "Old roommate?" Falcon asked. And then the upper class gentleman in him mentally cringed. He hadn't even been introduced to the man and he was asking impertinent questions. The Enforcer side of him, however, told the gentle born side to shove it.

Before Falcon could even begin to consider how to recover, Beatrice was smoothing things over, as she was so adept at doing. "Oh dear me, how very rude of me. Falcon, darling, come here. I'd like to present Mister Keene Kohli. And this is… apologies, Falcon, what's the shiny new title you just received?"

Falcon was grateful he'd managed to almost completely hide his limp as he approached—it was something he'd been working hard to accomplish. The current formalities, though, made him feel just as uncomfortable.

He cleared his throat before answering, "Steward of the Sage, but Falcon is fine, thank you."

Keene tipped his head to the side in a way that made Falcon feel he was definitely being assessed. The man's smile, though genuine, didn't hold nearly the same amount of warmth it had for Beatrice. "I should hope so, given that we'll be sharing the same house. Bit of a mouthful saying the whole title every time we see one another."

"Yes, I suppose so." Falcon rubbed the back of his neck. "And not a nice mouthful at that." The sentence he'd just uttered seemed to turn back on the air and stare at him in the face, questioning why it existed in the first place. "Not that…" he began, trying to recover before realizing he had no idea where he was going.

Stop before you make it worse, said his inner filter. *Please!*

Falcon coughed once before finishing, "Lovely to meet you. I'm sure we'll get on very well."

As they shook hands, Falcon got a whiff of spices from Keene. He didn't know cooking well enough to know what kind, but the scent was warm, as warm as Keene's chestnut skin, and reminded Falcon of pies during New Year's week.

"Rough hands," Keene said as the handshake ended. "Is that from holding a truncheon so much?"

That drenched the warm feeling like a bucket of ice water. Keene's tone hadn't been sharp, but Falcon couldn't tell if he'd just been making idle conversation either. The Enforcers had earned their reputation for cruelty hundreds of times over, true, but Falcon had always tried to be different. He strived to be better, to be a force for good from the inside. If Keene did despise Falcon simply on the basis of his job, then Falcon couldn't blame him. But the barb hit a tender spot inside and stung like Keene had been wielding a truncheon of his own, a verbal one.

I can fix this, Falcon automatically thought to himself. *Say something helpful.*

But before Falcon could think of anything, Beatrice put in, "Steward of the Sage is the name for the head of the Enforcers' new crisis response unit." Her tone made it sound as if she was dropping an interesting little factoid into the conversation over luncheon. Falcon couldn't decide if he wished he'd thought to say that or was glad he'd had the wherewithal not to. His new title did sound a bit self-aggrandizing.

"I know," was Keene's only reply.

Very well, I won't fix it by talking about work, Falcon decided. *But I can still fix this.*

Before he could venture down that path, however, a knock rapped against the front door. It obligingly opened under the force, which had not sounded particularly forceful, and Falcon scowled at the stubborn door. It seemed all too happy to let anyone just walk right in.

"Hello?" called a gruff but professional voice into the house. Whoever was on the other side was clearly confused but too polite to step inside. "Is there a Mister Falcon Smoke at home?"

"You're right on time," Beatrice chirped, sweeping over to the door.

The movers! Falcon had completely forgotten to think up an excuse for turning them away, what with being all distracted by handsome new acquaintances and all. Perhaps he could fabricate some tale about... *Oh, I don't know, floor gophers or something.*

He made a strangled sort of noise before blurting, "Never thank you!" He had meant to say, "no, thank you" before his mind switched to, "nevermind." His mouth hadn't been able to keep up, however, and thus he'd smashed the phrases together instead.

Both Beatrice and Keene gave him quizzical glances. Falcon rubbed the back of his neck again, mumbled an apology, and traipsed over to the door. Why, he didn't know. She was already taking command of the situation and giving the movers orders. Falcon stood by, however, wanting to be helpful and equally wanting to slink away as the pieces of his grand bedroom set were heaved into the house and up the stairs... or merely attempted to, in some cases. In the end, getting the headboard, a huge, solid piece of carved hardwood, up the skinny stairway was beyond both human ability and physics. Given that the rest of the four-poster bed would be tragically sloped without it, the movers set what they called chocks beneath the frame to level it. It turned out that "chocks" was just a fancy word for "hunks of wood," and Falcon thanked the stars for the dust ruffle, which would cover them. He also cursed the dust ruffle because the fine, hand embroidered fabric looked positively ridiculous against the chipped and pockmarked plaster walls and dusty wood floors of his new bedroom.

While everyone got to work—or in Falcon's case, watched everyone else get to work—Keene put on a pot of tea and laid on some sinfully buttery biscuits. Falcon took the opportunity to offer a hand, rough though it may be from truncheon swinging.

See, I'm helpful, and not a thoughtless lout.

But Keene seemed perfectly in his element in the kitchen and politely declined, barely sparing Falcon a glance. So then Falcon went and stood by Beatrice. Not that she needed the help. Beatrice was the kind of person who... well, if a steamroller was made of flowers and charm, that was her. It was best to stay out of her way and let her get on, but Falcon stood by, ready to assist should she call.

See, Keene, I know when to stand down, and I'm happy to do so. Falcon did have to remind himself not to stand quite so much at attention, though. That was at least made easier by the fact that standing at attention made his injuries complain. *See, I can relax too. I'm just as easygoing as you... alright, that might be a stretch.*

And when the tea was ready, Falcon jumped at the opportunity to serve the movers theirs.

Just look at how I think of others first.

They, in turn, happily took a break and removed themselves and their teacups out to their moving wagons. Falcon expected Keene to object, as it must have been Keene's drinkware the movers had absconded with—albeit, not far—but the man just sat next to Beatrice with his own refreshment in hand and left them to it. Only then did Falcon realize he'd fallen prey to one of the twisted beliefs his grandfather had tried to drill into him:

"The poorer classes are a drain on society. They'll steal from you as soon as look at you. They ought to put forth a little effort and better their situations instead of asking for handouts."

Falcon mentally shook himself. He'd worked hard to shed those so-called "lessons" and was grateful his parents, who had far better hearts and more sense, had, over the years, helped to undo the damage. Though any direct battles with the family's patriarch were few, far between, and carefully chosen, for it was he who controlled the Smoke family wealth.

Thus, with his moral compass realigned, Falcon too settled into the mismatched furniture of the sitting room. He must have been more drawn than he'd realized because he nearly groaned with pleasure as the restorative brew washed over his lips.

"This might be the best tea I've ever had," he said, unabashedly relieved by the reminder that there were still some reliable things in this world, things like good strong tea and rich biscuits.

"It's my own signature blend." Keene took a sip from his own teacup. Chipped, Falcon noticed, but Keene did not elaborate.

"I'd have had the chipped cup," Falcon said. Why he'd thought to fill the void with that, he didn't know. Clammy horror washed over him. Why was he pointing out the shabby state of Keene's teaware?!

Finally, blissfully, Keene granted Falcon a small smile. It was not as luminous as the one he'd given Beatrice earlier, but it was warm and genuine and made Falcon's clammy embarrassment evaporate like dew in the sun.

"What kind of host would I be if I'd served you a chipped cup?"

In a less than genteel move, Falcon shrugged. He immediately heard his grandfather's voice in his head, admonishing him for such a flippant gesture: "A man does not shrug. A man makes a strong answer."

"Given that we're roommates now," he said, ignoring his grandfather's voice, "I'd hardly hold it against you."

Beatrice smiled at them both and steered the conversation into amiable waters—the latest fashions, some new plays that had recently premiered, and other easy subjects. Falcon wanted to ask Keene a million questions. The man's manners implied he was gentle born as well, but why then was he living here with Falcon? Falcon's self-inflicted downfall had been painfully public. He had a feeling Beatrice knew the answer, as she kept their conversation neatly reined inside what were apparently safe spaces for the both of them.

The movers meanwhile were jolly pleased by the treats and all had a new spring in their step after they'd partaken. Maybe they weren't even judging Falcon as harshly as he'd imagined. It, and Keene's warming regard, gave Falcon a new lightness of heart. He wasn't even bothered when the head mover reported that some of the neighbors had come out and were sniffing around Falcon's fine things. The man had, in no uncertain terms, told them to shove off. Falcon knew his was a strange situation, but it was a situation he didn't expect to remain in. Once he was back on his feet and had saved up a little money, he'd move along to something more permanent… and far less dingy.

By the time the sun was going down, Falcon's bedroom set had been unloaded as best as possible. Beatrice had made her apologies and left by then, citing another engagement but promising to return soon to see how the two were getting on. Falcon's writing desk was upstairs with the bed now. And given how much room just those took up, he'd opted for his favorite chair to join the gathering of furniture misfits in the sitting room. Unwilling new denizens to the collection were Falcon's headboard, which he wasn't sure what he'd do with just yet, as well as his stately wardrobe, which had been even more of a lost cause than the headboard. Both had been painted in the striking blue-grey shades of a peregrine falcon, making them stand out like sore thumbs even more than they otherwise might.

The mover's payment had already been arranged, though it was apparently customary to tip. Falcon's funds, after putting down his deposit on the house, were severely diminished. Also, what was an appropriate tip after a gaggle of lads had just heaved your ridiculously oversized furniture from one place to another? Falcon had always hated tipping. It was such an odd affair—"Yes, let me pass judgment on your performance via this arbitrary amount of money and we'll both steep in the awkwardness of this moment together."

Just as Falcon was standing before the foreman and dithering, Keene glided over and pressed a tin of biscuits and a packet of his tea blend into the foreman's hands. A card was attached to the tin's top, and Falcon read just quick enough to catch the words "events catering."

"We're a bit light on funds, but I hope this shows our appreciation," Keene said, bearing another one of those magnificent smiles. He then lifted a hand to the side of his face and said in a stage whisper, "I've included some of my special chocolate and orange biscuits too."

The foreman thanked them both and left without seeming upset about the lack of extra payment. Again, why not just charge what you want to earn? That thought, however, was quickly replaced with a new realization: For the first time in his life, Falcon was *alone*. On his own in this new environment with no safety tether. Not even socially, and he looked at Keene, the stranger with whom he now lived. Falcon suddenly felt as if he was treading water and possibly or possibly not surrounded by sharks. If there were sharks, were they going to attack? Maybe, if he said the wrong thing.

No, Falcon assured himself, *You're being dramatic. All will be well.* No imagined real or nonexistent sharks existed... no, wait, that didn't make sense. He decided to leave the shark analogy for now.

"So, Keene, here we are," he said, and then immediately felt stupid for such an obvious statement.

"We are." Falcon got the distinct impression a different expression was hiding beneath Keene's easy countenance, but he couldn't guess what it might be. "Not for long, though. I'm heading out. Nice meeting you and all. Best of luck unpacking your things. If you need it, I've gotten some of my cookware set up in the kitchen already. It's not my good stuff, so don't feel like you need to be too precious with it."

Falcon swallowed a strangled noise of alarm. He hadn't even thought about the fact that he'd have to cook for himself, something he'd never done, not once, in his entire life. With everything else that had been happening, that hadn't occurred to him. No need for Keene, the blender and brewer of spectacular tea and creator of peace-making biscuits, to know how feckless he was in that area, though. Not yet anyway.

"Mind if I tag along?" he asked instead.

He didn't know if he had the funds to go out, nor even how expensive Keene's little excursion might be, but he didn't fancy spending the evening alone with his lack of cooking skills and surrounded by reminders of all he'd lost in the pursuit of doing the right thing. Falcon could always learn how to boil an egg or something tomorrow.

Keene gave him a sheepish smile—the first time Falcon had seen the man lose his cool and collected air—and Falcon knew the answer before it even came out. "Sorry, chap, but it's sort of a prearranged thing."

Falcon was already nodding, "Of course, of course. Apologies. It was rude of me to be so forward."

He'd broken eye contact, looking for anything in the flat that might provide even a halfway graceful escape. Maybe he could slip out a window or something without Keene noticing. Right, that seemed plausible. A warm tone in Keene's voice brought Falcon's attention back.

"Perhaps we can do something together tomorrow?"

Had Keene actually noticed how earnest Falcon had tried to be? He dared to hope that it had improved his new housemate's opinion of him.

Keene added with a kind half-smile, "We can make dinner and get to know one another."

The whole cooking affair was still very much a problem, and a part of Falcon couldn't help but wonder if Keene was avoiding introducing him, the horrible Enforcer, to his friends, but it was a start. Besides, how long could it take to learn to cook? And showing Keene he wasn't, in fact, horrible would happen along the way. Falcon would just pick up a cookbook on the way home, give it a skim, and problem solved.

He felt a smile bloom on his own face. "Tomorrow will be great."

~Chapter 2~

Tomorrow was anything but great. The night before, Falcon had taken one look at the stove in the kitchen—with all its knobs and warnings about petrolsene leaks and explosions and whatnot—gave up, and headed out alone to get himself some dinner. Unfortunately, the only food purveyors open at that time were proper restaurants—far too expensive—and street vendors selling all manner of dodgy-looking food from wheeled stalls. The latter hawked their goods as their rolling, cooking, steaming contraptions clattered over the cobblestone streets and through pools of soft, yellow petrolsene light thrown onto the road from street lamps and the occasional still-open eatery. Falcon had odd feelings about buying food off a cart in the street.

Was it clean?

What even was a bloater?

Were sheep's trotters exactly what they sounded like?

In the end, Falcon had given up and headed home and then to bed hungry, which meant he slept poorly. That morning, he'd awoken famished. And not just that but running late, which meant there weren't but scraps left at the Enforcer mess hall by the time Falcon arrived—via a hansom cab worth every precious copper for its quickness. The mess hall food wasn't free either, but it was extremely cheap… in every sense possible. There, he'd inhaled a cup of tea the color and flavor of old dishwater; a questionable sausage link; a lonely portion of egg white; and a bowl of the healthful but heavy, grey grain-mush also fed to prisoners at the Halls of Justice. It left him with just enough time to arrive last at his first shift of the morning—dueling practice.

Despite the fact that the newly-formed crisis response unit, which Falcon had taken to calling Cru for ease and to distinguish them from the rest of the Enforcer pack, was largely a peacekeeping and citizen assistance squad, the powers-that-be—First Iago most likely and possibly a few of his favorite Seconds—had decided that the Cru needed to remain as battle-ready as the rest of their Enforcer comrades. Thus, Falcon was dressed in full uniform facing off against his practice partner, Fifth Jones, jammy bugger and all around prat.

Funny enough, there was no grandfatherly admonishment in Falcon's head for swearing. Most Enforcers picked up salty language not long after joining the order. And his grandfather had never hesitated to use it, so long as none of the wrong people were around to hear. And, while Falcon admitted calling Fifth Jones names was immature and probably not quite deserved... some days, he really had gotten off easy compared to Falcon. Some of the injuries Falcon had sustained over the past year had occurred the night of the massive attack on the Halls of Justice, wherein pieces of that giant prison had been blown apart. Fifth Jones had ended up with a cane that night, just as Falcon had later—after Falcon had come out of his coma of course—but Jones had healed up beautifully. Meanwhile, Falcon was without his cane at the moment, and his body ached as he dodged and parried and thrusted and blocked with his practice truncheon—padded on the outside but weighted the same as their real ones. Before last year, Falcon had been one of the order's best duelists. Being good meant one had the control and skill to avoid causing undue harm. Now, just as he'd done three times already, Jones landed a hit against Falcon. This time it was in his ribs.

Sweat stung as it ran into Falcon's eyes, while the scent of crushed grass beneath their feet and the clean, cool smell of early spring air invaded his nostrils. Cold, cutting springtime winds blew all around, but the sun blazed enthusiastically down on the sparring field, seeming to celebrate the cloudless sky around it. Falcon grit his teeth and rolled with Jones' blow. He wasn't usually this badly off, but his performance had never gotten back to its old level since he'd woken up from his coma. Today must make it look like Falcon was getting worse instead of better. Just once this morning he wanted to get in a hit on Jones.

Around them, the heaves and grunts of other Cru and Enforcer members rang through the air. The sound of their efforts was punctuated here and there by the combat instructor—a man seemingly made of nothing but weatherbeaten skin, scars, and shouts: Second Winthrop.

"Steward Smoke," Winthrop bellowed, "where's yer head at today?"

Winthrop's accent betrayed his lower class upbringing, but he was proof positive that anyone could make a name for themselves in the Enforcer order.

Falcon was too tired to even try thinking up a snappy retort. Instead, as an answer, he feigned left and struck out, hoping to outmaneuver Jones. Jones quickly realized the ploy, however, and at the last second, blocked the attack.

"Good reflexes, Fifth Jones," Winthrop barked.

Falcon concentrated on his breathing as they continued. It didn't stop the pain, but it gave him something else to focus on. He didn't manage to land a hit, but neither did Jones.

After some time, Winthrop's voice boomed across the training field again. "Not my problem, Doctor."

That could only mean the good Doctor Philomena Allen had arrived for the Cru's next lesson. Falcon never heard anyone call her Philomena, and he suspected she swiftly corrected those who did. Instead, those closest to Doctor Allen knew her as Mina, who was currently raising her voice over the din of dueling Enforcers.

"I can make it your problem if you're going to have that attitude, Second Winthrop."

Doctor Allen's voice was an uncanny mixture of cool calm and ringing authority. Falcon tried to take mental notes on how she achieved this, all while dodging yet another of Fifth Jones' strikes. Falcon sidestepped and tried to get in a hit after that. Blazes! Another miss.

"Eh?" Second Winthrop called back, half his attention on a pair of younger recruits down the way. "What'll you do then? Come at me with leeches? I ain't scared of some wee worms."

Another voice replied this time, this one sweet and strong and not at all what Falcon was expecting. Camilla Hawkins, Falcon's dear friend and Doctor Allen's niece and apprentice, *never* came to the Halls of Justice, not since her father's funeral after the insurrection at the Halls of Justice. "Nothing so messy. A trepan would suffice."

Falcon had no idea what a trepan was, but he suspected it was a particularly nasty tool. Or maybe it was another word for tranquilizer? How Camilla made the most gruesome medical procedures sound so innocuous was truly a marvel, though she did sound a touch prickly today. In any case, he apparently wasn't the only one who was surprised at hearing Camilla's voice. Jones actually turned his head toward the sound—rookie mistake—and Falcon could see his eyes searching.

Jones would have had Camilla as a piece of decoration on his arm if he could. The Allen family and the Joneses had known each other for years. Camilla had even grown up with Fifth Jones' sisters, but she was too smart and ambitious to go for a prat like that. Though, to be fair, Falcon could see the attraction. Camilla was kind, intelligent, charming, and pretty. He'd fancied her for a time after her erstwhile, former-Enforcer beau, Dmitri, had disappeared. After Falcon had gotten to know her, however, he'd realized they weren't a good match and his romantic interest had faded. Camilla was the sort of friend, however, that, if you had any sense, you didn't let go of easily.

So, yes, truth be told, he had tried to swoop in after she'd broken things off with Dmitri. A man as not-charming as Falcon had to take his opportunities where he could, within the rules of gallantry and fair play of course. But Fifth Jones—who, unbelievably, was *still looking!*—would stab anyone in the back (metaphorically speaking anyway) to get what he wanted. With Jones rubbernecking like a goose, Falcon took his opportunity and slammed his training truncheon into the side of Jones' knee.

Falcon squelched a petty grin—all right, so the rules of fair play and gallantry were sometimes a little squiffy when it came to Jones. The proper attack, by Enforcer-recommended best practices, would have been a strike to the head. But people could end up dead that way, or at least severely brain addled, and Falcon believed an injured suspect was more helpful than a dead one. Fifth Jones let out a bright blue swear and stumbled back. Falcon didn't pursue or double down on his attack as he knew Second Winthrop would want him to. That wasn't the man Falcon wanted to be, though his insides squirmed, knowing this too would reflect poorly on his performance.

The same old argument Doctor Allen and Second Winthrop always engaged in had been going for almost a minute now. Doctor Allen must have gotten fed up early today because she abruptly turned toward the dueling grounds and clapped her hands.

"Alright, that's enough for today, gents. Crisis response unit, you're with Miss Camilla and me."

Second Winthrop sputtered on the sidelines. "You don't get to tell my recruits what to do."

"Given that you have failed to wrangle them in a timely manner, sir, the task clearly falls to me." To the Enforcer Fifths and Sixths on the field, she added, "Quickly now, please. We have to make up for lost time."

Falcon did a quick scan of the sparring field and identified those under his command. "Double time, Cru! Let's show the doctor what we can do!"

That set the Cru into motion—many might despise him after he'd publicly defamed his grandfather, one of their own, but they still had to follow the chain of command. Doctor Allen didn't have the authority to make them run laps, only set extra coursework, but Falcon could, had, and would. He followed his own instructions too, despite how his body protested.

It wasn't what he'd heard Doctor Allen or Camilla describe as acute pain, but rather it was a deep, constant ache in his joints that flared up when he pushed himself too hard. Perhaps if he hadn't jumped back into service so soon after coming out of his coma, had given his body more time to recover from being hurled through space and into a tree by an explosion, he'd be better off. He'd been offered a commission, though, a Cru squad leader, and his grandfather had insisted. He hadn't seen then how he could say no. That position had led to more injuries as, in order to protect citizens, he'd thrown himself into a hysterical, panicked crowd of sabotaged protesters. Then there'd been the raid on the catacombs to take down the Reaper's Collective, which had been several hours of highly compressed warfare. That, in turn, had earned him his newest rank, leader of the entire unit. So he'd hardly been able to let his body take the time it needed.

Thus, now, he pushed through the pain as he always did, forcing his breathing into long, slow breaths, and ran with his Cru. They automatically assembled into a two-by-two line and hustled into the Halls of Justice. Though it was a beautiful building, Falcon had never liked the Halls. Its creamy walls rose around them, thick and imposing. It was supposed to be magic-proof, but who even knew given that magic had been destroyed just over a century ago. Beneath the Cru's feet, white marble streaked with black and grey clapped back the sound of their trotting boots, echoing off the walls of the grand corridors.

It was all a very pretty lie, and Falcon preferred to call a spade a spade. The Halls of Justice was really nothing more than a grand prison. In the eyes of the law and much of society, once a criminal, always a criminal. Thus, higher up and further in, prisoners, all serving life sentences for crimes both major and minor, huddled and paced and slept inside their cells. Down here, though, on the lower and ground levels, were basic classrooms, more training areas, and the mess hall. Falcon led his troop into their designated lecture hall, where they'd spent the last few months learning how to save lives instead of destroy them. Though Falcon was no great student of medical care, this was by far his favorite part of the day. Not least of all because he got to sit down and rest his body.

Falcon had just watched his troop, barely over forty-strong, fill the room's seats, keeping order by his gaze alone. Finally, his turn. Just as he was creaking into his chair, however, Doctor Allen's voice called to him.

"Steward Smoke, I'd like a word, please. The rest of you, Miss Camilla will be teaching you today. Please afford her all the respect you would to me."

As Falcon re-creaked up to a standing position, he knew he shouldn't interfere, knew Camilla would want to earn the Cru's esteem on her own, but people often didn't take Camilla seriously simply because she was young and pretty and, most of all, female. And he was about to leave her alone in a room of forty-ish men, most of them also young and therefore predominantly stupid. He felt the need to protect his friend and therefore gave them all a long, silent glare. His instincts urged him to do more, to make a threat, but he restrained himself. She'd once told him she wanted partners to stand beside her, not shields to stand before her. He hoped his glare wasn't overstepping too much.

Then he followed Doctor Allen from the room, keeping one eye on his troop until the very last second.

"What can I do for you, Doctor Allen?" he asked, keeping his ears open for a disturbance.

She gave him a warm smile. "Falcon, I have said in the past you may call me Mina. I think we know one another well enough by now to do away with such formalities."

Falcon swallowed hard and tried to form the doctor's first name in his mouth. It blatantly refused to comply, and he shook his head. "I'm afraid you'll always be Doctor Allen to me."

She gave a conciliatory nod and clasped her hands across the front of her jacket, a smartly tailored wool creation of jade green, which matched her rose pink and tan striped skirt very well. Fashionable without being overstated. Her clasped hands, however, gave Falcon pause. He'd seen this move before, and it usually boded ill.

"I noticed your movements out on the dueling grounds," she said. "Are you doing the physiotherapy exercises we discussed?"

"Of course." That was an outright lie, and Doctor Allen's sharpened gaze said she knew it. Of course she would; she knew her business. So Falcon tried to salvage what regard he might have just lost with her. "Or rather, I am when I can. Moving house and whatnot has left me rather busy of late. And there's the Cru to manage as well. You know I want to see this endeavor succeed as much as you do."

"This endeavor" referred to the very existence of the crisis response unit. True, it had gained permanence with Falcon's promotion to Steward of the Sage, but it was still a nascent piece of the Enforcer order, having only been formed within the last few months. Falcon didn't know many of the details, but he'd gathered its formation had been largely a political move, with several people hoping to use the Cru to their own ends. And there was still plenty of opportunity for First Iago to decide it wasn't worth keeping.

Doctor Allen's eyes softened, but her voice remained firm. "I appreciate that you've been dealing with a lot of late. And I've been very impressed with how you've taken charge of the crisis response unit, as is First Iago."

Falcon blinked at her before blurting, "Is he? He hasn't said so."

Mina chuckled, and Falcon's cheeks heated as he realized he'd talked over whatever else she'd just been saying. He started to babble apologies but let them trail off when Doctor Allen raised a hand. "First Iago has a very different management style than you or I."

Turning people into verbal punching bags pretty much sums it up, Falcon thought to himself.

Mina went on, "And I think your men are grateful for how

you've chosen to handle them. It's a work in progress with all the regularly associated growing pains, but, Falcon…" Here her voice grew more serious. "If you and those around you are on fire, you cannot extinguish their flames without putting yourself out first."

"Um?" He felt his face move into an expression that matched this sentiment. "What?"

Doctor Allen laid a comforting hand on his shoulder. "You cannot help those around you if you fail to take care of yourself."

"Ah, I see." The advice was kindly meant but hit Falcon like a training truncheon. The word "fail" stung especially sharply.

Straightening back up, she said. "Do the physiotherapy exercises, please. Every morning and evening. You'll be glad you did."

Falcon nodded, feeling rather small. Doctor Allen seemed to be waiting for something, or perhaps hesitating? He doubted the latter; he'd rarely seen the woman not in command of a situation.

"Was there something else?"

She took a measured breath through her nose. "I'm afraid there is. I'm meeting with First Iago in a bit."

That can't be good, Falcon thought.

"The crisis response unit is standing at a crossroads," she continued.

"Are we?" If so, he couldn't see any of the directions.

Doctor Allen gave a sharp nod. "Yes. You see, some would simply have your troop folded back into the Enforcer order to do much the same as you always have."

That wasn't surprising, but Falcon's stomach dropped nevertheless. He'd never much liked what was required of him as an Enforcer. Their methods were brutal, thus why there had been such a large campaign for change last year. He'd joined the order because that's what his grandfather had expected of him. If he hadn't, the man would have disinherited him. Now that it had happened anyway, if the Cru hadn't been created and Falcon made a part of it, he wasn't sure in what direction he would have gone.

He'd always tried to make things better as he'd worked in the Halls of Justice and patrolled Springhaven's streets. It was how he justified his job to himself, and he sincerely believed people were better off dealing with him than they would have been with the usual sort who enlisted in the order. But the job had still never sat well with him.

The crisis response unit's creation was a beacon of hope, a

symbol of positive change, not just for the city but for Falcon too. But it couldn't just be symbolic. Even with the Enforcer reform bill ratified this past winter, the Cru didn't have a lot to do that was their own. Or rather, Falcon didn't have much for them to do that was any different from what they'd always done, save for the emergency response training. He'd always assumed Doctor Allen and either Lord Allen, her husband, or Lady Holmes, the co-founders of this little outfit, would give them directions. Mina's next words perfectly outlined his wishes for both the Cru and himself.

"There is an opportunity, however, for you all to become something different, something more separate and independent." With that, Falcon's stomach began pulling itself back up into its proper place, only for Doctor Allen to send it plummeting again. "In order for that to happen, however, *you* will need to take initiative."

Falcon gulped. Defaming his grandfather had been the hardest thing he'd ever done in his life, and it had put him in plenty of people's bad books. He'd tried to keep a low profile since then, and he had a feeling whatever Doctor Allen had in mind would put him front and center again.

Her face changed suddenly, warming as it bloomed with a pleasant smile. "Why don't you come round for dinner soon? We've seen so little of you of late, and Camilla has mentioned wanting to see you."

Falcon's confusion and worry garbled together in his throat and made his words sticky like toffee. "Erm, of… of course. That sounds… lovely?"

While Doctor Allen was never one to offer insincere hospitality, he was sure this dinner invite would involve more discussion of this "opportunity," all while closeted in the safety of their dining room. The pressure of it rather terrified him, and his brain scrambled for some kind of protection.

"May I invite my new housemate to join us?" A scheme of tactical genius, this was not. It was the result of panic, but actually turned out to serve him well. Doctor Allen couldn't refuse without showing her hand, and they couldn't discuss clandestine machinations, well-intentioned as they were, with Keene there. To add to the innocent effect, Falcon shut his mouth after that—Enforcer training had taught him silence could sometimes serve one better than a weak argument—and he blinked at her expectantly. He knew this expression on his own face was less pure innocence and more empty-headedness, but it had served him well in the past, so he went with it.

Doctor Allen didn't bat an eyelash at the less-than-artful parry. "Of course. We'd love to meet him. I'll send my card around with some dates and we'll sort it out."

With that, the conversation was ended, and Falcon was left in the corridor, alone, outside a classroom full of recruits who were depending on him for… something. He wasn't quite sure what yet, but he was certain it wasn't going to be easy.

~Chapter 3~

When Falcon headed home that afternoon, he felt as if his joints had transformed into rusty gears and the rest of him into ill-fitting iron pieces. He felt heavy and things seemed to be grinding against one another inside of him. Worry over the future, his and that of the Cru, had wrought his stomach into twists. His mind was leaden with questions.

Earlier that day, after his discussion with Doctor Allen, he'd had to arbitrate a disturbance he'd encountered upon reentering the classroom. It had been just in time to see a spitball flying through the air and into the back of Camilla's head as she wrote on the blackboard, but sadly Falcon had not witnessed the perpetrator. He and she had convened for a moment to discuss the best strategy— Camilla, being the spitball-ee in this situation, after all, should get to choose how she came off in the aftermath, and it was important for Falcon to publicly give her agency. He was more than willing to support her should she wish to appear either as a terrifying angel of vengeance or a beneficent goddess of forgiveness. In the end, Falcon explained to the class that Camilla would get to decide their punishment and he would use his rank to enforce it, whatever it may be. They let the class sweat for a few minutes before declaring that they would do line run drills outside whilst simultaneously having to answer pop quiz questions. Unfortunately, because he wanted to be a good example for his team, this meant that Falcon did a round of the drills as well too. But only one. Once upon a time, he'd have been able to do ten times that and barely break a sweat. Now, any more than the one and his legs might have seceded from the rest of his body and dropped off in protest.

Then there were their daily Enforcer duties, at which point the Cru broke up and Falcon was left with all the things he disliked about his job. He'd been assigned to prisoner feeding rounds, which sapped his soul rather than his body. All these people, jailed for life no matter their crime. Without even a proper trial, just a couple of Enforcers making life and death decisions for them. Falcon had long-ago determined to always be respectful during these tasks, saying please and thank you despite the fact that he was the one in charge. He told himself that he did it for them and avoided any thoughts that questioned whether it might also be to assuage his own guilt. Lord Allen and Lady Holmes were working on Springhaven's new justice system, and Falcon had heard whispers that people wanted all current Halls of Justice inmates reviewed for release. Stars, how he hoped that happened.

Thinking about Doctor Allen's request, maybe he could volunteer to be on whatever review team might eventually form. Maybe that would suffice for an effort on his part. He could hide in a little room somewhere and look over files. He would certainly be more lenient than many of his fellow order members.

For now, however, there was the problem of getting home. The Halls of Justice and Enforcer barracks were located in the Ivory district, along with most of Springhaven's other major governmental buildings. His family home was in the next district over—Rose. The different sections of the city had been named for the colors of the walls in each area, back before the War of Light. Back then, in the Old World, Springhaven had been called Prism, but the new world order had seen fit to rename the city along with so many other new creations. Or so Falcon's history lessons had taught him—he had never been a very good student, but at least that had stuck with him.

He'd actually begun walking West toward the Rose district, as he had so many times before, when he remembered that the Smoke family manor was no longer his home. His new residence in the Cobalt quarter was clear on the opposite end of Springhaven. Falcon's joints thrummed unhappily at the very thought of such a long trek. There hadn't been time to think about such things this morning, his sole focus being getting food and not being late to work. With a sigh, he reached into a pouch hanging off the side of his belt and extracted his telescoping cane.

He didn't like using the thing on any given day. It was one more reminder of what he'd lost in his misadventures this past year. But he especially didn't like using it when he was dressed in his Enforcer uniform.

"Don't show them your weakness," his grandfather would have said. "Be a man. Grit your teeth and bear it."

Now that Falcon was better—well, relative to the shape he'd been in a few months ago anyway—he'd kept his cane hidden as much as possible, only publicly pulling it out in the most desperate of circumstances. Doubly so, if he could help it, really only when he was dressed in his civilian clothes. A clever, engineering-inclined gent by the name of Lowell, with whom Falcon had a vague acquaintance via Camilla's adopted sister, Lenore, had gifted Falcon this collapsible version, thus allowing him to tuck it away into his side pouch whenever he liked. Today's circumstances, the long cross-city trek ahead of him, definitely counted as desperate.

The cane clicked merrily as Falcon depressed the release catch and it expanded, silvery steel and gleaming brass flashing brilliantly under the waning sunlight. His early morning start time meant he was usually home before sunset, but that looked like it might change starting today. At least he was good with directions. All those Enforcer patrols he'd done had acquainted him rather well with most every nook and cranny of the city, and he headed Northwest in the direction of Cobalt.

Not long into his journey, however, Falcon came upon a horse-drawn tram stop. He'd been aware of the public transport system, of course, but never in his entire life had he utilized it. If necessary, Enforcers had the authority to commandeer much swifter and more agile modes of transportation, such as a hansom cab or the larger growlers. Falcon knew several of his cohorts did this on a regular basis to get free rides about town. For his part, Falcon had never even considered exercising that arm of his authority.

Until now.

He'd always had the family's accounts to lean on, and so had paid for every cab ride he'd ever taken. As he looked at the small knot of people waiting at the horse-drawn tram stop, a small voice whispered in his head.

You could order a hansom to take you home. You've had a hard day. What's the harm?

But Falcon knew the harm. That was lost wages for someone else, wages they could be earning while they carted his, admittedly aching, sorry self around for free. Since his grandfather had cut him off from the family funds just over a month ago, and, more acutely, since he'd left the Smoke family manor yesterday, he'd become painfully aware of how precious every coin was. He didn't want to transfer that pain of his own to someone else. And so he trod toward the waiting group of people, trying to make his cane look more like an affectation than a need. It was ridiculous, he knew, but he'd rather look silly and rich than weak and hobbled. The shininess of the cane helped give the impression of the former.

The people gathered seemed to all spot him as one, and every eye clocked his movements, his expression, the location of his truncheon. Falcon wasn't surprised, though his face still began to burn, and he tried to be less purposeful in his gait.

Last year, unrest over the Enforcers' brutal tactics had heated over time, building steam and pressure within the city. The usually peaceful protests had turned violent a few times. Thank the stars those eager to stir the pot had remained few and far between. Since the Enforcer reform bill had been ratified this past winter, however, things had cooled considerably. Falcon had observed how many citizens' faces were less drawn by constant anxiety than before; they smiled and laughed more easily. But nothing had changed yet. And now there was a keen sense of... waiting. Waiting to see in what direction things tipped, full of both hope and caution. And Falcon sensed people looking at *him* with a keener eye too, given that his face was the one plastered on posters all over the city, promising the better future so many wished for.

As he approached the group, Falcon wished he could appear jaunty, though that was out of the question, even without his injuries. Gangly affability had been the closest thing he'd ever been able to achieve, and he tried to channel those happier old days, before explosions and canes and whatnot. The smile came easiest, and to the group he tipped his uniform's cap, an absurd round thing that was more helmet than hat.

Once he was close enough to be heard, he greeted the gathered people as warmly as his aching body would let him with a simple, "Afternoon."

Falcon took up a position a little ways from them, close

enough, he hoped, to indicate that he too was simply waiting but far enough away so as to not crowd them. Falcon had no idea if this stratagem was successful. There was a bench here, and after a few minutes, a man sitting there in a shabby greatcoat with the collar pulled up against the day's chill abandoned his seat to stand with the others. No one else took it. Falcon knew it had been left for him. He could have ordered someone to make space for him on the bench—not that he would have—but now that it was open, he couldn't bring himself to sit. It looked too weak. Or perhaps too spoiled. He didn't mind looking well-to-do, but he didn't want to appear entitled like so many others of his class believed they were. Though he felt his mealy muscles oozing toward the respite, trying to pull him along, he stiffened, ignoring the call of the empty seat. And all the while, it remained frustratingly open.

The horse-drawn tram eventually arrived. It was essentially a long box with a roof and wide, rattling windows. The body had been painted in bright red, the trim butter yellow, and a vehicle number emblazoned in white across the sides. A pair of massive draft horses pulled it along tracks cleverly built flush into the cobblestone street, so as to not pose a tripping hazard. The driver, positioned in a small niche at the front, pulled a lever, and a set of steps extended down to the ground. When they'd been pulled in, they'd formed a closed safety gate across the entrance.

Falcon made it a point to let all his fellow passengers board first and gave the driver a friendly nod as he hauled himself inside the tram. The driver's return nod was curt, but Falcon told himself the man was likely just a taciturn sort. He made a bit of a show of dropping his fare into the provided payment box, even though it was nothing more than two meager coppers. Thankfully, it wasn't quite peak travel time yet, and more than a few seats were left open by the time they set off again. Falcon was happy to let his mind wander into a nexus of non-thought as the tram trekked its path around the city. A tiny portion of his mind remained aware of where they were so he wouldn't miss his stop, and the sun was just beginning to dip behind the taller buildings and reaching smokestacks of Cobalt's canning factories when he arrived at his destination. Just a ten minute walk left, and his body even felt somewhat refreshed thanks to the tram's fortunate seating situation.

Falcon almost felt as if he might not need his cane as he went, but remembering Doctor Allen's words from earlier that day, he decided not to push it. Besides, he could pull off the silly and rich affectation act a little better now—acting had never been his forte, but he wasn't abysmal either.

His route took him around his back garden—he and Keene had been fortunate enough to procure a house at the end of the street, which meant their wee scrap of land was slightly less scrappy than their neighbors' and only shared a wall on one side. The back garden's rocky wall was tall, allowing Falcon to just glimpse the door to the lavatory—a thing Falcon had quailed at having to go outside to get to. Perhaps it was better that it wasn't open to the rest of the house, however, given that the plumbing, while modern, was not as new as that of his family's manor. He was no engineer by any stretch of anyone's imagination, but the considerable patches of rust on the pipes had told him as much. Over the garden wall, he could also just glimpse the thick, wooden back door, which led from the back garden into the kitchen. Falcon didn't have a key for the back door yet and hadn't realized to ask until now. He'd have to mention it to Keene later. Above, on the second floor, he could see the windows of both his and Keene's bedrooms. Falcon looked away, shaking his head. His Enforcer training had taught him to always study his surroundings, but honestly, he didn't need to examine his own house.

Voices met him as he came around the corner to the front of the house. One was Keene, the low, easy tones of his voice sounding as if they were trying to charm someone. The other was cracked and thin, a woman by the sounds of it. And a moment later, the two came into view.

Keene stood there with a smile that could melt butter. His hands were lazily half tucked into his trouser pockets, and he'd tied his hair back into a loose knot at the base of his neck. A gentle spring breeze toyed with a few locks that had come loose. Falcon found himself suddenly a touch jealous of that breeze, but the thought disappeared almost as soon as it had taken shape as his Enforcer training took hold once again and he began examining the woman.

She was stooped and made entirely of bent lines and wrinkles. Had those lines been straightened out, the top of her head might have come up to Keene's nose, but sloped as she was, she was eye level with his chest. Her pewter-streaked white hair had been piled into an amorphous shape atop her head. She wore a plain dress of dark blue cotton, and a shawl that had perhaps once been chamomile colored but was now dun wrapped faithfully around her shoulders. As Falcon drew closer, he saw the shawl was thin, threadbare even in a few spots. He also noticed a woven basket hanging off the woman's arm and, sitting inside of it, a flatish, round something wrapped in what might have been another shawl.

Both Keene and the woman turned to look at Falcon as he approached. Keene's smile cooled a little as his eyes roved over Falcon's uniform—he either hadn't been up by the time Falcon had left that morning or had already gone out; Falcon didn't know which—but Keene gave his housemate a nod of greeting that, by all appearances, was more than perfunctory.

"Mrs. Spoondawdle," Keene began as soon as Falcon was close enough. Despite his slight change in demeanor, the man had not lost an ounce of charm in his address. "I'd like to present my housemate, Steward of the Sage, Mister Falcon Smoke. Falcon, this is the honorable Mrs. Iphigenia Spoondawdle." He gave Mrs. Spoondawdle a cheeky wink. "At least, I assume she's honorable. We only just met after all. She might be a terrible flirt."

The woman chuckled, a curious sound with the way her voice crackled. She playfully batted Keene on the arm. "Oh, Mister Kohli. You do know how to make this old lady feel young again."

Falcon's lips twitched up into a fraction of a smile. He was so tired and achey, he wanted nothing more than to strip off the day and sink into a hot bath, but he felt this was an opportunity to show Keene he wasn't just what his uniform represented.

"It seems Keene is a terrible judge of character," Falcon replied. Keene shot him a curious look, smile fading a bit more, and Falcon added, "I'm sure you're an excellent flirt, Mrs. Spoondawdle."

A moment of silence ensued, wherein Falcon wondered where he'd gone wrong. Had he not actually said what he'd thought? He reviewed his words again. No, they seemed fine. Unless he was having a stroke and had said something completely different than what he'd meant to. He could just feel perspiration prickling in his hairline when both Keene and Mrs. Spoondawdle burst out laughing.

"What a delight it'll be to have both of you living here," Mrs. Spoondawdle said.

They chatted for a little while longer. Mrs. Spoondawdle, it turned out, knew the area well and gave the gents all sorts of advice as to where to get the best produce, which shops to give a miss, and more. She also handed the flatish parcel in her basket to Falcon with strict instructions.

"It's still cooling, so save it for dessert tonight."

"Would you like to join us?" Keene offered. "We should share and have a bit more of a gossip."

Mrs. Spoondawdle chuckled again. "I'd love nothing more, dear, but I have my whist club tonight." She looked at Falcon as she added, "Nothing untoward, I assure you. We're all just there for friendship."

Falcon felt his insides turn in on themselves. Though Mrs. Spoondawdle's tone was nothing but friendly—she'd even patted his arm as she'd spoken—he was, despite this merry gathering, still, at best, the resident killjoy. And at worst, the overseer of oppression. Mrs. Spoondawdle was, of course, referring to the bidding that went with whist. Gambling was, according to a handful of obscure city codes, supposed to be reserved for clubs and other officially licensed venues, though literally no one followed those rules. Not at friendly get-togethers, high society soirees, or even at the Enforcer barracks. And given that it wasn't even really a law, no one, thankfully, was ever arrested for it, though they could be fined. That was, assuming there was at least some evidence or multiple credible witness statements—not even the Enforcers could quite get away with imprisoning people on nothing, thank the stars.

Options ran through Falcon's head. He could tell her even if they did bet, he wouldn't tell anyone. Or simply admit that he'd been gambling his own pocket money since he was small, just like everyone he knew had done too—though he rather more enjoyed Hazard, a game played with dice instead of cards. But either option would undermine his position and authority. And what would happen if Mrs. Spoondawdle then went and told her friends about the Enforcer Cru leader who openly admitted to breaking... well, not the law. But flouted the rules anyway. And what if that somehow got back to his superiors. He was spiraling, he knew.

"Do I detect a hint of nutmeg, Mrs. Spoondawdle?" Keene's voice was suddenly close to Falcon's ear. Close enough that he could just feel the warmth of the man's breath on his cheek.

Falcon had been so engrossed in his own private panic that he hadn't noticed Keene lean close, eyes on the still-wrapped parcel. Keene's shoulder pressed against Falcon's. The latter had been trained to stand his ground; others had to move around him.

Though that wasn't the reason Falcon remained where he was now, and his housemate didn't back off either. Though Keene had a slimmer build than Falcon, his shoulder wasn't bony. It was supple, even a little soft, and Falcon wondered what his felt like to Keene.

The man in question took another deep breath through his nose before releasing it through his mouth. More warmth on Falcon's cheek, warmer somehow than even the pie tin seeping heat through its thin fabric wrapping.

"*And* cinnamon?" Keene went on, an exaggerated affectation of shock in his voice. "Mrs. Spoondawdle, you spoil us!"

She laughed. "Welcome to the neighborhood, loves. I expect to have that treat and tittle-tattle another day."

Keene flashed another winning smile at her. "It's a promise."

"I see everything around here, so prepare yourselves." She shook a finger at them.

"You absolute tease," Keene laughed.

Falcon, despite wondering if there was more to Mrs. Spoondawdle's "I see everything," statement, smiled at them both. He could get used to this place. Yes, he could. At least for while he had to be here.

~Chapter 4~

"I didn't expect you to have a sense of humor."

The statement came from Keene as they were getting settled for their evening in. Falcon had changed clothes and splashed a little water over his face—a proper wash would have to wait since he was meant to help make dinner. Something he hadn't, in fact, found time to learn anything about that day. Keene was in the kitchen assembling cookware and the like. Meanwhile, Falcon was leaning against the doorframe, hoping he appeared ready to help and not nearly as clueless and bone-tired as he really was. Keene's words had not been said unkindly, but they still prickled.

"Oh?" Falcon replied, though he expected he knew the answer that was coming.

As Keene looked up from setting out several bowls, a large knife, and a deep pot beside it all, he gifted Falcon a smile. "Are Enforcers really allowed to make jokes? It might mar the whole…" He circled his hand through the air, fingers and thumb all pointed toward Falcon to indicate his whole self. "…stony image you all seem so eager to purport."

Alright, not quite the response Falcon had expected. Not as scathing as he thought Keene probably really wanted to be, but he'd take a gentle touch where he could get it.

Falcon gave his housemate a smile to show he hadn't taken

offense—not that he was certain whether Keene was worried about such things. "We're told to do whatever it takes to keep the city safe. I happen to think that requires a carrot far more often than a stick."

Keene's smile grew. "If only your cohorts felt the same."

Falcon bobbed a nod. This was getting a touch close to badmouthing the order. Granted, *he* could have diverted the subject and hadn't felt the need to, but still, probably not something he wanted to encourage for a multitude of reasons, especially in someone like Keene—Falcon was beginning to notice the man gave his opinion very freely.

Quiet fell between them, and Falcon studied the various implements being arranged on the kitchen's worktable. He'd been in kitchens before. Of course he had, but now that it was on him to help transform raw ingredients into something edible, the individual tasks of chopping and heating and whatever else went into it seemed complex and mysterious. He wasn't certain he'd ever even read a recipe, nor did he see one helpfully lying anywhere around Keene. A knitted sack with a stalky, light green vegetable sticking out of the top sat at the end of the work table. Falcon spied carrots through the weave of the sack as well, but realized he hadn't the foggiest as to what one actually *did* with carrots. He internally quailed at the growing, looming awareness of his own lack of knowledge.

Falcon took a deep breath, screwing up his courage. He'd approach this like he did any difficult situation.

"ADE-ing a situation will always aid you," he'd heard countless commanding officers say during training. "Assess, determine, enact."

And Falcon pushed himself off the wall, ready to do just that. Except a part of him was apparently done with today. Somewhere between his upper thigh and his lower back—it was hard to tell the source of pain sometimes, what with the way human parts were all intertwined—a muscle, or perhaps a tendon, twinged. *Sharply*. He wasn't ready for it and stumbled. He'd left his cane upstairs, thinking surely he wouldn't need it now that he was home and could relax. Thus, he shot a hand out and grabbed the doorframe. It was not a terribly prepossessing move, hunched as he was now to appease the twinge and grasping the wood of the casing so hard his knuckles had turned white. He looked up to find Keene staring at him, frozen, with a question in his eyes: What should I do?

Get up, lad! Falcon heard his grandfather's voice in his head. *Do you want everyone to think you're a bloody, swooning nancy?*

Well, he was a bit, according to his grandfather's definition anyway. But that wasn't why he immediately tried straightening up again. Falcon had never let himself get much bothered by the slur. No, he did it because these blasted injuries made him weak, infirm far sooner than was right or fair. Unfortunately, the hasty correction only made the twinging bit of him angry. This time, it flared hotter, and real pain rather than mostly surprise hit him. He refused to surrender ground to the pain, though, and paused. After a moment, albeit much more slowly this time, Falcon tried again. He couldn't help but grimace as he did, pushing through deep discomfort, until he was properly upright this time. He met Keene's eyes and forced a laugh—it sounded every bit as hollow and strained as it felt.

"Apologies," he said, trying to sound blasé about the whole thing. "Just a little stiff."

He chose to ignore whatever snippy comment his inner dialogue might offer. He knew how he sounded.

Keene tipped his head in a way Falcon found endearing, his gaze a mixture of curiosity, sympathy, and something maybe a little wry. "I was there, you know? At the protest where those Reaper's Collective people used the pepper gas."

Falcon's throat tightened. The protest Keene was referring to had been, for better or worse, a tipping point for Falcon's career. At the time, he'd worried that one, small canister of pepper gas—launched by a member of the Reaper's Collective disguised as an Enforcer—might make Springhaven tear itself apart. The device had spewed red smoke that had made Falcon feel as if his eyes and throat were being carved out by invisible hands. He'd been in charge of the Enforcer squad patrolling the protester crowds that day, and it had taken everything in him to keep shouting at his men to protect the demonstrators, to push himself through the panicking crowd to get to the canister, to enter fully into its noxious plume, grab it, and throw it beyond the crowds to where it could do less damage.

And all while he'd fought against his own instincts to turn and run, resisted the agony caused by the pepper gas, the people he'd sworn to protect had turned on him. Falcon's mind traveled back to that day. He felt the tension in his jaw as he grit his teeth through the pain of someone jabbing him in the ribs, kicking him in the back of the knee, forcing him to strain through other injuries he was still healing from. He didn't blame them for their fear; he'd been terrified too. His job had been to keep the peace, and by the very barest definition he had—no one had died anyway—but it had hurt more than anything he'd ever experienced.

Keene's voice pulled Falcon from his dark memories back into the light and warmth of their shared kitchen, shabby though it was. "I didn't see a lot of what happened after everything went pear-shaped." Keene was looking thoughtful now, clearly dwelling inside his own thoughts. "I admit, I was too much of a meater to stick around. It did all get a bit manic."

Falcon wheezed out something that was like a laugh but devoid of mirth. "You can say that again." More seriously, he added, "You're not a meater, though. There's no shame in running during an attack like that. If anything, you helped by clearing the field. Maybe you forged a path for others to follow and stay safe as well."

Keene gave a sardonic half smile. "That's very generous of you. I read the reports, though. In the newssheets. The pepper gas didn't get me. I was lucky enough to be at the edge of the crowd when it happened, but I've heard others' accounts of it." He paused. "And I read about people getting … what was the word the papers used?"

"Turbulent," Falcon said.

Writers certainly could pick their battles when they chose to. The description had done everyone a favor by blaming no one and making the crowd's hysteria sound more like a force of nature than the result of anyone's choices.

Keene finally looked to Falcon again, meeting his eyes. "That's right. Turbulent."

He knows I was injured that day, Falcon realized.

Falcon's first reaction was to feel shame. The Enforcers didn't have control over the newssheets, thank heaven, but in regards to the pepper gas attack, they'd requested that any reports of Enforcer injuries be omitted. And for some reason, the various newssheet agencies had agreed. Yet here, an almost total stranger, had sussed it out. Falcon realized his infirmity must show worse than even he'd realized, and cold, clammy embarrassment prickled over his skin.

He shifted, still fighting to remain straight and steady. Falcon wasn't certain what Keene was getting at, and he wasn't sure he wanted to know. People, Enforcer-supporters mostly, had lauded Falcon for his actions that day. It was the first time the newssheets had called him a hero. Given that Keene clearly wasn't an admirer of the order, however, that could only mean…

"It couldn't have been easy to do what you did."

The softness of Keene's gaze, the compassion and, unbelievably, sincere respect in his voice swept Falcon's shame away like a broom clearing cobwebs. And Falcon was left feeling too surprised to speak, but pleased nonetheless.

Keene shook his head. His voice was forthright but not unkind as he said, "Enough of this beating around the bush. Look, I've seen your cane, you have a job that keeps you active—"

Falcon's internal commentator whistled at the factory-sized mound of things that "a job that keeps you active" said without actually saying them.

"—Why don't you sit while I make us dinner? Rest your legs a bit."

Presumptuous, pitying pup! Who does he think he is? That was Falcon's grandfather in Falcon's head. He cringed to think what else the man would say if he were here to witness this exchange.

Nevertheless, Falcon's mind whirred through objections, doing his best to filter out all of those that smacked of his grandfather's views. That proved difficult given the way ideas about how to "be strong" got entangled with not wanting to put extra work on Keene. As Falcon was doing his mental sifting, seconds passed by, and he became increasingly aware of just how long his silence was stretching. It made him feel stupid and weaker than ever—was he as broken mentally as he was physically?

Then Keene was tipping his head again and giving Falcon an entreating smile. If Falcon was a cat, fur bristling and backed into a corner, Keene's smile was the soft voice and offered treat that soothed his fur smooth again and drew him out.

"I'll make you a special cup of tea."

That did it. After experiencing Keene's special blend yesterday and the strain of today, a cup of tea sounded like heaven. Falcon didn't know what would make it special, but he had only happy expectations.

In an attempt to both throw off his prickly feelings from the last few minutes and to convince his housemate that it really hadn't been as dramatic as all that, Falcon swiveled his head around his shoulders in an exaggerated manner, rolling his eyes and releasing a theatrical sigh. "Oh very well. As you are so very insistent."

Keene cocked an eyebrow at him that said he knew very well what Falcon was trying to pull off and failing abysmally, but Falcon couldn't bring himself to care. He had tea coming his way and had gotten a reprieve on showing Keene just how useless he was in the kitchen.

At the opposite end of the kitchen, in between the door to the pantry under the stairs and the door that led out to the back garden, was a skinny bit of wall. A small, currently collapsed fold-up table was attached to the wall and a duo set of chairs stacked against it. To show how definitely not an invalid he was, Falcon set all these up into the little eating nook they were meant to be—carefully, so as to not anger his cantankerous muscles again. Of course, that took up more space and left just barely enough room for Keene to shimmy between a chair and the pantry should he need to. Thus, Falcon took the seat by the door, which was drafty and cold. And Keene immediately piped up about this arrangement.

"Don't be daft. Sit close to the fire and warm up."

Falcon chuckled. "Has anyone ever told you you'd make an excellent stand-in for a mother hen?"

"I'm sad to say they haven't. Hens are a gift. Speaking of, what would you say to getting some?"

Falcon blinked. "Some what? Hens? As in, living ones?"

Keene had turned his focus to the fire. He was fiddling with a rotating arm sort of contraption, hanging a kettle onto it and swinging the entire thing back into the fireplace, all with the help of some small levers at the base of the thing. Falcon's legs were stretched out before him, and snug as the kitchen was, he could have tapped his shoes against Keene's leg as the man knelt there.

Occupied as he was with his work, Keene's answer came out only half-focused. "Mhmm. For the back garden. And eggs."

It took Falcon a moment, but he realized that meant hens—yes, living ones—providing them with eggs daily. Daily? How often did hens lay eggs? His family estate had a chicken coop, but he'd only ever seen it from a distance. Falcon wasn't exactly what one would call an animal person, and it had only taken one instance of being chased out of the chickens' enclosure as a small child by a very angry rooster to convince him that the only thing he needed to know about the fowl beasties was that they were delicious.

"As long as there are no roosters, certainly. Wait, do hens need a rooster to lay eggs?" Heat crept into Falcon's cheeks. This was getting into delicate and private matters best left between poultry.

Keene's attention was still on tea-making as he replied, "That's fine. No roosters necessary. Loud little blighters anyway. And cranky."

That pleased Falcon, so long as he wasn't expected to help with the proposed chickens. Not that he planned on staying here any longer than necessary, though he had no idea yet how long it would take him to build up the funds for that next step. And there was the question of how much this hen-keeping venture might cost too, but he was certain they'd get to those details in time. For now, a silence far more comfortable than the earlier one began, but Falcon found he was curious about his kindly new housemate.

"So, Keene, what do you do?" It was a conversational go-to Falcon sometimes used at parties, but not one of his favorites, given that the rules of polite society dictated people would then have to ask him the same. Which then led to either awkward silences or overenthusiastic launches into political conversations. Neither of which Falcon counted as much fun. Even now, he sort of regretted asking. It sounded as if he was interrogating Keene as to how he was going to pay his half of the rent.

Thankfully, Keene's smile flashed brilliantly. "I'm a caterer."

"Huh?" That was all the oh-so-eloquent response Falcon's brain initially gave him, and he hurried to add, "I mean, interesting. Do you enjoy it?"

Truth be told, he'd never had much cause to think of caterers in his life. He knew people hired them for events, but his family never had. They didn't host many parties and those they did were usually smallish affairs for which the regular Smoke manor staff cooked and served. And the Enforcer order didn't have anything like enough funding for galas. If a support event needed organizing, one of First Iago's rich friends, or someone who traveled in similar circles, offered to host the bally thing. Falcon's grandfather had dragged him to a fair few of those throughout his life, and Falcon had hated them all.

Catering was apparently a marvelous profession. Keene's face lit up as he talked about creating menus and seeing people shocked, actually shocked, as they tasted something unlike anything they'd ever tasted before. By now, Keene had moved from the fireplace to the worktable. And all while he talked, he went on preparing the tea.

From a small, square bag on his belt, he produced a vial full of what looked like mostly yellow pickings from someone's garden. He carefully measured some out before sprinkling them into a somewhat worse for wear looking teapot with white violets painted on it.

Falcon wondered what it felt like to not just simply enjoy, but to love one's vocation so intensely it made their eyes shine and completely changed the way they moved and looked. He'd seen something similar in Camilla and Doctor Allen, in the staid way they handled their patients, the soft yet confident look in their eyes as they addressed hurts and concerns. But Keene's expression was a sort of exhilaration.

While the tea brewed its rather long steeping time, Falcon asked questions. What sorts of events did Keene victualize—a joke that earned Falcon a warm, rolling laugh from his housemate.

"All sorts," Keene explained. "Anything people will hire me for really. Weddings are my favorite, though." At this, a smile positively made of sunshine bloomed on his face. "And engagement parties."

Falcon couldn't help but smile too. Keene's joy was infectious, and the fact that he was apparently more than a bit of a romantic was downright adorable. Given how idyllic it all sounded, Falcon wondered aloud if things ever went wrong? Of course they did, but Keene had never let a client down and didn't plan to.

Despite Keene's evident expertise, Falcon had concerns when his housemate finally served Falcon's tea. Rather, one major concern. It was *yellow*. Not faintly yellow as if the petrolsene lighting could be blamed. No. Unlike yesterday's normal mahogany-colored brew, this was the bright golden yellow of corn or baby ducklings. Falcon didn't want to be rude, but also couldn't stop himself from giving Keene a look that demanded, "What is this nonsense?"

"It's a tisane," Keene said, as if that explained anything at all. When Falcon said nothing, Keene stood straighter, a move Falcon realized was likely him shifting into his food service role. "It's a proprietary blend of anti-inflammatory herbs, spices, and plant life that just happen to make the tea yellow."

Another moment of uncomfortable silence was spent with both men staring one another down. Keene's face was kind but firm, while Falcon, who really, truly wasn't trying to be rude but had never seen a tea—cheeky of it to even call itself that—so enthusiastically, unarguably *yellow*. Finally, politeness won out. When someone was kind enough to serve you food, you didn't turn your nose up at it. At least not without giving it a good and proper try. So Falcon thanked Keene as he would at a friend's luncheon and lifted the teacup to his lips. Steeling himself, he sipped.

It was... glorious. Warm and a touch spicy, earthy though extremely gentle in flavor, it soothed all the way down. Falcon wasn't embarrassed as he let out a relieved sigh. The sip had turned into a deep draught, and he'd nearly emptied half the little teacup in one go. He noticed Keene had still not given him the chipped one.

"There now. That wasn't so bad, was it?" Keene said, a look of deeply smug satisfaction on his face. "Make sure to drink the entire pot. It'll help those achey joints."

"Mother hen," Falcon muttered, but a smile was playing at his lips.

"Bok bok," Keene replied playfully over his shoulder.

The two chatted amiably while Falcon drank more tea and Keene prepared their dinner. It was some kind of soup with lots of vegetables and flavored by bits of chicken that were more bones than meat. When Falcon asked about it, Keene explained that he'd met their local butcher that day and had haggled for some carcasses they'd just broken down. Keene was certain he'd develop a rapport in no time.

So he must have lived in a different neighborhood before this, Falcon surmised.

He wanted to ask about Keene's former living arrangement, especially given that Beatrice had said Keene needed new lodgings as soon as possible, thus his current occupancy here. Falcon was curious about Keene's family and all that too, but, in the course of their few conversations thus far, Falcon had noticed how Keene had deftly avoided all mention of those subjects. And fair dues, Falcon wasn't eager to discuss his own fraught familial relations either. Keene's manners and speech indicated that he was well educated, likely either upper class or at least upwardly moving middle, though those traits could be changed and honed through practice. Keene's mode of dress, not counting his casual hair styling, pointed to the latter class, however. To change how you sounded cost only time and applied effort. Clothing cost actual money, so perhaps his family was involved in trade?

And Falcon definitely didn't want to appear as if he was interrogating the man, especially since Keene seemed to be warming up to him, so Falcon didn't pry. Instead, the conversation drifted to the latest local gossip, most of which went over Falcon's head. He didn't know any of the participants, so the names Keene rattled off meant nothing to him. Mister Snodgrass, the candlemaker, was finally getting over a bit of a cold that had been plaguing him for weeks. The local bakers had tattled about a secret tryst between their neighbor's daughter and a young gent in the neighborhood. And the blacksmith, Mister Halpern, just hired a new farrier. Apparently, something hadn't worked out with the previous one. Falcon was thoroughly impressed. Keene's talent for harvesting from the local grapevine apparently rivaled Beatrice's—no mean feat indeed.

All too happy to simply sit and listen to his new housemate prattle on, Falcon enjoyed getting to know the man in such an easy and relaxed manner. The world seemed a little less sharp and difficult while inside the bright sphere of warmth Keene gave off. It was one of the most pleasant evenings Falcon'd had in a long time.

"By the way, you and I have been invited to dine with the Allens." Falcon thought this chummy setting seemed like the best time to bring up Mina's invitation from earlier that day.

"The Allens?" Keene asked. He didn't look away from the seasonings he was measuring out into his hand. "As in, Magistrate Allen? That fellow who worked with Lady Holmes to get the Enforcer reform bill through?"

Keene didn't try to hide the surprise in his voice. Falcon knowing Beatrice, Lady Holmes' socialite daughter, could be easily explained: Beatrice knew *everyone*. This, though, was something else. Falcon, an *Enforcer* of all people, had been asked round to the coauthor of that bill's home. True, Falcon was fairly certain part of the reason was because there were still things to be gained from his cooperation. But he was also on genuinely friendly terms with the family, and Falcon couldn't help but feel pride start to glow in his chest.

"The very same," he replied. "Though, just so you know, Engineer Allen *hates* his magistrate titles. He prefers 'Engineer,' for his work outside of the magistrate council."

Keene nodded, and Falcon caught a smile creeping up his housemate's cheeks. "I'd be delighted to join. Thank you." He finally looked back over his shoulder. "You do run in some surprising circles, Falcon Smoke."

That made the pride in Falcon's chest glow even brighter, and he returned a smile that was pure, unadulterated joy. "Spiffing. Just spiffing." It was a silly, toffee-nosed expression—definitely not one fitting for a serious Enforcer to use—but Falcon was too pleased to care.

At last, dinner was ready. The soup was hearty and restorative and exactly what Falcon needed after a day like today. He didn't reserve his praise and insisted on doing the clearing up after they'd finished. After all, Keene had done the really hard work of cooking. Falcon took it slow, though. His body still wasn't entirely happy, even after its respite, and he was rather tired of playacting like everything was fine. Besides, with them living together, how long could pretending really last?

"I'm surprised you don't have stretches or something you can do to help your pain," Keene commented. He was taking his turn to rest at the table.

"It's not proper pain," Falcon replied automatically. That was only halfway a lie. He'd experienced truly painful ordeals, and this wasn't that. But he also couldn't deny that it was more than a little uncomfortable. "And I do have some exercises that are supposed to help. Things have been a bit busy of late, though. You know how it is." He didn't elaborate, nor did he wait for Keene to agree. "I'll get back into them."

"Let's do them now."

Keene's sudden statement made Falcon stop and look back at him, brows squinching together. "Pardon?"

Keene smiled and motioned between the two of them. "Let's both do them together. It's always helpful to undertake a challenge with someone else."

"That's…" Falcon was flummoxed as he looked for the right words. They came spilling out of him while surprise still had hold of his wits. "That's extremely kind of you." Falcon shook his head, wrangling said wits back into place. "Thank you very much, but no. This is something I need to do alone."

"Why?"

Surprise sucker punched Falcon again, keeping him from dodging the question as he might have usually done. "Why what?"

"Why do you need to do it alone?"

Falcon studied Keene's face. What a curious inquiry, and he

wondered if his housemate might have some kind of ulterior motive. Did he want to see the cruel, heartless Enforcer brought low? As soon as that idea entered Falcon's mind, good sense swatted it away. Keene wasn't like that; he'd made Falcon tea and dinner. The man's expression was open and sincere. Feeling really rather chuffed about Keene's kindness but unable to bring himself to accept the offer—the exercises looked absurd, after all—Falcon chuckled nervously.

"Thank you anyway." He placed their bowls in the sink for washing up.

"Make sure you do them." From the corner of his eye, Falcon could see Keene playfully shaking a finger at him. "You can't depend on me to make you dinner every night."

Falcon's chuckle was easier this time, and not a little bit wry. At least dinner with the Allens—the date for which they'd sort soon—was one more night Falcon was off the hook.

"I'll do them. I promise," he said.

"My offer's still on the table if you change your mind."

"Duly noted. Thank you."

Falcon was definitely *not* going to take Keene up on that offer. It was bad enough the chap had to see him hobble about like an old man. He absolutely didn't want Keene seeing him lie on the floor and stretching his limbs to and fro like a swan who'd gotten drunk and fallen over. He caught a mischievous glint in his housemate's eye just then, a glint that made Falcon decide he might want to close his bedroom door while he did said ridiculous exercises.

~Chapter 5~

Unsurprisingly, Mina's card came round the very next day with a list of her and Engineer Allen's availability and a request for dates that might work for Falcon and Keene. The gents coordinated their calendars and came up with a scant handful within the next fortnight. Keene was, to Falcon's interest, the harder of the two to nail down. He had some catering events coming up, several of which ran into the evening, but they were finally able to settle on something that worked for everyone.

The two men fell into a bit of a routine over the next few days. Falcon always came home from work aching, and Keene took on the kitchen duties, either making dinner fresh or having left a prepared plate in the icebox for Falcon. Falcon made a few weak protests, but he couldn't maintain them. He wanted to. It didn't seem fair that Keene was always the one who cooked, but Falcon was also infinitely grateful that he hadn't had to reveal how useless he was in that area yet. All his plans to learn to cook had gone down the pipes as his regular Enforcer duties and Cru training kept him busy enough for two people.

He hadn't heard anything about the results of Mina and First Iago's meeting, which suited Falcon's goal to keep a low profile just fine. Thankfully, he had some leave time coming up—a somewhat tiresome family holiday he, his sisters, his parents, and his grandfather took every year. No one had needed to say that Falcon was no longer welcome on that trip, and to be honest, he wasn't terribly sad about missing a train ride to the bordertown of Dogwood Lane, just so they could eat out at different restaurants and hear his grandfather bang on about how much better things used to be. The leave had been approved, though, and Falcon was happy to step out of everyone's sightlines for a while. And he was certain he'd finally be able to brush up on his nonexistent cooking skills.

In preparation for this goal, he tried observing the cooks in the mess hall at the Halls of Justice, but frying everything in grease or, more often, stewing it into an unrecognizable mash seemed to be the only two methods they used. That just wouldn't do. Not when Keene had made them lovely soups, baked fragrant breads, and roasted tumbles of colorful vegetables.

"Roasting covers a multitude of sins," he'd said one cold, rainy evening.

Falcon had barely heard him while trying not to drool over the delicious melange of stewed broad beans plus roasted parsnips, leeks, and tiny cabbages he couldn't remember the name of on his plate.

Falcon had grown up on rich meats like duck and beef, dripping fat and juices. Desserts were on offer every night—dense plum puddings and fluffy cakes dressed with sprinklings of featherlight sugar. And yet, Keene's simple, frugal meals shone as brightly as any of those decadent delights had. Some lucky mornings, rare instances wherein Keene had neither gone out early nor had been kept late working, he was already up and making a breakfast of tea and either eggs or toast. This morning was especially lucky, as Keene served up leftover bread slices fried in chicken fat with an egg and roasted tomato on top.

As they sat together and ate their breakfast, Falcon already dressed for work and Keene reading a newssheet, Falcon couldn't help but laud Keene's cooking for what was probably the thousandth or so time. He'd considered asking Keene where he'd learned to cook, but thought better of it. What if the answer was something Falcon should already know? Something like, "The same place everyone else learns." Where that ubiquitous place might be, Falcon hadn't the foggiest. No matter, he'd get there soon. And then *he'd* be the one making scrummy breakfasts just like this one! This future prospect was very appealing indeed.

Thinking of the upcoming opportunity, Falcon mumbled between bites, "My leave time can't start soon enough." He didn't mind showing how keen he was. Who didn't get excited about time off work? "Just today to get through"

They'd discussed it while figuring out a day to join the Allens for dinner, so Keene was already aware too.

In the way that had become familiar, Keene made a hard left turn in the conversation. "We should go shopping together. Tomorrow."

Mouth full, Falcon tipped his head to the side curiously, and he suddenly realized he might have picked up the habit from Keene, though he doubted he looked as charming doing it as his housemate did. Seeing Falcon's expression, Keene smiled and went on to explain.

"You've been here over a week now and you've only gone to work and come back. You need to get to know your neighbors, learn the neighborhood. And *I* will be your guide." Keene pressed a proud hand to his chest as he said this last sentence.

Falcon rather doubted any of their neighbors wanted to meet him. Well, he'd met Mrs. Spoondawdle without incident, but she seemed the sort to like everyone, right down to the ornery, yowling alley cat that prowled around the rubbish bins at night. He felt bad about barely having spoken to her since their initial meeting, especially since her apple pie hadn't stood a chance against two young blokes armed with forks and big appetites. Falcon had enjoyed an especially large slice one of the mornings Keene hadn't made breakfast. Falcon had seen her in passing most days, though, either on his way to work while she watered a small window box of flowers on the front of her house or on his way back, chatting to neighbors he didn't know.

He couldn't deny that it would be good to get to know the area. He really should have already, or so his Enforcer training said:

Always know your surroundings. The better you know them, the quicker you'll know when something's off.

Falcon didn't suspect nearly the level of wrongdoing around every corner his superiors insisted existed, but if someone was looking to cause trouble, he wanted to be able to protect his home, temporary or not. And having Keene show him around, given that Keene was becoming quite the local expert, would be wise. So Falcon agreed they would go shopping together tomorrow, and he found himself looking forward to it, despite the high likelihood that most of his neighbors would despise him as soon as he answered that dreaded but all too common query, "And what do you do?" Keene had warmed to him after all; perhaps Falcon could engender similar trust from his community.

As he left that morning, he gave a cheery greeting to a man leaning against a nearby lamppost, tipped his cap to a passing woman going the opposite direction on the footpath, and swung by Mrs. Spoondawdle's house to remind her that they really must get together soon. Perhaps tomorrow after his and Keene's shopping trip? He'd have to remember to tell Keene, and maybe they'd be able to afford to get the old woman something yummy while they were out.

Work too went better than he'd expected—though that wasn't saying much; he never had great expectations for work. His body wasn't complaining throughout the day like it usually did anyway. Perhaps that was because he'd remembered to do his stretches both last night and this morning. Truth be told, he hadn't done very well keeping his promise to Keene about doing physiotherapy regularly. Falcon chuckled wryly at himself as he admitted that alright, perhaps, maybe, just possibly there was more than a little benefit to being disciplined about his exercises.

He smiled warmly at the folks at his tram stop that afternoon. He'd even begun to learn some of their names, though that had commenced carefully. He didn't want to give anyone reason to avoid him and make their daily travels a burden. He gave the tram horses pats on their necks—Artax and Hwin, he'd learned they were called—and asked after Marty's, the driver's, shoulder, which had been giving him trouble. The two had bonded over achey joints, though not much else.

With all the feelings of such a good day floating around inside of him, when Falcon walked into his shared house that afternoon, he suddenly felt as if it had all been a dream. Everything looked utterly, unequivocally *wrong*. Or perhaps his day had been real and this was a nightmare. Stars, he hoped for the latter.

ADE: Assess, determine, enact.

Falcon whipped out his truncheon from its holster at his side and then stilled. His eyes roved over the front room, taking in the details of the wrongness. The most blatant issue, and that which had slapped him in the face upon entering, was that the front room was now entirely empty. Even his ridiculously oversized wardrobe and headboard had vanished. Through the fireplace, which he noted was cold, he saw the cooking implements that usually lived there gone as well. He couldn't remember if those were some of what Keene considered his "good" cookware.

The thought of his housemate splashed ice, heavy and sharp and frigid, over Falcon's insides.

He just stopped himself from calling out Keene's name. He was often home. This heist job would have required at least two, if not more, people for lifting the larger furniture. Definitely enough to overpower one person. In a situation like this, an Enforcer's first priority was to keep the crime scene pristine. Not a dust mote should be unsettled if possible; catching the perpetrators was paramount. Everything else, including the health and safety of potential victims came after.

Falcon promptly ignored this knowledge and began a quiet—lest the burglars were still around and feeling stabby—but thorough search of the house. Keene was nowhere to be found, and the thieves were similarly absent, though Falcon did discover that the rest of the house had been looted almost as completely as the front room. Only his bed, his idiotically large four-poster bed, remained. Likely because it was too heavy to move and the thieves hadn't wanted to bother with disassembling it. Keene's room was the most difficult to assess. Falcon had never seen inside his housemate's room and therefore had zero context for how much had been stolen. Keene's bed was entirely missing, as was any other furniture he'd had. Papers scattered across the floor, bootprints patterning across tightly written lines. Boxes containing various cooking implements and serving ware had been riffled through and scattered. A single teapot painted with chamomile flowers lay shattered on the floor.

As he was taking in this scene, Falcon heard the front door open, shut, and, faintly, Keene's disbelieving voice.

"What the bloody blazes…"

Falcon hurried back down the stairs and found his housemate gawping at the front room as he leaned back against the front door.

"Leave everything exactly as it is," Falcon ordered from the opposite doorway. He'd assumed the voice he used for commanding the Cru: firm and confident. He felt it too; *this* he knew how to handle. "They might have left evidence."

Keene, presumably because he had never had to learn to fall in line and follow orders, immediately did the opposite and ran into the kitchen, pushing past Falcon, and began tearing through the cabinets and drawers.

Falcon could hear him muttering to himself, mostly versions of, "You've got to be joking," and, "They didn't. They couldn't have. They did!"

"Those ratbags!" Keene came marching back to the little corridor between the door to the kitchen and the door to the living room.

Falcon had shut the latter as a way to try and slow his housemate's tirade, leaving them in quite a tight little space at the foot of the stairs. This corridor, after all, was only as wide as the stairway. Keene looked at the closed door, to Falcon, and back to the closed door.

"Well?" he asked expectantly.

They were no more than a foot apart, energy crackling almost audibly in the air. Falcon had seen distress countless times before in all its forms. This was the sort liable to explode, and he reached out, palms down, and made a show of taking a deep breath in the hope that Keene would follow his lead. If he knew Keene better, he might have patted his shoulder. Touching was something that had to be earned, and Falcon hadn't earned the privilege.

"We'll need to make a list of everything that's been stolen. With that, the Enforcers will know what to look for when they investigate."

He decided against telling Keene that the Enforcers likely wouldn't give a fig about this case. Break-ins at private homes were difficult to solve and, if no one had been a victim of violence, the case was even less of a priority. The order might care a bit that it had been one of their own who'd been robbed, but Falcon was in enough people's bad books that they might also happily look the other way while the case went cold. Still, he and Keene would go through the proper channels. At least, Falcon assumed they would until Keene started shaking his head.

"No. We're not tattling to your boys in blue and grey." Keene's tone was as firm as Falcon had ever heard it.

"Why ever not?" Falcon replied. Unexpected anger began to rise in him as he gave voice to what had happened. "They *broke into* our home, *stole* our things. It's not like we have the money to just buy new furniture." Falcon tossed a wave toward the kitchen. "I can't imagine your cookware was cheap."

Now it was Keene's turn to be conciliatory. He extended a

hand, fingers stretched toward Falcon just shy of touching his forearm, but he never quite made contact. More of an offer than an actual gesture. "I'm angry too, but in the end, that's all they are: things. I don't want someone locked away for the rest of their lives over mere stuff."

Falcon's anger bristled as hot shame washed over him. "That's not what I meant. I don't want... Trials are coming. And reform." He wanted to retreat and steamroll ahead all at once. He knew the call he should make. He far outranked Keene, a civilian, in this situation. The decision was Falcon's to make. And he knew Keene knew it by the way his housemate's dark eyes beseeched him.

Most people looked away, became deferent, when an Enforcer locked eyes with them the way Falcon had. He'd done it without even thinking about it. And more shame churned in his stomach. Keene's eyes were soft. They weren't judging Falcon, but they wanted what he did not. He shifted his weight, and when he did, his arm brushed Keene's fingertips where they'd been hanging in space, offering comfort to Falcon despite... despite everything the uniform he was wearing meant. Still, the violation of the break-in sent a twang of thorny uncertainty through him. It had stolen his peace of mind, his feeling of safety, as it would anyone's, and that was inexcusable.

"Trials are coming," he repeated, more confidently than before. "Reform is happening."

Whether accidental or purposely, Falcon didn't know, but Keene's fingers tensed against his arm. "But how quickly? And what guarantee is there for anyone arrested before it arrives?"

None. There was no guarantee. And Falcon sighed. He leaned further into Keene's touch, letting the man properly grasp his arm. Keene gave it a little squeeze, and Falcon gave the hand an affirming little pat.

"Very well, we won't report it. But I have to do something. This is a violation; it cannot stand."

Keene gave him the gentlest of smiles, and Falcon thought he caught a wobble in it. "Let's make that list then."

During the process, Falcon had to tuck his personal feelings into a box. It was similar to what he'd heard Camilla and Doctor Allen describe they had to do in their own line of work. The small notebook he always kept in one of his uniform's pockets served as an anchor, full of cold, hard facts and sketches of Falcon's observations around the house. A magnifying glass and tape measure made up part of his evidence kit too, and he took measurements of everything, even if it seemed insignificant. He might have decided not to report the break-in, but he couldn't keep himself from following the steps for a proper investigation.

Deep scratches on the back door's frame told him the thieves likely used this as their entrance and exit. Smart, given the fact that they'd committed their crime in broad daylight. Falcon had initially suspected the front door, given its propensity to pop open when it wasn't deadbolted, as he'd learned the day he'd moved in. But no, he'd had to unlock it when he'd come home. True, the back garden faced another back garden across the road, but both were surrounded by high walls. The street behind the garden wasn't often used in midday, as it only led deeper into the thicket of houses in this area.

Falcon skirted the inside of the back garden's wall, careful to preserve any clues left in the yard as he scrutinized the ground. A herb garden had clearly once existed here, but it hadn't been kept up, leaving the remaining plants to duke it out for dominance—mint was winning by leagues. He felt confident that the semicircular, pockmarked divots in the ground had been left by the clawed feet of the longest couch that had, until today, resided in the front room. The length between them matched the length of the couch, and other, though less distinct marks scattered along the skinny dirt path that led to the back gate. Thank the stars for the rain that night Keene had made stewed broad beans and roasted vegetables, leaving the ground softer today than it might have otherwise been.

Several sets of bootprints had been preserved as well, but Falcon could only draw those. Image-stills were both time consuming to produce and expensive. Even if he had one that captured each distinct print—and he still had yet to determine how many different sets there were—he'd need more to prove that the prints were from his back garden. He'd face similar problems if he cast them, and that would also require him to know how to create casting material in the first place. Once more rain came and washed the evidence away, the drawings and Falcon's word would be all that remained. And his word wouldn't carry much weight since he'd flouted the standard practice of immediately reporting crimes. Perhaps Keene might consider...

Keene's room!

The papers strewn about there had bootprints on them. It

wasn't much, but it was better evidence than drawings. On tiptoes, Falcon speed-minced his way back inside, still careful to preserve evidence, and hurried up the stairs.

"Don't bin anything!" he commanded, bursting into Keene's room.

His housemate, he was surprised to discover, was sitting on the floor beneath one of the room's windows, next to an open hat box and surrounded by the devastation of the break-in. His eyes were red around the edges, and though he tried to quickly wipe them away under the guise of scratching his nose, Falcon saw the tears slipping down Keene's face.

"Keene?" he asked softly. Falcon thought maybe he ought to leave. He had, after all, just burst into the man's room. The very height of rudeness, but Keene looked so small sitting on the bedroom floor, so forlorn.

Keene flashed a smile, and Falcon easily read it as an automatic reaction. It didn't reach his eyes. "Sorry, mate. Just trying to take in the damage." He looked around and drew a shaky breath. "It's hard to know, where does one even start?"

Falcon muttered some apologies, sincere but garbled as he began to back out of the room. He'd decided he'd leave Keene to it before his brain registered what Keene's words had meant. Then Falcon realized, had he not been trained how to assess a crime scene, he might very well feel the same as Keene did: lost and staring up from the bottom of a seemingly insurmountable cliff face of a task. It wasn't that Keene needed more time, he needed help. Help that Falcon could offer. He slipped back around the door and, still careful to avoid disrupting the evidence, sidled up to Keene before dropping into a cross-legged sitting position next to him. Keene acted as if he was looking back at the mess around them, but Falcon followed the line of his gaze to a bare spot on the wall, away from the aftermath of invasion around them.

"Oy," Falcon said, budging his shoulder against Keene's. The word fell awkwardly from Falcon's mouth. It wasn't part of his usual vernacular, but he wanted something casual, safe, to approach Keene with.

Keene looked at him, and a tiny, questioning line creased between his dark brows.

"I know it looks bad, but we can sort it. I'll help if you want." Falcon's tone was soft and low.

Keene's eyes grazed the edge of the mess around them before

meeting Falcon's again. "Have you ever dealt with a situation like this before?"

Falcon nodded. "Many times." His voice held no conceit. It was simply a fact, but one Falcon delivered with a note of sadness. He always felt for anyone who'd had their sense of security taken from them. He paused, considering how his next suggestion might come off, and added an addendum to his query. "Are you certain you don't want to open an official case? I understand your issues about it, but I also don't want you to feel alone in this."

Keene shook his head. "No, I can't condemn another human being to a life in prison." There was no judgment in his voice, but Falcon still felt a pang. It faded like mist when Keene smiled at him. And this time, the smile lightened the umber tone of his eyes to walnut. "But thank you. I'm not alone, not with you here."

He budged Falcon's shoulder back, and Falcon's stomach did a flip inside of him. He couldn't stop himself from smiling in return, and a nervous chuckle slipped, without permission mind you, past his lips. Looking away, Falcon cleared his throat and began to assess the room.

"You'll have to let me know if I overstep anywhere. I can get a bit bossy, you know."

"Oh, I know," Keene said far, *far* too quickly.

Falcon laughed properly at that. His sisters had informed him of this character flaw too many times for him to deny it, and then he laughed harder at a sudden mental image of Keene meeting them and all three comically shaking their heads at Falcon's bossiness problem.

Night fell with a slow, respectful tread as the lads tackled the room. Rather, less of a tackle and more of a meticulous cataloging of all the bits of paper and other debris around the room. In addition to the chamomile teapot, more dishes and pieces of serving ware had been broken. Keene, it turned out, had quite the extensive collection of tureens, pudding molds, cake and dessert stands, platters, and tea ware. Stars, the amount of tea ware! Most of the sets had been selected for the specific flower motif decorating each one, as flowers were a language unto themselves. All the silverware was gone, but thankfully many small, common items that either weren't worth much and/or couldn't be melted down or safely transported without considerable care had been left behind. As had Keene's collected documentation, marred and damaged though it was.

The papers scattered everywhere were mostly Keene's recipes, contact lists, business records, and the like. He'd kept them in separate binders based on category, and the thieves had seen fit to, instead of simply flipping through the binders, tearing out the pages and flinging them like giant confetti.

"Why would they go to all the trouble?" Keene asked.

Falcon was examining one of the pages bearing a well preserved bootprint. He'd separated out specimens like this, though ideas for how he'd use them were still forming. Thus, he was distracted when he answered matter of factly, "They might have been looking for sensitive information, like safety deposit box information or safe combinations." He turned his scrutiny to the slowly shrinking mess around them. "Or they were trying to cover their tracks, use the mess to mislead us somehow."

As he searched, his gaze fell on Keene, whose shoulders slumped, chest tight and brows knotted.

"You know," Falcon said, making a show of looking at his pocket watch. "It's getting on. We should break for dinner."

In response, his stomach growled. That brought out a whisper of a smile on Keene's face, and he looked to the door.

"They ransacked the fridge. I'll go out and get us something."

"We can go together if you want," Falcon offered. He didn't really want to leave the house, but he wanted Keene to know he wasn't alone.

His housemate's expression turned cheeky, one eyebrow arching playfully. Seeing cheer in Keene again made the whole room seem a little brighter.

"We've still got a lot of work ahead of us, so you do what you're good at and let me do the same."

"Are you certain?" Falcon asked, more than anything as another show of solidarity.

Keene nodded. "I wouldn't mind some time to sort my thoughts. Away from here."

That last sentence said volumes with just three little words. Falcon understood. Distance could be a wonderful crystalizing agent. While Keene was gone, Falcon continued to gather what evidence he could and hoped that tomorrow's daylight would reveal yet more.

Darkness thoroughly blanketed the back garden now, but Falcon returned to give it one last look in case he'd missed anything before he'd rushed back inside. Sweeping an oil lamp back and forth, he'd nearly finished inspecting what he could when a bit of movement at the gate caught his eye. It was a small piece of fabric caught on a decorative wrought iron vine. The vine's weld points had rusted away, leaving the vine to stick out from the rest of the gate. More specifically, it stuck out into the *inside* of the garden. Falcon carefully removed the bit of fabric. It was reddish brown with black pinstripes—an interesting design choice since the stripes were nearly invisible against the brown. The fabric's shade was similar to the color of the gate's rusty metal. Thus why he'd missed it before, but it fluttered and threw excitable shadows in the lamplight any time the barest breeze came by to tickle it. Falcon supposed it was possible it belonged to an unfortunate passerby, though that seemed unlikely given that the scrap had been caught inside the gate. And he wouldn't discount any possible lead. As he headed back inside to wait for Keene, Falcon considered the evidence he'd collected so far. He might not have plans to report the robbery to the Enforcers, but he wasn't planning on just letting the thieves keep his and Keene's things either. Not without a fight.

~Chapter 6~

"I'm sure it'll be fine." That's what Falcon and Keene had both said when they'd realized there was now only one bed in the entire house.

And it mostly was fine. In fact, Keene was downright blasé about the entire affair. His only follow-up question had been which side Falcon preferred. If he'd grown up on the lower end of middle class—Keene's background was still a subject they hadn't broached—it was possible he'd had to share a bed with siblings. And, though Falcon had never had to share a room with anyone, much less a bed, he'd had to share close quarters with other Enforcers during stakeouts, during which two or more of them often had to squash inside a hansom or hide just inside the mouth of an alley for hours at a time. What Falcon was not used to, however, was being awoken in the middle of the night to the dim light of an oil lamp. Not just the light, though, but the feel of someone shifting next to him and a soft, semi-regular clicking noise. It took Falcon's groggy brain a moment to remember what had happened that day, and he turned over, grabbing his cane from beside the bed as he went. This was before he realized the thieves would have to have heads made of melons to return to the scene of the crime. Instead of melon-headed rapscallions, he found himself looking up at Keene, who was wielding nothing more dangerous than a ball of yarn and a pair of knitting needles.

Keene was looking back down at Falcon with a definitive, "Oops," written across his countenance.

"Sorry," he said. The oops expression flattened into a grimace. "You were sleeping so soundly, I didn't think I'd wake you."

Falcon warmed as an image of Keene watching him sleep floated across his mind's eye. Then, slowly, slogging through the clearing cobwebs of consciousness, he levered his elbow beneath him to lean his head on his hand.

"Everything alright?" Falcon asked.

Keene gave a shrug that was nowhere near as easy as his usual manner. "Knitting helps me think."

"And what are we thinking about?" Falcon asked. He hadn't meant to sound as playful as he had. Sleepiness made his mind bleary.

In return, Keene gave a small but equally playful smile. "You're certainly right to say 'we.'"

That woke Falcon up a bit more, and he pushed himself up to a sitting position. "Why is we right? I mean, why am *I* right?"

"So proper," Keene teased before setting his knitting down. He took a moment to count his stitches, nodded approvingly, and said to himself, "Twenty-seven." Then he squared a look at Falcon. "I want in on solving the crime."

"What? No! Absolutely not. I mean... I'm not trying to do that."

Falcon couldn't have been more unconvincing if he'd been wearing an oversized, steam-powered badge that spun and puffed smoke when he lied. And, in the case of this humongous fib, it would have exploded in a tiny fireball. In addition to his flub just now, Falcon had already outed his intent several times over. Every time he'd told Keene, in one way or another, to preserve the evidence. Or the way Falcon had muttered theories and thoughts to himself while he'd recorded the details of the crime into his notebook.

Keene fixed him with a dubious look, but had the decency not to decry what a terrible liar Falcon was. Instead, he pointed at the small stack of bits that Falcon had collected over that afternoon and evening. "I see what you're doing. You're building your case. Every mystery novel hero does it."

Falcon tried to shoot back a withering glare, but what came out, what *always* came out when he tried this tactic, wouldn't even

Falcon's Favor

make a parched daisy wilt. He couldn't bring himself to lie again, though. Not just because he knew he was rubbish at it, but also because he realized he didn't want Keene to start thinking that was his fallback mode of operating. And that certainly wasn't who Falcon wanted to be either.

So instead, Falcon said, "I'm not letting you put yourself at risk like that." And he immediately hated himself for it. Stars, he sounded pompous.

"Not letting me?" Keene chortled. "What do you think I am? Some swooning dandy?" He then melodramatically pressed the back of his hand to his forehead and wailed, "Heavens, why?! Why couldn't they have left me my fainting couch? What I am without a couch upon which to perform my many oodles of faints?"

Keene then proceeded to fling himself across Falcon's legs, the very picture of delicate nerves brought low by ne'er-do-well-iness.

Falcon raised an eyebrow at the hammy cad sprawled in his lap, an experience both entirely new to him and quite fun. "You are a bit of a dandy, though."

"Thank you!" As Keene opened his eyes again, his smile looked genuinely chuffed. He lifted himself back to an upright position and added, "I do try, but clothes cost money I could be spending on tableware. It's a struggle."

Despite Keene's light tone, Falcon's insides twisted. He couldn't imagine how much money it would take to replace all of Keene's stolen cookware, not to mention the silver, table, tea, and every other kind of ware too. For a moment, he considered asking his family for money. But, again, he didn't want to lie, and telling them the truth made the twists inside of him turn double knots around themselves. What would they think? He had failed at this whole living-on-his-own endeavor barely a week in.

"You alright, mate?"

Keene's gentle voice pulled Falcon from his thoughts. He realized he'd been staring down at his hands, fiddling with the handle of his cane. He looked back at his housemate and tried to summon a smile. Falcon felt the thinness of it on his face.

"Fine. Just thinking."

"Do you want to talk about it?" Keene craned his neck around to look Falcon more directly in the eye.

It felt oddly intimate, looking eye to eye with this kind person who was open to hearing Falcon pour out his feelings. Though, that could be down to them sharing a bed too. And anyway, Keene was probably just being courteous. He likely didn't really want to hear Falcon whitter.

Falcon straightened up against the wall where the headboard should have been. "Let's get back to the subject at hand."

Keene nodded like he completely agreed, but his eyes were still clouded with what looked suspiciously like concern. "Right. The case. The case we're going to solve together."

He picked his knitting back up and paused. Keene mouthed something to himself and started tapping his thumb and fingers together like he was counting.

"Twenty-seven," Falcon supplied.

"Ah, yes, thank you." And Keene began his work again.

"You can't help me with the case." Falcon tried piercing Keene with his gaze, but the man wasn't looking at him to notice. So, Falcon leaned in to try and intensify the power of his stare. "You're a civilian."

Quick as a flash, Keene turned to face him, a mischievous gleam in his eye. Their noses were inches from each other thanks to Falcon's lean. "And *you're* investigating as one too." He waggled his head smugly. "Since it's not official Enforcer business, even stevens, ducky."

Falcon didn't pull back, still hoping to win the argument by the force of his determination. Even though he was extremely aware of Keene's breath on his cheeks. How did he always smell of warm spices? Was it a hair oil he used or something? Keene's hair hung loose around his face now, framing those deep, dark eyes locked on Falcon's own honey brown ones. Honey and walnut, each waiting for the other to budge. When Falcon's gaze dipped to Keene's lips, he realized he was letting the situation get away from him. He needed to focus on the problem at hand, nothing else, though he still held his ground.

Falcon wrinkled his nose to show his distaste. "Alright, first, don't call me ducky. Ducks are horrible creatures—"

"Ducks are delicious creatures," Keene interrupted.

"Fine, granted. And second—" He slowly arced his open hand over Keene's project and pushed it down. "—no more knitting. You're right; it's clearly helping you, and that's an unfair advantage."

Keene threw back his head and laughed, a pure, golden sound of amusement. After the day they'd had, it was like music. Falcon pulled his hand back, but kept it ready.

"Why shouldn't I get to use handicrafts to my advantage?" Keene asked, still laughing.

"Because I'm not that clever to start. I need you to have some kind of handicap." A yawn overtook Falcon just then, and he added mid-yawn, "Plus, I'm tired." Keene gave him a sympathetic sideways tilt of his head before lifting the knitting project back up. "Ah!" It was more a noise than a word, and Falcon pushed Keene's needles down again.

Keene laughed some more and had to lean back against the wall, placing a hand over his belly as he tried to get his breath back. Falcon chuckled, and they enjoyed the moment of levity together for a few minutes, neither saying anything more. When Keene had mostly collected himself again, Falcon continued more seriously.

"Look, yes, this case isn't under Enforcer purview, but *I'm* still an Enforcer. So it's my job to keep people, you included, out of danger. That means I have to do this alone."

Keene rolled his head around on the wall to face Falcon, a quizzical look squinting one eye and quirking up his mouth. "I thought 'keeping people safe'—" He made little quotes in the air with his fingers. "—meant arresting baddies." Sardonically, he added, "As well as anyone who could potentially be a possible baddie. You know, for *safety*."

Falcon released a sighing groan that expressed his frustration with the order fairly succinctly. Unfortunately, that didn't really translate into words, so he added, "I have a different idea of how to protect people than... some of my cohorts." Falcon then had to resist the urge to squirm at his own statement. It felt both like painting with too broad a brush and more than a touch self-aggrandizing to lump the entire rest of the order together whilst simultaneously excluding himself.

Surprisingly, Keene softened. "I see that."

Falcon might have reeled back in surprise if sleep weren't calling to him again, making his limbs and mind sluggish. As it was, he simply appreciated the sentiment and wriggled down beneath the covers once more. Not his covers, unfortunately. No, the thieves had taken his fine, soft bed linens, but a spare set of Keene's, which had been stored away, had escaped their notice. They were warm, though a little scratchy. As were the pillows, which were also Keene's and nothing more than old flour sacks stuffed with straw, or perhaps reeds. They were some of the items that had, thankfully, been deemed not worth stealing.

"So we have an understanding then?" Falcon asked, his words partially muffled against the pillow. "No investigating for you." He yawned again. "Leave that for your mystery novels."

Keene didn't answer, and Falcon looked back up to see his housemate counting stitches again. He reached an arm out from under the sheets and batted at the hanging work.

"Did you hear me?" Falcon mumbled.

"I heard you," Keene said, clearly distracted by counting. "Are we still on for shopping tomorrow?"

Falcon wasn't really thinking, eyes closed and sleep already darkening his consciousness. They'd let a good bit of heat out from the blankets with all their shuffling around. Like a moth to a petrolsene lamp, he wriggled closer to Keene for warmth. Falcon was vaguely aware of the feeling of Keene pulling the covers up over his shoulder.

Just before he nodded off, to Keene's question he answered, "Of course."

)(

Falcon had never stepped foot in a butcher shop before. He considered himself to have a pretty strong stomach, especially considering the things he had witnessed in the line of duty—torture during interrogations, public punishment displays meant to deter others from wrongdoing, and the injuries wrought both by the night of the attack on the Halls of Justice and the protest that had gone wrong—but seeing slabs of meat dismembered from the bodies they used to belong to and put on display was unlike anything he'd seen before. In his experience, meat came pre-cooked. Even when he'd watched Keene make food, Falcon hadn't had to see many raw body bits.

Here, on his first day of what was supposed to be a relaxing bit of time off work, salty hams hung from hooks attached to rails that crosshatched the ceiling. Entire ducks and chickens bereft of their feathers did the same from more rails that striped horizontally along the walls. Sausage links, which looked the most like what they were supposed to, looped along more hooks across the front window like New Year's garlands. A glass and wood case stretched across the front and around one side of the small shop. Within it, nestled in ice, sat smaller cuts of meat. And all along the back, behind this counter, were the huge, hanging carcasses of entire cows and pigs.

Despite the nature of the shop, the floors and glass surfaces were all clean. Falcon had expected there to be a sort of rotting smell hanging in the air, even a faint one, but it mostly smelled of sage, rosemary, and other herbs Falcon couldn't name, which clustered in small jars around the shop. Attached to the jars were small notes that read:

Herbs generously provided by Ms. Begonia Perez, florist

Small bundles of the same had been attached as fragrant decoration to the ends of the grease pencils the employees used to write orders and label customer packages. The scene had been disconcerting at first, but Keene's decadent descriptions of ways he'd like to use some of the raw meat around them quickly banished Falcon's unease—a chicken dressed in forty cloves of garlic, roast lamb artfully decorated with spikes of rosemary, duck breast smothered in cherries and port wine. Beyond the shop walls, Falcon heard the distant noise of ships' bells in Cobalt Bay, horse hooves clopping on the cobblestone street outside, and the murmur of the occasional group of chatting passersby outside.

Shopping had turned out to be a test he wasn't prepared for. Falcon had never been much good at exams in school, even when he'd studied, but he'd managed well enough. This, though, was like one of those trick word problems.

There are twelve apples in the basket. Four are the Dumelow's Seedling variety, two are Wyken Pippins, and six are Golden Spires. If you buy three, how many will be fresh? Bonus: Which is the best for making pies?

Except Falcon'd had to do different versions of it over and over again. With vegetables at the greengrocer's—an elderly, spindly man built like a stalk of celery—a quick inquiry about tools with the blacksmith, candles at the candlemaker's, breads at the bakery, and now cuts of meat. The last of these were far more expensive than Falcon thought they should be. Not that he had any basis for this belief, given that he'd never shopped for his own groceries. Nevertheless, he'd mentally balked at seeing the prices. *How much* did it take to grow a cow? He might have verbalized his shock if Keene had not been there. His housemate was clearly chummy with the man and his wife, however, so Falcon was trying to make nice as well. He remembered Keene saying he wanted to develop a rapport with the butcher and didn't want to spoil that.

Keene was currently telling them about the rather nice spread he'd fixed up for himself and Falcon that morning. Falcon had awoken to the smell of sizzling bacon and freshly brewed tea and had come downstairs to find Keene cooking. Despite complaining that the cookware he'd been left with was fussy and full of hotspots, whatever that meant, Keene was clearly a dab hand at making the petulant cookware bend to his will. Falcon suspected this relatively indulgent breakfast had been a strike against the bad feelings yesterday's robbery had created.

This suspicion was all but confirmed when Keene had, upon presenting Falcon with his plate, pointed a wooden spoon at him and said with the air of a commander in battle, "Don't let grey skies get you down, my friend. Eat, drink, and be merry!"

Falcon had smiled at his housemate and had the wisdom not to ask whether this bolstering speech was more for his benefit or Keene's. Nor did he quibble about how much this meal likely cost and how they'd have to really start pinching their coppers. Instead, he lavished praise on Keene's cooking. Not that it proved difficult. As usual, Keene's food was spectacular, though this meal'd had a little extra something to it.

Keene had dipped toast in a mixture of eggs and milk seasoned with some sort of warm, fragrant spices and then fried the soaked and dripping slices in fat leftover from cooking the bacon. If not for the need to track down and get his and Keene's stolen possessions back, Falcon could have died happy right there.

That need began sniffing again as Falcon listened to Keene share the tale of his culinary victory with the butchers. He didn't mention the robbery, which Falcon found curious. They hadn't discussed whether they'd mention it to anyone else, and Falcon had abstained so far, preferring to get a feel for his neighborhood first. He knew this might be a mistake. If anyone had seen anything suspicious, it would be better to ask them about it now, while it was still fresh in their minds. The shops they'd visited so far were all within a few minutes' walk from their house, but was that close enough for anyone to have seen anything?

"And you remember what I told you about my silver tea set?" Keene was saying. The mention of such an expensive item grabbed Falcon by the ear and yanked his attention that way.

The butcher looked confused, glanced at his wife, and then back to Keene. "No, I don't remember you mentioning it." The man was built like a bear and had a voice to match. The lush layer of hair on his arms likely helped keep him warm through the winter, as did his bushy beard. In an odd contrast, the man was bald.

"Didn't I?" Keene asked. "I could have sworn... hm, I must be thinking of Mister Snodgrass. Or perhaps Mister Halpern's new farrier? Anyway, I have a theory on using silver versus porcelain for serving tea."

As Keene expounded on his theory, Falcon decided it was time to make a move. He walked away from the little huddle and pretended to inspect some of the lamb shanks further down the display case. The butcher's wife, who had been introduced to Falcon as Mrs. Bellows, minced down the row after him.

Mrs. Bellows had the look of someone who would not and could not do as her surname suggested. She was thin and petite, only coming up to Falcon's shoulder, though her auburn hair, coiled into a tidy, practical braided bun gave her a few extra inches. She was round and reminded Falcon of a cream puff with chocolate icing. Her blue eyes sparkled as she smiled with motherly affection at him.

"Anything I can help you with, dear? Anything to put some meat onto those bones?" She chuckled to herself, and Falcon smiled.

"Getting to know the place," he replied. He always did best when his answers were rooted in truth. "I'm new to this area."

"Yes, Keene told us. Him too."

Falcon leaned against the case, trying to be subtle about it. He'd left his cane at home and was regretting it. He hadn't thought a little shopping trip would tax him so, but it had gone on longer than anticipated. Mostly because Keene wanted to introduce him to simply *everyone* and ended up in longish conversations about family happenings and neighborhood gossip and all manner of local subjects. Mrs. Bellows patted Falcon's hand.

"It's sweet the way you lads are making your own way in the world. I'm as proud as a mother sparrow watching her babies fly for the first time."

Falcon didn't much like that analogy. His parents, both of whom had made careers of studying birds at the Springhaven Museum, had often threatened to kick him and his sisters "out of the nest" when they'd misbehaved. It was believed birds did this to force their babies to learn to fly. He knew no one liked a pedant, however, and smiled back at the woman.

"Thank you. It's not easy starting out on your own, you know?" Mrs. Bellows nodded, and he added. "Do you know of anyone else new to the neighborhood? Maybe you've seen a moving cart full of stuff recently?" He knew how he sounded. To try and make it seem less like he was questioning her, he added, "Shared experiences and whatnot make for fast friendships, don't you think?"

Mrs. Bellows placed a thoughtful finger to her chin and cocked her head. After a moment, "Not that I can think of, dear." She then flashed a smile, "But you know who you should talk to? My daughter. Oh, Candy, darling. Come here for a moment, would you?"

Mrs. Bellows motioned toward a young lady about Falcon's age who'd just entered the storefront through a door that presumably led from the backroom. Candy, who shared her mother's build and hair color, looked to her mother, looked to Falcon, and started to turn back the way she came, but Mrs. Bellows was too quick.

"Now, please, young lady."

Falcon had been right. Mrs. Bellows was one of those people who could wield authority without raising their voice. Candy's shoulders stiffened, but she did as she was told, raising her head high despite her apparent displeasure.

"Candy, this is Mister Falcon Smoke. He's the Enforcers' new Steward of the Sage." Mrs. Bellows said the title with the same gravitas as introducing royalty.

Falcon cringed internally, knowing exactly where this was going. It wasn't the first time some mother, keen on marrying off her daughter, had thrown said offspring at him like this.

"Mister Smoke will do." The only people Falcon wanted calling him by his title were other Enforcers. This was still a bit uncomfortable, as he'd initially told the Bellowses to call him Falcon, but he hoped to dissuade the well-meaning woman with distance.

Mrs. Bellows was undeterred. "Lovely. And this is my daughter, Candy. Because she's so sweet." She smiled for a moment before grabbing the grease pencil Candy had stuck behind her ear. "Oh, dear, I've told you not to do this. You'll get marks on your lovely face."

Falcon could see the poor girl suppressing a groan as she wordlessly took the pencil from her mother. Candy must not work with the meat very much, because she wore a set of black leather gloves, unlike her parents, who simply handled the pieces with their bare hands. Or perhaps she subscribed to the same sort of hygienic methods as Doctor Allen and Camilla. Or her hands might just have been cold.

Mrs. Bellows fussed with Candy's hair for a moment before saying, "There now. Much better. Mister Smoke had some questions for you, Candy, and I expect you to be helpful."

"Of course, Mama," Candy replied, her tone flat.

"Good girl." And with that, Mrs. Bellows flitted off to help other customers.

An awkward silence passed between the two young people.

"Sorry about that," Falcon said at last. "I know your mother means well."

"She does," Candy replied, voice still flat. With a quick glance to ensure her mother wasn't watching, Candy replaced the pencil behind her ear.

Falcon couldn't blame the girl for being irate. No telling how many chaps Mrs. Bellows had slung Candy's way, expecting her to put on a show to win him over. And the way Mrs. Bellows had said his title made him suspect she assumed he made a nice fat salary, sufficient for supporting a wife and a couple of children to boot. He almost laughed to himself at how wrong that notion was.

"So how long should we stand here and pretend to talk?" he asked. "You know, to appease your mother?"

"For as long as you'd like, Mister Smoke." Candy said his name like it left a bitter taste in her mouth. "I believe you had some questions for me."

Falcon nodded, deciding perhaps a Doctor Allen-like approach would be best here. It wasn't exactly genteel, but it should be effective. "Alright, well, so we're clear, this little meat-cute your mother's arranged…" He waited for the joke to land, but Candy simply looked at him, stone-faced. Falcon pulled at his collar and cleared his throat. "It's not going to lead to anything."

"Noted."

Another awkward pause, and Falcon said, "Um, alright. It was lovely meeting you, Candy. Best of luck with…" He glanced at Mrs. Bellows, who was, thankfully, occupied. "…everything."

He tipped his hat to her, and she returned a perfunctory curtsey. Then, he ambled back over to his housemate and watched as Mr. Bellows wrapped something up for Keene.

"See anything you'd like?" Keene asked.

Falcon shook his head. As Keene paid for his purchase, Falcon felt his heart sink a little. They'd accomplished nothing in regards to the case. If he'd been investigating as an Enforcer, he'd have authority to search back rooms, question people at length, but that also meant at the end of the journey, somebody would end up locked away in the Halls of Justice, probably forever. Possibly not even the right person, just so long as *someone* paid the price. The reform he and so many others were hoping for was nowhere near complete, and what it would look like at the other end was anyone's guess.

Back outside, Falcon and Keene pulled off the main walkway and leaned against the side of a building. It wasn't raining, but the sky above was heavy and grey, threatening a spring storm. Gusts of wind whipped by, making people huddle and pull their cloaks and greatcoats and mufflers tighter around them. Falcon dearly wished for some sunshine to keep him warm.

The buildings in Cobalt were a mix of red brick, white plaster with dark beams, and even the occasional heavy stone Old World building, though those were rarer this close to the Agate quarter, which had suffered badly during the War of Light. This building they sheltered next to, just a few down from the butcher shop, was one of those with dark beams, but smoke from the nearby canning and other processing factories had coated the once-white plaster with soot, turning it a dove browny-grey color. To avoid smearing their clothes with the grime, Falcon and Keene shared one of the timber beams to lean against while they went over the list Keene had made.

Something said in the butcher shop kept nibbling at Falcon's brain, and he began gently, "Keene?"

"Hm?" He didn't look up from his list, trying to hold it between them and keep it from the wind's grabby grasp.

"How, um…" Falcon searched for a less accusatory way to word his question, but came up empty. He hoped his tone would help. "How many people did you tell about our things?" Keene finally looked up from his list and fixed Falcon with a quizzical stare. This had been easier when Keene'd had his head down, Falcon realized, and he swallowed hard before soldiering on, still as gently as he could. "The nice bits, I mean. I know you wouldn't do anything to... That is, I'm not saying it's your fault. I just wonder, well, perhaps... It's possible someone heard you mention that silver tea set, for instance, and got it into their head to, you know..."

Keene raised an eyebrow and finished for Falcon, "Plot a heist."

"Yes," Falcon said.

He couldn't read Keene's expression. He'd only ever seen him distressed once. That had been yesterday, and it had been fraught and fast.

Before Falcon could begin trying to smooth things over, before he knew whether or not that was really necessary, Keene shot straight to the heart of the issue.

"You said you weren't saying so, but do you *think* it's my fault?" His voice was level and serious, though Falcon still couldn't tell what he was feeling.

"No."

Keene nodded. "Good. Nor I." Falcon's shock at such a forthright statement must have shown on his face because Keene's gaze flicked over his features. In that same even tone, "What kind of life is it to always be watching what you say? For fear of someone else using it against you? Down that way lies madness. I won't take responsibility for someone else's bad behavior."

Falcon gawped. On the one hand, Keene was, quite possibly, the most outspoken person he'd ever met. Surely that sort of attitude caused problems. Or did it? Between his upper class station requiring perfect propriety from him at all times and his position as an Enforcer demanding that he tow the party line, Falcon had always had to watch his words. Perhaps Keene had never had such demands placed on him, so he couldn't possibly know what that was like. Falcon's mind marveled at the idea. And on the other hand, his words struck a chord with Falcon.

I won't take responsibility for someone else's bad behavior.

He didn't know what to do with that yet, but it settled inside of him and began making a nest.

"You are very forthright," he finally spit out, dumbly, as if that wasn't glaringly obvious.

Keene's lips crooked into a smirk, but he didn't reply. Then his head dipped again, and he began moving his fingers as if counting, or perhaps looping yarn around them.

"So you think one of the folks I've been hobnobbing with did it?" he asked.

Falcon returned a reluctant nod. That expanded the suspect list greatly, especially given how friendly Keene was. He rubbed his face, reviewing just those places they'd visited today. Without his Enforcer authority behind him, he didn't know how he was going to get straight answers from them, much less explore their homes and shops.

"Let me think on it," he said. "We haven't got many cards in our deck."

"Our?" Keene cocked his head in that endearing way he did.

"Don't start getting ideas," Falcon warned, though he couldn't help smiling a little at Keene's hopeful expression.

"Oh, I'm full of ideas." And, before turning away, Keene gave a cheeky little wink that made Falcon wonder if the man wasn't already plotting something.

~Chapter 7~

It was while they were back at the house and putting away their goods that a new idea hit Falcon. Specifically, while he'd been crouched before the fire in the kitchen, stoking a little life back into it. It was a skill he'd actually picked up back at his family manor. Though they'd had staff for that sort of thing, Falcon had always thought it silly to wait for someone to come poke at the logs a bit when he could do so just as easily. He was pleased to show off this skill when Keene was around, to prove, toff though he may be, he wasn't a completely useless one.

As Falcon stooped at the hearth, letting the heat seep into his skin and melt away the complaints scattered around his body, he looked through the open firebox into the parlor. The pillaged space gazed emptily back at him. When he'd taken up this spot before, his absurdly oversized wardrobe and headboard had always looked like a mountain range, surrounded by a landscape of other, far more sensibly sized furniture.

His eyes grew wide as the realization hit him. It might have made him jolt upright, but, between his aching joints and the lack of his cane at the moment, jolting was out of the question.

"My uniforms," he said, and turned to Keene, who was halfway inside the pantry cupboard.

Keene leaned backward out of it to look at Falcon. "Beg

pardon?"

"My uniforms," Falcon repeated. He was so startled by the idea, he didn't realize his words explained nothing.

"Ooh," Keene said sympathetically. "Were those stolen too? Will your supervisors be able to tell if you wear the same one over and over again? Since they're identical and all?"

That hadn't been Falcon's line of thinking. In truth, he had several hanging upstairs. Not all of which were clean because, in truth, he didn't know how to wash them. Yet another problem he'd been meaning to sort but hadn't found… alright, he'd been waiting for Keene to leave the house long enough for Falcon to learn to use the washing tub out in the back garden. The opportunity had presented itself during those few evenings Keene had been gone, but Falcon had been so tired and sore that he'd put off the task.

It was no surprise the thieves had left them. Since the attack on the Halls of Justice, proclamations had gone out promising severe punishments for anyone caught impersonating an Enforcer. That was how the Reaper's Collective had infiltrated the Halls in the first place. And how they'd tried to sow discord at the protest assembly where they'd released the pepper gas last winter. Thus, the uniforms might have been more of a liability than they were worth. He had been storing a few in the wardrobe, though.

Falcon ignored Keene's comment in favor of chasing his own thoughts. "My dress uniforms were in my wardrobe. If the thieves try to sell those, it might attract some attention."

He needed to speak to a criminal. Unfortunately, all those he'd ever crossed paths with, well, he'd arrested them.

Wait. All those except…

Falcon's mind slowed as he considered his options. He stared into the crackling fire as he realized he did have a card to play. He stood, carefully, supporting himself on the fireplace's apron and then mantel as his joints creaked unhappily.

"I need to go back out," he said, trying to sound casual.

"Excellent," Keene replied, a jot too cheerily. "Where are we going this time?"

He can't come, was Falcon's knee-jerk thought. *Right, now tell him why.*

But an actual reason failed to present itself. It wasn't like he could say, "No, you stay here and don't ask me why. No, that's not suspicious. Why would you say that?" He could always claim some sort of personal matter, but Falcon wasn't as open as Keene about things—proper gentlemen certainly didn't trumpet their private matters. And anyway, a half-truth like that was liable to lead to more questions, which meant Falcon would either have to fold or lie. So he folded.

"Have you heard of that new clothing shop in the Sand district? Hollow Ensembles?"

Keene's face brightened. "Yes! Run by that disgraced Pendragon chap who changed his name." He looked absolutely delighted when he added, "What a scandal. I've been meaning to go, but—" He cut himself off as he waved a hand through the air. "No matter. I'll get your cane."

)(

Falcon read the sign above the shop's window and cocked an eyebrow.

Hollow Ensembles. Filling your everyday and every occasion apparel needs at criminally low prices.

Varick Hollow, proprietor of Hollow Ensembles, was formerly of the vastly rich, vastly influential, and just plain vast Pendragon clan. That is, until last winter when he'd publicly split from them and changed his name in what some suspected of being a bit of a publicity stunt. He was also a former criminal—importing and exporting goods illegally, weapons mostly—but had paid his debt to society through the brutal process known as purging—in short, torture to both "cleanse" a person of their criminal desires and punish them for the harm they'd done to society. It was a "gift" offered only to those who willingly turned themselves in, however.

To Falcon's mind, that had never seemed a great incentive. He was frankly surprised and impressed at the callback to Varick's criminal past on the shop's sign. The few Falcon had heard of who'd both submitted themselves for purging and survived seemed to want to put their past behind them. He couldn't help but wonder if this was a taunt toward the Enforcers. Given that Varick had been with the AWOL former Enforcer, Dmitri, at the Halls of Justice the night of the attack, Falcon also questioned whether the former had really cut ties with Springhaven's criminal underworld. Then again, Camilla and her sister Lenore had been there too, so maybe that didn't automatically point to continued nefarious activity.

It was also possible Varick simply didn't give a toss about

appearances and was capitalizing on his infamy for profit. Given the number of people Falcon had watched go in and come out during the time he'd been standing there to read the sign, this second theory was seeming far more likely by the minute.

The shop window displayed men's suits in the latest fashions with high collars starched stiff enough to cut and sharply notched double-breasted waistcoats. Tall top hats in both silk and beaver fur, as well as bowlers graced the heads of mannequins that could be made taller, shorter, wider, or thinner just by turning a few small hand cranks. By the prices on display, Varick was clearly marketing to a broad spectrum of incomes. Overcoats, frock coats, and morning coats were showcased with each ensemble as well. A late afternoon gust of wind rushed past as if it was in on the advertisement. One ladies' ensemble was on display as well: a sensible cerulean, slimline dress without a bustle and including practical, fitted sleeves—nothing like the puffy monstrosities in fashion elsewhere. Though it was not plain. Scarlet bows adorned the cuffs at the wrist and elsewhere on the piece, adding a tasteful bit of flair.

Beside Falcon, Keene craned his neck, even going so far as to stand on his tiptoes, trying to see further into the shop through the window.

"You say you actually know this Varick cove?" he asked.

Falcon waggled his head, sifting out the most incriminating bits. "We have some shared acquaintances. Crossed paths a few times, you know how it goes."

As if to intentionally undermine his rather blasé description, the man in question chose that moment to appear in his establishment's doorway, crowing and sweeping his arm in an arc as wide as his smile. "Falcon, my man!" He strode over and clasped Falcon's hand without being offered it. "So good to see you! I was wondering when you might darken my humble doorway." He turned to Keene. "And who is this? I demand you introduce me at once."

Varick was, as befit his business, consummately dressed, but not as flashy as a dandy might be. An evergreen brocade waistcoat, cut in the latest fashion with perfectly pressed lapels, paired beautifully with an indigo cutaway coat. From a belt slung around his hips hung several tools of his trade, almost like a lady's chatelaine, though no lady would have scissors so very large or deadly-looking. Why Varick needed several of these, Falcon couldn't guess. The bold colors he wore matched his dark hair and eyes well without being ostentatious, a look Falcon was certain had been carefully crafted.

Despite how glad he was that Varick had been easy to wrangle, Falcon had to swallow a sigh. He'd forgotten how exhausting salesmen could be, especially exuberant ones. Still, he was a gentleman and an Enforcer, so he straightened up.

"Mister Varick Hollow, I'd like to introduce my housemate, Mister Keene Kohli."

Varick shook Keene's hand as warmly as if they'd been friends for years. "Chuffed to meet you, sir. Simply chuffed." He then clapped Falcon on the back. "This one, though. So proper. Please, call me Varick." He then motioned them toward the shop. "Come inside. I'll have tea brought out."

Keene wasted no time in pouncing on the opportunity. "Could you brew us up some of this?" He produced a small bag of his custom blend from a pocket. Attached to the top was one of Keene's business cards. "It's my treat."

Varick started to politely wave away the offer, being a good host, but Falcon interrupted. "Trust me, you don't want to miss out. His tea is outstanding."

Varick raised his eyebrows, one looking impressed and the other dubious, before taking the proffered bag. "Very well. We'll see if your tea is as strong as your claims."

While Varick sauntered back into the shop, Keene leaned toward Falcon and whispered, "You two just share some acquaintances, hm?" He gently poked Falcon's ribs with his elbow. "No need to be so coy about your famous friends. I'm not surprised."

Falcon began to protest, that he didn't have famous friends, that there was no reason for him to. But his words tripped over themselves on their way out, stumbling into nonsensical syllables. Between him knowing Beatrice, one of Springhaven's most beloved socialites, his public statements against his grandfather last winter, and now this, he really didn't have a leg to stand on.

Inside, the shop was neat and orderly. It was not a large area, but the space was used well. Tall rows of cubbies and drawers lined the walls, each one labeled in neat painted letters as well as painted pictures of what hid inside. Mannequins stood on display platforms here and there, dressed in fashionable apparel and arranged in positions that best showed off the garments. Keene was already eyeing a honey-yellow cravat and striped trousers, perfect for the coming warmer months. The stripes reminded Falcon of the bit of fabric he'd found attached to their back gate, and he cursed himself for not having thought to bring it. It was a long shot, but perhaps Varick could tell him something about it, given his new line of work.

Speaking of the man, he was talking to someone near the back of the shop, someone who looked vaguely familiar, but Falcon couldn't place why. He tried to look harder, but with so many people milling about, his view kept getting obscured by a bloke's head or a lady's feathery hat. The familiar man disappeared into a back room, and Falcon wondered where exactly they were meant to take their tea with all the people around. Meanwhile, a petite shop boy zipped to and fro, bringing customers items and taking money for purchases. The system likely wouldn't have worked if the shop had been larger, but its cozy size leant itself to feeling like everyone was shopping together. Keene, friendly as ever, was complimenting another gent on his choice of ribbon for a boater hat. The shop simply had that sort of communal air about it, and Falcon decided he was going to have to come back when he wasn't trying to solve a robbery… and when he had a bit of money saved up.

"Over here, chaps." Varick had wound his way back over to them, in between checking on customers, and was motioning for Keene and Falcon to follow him.

In the furthest corner of the store, behind a trio of mannequins dressed in variously colored ladies' high-low skirt and trousers combinations, nestled a little hideaway of chairs and small tables. Plush damask curtains attached to a rail across the ceiling could easily close off or open up the space with nothing more than a tug on the curtains' tasseled rope-pulls. Varick gestured for his guests to sit, and Falcon was pleased to find the mannequin trio's clothing, even without the help of the curtains, soaked up a good deal of shop noise, turning it to a pleasant background hum.

A moment later, as if perfectly orchestrated, the somewhat familiar man approached with tea service in hand. And, knowing Varick, it might have been arranged, though Falcon didn't give more than a moment's thought to that. He was studying the man with the tea service. He had plain, almost forgettable features, with blond hair and fair skin. Only when he bent to set it down did Falcon realize what he recognized. It was the man's bearing that

Falcon's Favor

was familiar. So stiff and measured, like a wind-up toy soldier.

"So what can I help you gentlemen with today?" Varick asked, pulling Falcon's attention from the nameless employee, who was already striding back from whence he'd come. "New waistcoats? Removable collars—really quite convenient, if I may offer my two coppers. A change of shoe perhaps? Square toes are coming strongly into fashion, you know." While Varick talked, he served tea for his guests. "My, that does smell delicious."

Before Falcon could divert the conversation into more useful waters, Keene jumped in. "Thank you. As I mentioned before, it's my own custom blend." He removed a business card from his jacket pocket and offered it to Varick. "If you ever need an event catered, please do keep me in mind."

With the grace of a master prestidigitator, Varick summoned the same to his hand, grasping it between two fingers. He must have pulled it off the tea packet. "I surely will."

He took a moment to sip his tea, and Keene kept his mouth shut all during the tasting. Falcon too watched silently. He smiled a little as Varick's eyes lit up in genuine surprise. The man gave an air of rarely being shocked, and Falcon was pleased to have witnessed it.

Varick looked to Falcon. "You weren't joking. This is spectacular." He turned his attention back to Keene. "You and I should talk later, but let's focus on what brought you gents here in the first place."

Keene didn't look to Falcon, instead turning his attention to his tea with the satisfaction of a proud father. Falcon, however, even with the incredible brew in his hand, felt lost. He took a sip to give him an extra moment to think. He hadn't wanted to bring Keene because that would mean involving him in the investigation. Falcon hated that, even with hindsight, he couldn't see what he should have done instead. He just knew he'd probably handled things wrong. One more fortifying sip. There wasn't anything else for it now.

To Keene, he said, "I'm doing this alone. Do you hear me?"

"I hear you," said Keene. But the expression on his face said he didn't agree.

Varick's eyes darted between the two, the whisper of a smirk pulling at one corner of his mouth.

Falcon decided not to waste any more time arguing and cut right to the chase. Looking to Varick, "I'm going to be honest with you…"

He trailed off as Varick raised a hand, got up, and untied the braided gold cords holding back the curtains. With a heavy *whump*, they fell closed exceptionally fast, but Falcon worried they still wouldn't be sufficient. Just this past winter, he'd seen the effects of a curtain failing to keep conversations secret. Granted, that had worked in his favor—it was how he'd learned of his grandfather's nefarious history—but now he was the one hiding behind one, and, if one believed the Old World tales, the universe liked to keep balance.

As if reading his mind, Varick tapped one of the curtains, which did not ripple as Falcon expected it to.

"Honesty requires protection. The inside is lined with extra material. I've tested it myself, so not to worry."

Falcon couldn't help but wonder if Varick had learned what had transpired the day Falcon had just been thinking about. It wouldn't surprise him. Camilla had been there, and Camilla was Lenore's sister, and Lenore was Varick's… well, Falcon had never really been certain what they were. But Varick and Lenore were definitely close. In any case, Falcon was grateful.

Varick was already swanning back over to his chair, suddenly all nonchalant again. "Besides, this space doubles as our changing room. We are a small operation and, thus, have to make do, but our clients' privacy is a paramount concern. Please, continue what you were saying."

Falcon nodded. If Varick said their secrets were safe here, he believed it. "Our house was burgled yesterday. They stole…" He sighed but straightened. "Well, they stole nearly everything. One of the items being my wardrobe, which contained several of my uniforms, including two dress ones." Falcon watched Varick's face for changes, but he remained stolid. "I realize you have moved beyond your past, but if someone were to try and sell such unique items, where or to whom might they do that?"

Varick slowly lowered his teacup onto his saucer. A calculated slowness, if Falcon didn't miss his guess. He knew he'd risk offending the man by coming here with his questions. Thus, why Falcon had made sure to mention his surety of Varick's wholesome and crime-free lifestyle now, but Falcon realized that might not have been sufficient. Or perhaps he hadn't been clear. Or—

"As you say, I've left that life behind." Gone was the congenial salesman Varick had been mere moments ago. Now he was stone cold, cold enough to place his saucer back onto the table and push it away from him. A silent signal that he was finished. "I don't appreciate you endangering the progress I've made by—"

"This isn't an Enforcer case," Keene broke in. His eyes flicked between the rejected cup and Varick, a look of open concern on his face. "We're investigating privately. We haven't even reported the robbery, nor do we intend to."

Varick looked Keene up and down, eyes sharp. Falcon had read the former weapons dealer's file when he'd turned himself in for purging, and Falcon had always found Varick's confession a bit light on details. He'd not cited any criminal accomplices, claiming to have worked solo with anonymous buyers. Whether that was true or not, Falcon couldn't imagine what Varick'd had to do to survive in Springhaven's seedy underbelly.

Silence swirled around and between them, as thick and heavy as the curtains. Keene's expression hardened. Not nearly as flinty as Varick's, but enough to add weight to his next words. "We don't want whoever robbed us going to the Halls of Justice. No one should have to endure those horrors."

The intensity of Varick's gaze softened, though he was still clearly assessing them both. Finally, he leaned back in his seat, hands clasped in his lap. "It's been a long time since I've had contact with that world. A very long time. I can't stress that enough. I might not be able to remember names very well." He spread his hands innocently before him. "Or the players may have changed since I've been gone. *However…*" At this, he fixed Falcon and Keene with another hard glare. "*If* I'd ever done any work like that—getting rid of stolen items, I mean—I'd have talked to someone called Twigs. He's easy to spot. Looks a bit like a living candle."

Falcon had removed his little notebook from his pocket and wrote down the name without context. He didn't want to incriminate himself should anyone ever see his notes. Varick was eyeing it like a venomous snake.

"Burn that as soon as you don't need it anymore," he said. "And don't write down anything you don't have to. The best criminals, the ones who live the longest, don't keep evidence around." He pointed at the notebook. "That'll call you out as an outsider in a blink. And *don't*, under any circumstances, tell a soul I told you any of this." An unspoken threat wound around the words, underscored by the steely glint in Varick's eye. "I shouldn't need to tell you they won't welcome an Enforcer amongst them."

"Of course," Keene agreed. "But where do we find this Twigs chappie?"

"*You're* not," Falcon put in, cutting his eyes to his housemate. Keene didn't look back.

"He's got a storefront in the Sand quarter, a place called Bits for Bobs," Varick said. He pulled his fob watch from his waistcoat pocket and opened it. "He won't be open for much longer today." Varick gave them both another assessing look, but his eyes lingered on Falcon and traveled to the cane resting against the chair next to him. "I don't recommend going alone. If things go south… well, you don't want that."

Falcon's face heated. Before he could stop himself, he shot to his feet and blurted, "I'm perfectly capable of taking care of myself, thank you. Enforcer training is—"

"Keep your shirt on," Varick cut in, waving a lazy hand. That hand then swept toward the outside of the dressing room. He was suddenly smooth as oil again. "Or try a new one on. Either way, I wasn't calling your abilities into question. I just mean that you, a rather famous member of the Enforcer order, should take extra precautions."

"I'll go with him," Keene said.

In his anger, Falcon had temporarily forgotten he was there. He spun on the man. "No! Absolutely not. This is only getting more dangerous, and it would be grossly—"

"I know, I know." Keene stood too, though he did it with the fluid grace of water, unfussed and entirely too confident given what they were discussing. "But Varick has made it clear you can't risk going alone. Who else are you going to take?"

Falcon looked around the room like a good volunteer might pop out from under one of the tables. For a split second, his eyes rested on their host, who instantly shook his head.

"Nope. We're not even having this conversation, remember?"

Falcon put out a reassuring hand. "I wasn't considering that. I wouldn't ask such a thing, not after everything you've been through to restart your life."

If Varick had a response to that, Falcon didn't see or hear it. He was already redirecting his attention back to Keene. The men locked eyes, Keene cool and immoveable, Falcon determined and beginning to feel frenetic. Keene had made a good point, but it would be inexcusable. What else could he do, though?

Think. Think. Think, rang through his head.

Keene was the first to move. He wasn't folding, though. He was softening, in a way. He gave Falcon a crooked little half-smile and raised his eyebrows. It was annoyingly charming, and Falcon was in no mood to be charmed. So in response, he folded his arms over his chest to show just how unimpressed he was.

"Have you ever considered that you *don't* have to be the hero?" Keene asked, his voice a quiet nudge.

Falcon was so taken aback by the accusation he dropped his arms again, opening the wall he'd been trying to build. "I am *not* trying to be a hero. I am simply trying to set a wrong back to rights."

Keene waggled his head and twisted his lips, cinching them closed to keep a retort inside. His expression, however, spoke for him well enough: *Sort of the same thing.*

Falcon threw up his hands. "You *can't*. You're a *civilian*." He over enunciated the last word.

Keene returned a smooth shrug. "And you can't go alone, so where does that leave us?" He rolled his eyes. "Pardon. Where does it leave *you*? Are you going to give up?"

Falcon took a deep breath and shook his head. "I'll just have to figure out something else." He looked back to Varick. "Is there anything more you can tell us?"

Varick was looking between his two guests with an expression Falcon couldn't identify, but the corners of his mouth were twitching upward. He leaned forward and took his teacup back. Taking a sip, he said, "This really is lovely. But no. I think I've given up enough today. Now, shall we discuss how I can help you gents replace some of your purloined clothing?" He gestured with his teacup at Falcon and gave him a knowing wink, "Given our history together, I think a steep discount is in order."

And just like that, Falcon understood. The subtle reference to Falcon having been there with him—and not just him, but Camilla and Lenore and Dmitri too—during the Halls of Justice attack, having tried to help two prisoners escape and all that followed. It was a veiled reminder that betrayal on either side meant mutually assured destruction. Falcon gave an understanding nod in return. He hadn't been planning on double-crossing Varick anyway, but he now saw how the man had survived so long in the criminal underworld. Turning the conversation to apparel was a welcome respite. That and several more cups of tea.

~Chapter 8~

Falcon sat before the fireplace back at the house. On the floor, given their new lack of furniture. It wasn't so bad, or so he told himself. It could be worse anyway. Yes, that was the bright spot he could hold onto. He knew he was being maudlin, but Keene had been withdrawn on the trip home.

"I'm thinking, that's all," he'd said when Falcon mentioned his unusual quietness.

Falcon couldn't help but think Keene was upset with him. He wasn't trying to be overbearing or unfeeling or whatever it was Keene was probably thinking about him. The feeling of distance was made worse by the fact that Falcon had his back to the fire. Otherwise, he might have been able to watch Keene work on dinner in the kitchen. Or at least his legs. Falcon could hear the soft hiss of the petrolsene stove at work, the clunk of one of Keene's pans atop the hob as he moved said pan around. But Falcon didn't want to risk the fire's heat damaging the evidence he had laid out before him. And he didn't want the sight of it reminding Keene of their disagreement from earlier.

Falcon had so little to go on. Some bootprints. A scrap of fabric that might not even be related. A list as long as his arm of items stolen. Falcon sighed. None of this helped; he should follow the lead Varick had given him. But then there was still the problem of going alone, of his face being known. Falcon grumbled inwardly as he thought of the posters around town that bore his picture and name, promoting the new Crisis Response Unit. Who weren't doing *anything* differently from the rest of the Enforcer order. Except for the emergency response classes, at least, which weren't being used in any way. Not anymore now that the protests were over. The posters were meant to inspire new confidence in the order, to tell the citizens of Springhaven about the positive new direction in which their city's protectors were headed. It was all lies.

Of course, if Doctor Allen... Mina—Falcon was still trying to make himself call her by her first name—had her way, the Cru might become something better. But that would require something from Falcon. He didn't know what. And he really didn't think he was up for it anyway.

Falcon was good at tearing things down, not building new things up. He'd disgraced his grandfather, helped lead the raid on the Reaper's Collective's hideout, arrested people...

He sighed again and dropped his head into his hands. Falcon focused on his breathing, on the feel of the fire's warmth against his back, clearing his mind of everything but those things. He could hear his grandfather's taunts in the back of his mind. Distant, but still there.

Get up. Bloody do something, boy. Don't be such a weak, little milksop.

But Falcon was tired. Bone-tired. And he'd learned the hard way what happened when he pushed himself too hard. That was how he'd ended up always needing a cane, and now he might need it forever. He didn't know. If he found time to take a nice long holiday, a *proper* holiday, maybe one of those restoration retreats people did up north in hot springs and steamy wooden rooms—what were they called? Saigas? Songas?—maybe then he'd actually have a chance to heal properly. But he couldn't. Not now that he was the Steward of the Sage. Not when he was trying to solve this robbery with next to no evidence. Not with what was essentially an entire neighborhood's worth of suspects.

"Falcon?" he heard distantly, though it was probably his imagination. Probably just some other responsibility he'd forgotten to list calling out to him.

He jumped when something touched his shoulder. Eyes darting, he closed his hand around nothing as he reached for his truncheon that was not there. Keene was, though, kneeling next to Falcon, hand hovering above his shoulder. Keene must have done the touching. Concern was written across every inch of his face, and here Falcon was wallowing in his own problems. The physical reminders of their earlier argument lay scattered between them, but Keene's gaze wasn't on them. It was on Falcon, searching.

"Are you alright?" Keene's voice was so soft, almost a whisper.

A second passed, and he placed his hand on Falcon's shoulder again. Stars, it was warm, almost as warm as the fire at Falcon's back. Had Keene been handling the hot pan without protection? Falcon had a sudden urge to take his hand, to check it for burns, maybe even apply some of the skills Doctor Allen had taught him and soothe away any damage he might find. Keene was always so kind, a kindness Falcon was feeling less and less like he deserved. He'd shut Keene out *and* was failing to make progress.

Falcon didn't know what to say. Though he knew it was the wrong move, he dipped his eyes, looking away from Keene. He was an Enforcer; they *never* broke eye contact first. In the back of his head, he could hear a rant in his grandfather's phlegmy voice start up, but a different one rose at the same time. The voice that was here, with him, and it drowned out the angry mental tirade.

"It's okay to not be okay." Keene gave Falcon's shoulder a squeeze. "And I'm here if you need to talk."

A wall inside of Falcon, one he felt he'd always been holding up, cracked and began to crumble. It wasn't a wall he'd asked for, but rather one everyone else—his family, his superiors in the Enforcer order, his station in life—had always expected him to uphold. And the crumbling hurt, in a way, but somehow, it also felt so good, like the new cracks in that wall were letting in fresh breezes to blow away old air he hadn't realized had grown musty and stale. But the wall was familiar too, known and safe, and Falcon wasn't ready to let go. He felt his throat tighten, and he swallowed once, twice, before he felt like he could keep his voice steady.

With an emotional heave, he managed to summon a weak smile. "Thank you. That's very kind, but—"

"But what?" Keene's voice was firm now. Not unkind, but...

Stars, no. Please don't let him be disappointed in me too.

Keene's hand was still on Falcon's shoulder. He wanted to straighten up, shake off his housemate, but he couldn't find the strength through his exhaustion.

Keene seemed to study Falcon's face for a moment. Then he sighed and sat on the floor opposite. He had to pull his hand away, and the absence hurt more than Falcon wanted to admit. Keene was supposed to just be his housemate, but Falcon found he cared what Keene thought of him more than that.

"I'm sorry," Keene began again. "I didn't mean to push. I know not everyone's as…" He rolled his head around, eyes searching like the right word was spidering its way along the ceiling or something.

"Confident? Likable? Pulled together?" Falcon offered. He tried for a wry tone, but worried it came out more defeated than anything else. "I assume you were going to say not everyone's as something-something as you anyway."

Keene let out a weak chuckle. "Now you're the one being kind."

That was taking humility to an almost unreasonable level, in Falcon's opinion, but there was nothing insincere in Keene's tone. Falcon didn't really feel up for arguing, so he let it go.

Keene crossed his legs before him, hooking his knees in the crook of his elbows on either side, wiggling his socked feet. "Anyway, I just think you're being unfair to yourself. There's nothing wrong with needing to lean on others once in a while."

"Truly, I'm fine," Falcon insisted.

Believe me, he mentally urged. Because no one else had ever offered him any other options than the one where he had to be strong. He wasn't sure what to do with the alternatives, and dear heavens, he didn't want to risk falling on his face any more than he was already doing.

Keene folded a little, looking off to the side. He was twisting his lips in that way Falcon was learning to recognize meant he was keeping some comment or other to himself but wasn't happy about it.

Falcon made a tired beckoning gesture with his hand. "Let's hear it then." When Keene didn't immediately answer, he added, "You're squirming like a child in stiff New Year's clothes. No one is fooled, so let's just have it in one go."

Keene stilled. He held a hand up requesting a moment. When he finally spoke, his tone was careful but hopeful. "I'm trying to be gentle when I say this. It's not a judgment; I think you're a terrific person."

Something in Falcon's chest flared to life, all warm and squishy. He couldn't stop a smile from spreading across his face and nodded.

"So please don't take it badly when I point out that, when I came out here, you looked like a droopy bag of flour." He injected a playful lilt into his voice when he said this, but his eyes searched Falcon's expression. "I could be wrong, but I don't reckon that's the behavior of someone who's 'fine'." He made little finger quotes around the last word.

Falcon sighed. He really shouldn't have let Keene catch him out like that again, but he was just too bloody tired. Falcon shrugged.

"Sorry. I suppose I've got the morbs over everything that's happened lately." He'd chosen the jaunty little phrase to try and make light of the matter. And using such a vague description hadn't been on accident either; let Keene decide what he thought "everything that's happened lately" covered.

"Hmm." It was more a noise of disbelief and dissatisfaction. "Maybe. Well, in any case, I always find a good meal helps. And if you decide later you want to talk about it, I'm all ears. Only if you want to, though." Keene held up a finger. "Think about it for a moment while I grab dinner."

While Keene stood and hurried back to the kitchen, Falcon turned to the fireplace and watched through it. As expected, all he saw were Keene's socked feet trotting back and forth, accompanied by the sound of metal cookware.

If Falcon was brutally honest, he'd say he wanted to curl up and let someone else be the strong one for once. But that wasn't his role. Life had dealt him a different hand and he needed to make do with that. Still, Keene was here, and Falcon didn't want to hurt the man by making him feel shut out again. So he'd compromise.

When Keene returned a few minutes later, he carried one of his larger cast iron skillets with a part of a tea towel wrapped around the handle for protection. The pan had a warped bottom, Falcon noticed, and he felt a pang of regret for his housemate. Two spoons, artfully folded within another tea towel, stuck out from one of Keene's waistcoat pockets. The skillet was still hot enough for its contents to bubble around the edges, and he was careful to protect the wooden floorboards as he set it down.

Keene sat, cross-legged again, and flourished a hand over the meal. "Chicken and dumplings." He handed Falcon the artfully packaged spoons, waited for him to select one, and then took the other for himself. "Just the thing after a long day of shopping."

Falcon nodded, but his mind was still on Keene's offer. He appreciated the man giving him space, the opportunity to move on if Falcon wished it, but Falcon wanted to address one point before they did.

"I wasn't trying to be a bully about the case," Falcon said. "Back in Varick's shop. I just can't risk endangering you."

Keene pointed a spoon at him. "Or yourself. Varick made a good point. Your face is too well known." Keene then leveled a firm look at Falcon. "Tell me you're not still considering going."

Falcon shook his head. "Not without a plan. I hate to admit it, but I think you and Varick are right. It wastes valuable time, but…" He sighed. "I don't think I have much of a choice."

Keene nodded. "We'll figure something out." And before Falcon could object to his use of the word "we," Keene continued. "For now, dinner!" And he flapped his hands to waft the steam rising from the pan toward Falcon. The scent of black pepper, chicken broth, and vegetables melting together underneath savory dough speckled green with chopped herbs wended its way into Falcon's nostrils. He swallowed quickly as he began to salivate.

Unfair play! objected Falcon's wits. But his hunger grabbed his rational brain by its metaphorical face and shoved it away.

They couldn't afford new dishes yet, and Falcon cringed at the thought of how long it would take to replace everything. For starters, he'd have to wait until next time he got paid. Keene had said he could get some things after a client's pre-event payment deadline in a few days, but Falcon had feelings about that too. Keene already did so much for their little household; Falcon wanted to feel like he was doing his part. And he would. He'd promised that to both himself and to Keene, who, unsurprisingly, had received the vow with easy, reassuring gratitude. Until then, though, eating straight from the dish would have to do.

The idea was strange for Falcon, and Keene was waiting for him to go first. He'd heard of some practices both to the north in Duskwood and the south in Bone Port wherein people ate from and even cooked their own food in large, communal dishes. The practice had never caught on in Springhaven, though. And even if it had, his family wouldn't be caught dead supping in such an environment. The fact that Keene was waiting on him pushed Falcon to just hurry up and do it, and he drove his spoon into the gooey, savory mixture.

Keene almost immediately followed suit, his spoon diving easily into the pan like he'd done this a hundred times, and maybe he had for all Falcon knew. The creamy broth in which the veggies and sparse chicken bits were suspended dripped, and both gents had to scooch close to hold their heads over the dish, lest they risk wasting some of their delicious dinner by dropping it onto the floor. The physical closeness felt easy by now, given that they'd shared a bed last night and had huddled against gusting springtime winds through much of the day. With a delicious meal between them and the offer of emotional support on the table, Falcon softened more. Keene really was nothing but kind; he wouldn't judge Falcon for a moment of weakness. So he decided he could share just one more tidbit with his housemate.

"Thank you," Falcon said between spoonfuls. Which was just as delicious as the scent had promised. Keene, mouth full, looked at him with questioning eyes. A drop of gravy glistened at the side of his mouth, and Falcon pointed at it, but didn't touch. "You've got a little something there."

Instead of using his napkin, Keene's tongue flicked out to wipe it away. Falcon's stomach did a strange little shimmy, but it wasn't unpleasant.

He smiled and went on, "Thank you, for distracting me from my melancholy."

That wasn't the extent of his feelings. He'd actually been thinking something along the lines of, *Thank you for creating a space for me where I feel safe to share, where I don't feel like I always need to fit a certain mold. Thank you for encouraging me to be what I want and for understanding when that's not what you think might be best.* But that was an awful lot of words, and the last thing Falcon wanted was to scare Keene off by being *too* open. So "distraction" covered a multitude of meanings, and Falcon looked earnestly into Keene's eyes, hoping to convey the rest.

Keene gave him a smile as warm as the pan between them, and he bumped his shoulder against Falcon's.

"I am happy to distract you any time you want."

Falcon's stomach did that same little shimmy, and he welcomed the warmth of it, which ebbed up into his chest, into his arms and legs. It flushed into his face, and Keene, still smiling, went back to eating.

After a few more bites spent in companionable silence, Keene burst out with a new topic. "So things got a little intense with Varick, didn't they? What do you suppose he meant by your *history together*?" Keene bobbed his eyebrows for effect.

Falcon sucked air through his teeth. "He turned himself in for purging, remember?" Falcon left it there. Just that simple statement came loaded with implications—Varick's punishment, the secrets he might have shared during his incarceration, and the methods the Enforcers used during that heinous process. The purging wasn't actually what Varick had been referring to, of course, but Falcon hadn't technically said that was the answer to Keene's question either.

Keene gave a knowing nod. Purgings weren't considered polite conversation in any level of society. Instead, he asked, "You must at least tell me about your mutual acquaintances then"

So Falcon spent most of the rest of dinner explaining how he knew Varick—they had both been Doctor Allen and Camilla's patients at one point, though not at the same time, and both had attended the same wedding—all after the whole purging business, of course. And he shared what little he knew of a man called Lowell Thorne, who was friends with Camilla's sister, Lenore, so Varick probably knew him too. Lowell was of note because he had, out of the blue, sent Falcon's cane to him a little less than a month ago.

Keene was instantly enraptured by the intrigue of the mysterious cane-building gent and excited to meet some of the other players in this little tale when they went to dine with the Allens tomorrow.

~Chapter 9~

Falcon awoke early the next morning, as he always did. It was a long-ingrained habit. Not even his coma had broken it, though he took lots of naps those first few days after he'd awoken. No scent of cooking breakfast met his waking senses, though—strange given that Keene hadn't gone out last night, and he basically always cooked breakfast on days he didn't have reason to sleep in. But he wasn't in bed next to Falcon either.

Worry tugged Falcon from bed faster than he might have otherwise gotten up, and he hurried downstairs, cane in hand. His muscles, without warning of changing modes or a good stretch, complained every step down, but Falcon ignored them. Keene wasn't downstairs either. Nor did Falcon see him when he poked his head out into the back garden. He called through the house, even checked Keene's ransacked bedroom, but the man had vanished. Only when Falcon headed downstairs again did he spot the small piece of paper folded into a swan shape on the parlor-side fireplace mantel. Written in tiny letters across the swan's left wing was Falcon's name. Thankfully, the little creature unfolded easily, because Falcon's hands were shaking, though he refused to consider why.

I've gone out to run some errands. Be back soon.

—Keene

"Where would he have to go?" Falcon wondered aloud to himself. "And why would he go so early?" The answer hit him like a truncheon across the head. Falcon actually gasped as he said, "So I couldn't go with him! He's going to Bits for Bobs."

Keene was industrious, to be sure, but scarpering off with the sun barely up? Sneakily enough to not wake Falcon, who wasn't exactly a heavy sleeper. And without a whiff of food? The fireplace hadn't even been fed; only barely warm embers remained. Falcon hurried back upstairs as fast as his aching muscles would allow, changed, and then charged out of the house.

It was a short tram ride to the Sand quarter, but the wait nearly killed Falcon. He considered commandeering one of the horses pulling the tram and racing it across districts like some doomed penny dreadful hero. That, however, for one, would massively inconvenience who knew how many people. And, for two, create quite the scene. They were trying to keep this investigation under the echoscope, after all. In his haste, however, he tripped up the short stairway into the vehicle.

"You alright, mate?" asked Marty, the tram driver. "You're looking harried this morning."

The man's sun-weathered face was hard as leather, but concern glimmered in his eyes. Those same eyes took in Falcon's clothes. His street clothes, as most Enforcers referred to their civilian dress, not his uniform today. Thank the stars the thieves had left Falcon's basket of dirty laundry mostly untouched.

"Yes, sorry." Falcon wasn't sure why he was apologizing, but there it was. "Just being clumsy."

Marty nodded, and Falcon, grateful he had the grace not to press, took a seat behind him.

"I'm Falcon, by the way." He'd never properly introduced himself, just exchanged light conversation in passing, as was so often the way with people regularly crossing paths.

Falcon knew he should give his surname too; his mother would be appalled at his manners if she were here to see him—not that she'd ever be caught dead on a tram, not even if it had been pulled by the extinct dragons of the Old World. He swallowed the urge, though. In his old life, given his station—which his clothes, even old and out of fashion, indicated—Marty would be expected to call him Mister Smoke, and Falcon didn't want to make the driver feel as if he had to stand on ceremony.

"Falcon, eh?" Marty asked, pulling the lever to retract the stairs and urging the horses forward. "That's not a name you hear often."

Falcon gave a tight smile and swallowed a groan. That was the first comment *everyone* made upon meeting him. He must have heard it a million times throughout his life, and though his inner gentleman clutched his chest in horror at the rudeness, Falcon sped through the explanation. "Yes, my parents are avian specialists at the museum. My sisters are called Lark and Wren. You wouldn't have happened to see a certain chap early this morning during your route, would you? Dark hair and eyes, brown skin, about my age but a little shorter.

"Do you mean Keene?" Marty replied. "Yeah, I picked him up on the round before this one."

Falcon felt like a heel. Of course Keene had introduced himself. He'd probably done it upon first meeting Marty. Why hadn't Falcon? If Falcon was honest with himself, he didn't make a habit of getting to know people in service roles. Well, that was going to have to change. Starting today, he'd be more like Keene. Though he was certain he'd never match his housemate for congeniality. Still, he was going to make an effort. But first…

"Brilliant. Yes. At which stop did he get off?"

Marty told him, and Falcon spent the rest of the trip chatting with his new acquaintance, being careful not to interrupt the man's work, of course. Two minutes in, Falcon was reminded at how bad he was at making conversation, but Marty made up for it by being an absolute chatterbox. He nattered on about his favorite places to eat—"You ever tried Bags o' Mystery? Not a lot of choice, by which I mean none. You pay a copper, you get some sausages, a good drink, and whatever else they've got on offer that day, but after a long day, sometimes that's all you want."—and his shoulder complaints, of course, since that was what had first bonded him and Falcon.

"I've got these exercises I'm doing. They're helping a bit, but blazes this cold ain't."

Falcon pulled his coat tighter around him and grumbled, "Yes, I've got a similar prescription." He didn't say that he hadn't done any in the last day and a half or so, though his creaky joints seemed to be clucking their disapproval at him.

"Tell ya what," Marty replied with a smile. "I'll keep after you about yours if you'll keep after me about mine. Deal?"

Falcon tried to smile, though he worried it came out more of a grimace. That was a grand idea, except it meant he had to be accountable as much as he kept Marty so. Still, the camaraderie was nice, and he put his hand forward. Marty took it over his shoulder and shook.

"Deal."

The conversation helped distract Falcon during the ride from Cobalt to the Sand district. When he disembarked at the stop Marty had mentioned, the tram driver promised to check up on Falcon the next time they met.

"You'd better have good news for me," Marty warned. His face was still stern, but there was an air of joviality in his voice.

"You too," Falcon replied, giving the man an admonishing look. "Don't think I'm going to go easy on you."

Marty drove away chuckling, and Falcon felt encouraged as he turned to search for the infamous shop. He had allies. If anything happened to Keene... no, he couldn't think about that.

Focus on the mission, he told himself, parroting the various C.O.s he'd had over the years. *Maybes and what-ifs will get you killed.*

Falcon pulled his collar up against the cold and plodded forward. Shop names with directional markers were painted onto the sides of nearby buildings. Posters with advertisements and addresses for those stores further away were plastered next to the painted signs. Here in Sand, it was a bit of a free-for-all, unlike its somewhat more upscale sister quarter, Copper, where things were a bit more regulated. Thus, it wasn't but a few minutes before Falcon knew where he was headed, and a few minutes more before he was there.

Bits for Bobs turned out to be a rather vast secondhand dealer of, well, anything. Anything of moderate to considerable value anyway. The entire place consisted of three or four store spaces that had been combined via some knocked-down interior walls. Long signage outside stretched over multiple doorways, unifying them. The painted words let customers know through which door lay what types of items, or at least what was closest through each one.

The place was packed with merchandise, but in an organized chaos sort of way. Clothing had a section over on the far side of the store, which was further subdivided by style, gender, and age.

Furniture took up a good bit of real estate at the back, while dish, tea, cook, and flatware inhabited countless shelves and even some of the furniture nearby. Books looked hopefully out from a corner near the door, and displays of especially fine or interesting items graced the entrance areas of the store, near the registers where employees could keep a close eye on them. Mannequins scattered around the entire place, though these weren't on raised stands like in Varick's shop. Rather, these exhibited ensembles and other items that customers could remove as they pleased. Falcon had expected such a huge collection of people's former possessions to either smell stale or reek of too many households' scents frothing into an unpleasant melange. Instead, however, it smelled of... nothing. Like a blank canvas of endless possibilities.

The air was still, though plenty of other patrons were already perusing the racks and shelves. Only then did Falcon realize why their conversations weren't bouncing off one another like billiard balls. Above, swooping overhead in great swaths were coverless duvets. They looked like clouds, each one creamy and unblemished. The items that came into Bits for Bobs must go through some kind of intense vetting process. That, or Twigs knew secrets for cleaning that every housemaid and washer woman in the city would sell their souls for. The duvets soaked up noise like sponges, and Falcon, even knowing that underhanded dealings of some kind happened here, considered coming back to this place one day just to see what hidden treasures might be on offer. When he wasn't trying to solve the mystery of his own pilfered home goods of course.

Scanning the store turned up nothing. Heads of dark hair were fairly prevalent, but most were coiffed in a way that couldn't be Keene. So into the sea of gently used this-and-that Falcon dove. He went methodically, starting at one end, near the clothing, and skimming every aisle. He remembered Varick's warnings about his poster-boy-face and kept his collar turned up. It really was shocking how many people were in here at this early hour. Until he overheard a middle aged woman in a simple calico dress telling her friend how the shop worked. This was apparently the friend's first foray into the place.

"They've got staff working round the clock to restore items they've bought from other people. Then, at night while the place is closed, they put out all their new bits. And once they're gone, they're *gone*. They don't do holds, don't haggle. You've got to get in early and strike fast. Now come on. I see a new harmonoloq that's calling my name."

The ladies giggled over the joke, as a harmonoloq could play music or other recordings from an etched cylinder.

Falcon also spied shop hands in matching dark blue and brown checked outfits prowling around the place—offering help or watching for thieves, he didn't know. They didn't look too friendly, however, and so Falcon gave them a wide berth. It was a bit like a game, trying to cover each aisle quickly whilst avoiding people. A game with possibly dire consequences, and Falcon wished he'd given some forethought to a disguise. Not that he knew the first thing about subterfuge, but still. About ten minutes in, while Falcon stood beside racks of women's winter coats on one side and evening dresses on the other, he found himself trapped longitudinally between two of the shop hands, one on either end of the long aisle. He didn't think they'd spotted him yet, or at least weren't headed for him, but he also didn't want to risk having to lower his collar or answer questions, so he dove into the rack of ladies' coats beside him. When he emerged on the other side, between a lambswool trimmed velvet coat and a cape with attached fur muff, he spied a familiar figure examining some gentlemen's dinner jackets further down the aisle.

"Keene!" Falcon hissed.

His housemate turned, smiled, and then looked confused—fair dues since all but Falcon's head was still hidden within winter wear. Then the confused expression turned concerned.

Keene swiveled his head once before stepping close and hissing back, "Falcon, what are you doing here? You know it's dangerous."

"Oh, but it's fine and dandy for *you* to come alone?"

"I'm not an Enforcer. They have no reason to hate me."

As he spoke, Keene's eyes searched amongst the women's coats, and Falcon suspected him of not saying everything he was thinking. Heat ran up Falcon's neck, and he brought out his cane from within the coats, tapping it angrily on the floor.

"And you're also not impaired." His voice was flat and cold when he said it, and he found himself looking away from Keene without meaning to.

"Falcon, no." Keene's voice, in comparison, was a low croon. Hurt swam in his eyes.

He looked around again, and Falcon felt even stupider for

making so much noise with his cane. He was just considering melting back into the coats when Keene stepped closer and put a hand atop the one with which Falcon held the cane. A different kind of warmth spread from where Keene's skin touched Falcon's. It traveled up his arm and into his face, replacing the heat of shame from just a moment ago, gently pulling Falcon's gaze back toward his housemate's.

"I'm just worried for your safety. Nearly everyone in the city knows this handsome mug." In a move so swift Falcon would have questioned it had he not seen it happen, Keene tapped a playful finger against the tip of Falcon's nose. "Everyone we saw yesterday mentioned it."

Falcon's mind twisted around itself like the dough he'd seen Keene form and then bake into fragrant loaves of warm bread. And he was suddenly full of heat, like the kitchen got when Keene had the stove and fire going at once. Falcon couldn't sort all the sensations tumbling through him. He swallowed hard, grasping for sense.

"Th-They mentioned my face?" he bumbled.

"No, not your face," Keene replied. And now he grinned cheekily. "Well, sort of. They all asked if you were really the Steward of the Sage."

"I didn't hear them." Falcon blinked at Keene, still trying to regain his mental footing.

"Of course not. They were too polite to ask you. Didn't want to put you in an awkward spot, so they asked me." Keene's smile faded. "You need a disguise."

Both gents looked around them. Falcon came up empty, but Keene uttered an excited, "Aha!" and pounced on an unsuspecting mannequin nearby. From its head he snatched a bonnet with trailing satin ribbons and, in what was hands down the most confusing moment of Falcon's life, popped it onto the baffled Enforcer's head.

"Keene, what *are* you doing?" Falcon was too stunned to move.

"Just follow my lead," Keene replied.

He then stripped Falcon's coat off of him, shoved it into the women's coat rack to hide it, and pulled a bright blue cape off of the same rack. Like Falcon's coat, it had a high collar, which Keene made certain was standing as tall as it could. Falcon could feel the friction of the bonnet's bottom edge and the cloak collar's rim brush against each other, and he finally caught onto Keene's scheme.

"Keene!" he hissed. "You cannot dress me up as a lady!"

"Why not?" He motioned at the bonnet and cloak. "Instant disguise."

Keene went about tying the bonnet's ribbon's beneath Falcon's chin, and where his hands brushed gave Falcon more of that warm kitchen feeling. He began to do-up the ties on the cloak lower down while Keene started on the ones at the top.

Despite helping the outfit come together, Falcon still protested. "I'm taller than you. Ladies aren't tall."

"Some ladies are tall. Look at Magistrate Holmes."

He had Falcon there. Lady Katerina Holmes, Beatrice's mother, was an imposing woman, nearly as tall as Falcon.

Keene leaned around the rack and grabbed a pair of buff-colored men's gloves from somewhere nearby before handing them to Falcon, who begrudgingly pulled them on. They were leather and looked close enough to a lady's kid leather daywear. At least, Falcon hoped they did anyway, as he doubted any gloves actually meant for a woman would fit his hands. They also did a good job of hiding his Enforcer number tattoo, which striped across the inside of his wrist and, since his sleeves were a touch too short, had been peeking out all morning.

"Why can't *you* be a lady?" Falcon grumbled, knowing even as he spoke it wasn't his best argument.

Keene motioned to his own face. "With facial hair?"

He didn't have the muttonchops like a lot of older men, nor the more extreme ear beards or side whiskers of yet older gents, but Keene did sport a pair of neatly trimmed sideburns. Falcon's face, due to Enforcer order regulations, was entirely clean shaven.

All the strong emotions from this morning, ebbing and flowing as they were, began to make Falcon feel giddy. He'd sincerely worried Keene was in danger, only to find him safe, but then to have to face his own danger. And now, with all the squishy warmth Falcon found himself wanting more of…

He weakly flapped the thought away. He was on a mission, but blazes. He'd heard people say adrenaline was quite the drug, and they were right. It was a bit like those times when Falcon'd had a touch too much to drink, and it gave him the same sense of quick courage. He twiddled the end of Keene's sideburns with a finger.

"You jammy little sod. You'd make a lovely woman, though.

Sideburns and all."

Keene chuckled and caught Falcon's fiddling hand in his own. "Focus," he said, though he was clearly trying to suppress a laugh.

Yes, that's what he needed to do. And Falcon pushed the silly feelings away, though they bayed close by, like eager puppies wanting more fun.

Keene held up a finger and took one more item from the nearby mannequin: a lacy hand fan. Snapping it open, he declared, "There! The final piece."

Falcon caught on instantly and took it, covering his face. And just in time too, for one of the shop assistants who'd been prowling down the adjacent aisle came near. His eyes alighted on the two gents, and Falcon desperately hoped the man didn't see through his disguise.

"Can I help you two?" asked the man in a gravelly voice. It sounded as if helping was the last thing he wanted to do.

"Good morning, my good man," Keene replied more cheerily than should be allowed at this early hour. He tipped his top hat and deftly nudged Falcon with an elbow in one smooth motion.

For a moment, Falcon considered how Camilla or Beatrice might address the man. And then realized they didn't exactly fit the mold of how proper young ladies were supposed to act… or rather how people *believed* ladies should act. Desperately then, he instead thought about what a man might like to hear from the fairer sex and released a high pitched titter.

"Teeheehee!"

Falcon immediately felt dirty. Is this what his lady friends had to deal with? Ugh, always trying to please men. He'd consider that later, though. The shop assistant was eyeing him with naked suspicion. Should he extend his hand for a kiss? No, that sounded utterly foul. And he didn't want to tempt fate by flashing his gloves in the man's face, so he just released another ridiculous titter and bobbed something that he hoped passed for a cloak-covered-curtsey. On the way back up, he kept his knees bent, masking his height and coming level with Keene. His knees didn't like that at all, and he leaned more of his weight onto his cane, which he kept hidden beneath his cloak. All the while, he kept the fan in front of his face, only letting his eyes peek above it. Falcon didn't know if Keene noticed the man's suspicious look, but he took the reins of conversation again.

"I'm in the market for something special, you see," Keene

said, swirling an airy hand. "I've got a gala coming up and I need something that makes a statement. I quite favor grey and blue. Oh, and some gold braid wouldn't go amiss, so if you could point me in the direction of something fitting that description, that would be smashing."

Keene flashed a winning smile, but the shop assistant's eyes barely left Falcon. Keene looked between the two with puzzlement painted across his features. Falcon tried to demurely avert his eyes, which was difficult considering his instincts all shouted at him to keep this man in his sights.

"Is there a problem, sir?" Keene asked. When the man didn't reply, Keene shook an indignant finger in his face, finally catching the man's attention. "Now see here! I won't have you ogling my wife. I know she's lovelier than a dogwood tree in bloom, glows more radiantly than the sun, is more captivating than the full moon's pearly luminescence against freshly driven snow—" With each description, Keene made larger and more elaborate gestures. "—but that's no excuse for poor manners."

A laugh… no, a full-on guffaw was crawling its way up Falcon's throat. He released the most exaggerated tittering yet, easing the pressure off his amusement, and said in a high-pitched voice behind the trill, "Oh, darling, stop. You're being indecorous."

Keene leaned into Falcon and looked at him with enough adoration to put a romantic novel's hero to shame. "I'm sorry, my dearest. I just can't help it. You're too intoxicating." He then, in a scandalous public display of affection, kissed Falcon's cheek.

Heat rushed up to the top of Falcon's head, down to his toes, and everywhere in between. "*Darling*!" he protested in that same voice.

The shop assistant, however, was averting his eyes and looked like he wanted to vomit.

"Go have a look for treasures, my treasure," Keene said. "I'll see what I can find here."

Falcon wanted to protest, to stay by Keene's side in case he needed protection, but as a wife… erm, might it look suspicious if he defied direct instruction from his husband? Yes, indeed, he certainly had a new appreciation for his female friends' struggles. Reaching with two fingers from underneath his cloak, he gave Keene's hand a squeeze and hoped his housemate understood the meaning:

I'm here if you need me.

And with that, Falcon toddled away, trying but mostly failing to keep his cane from tapping on the shop floor, all while continuing to feign being shorter than he really was. Not to mention avoiding people like there was a plague on. He made a beeline—alright, a drunken and directionally challenged beeline—for the furniture at the back. A quick glance told him none of his and Keene's furniture was here. Falcon worried it had already been sold. Based on what he'd overheard that other customer saying to her friend, it was possible. Despite some impressive success in keeping away from other customers and roving shop assistants, he kept his fan in place before his face like a shield. He could and certainly would claim he was shy if anyone mentioned it.

Upon inspecting the row of furniture closest to the store's back wall, Falcon spied a door there. Above it, a sign in red, foreboding capital letters said, EMPLOYEES ONLY.

Well, that seemed like an area he definitely needed to inspect.

Armoires, hat racks, and bookshelves obscured his view back out to the rest of the sales floor. But that meant he too was hidden from view. So he made for the door, head swiveling to and fro. And when he was certain no one was looking, he slipped in, keeping close to the wall.

~Chapter 10~

The world on the other side of the door... well, it wasn't that impressive, to be honest. It wasn't even that different from the sales floor. Perhaps just a bit more haphazard. More furniture, racks of clothing, steamer trunks of books and jewelry, and tables laden with housewares littered the enormous backroom space. Each individual piece, however, had a bit of paper stuck to it. Not a price tag like out front, though. It didn't look terribly busy back here at the moment, and Falcon suspected most of the employees were out with the customers assisting... lurking... whatever.

Still keeping close to the wall, Falcon sidled up to the closest set of bits and bobs—a vanity table with empty perfume bottles scattered across it—and inspected the attached paper.

Donation
Inspected: JRF
Refurbished: Air23Y12NA
Display: Air30Y12NA

The dating system was easy enough to interpret. Refurbished the twenty-third day of the Air, the first month of the new year—this month in fact—in the twelfth year of the New Age. That refurbishing, which Falcon took to mean shining up the piece for new buyers, had only taken place a few days ago. And it looked to be scheduled to go out onto the sales floor on the thirtieth, tomorrow, the last day of the month. Alright, that made sense. An operation of this size must require things to move on a schedule. Otherwise, they might end up with a day where too much stock goes out, or vice versa. But why would someone *donate* such a nice piece?

Falcon stroked the gleaming varnished wood. He was no expert, but he guessed the piece wasn't made of mahogany or one of the other fine woods his father was always banging on about. Falcon's father, in addition to being an avian specialist, had a keen interest in the types of trees they lived in and the qualities thereof. Falcon had learned to tune his father out long ago, lest he actually die of boredom, but some of that knowledge must have seeped in because he began to remember things. Pine was a poor quality wood, and this vanity table didn't seem that either. The piece had been stained a deep red like cherry, but the grain was fairly light and even. He didn't know what that meant, but he clearly remembered his father once emphatically pointing to a cherry wood table whilst they'd been visiting a friend's house for tea and excitedly praising the clear, striped woodgrain.

Suffice to say, Falcon didn't think a piece of furniture like this was the sort of thing someone would just give away. It wasn't high enough quality to belong to a household that could afford to simply fob off their old belongings for nothing. And who would? Falcon's family was wealthy by anyone's standards and not even they would be so careless with their money. When they did donate to charity, it was only ever small items. It was more economical to fix up and sell off their unwanted goods. No, something was fishy here.

He looked at the perfume bottles too, each with their own notes attached. Only one of them had been refinished—probably a new squeeze pump if the quality of the one attached was any indication—and most of those had been donated too, save one.

Consignment

Falcon wasn't certain he knew what that word meant, at least not in this context. He wracked his brains, but no new understanding floated to the top. He scanned the backroom again. There had to be something here. Maybe it was false hope talking, but he refused to believe they'd hit a dead end. Something familiar peeked over the edge of a tall bookshelf. He checked his surroundings again. His new target was beyond the center of the vast backroom, and doors on either side led to who knew where. If anyone came out whilst he traversed the field of scattered furniture, this investigation would be over. And worse...

No one was around. Swallowing hard, Falcon decided to go for it, dropping his fan to hang from a loop around his wrist and opting to use the various furniture pieces as cover instead. And within one second of setting off, Falcon regretted so much.

"Blazes, mate, you've really got to start doing your stretches," he muttered at himself under his breath.

His joints ached more fiercely than usual, probably from all the tension he'd been holding in this morning. As he crouched beside a lovely clawfoot tub, Falcon fantasized about a nice hot bath in it. Thoughts of his pain fluttered into the background, however, as he properly clapped eyes onto his target.

His wardrobe! The corner of his ridiculously overlarge wardrobe had been peeking over the bookshelf. That's why he had recognized it; he'd seen that corner every day of his life. Thank the stars it hadn't yet been "refurbished." Another quick check for shop assistants and Falcon scuttled from the tub, to the bookcase, behind a changing screen, and to the wardrobe. He very nearly ripped off its notepaper in his haste to read it.

"Donated?!" he hissed to no one in particular. "Donated?" He couldn't help but say the word over and over again, barely remembering to keep his voice down. "Donated my eye!"

But why would a stolen item be listed as donated? What could the thieves possibly gain from giving their ill-gotten goods away for free? Then he remembered the source of his information. Varick, former criminal.

"Getting rid of stolen items," Varick had said.

This Twigs chap he'd mentioned was a fence. Payments for stolen goods must obviously be off the books, but they listed these items as donated as a cover. Falcon didn't know the first thing about taxes, but he knew when his parents did donate to a charity shop, they got a receipt they included with their tax filings. Was this place committing tax fraud on top of being a fence? And why didn't the Enforcers know about it? An operation this big...

Falcon shook his head. Too much at once. He needed to focus on the mission at hand. But now that he'd found where his and

Keene's stolen possessions had ended up, what to do about it? It wasn't like he could hide the wardrobe under his cloak and sneak out with it. Maybe he could put on one of his dress uniforms and use his authority to do something. He'd said he wouldn't make this an Enforcer issue, but...

Unfortunately, when he opened the wardrobe doors, only empty space stared back at him. They'd cleaned the thing out, the ratbags. Even the hangers were gone. Falcon released a low growl. He knew he should be happy; he'd made progress on the case. But now what? The wardrobe's back wall was a bleak physical representation of the dead end he'd hit. He lifted his head and then let it hang, taking a deep, calming breath.

Odd. A plant stared back up at him.

No, not a plant. A small sprig or stem or something. He bent down to pick it up, moving slow to give his muscles time to adjust to the new position. Tiny leaves sprouted from the twig, light green in color, and they gave off a fresh, woodsy odor. Crouched there, he also caught sight of something strange about the wardrobe's feet. They were dusted with a fine, white powder. Not much, just enough to muss the bottom edge of the feet. And they'd even chipped one! The nerve of those shoddy thieves.

"There you are!"

Falcon quickly stood and spun, stuffing the sprig into his pocket and holding his cane out like a weapon. His muscles twinged, but fear drove pain into the background for now. Not his best move, considering he was trying to remain incognito, and he tensed, waiting for a shop assistant to come flying at him now that he'd blown his cover.

"Blazes, I've been all over this bloody store looking for you."

Falcon's vision registered Keene before him. He lowered his cane, but his eyes darted around them now, keeping it ready just in case.

"Put that away," Keene said. He pushed Falcon's cane back down and tucked the cloak around it. "I didn't get anything out of the bloke I was talking to. What about you?"

"You questioned him?" Falcon asked. Keene was smooth, to be sure, but smooth enough to interrogate someone without raising suspicion?

"I didn't *question-him* question-him," Keene replied, which clarified nothing at all. "I just acted like I really wanted a suit in grey and blue. Something *like* an Enforcer uniform to, you know, really add some panache to my look."

Falcon grimaced. He wasn't convinced Keene's queries had come off as casually as his housemate made it sound. Then again, he hadn't been there to witness the exchange, so maybe it had. Either way, he had yet to share his own discovery.

He waved his fan behind him. "My wardrobe's been *donated*."

Keene looked in confusion at him, at the wardrobe, and back at him.

"The store is a front," Falcon explained. "Some of the pieces are legitimate, but some are disguised stolen goods."

"Oooh." Keene looked around as understanding dawned on him. "That's really rather clever. In a dastardly kind of way, of course. How can you tell what's stolen?"

Falcon pointed at the notes written for his wardrobe. "I think it's the ones that say donated, though there could be some legitimate donations here too."

"Like a charity shop," Keene offered.

"Right. It would muddy the waters and help cover their tracks if they really did take in donated items. Although…" The gears of Falcon's mind were turning again. There were a couple of different ways "donated items" could come into the shop, including having employees genuinely buy items on the business' account and then "donate" them. He shook his head; there wasn't time for that now. "There are items labeled as consignment too, but I don't know what that means."

"Split profits," Keene supplied. Now it was Falcon's turn to look confused, so Keene explained, "Someone brings in an item, and when it sells, both the original owner and the shop get paid."

"Aha! Those must be on the books. I…"

Falcon trailed off as he heard a door bang shut. Along with the sound, voices began to approach. They were coming from the far end of the room, and Falcon's head swiveled, looking for a place to hide. The answer stared him in the face.

"In here!" Falcon hissed to Keene, who was staring in the direction of the noise.

Keene was inside the wardrobe in a moment, but Falcon tripped on his cloak as he stepped up and over the lip. He stumbled and, a moment later, found himself caught in Keene's arms. Keene dragged him the rest of the way in and then shut the doors behind them, being careful not to make any noise. Falcon blessed the house staff back at the Smoke family manor for always keeping the door hinges well oiled.

Then he realized he was still leaning against Keene, surrounded by his usual warm spices scent while Keene held Falcon against him.

"You alright?" Keene whispered.

The dark around them was thick and heavy, as if it went on forever. They were hidden here. Alone. This was the sort of space where secrets were born, and Falcon's mouth went dry as he imagined what some of those secrets could be, as Keene's lips brushed against his ear when he'd asked if Falcon was alright. Falcon could still feel the warmth of his housemate's breath against his own skin.

Oh stars, he'd better get off of the man. Falcon's fantasizing was starting to have a bit of an effect in a particularly delicate area. He retreated, whispering a garbled affirmation, and half a step back found the wardrobe's opposite wall. Strange, it had never seemed so cramped from the outside. Then again, he hadn't used the wardrobe as a hiding place since he'd been a boy. Now, stuffed with two full grown lads, there wasn't even room to move without jostling each other.

Falcon stood up straight, trying to give them both some more room, and he sucked in a breath as a muscle in his back twinged, sharp and angry. Keene repeated his query from before, and Falcon nodded before remembering that Keene couldn't see him.

"Fine," he whispered. He tried to sound light as he added, "Just the old battle injuries playing up. I think I just need to massage it a little." He tried reaching around to rub the spot, but his elbow bumped the wall, sounding far too loud. Both gents froze and listened. The voices were getting closer, but slowly, and with such thick wooden walls around them, Falcon couldn't make out what they were saying. Still, they didn't sound alarmed, and Falcon released a grateful breath.

"Here, let me," Keene said.

And before Falcon understood the offer, Keene was reaching his arm around Falcon and pressing his fingertips into the aching muscles there.

"Here?" Keene asked.

Falcon swallowed hard. Excitement was growing in his trousers, but blazes, Keene's hand felt good gently but firmly pressing into him.

Falcon shifted to hide his pleasure and then tentatively

summoned his voice again. "A little higher?"

Keene obeyed and soon his hand found the right place. "I can feel a knot there." He placed his other hand on Falcon's hip for leverage. "Just hold onto me. I'll be gentle."

Falcon tried desperately not to imagine Keene saying those same words in a different context. Tried and failed, and he was very glad indeed he'd shifted. Keene's hand pressed into Falcon's back and massaged the knot. Falcon made himself breathe deep and slow. Keene had been right. It ached, but also somehow felt good. As Keene worked, tension released from the knot, and it slowly began to unwind.

It wasn't but a few minutes before the pain was fading into memory. All the while, Falcon had kept an ear out. As the voices had gradually grown closer, he realized the two speakers—men, by the sounds of their voices—were discussing the backroom's various pieces. As long as he and Keene were quiet, the Bits for Bobs employees should have no reason to suspect anything amiss about the wardrobe.

Something rubbed against Falcon's leg, and his eyes widened in the dark as he realized it was Keene. Or rather, Keene's own growing excitement, which only served to make Falcon's practically leap in celebration.

It's natural, he told himself, trying to calm down. *It's not about you anyway. It's just the friction. And besides, he can't be anything more than a friend to you... certainly not* that.

A little voice inside Falcon asked why. There was nothing wrong with a man loving another man, or a woman loving another woman—assuming one didn't hold with the idea that the former was unmanly, like Falcon's grandfather and others like him did. Rather, it was Falcon's own sense of responsibility that tugged at him. Fine, gentle born ladies and gents found a suitable match in order to spawn more fine, gentle born ladies and gents. And if a member of the upper-crust happened to possess preferences that didn't align with that, they were perfectly welcome to indulge those needs, just so long as it was kept a secret. Falcon wouldn't, he *couldn't*, do that to Keene.

Then again, Beatrice didn't live by that edict. She took multiple lovers. Though she didn't crow about them, of course. That would be very gauche, but she also didn't hide the fact that she dealt rather more freely in her romantic relationships than some more traditionally-minded folks would deem suitable. Why couldn't Falcon also choose a path that would make him happy, a path with Keene? Only if Keene wanted that too, of course. Then again, how would it look for an Enforcer—and not just any Enforcer, but the the newly-appointed Steward of the Sage—to…

Keene clearing his throat brought Falcon's attention back around. At least his mental spiraling had served to calm the inconvenient vim within his trousers.

Keene removed his hand from Falcon's hip but left the other against his back for now. "Feel better?"

Falcon leaned back a touch, testing his muscles. "Yes, thank you," he sighed in relief.

Instead of lifting straight away, Keene's hand slid from Falcon's back and around his side before disconnecting, which sent a minor thrill up Falcon's spine, but he said nothing.

They were both quiet as they continued to stand there, listening for the voices to pass, waiting until they could escape. The two chaps speaking outside really were taking their time. It almost sounded like they were running an inventory of sorts. And, unfortunately, not a single thing they said was incriminating. Next to Falcon, Keene's breathing grew louder, began to quicken.

"Keene?" Falcon whispered.

He heard his housemate catch his breath before answering so softly Falcon had to strain to hear him. "Does your wardrobe have any vents?"

"Vents?"

"Air holes, as in for breathing. It's just that it feels like it's getting awfully stuffy in here and… and… and…"

When Keene trailed off, it sounded like he was embarrassed to finish, and his voice contained a tremor Falcon hadn't heard from him before. To Falcon, their little hidey-hole felt the same as ever. Was it possible that Keene, calm and collected Keene, was one of those people with a fear of small spaces?

"It's alright," Falcon said gently. "There's plenty of air in here." He didn't know if it would help, but he raised his fan above their heads and blew a tiny gust down onto Keene. "I used to hide in here for hours when I was small, as have my sisters. We're fine, I promise."

Thinking of his sisters reminded Falcon of something he used to do to soothe them when they'd been little and were frightened. He leaned his cane against his leg and moved slowly, lest he accidentally jab Keene in the eye or something. Falcon felt for

Keene's face and tenderly brushed his hair back. He listened for the rhythm of his housemate's breathing.

"You're okay," Falcon assured him in whisper-gentle tones. "I won't let anything happen to you, alright?"

Keene's breathing did slow, and Falcon felt tension beneath his fingers ease as he stroked Keene's face and hair. Both were soft and supple.

To try and further distract Keene from his fear, he said, "Your hair feels so nice. Do you use something special for it?"

And to his great relief, Keene chuckled. "Just born under a lucky star, I'm afraid."

"Heavens, that's annoying," Falcon replied. He was pretty sure, even bathed in darkness as they were, that Keene knew he was rolling his eyes.

And suddenly, he felt Keene's fingers on his own face too, tracing their way upward. Across his cheek and until they found their way under Falcon's bonnet and into his hair.

"Yours is nice too," Keene whispered. "Don't sell yourself short."

Falcon's voice stuck in his throat. *Say something clever, something charming,* his brain urged. But nothing came out. He shifted his weight, and his cane slid off his leg, falling the short distance to the wardrobe wall and making a loud *thunk!* as it connected.

Keene froze. Falcon grabbed his cane and covered his face with his fan just as angry footsteps approached the wardrobe. Light sloshed back inside as the doors were thrown open.

If he'd wanted to get caught in a compromising position, Falcon couldn't have done better if he'd planned it. No more than a few finger breadth's worth of space separated him and Keene, so close that the fan covered both their faces.

Before them stood two men. One, as previously described, looked exactly like the living embodiment of a candle. A shock of bright red hair struggled against whatever product the man had used to try and smooth it down. Freckles spattered his pale skin like countless tiny sparks, and he was impossibly thin, which only served to make him look taller than he already was. The man wore a suit in the same blue and brown check pattern as his employees, but the cut clearly defined him as the man in charge. Twigs, Varick had called him, but Falcon realized that might not be the name he went by in public.

The man with him was another shop assistant, though this one wore a slightly different uniform than his comrades. It was nicer than the bloke's they'd run into before, but not quite as nice as Twigs'. Probably some middle manager, but if he was in on the scam, that might mean he was more dangerous as well.

Twigs glowered while Falcon and Keene stared silently back at him from behind the fan.

"Out," Twigs ordered as he jerked a thumb behind him.

Keene gave a surprisingly graceful nod, given the compromising position they'd been caught in, and glided out of the wardrobe. He took Falcon by the elbow and helped him down. The latter, not certain what else to do, began whittering garbled apologies in the high-pitched voice he'd established for his character. Falcon could just hear Camilla's words if she'd been here now:

"Is that really what you think women sound like?"

He was apologizing in his head already.

Once Falcon's feet were on the floor again, with Middle Manager and Bits for Bobs' owner glaring at them, Keene flashed a winning smile. "There we are, out of the closet now. I'm so proud of us."

Falcon tittered a laugh, playing along with Keene's attempt to lighten the mood. "Oh darling, you're so droll."

Neither Twigs nor Middle Manager were amused. They continued to stare with eyes so cold and stony they could have been made of granite.

Keene gave a weak chuckle to his own joke and gestured around them. "We thought back here might be where the paper products are kept."

"Paper products?" Twigs asked.

"Of course," Keene replied as if it were the most obvious thing in the world. "You know, extra New Year's cards people had leftover after sending theirs out. Old maps. Antique letters from the Old World. I'm quite a keen collector of such things. So if you could just direct us—"

"We don't deal in paper products," Twigs said flatly. "Not profitable enough and too easily damaged."

"I see." Keene looked genuinely crestfallen, and Falcon wondered if his housemate had ever ventured to tread the boards, as some of Beatrice's theater friends often said. "But if you got some, what would you do with them? Do you throw them in the bins maybe or just... burn them?"

"We don't accept them," Twigs said.

"Right-o," Keene said. "In that case, what about strong box —"

"You're not here for any of that," Twigs snapped, cutting Keene off.

Falcon felt a line of sweat pop out across his brow, and he fluttered his fan to get rid of it. Next to him, Keene seemed lost as to what to do next. Falcon began to do the math. He didn't have his truncheon, but his cane would do well enough in a fight. But it was two against one, as he neither wanted Keene in a fight nor could presume that Keene knew how to. As carefully as he could, Falcon slid one foot back into a defensive stance, using his cloak as cover.

"You two came in here to canoodle." Twigs sneered as he said it. "What was it, some kind of dare? Did you think the excitement would increase—"

"Sir! There is a lady present," Keene cut in.

He swished a pointing finger around toward Falcon as if they might need a reminder as to who the lady among them was. Fair dues, Falcon was now fully convinced he made the worst lady in history. Meanwhile, Keene went on.

"Now, I apologize for being where we shouldn't. We'll remove ourselves from your premises immediately." He tipped his hat. "Good day." Twigs began to object, but Keene threw back a stern, "I said good day!"

The housemates then hurried out of the backroom and back out to the sales floor, stopping where they'd initially met to shed Falcon's disguise and reclaim his greatcoat before escaping the store. Stepping back out onto the street, Falcon felt as if he were leaving a dream. He couldn't believe they'd really done it; they'd found new evidence. Nor could he believe much of the rest, especially that which had transpired inside the wardrobe, and try as he might, he couldn't stop replaying it in his head.

~Chapter 11~

"Well, that was something else," Falcon said as they made their way off the horse-drawn tram and began down the footpath back home.

On either side of them, people passed. It was peak morning travel time now, with fellow Springhavians heading to work, off to shop and run errands, and shuffling children to school. Falcon had to move slowly, given how much he'd already put his tightly wound muscles through today. Keene was keeping pace next to him, eyes skyward as if in thought.

"It certainly was," he replied blandly.

"Everything alright?" Falcon asked.

Keene finally looked at him and smiled, but it didn't quite reach his eyes. "Sorry. I just can't quite believe we pulled that off."

Falcon laughed, surprising himself. "I'm still not certain they believed I was a woman. They might have just thought I was mad and didn't want to upset me."

"No," Keene teased. "You also make a lovely woman."

"I think I prefer being a man, though."

Keene gave a playful shrug. "Whatever you like, as long as you're happy."

Falcon expected more, but Keene's gaze had wandered again. Falcon hesitated, not certain if he should pry. Clearly something was bothering his housemate, and it wasn't just discombobulation over what had happened. Was Keene bothered by something that had transpired in the wardrobe? Had Falcon crossed some kind of boundary? He began to mentally sift through the events, wondering where he might have gone wrong. He hadn't asked Keene to rub his back, nor play with his hair. Still, Falcon was convinced he'd done something wrong.

"Keene, if I..." Falcon began. Keene brought his eyes back to Falcon, but his words tripped over themselves as he realized he didn't know how to articulate his concerns. Especially in public. Everyone around them was rushing to some other destination, but discretion was still a concern when discussing sensitive matters. He decided to follow a more vague route, hoping he might still get his meaning across. "If I ever do anything to offend you, anything that makes you feel uncomfortable, I want you to tell me. Alright? I don't... um, I want us to feel comfortable being honest with one another, whether it's good or bad."

Bollocks, he was making a right meal of this. Still, Keene's mouth tipped up into a smile.

"I appreciate that, Falcon. Thank you. I want that for us too."

Falcon hesitated. Then dared to venture, "So have I... offended you at all?"

"What?" Keene replied, and Falcon nearly slumped with relief at the sincere confusion in his tone. "How would you have offended me? Why would you think that?"

"Uh," Falcon answered.

Eloquent as always, he thought.

Falcon looked around as he searched for how to explain. Not just that, but how to do it without being completely inappropriate in public. And as he looked, he realized they weren't where he expected. Falcon really hadn't been paying much attention to where they were going, what with so many other things on his mind, and they must have turned somewhere without him realizing it. They weren't headed home as he'd assumed, but rather into their neighborhood's little shopping district.

"What are we doing here?"

"I've got a pickup scheduled," Keene replied.

Ah, probably something for his next event, Falcon thought. He decided he was content to let Keene's questions go unanswered and let them fall into comfortable silence.

The two soon arrived at the bakery, which Falcon found odd

considering they'd only just been there the day before. Keene must have placed a special order at some point.

The bakery smelled of warm bread, vanilla, and yeast. A row of long wooden worktable-turned-displays ran all down the length of the shop at the back. The tables were piled with freshly baked loaves, pies both sweet and savory, the last of some New Year's figgy puddings, and what looked like miles of biscuits if they were laid end-to-end. Everything was arranged to be a treat for the eye, tiered so customers could see everything at once, and small stands holding cards with prices written across them popped up all over the worktables, like cheerful daisies asking for money.

Falcon had learned yesterday that the bakery was owned by a Mister and Mrs. Strongbow. Mister Strongbow was currently helping customers at the till, which made a pleasant *ting!* every time a sale completed. Meanwhile, further down the row, Mrs. Strongbow, along with a lad of about fifteen, were kneading great slabs of dough flecked with green bits. Another customer chatted with Mrs. Strongbow while the boy glared down at his dough like he could stare it into submission. Falcon assumed he was the Strongbow's son, given the uncanny resemblance he bore to Mrs. Strongbow, both squat with thick builds. The entire family had rosy skin and dark hair, which Mrs. Strongbow currently had tucked up into a mobcap. Falcon wondered if all the flour they worked with had dusted them and made them look paler than they actually were. Their worktable was absolutely covered in the stuff, and it had lightened the sleeves of Mrs. Strongbow's cinnamon-colored work dress to more of a sepia tone.

Both Mrs. Strongbow and her son had their sleeves rolled up, something that would be looked down on if they weren't currently engaged in their livelihoods, and Falcon was impressed by the biceps on both of them. Even Mrs. Strongbow, whose petite stature belied her strength, could probably take Falcon in an arm wrestling contest. He wondered for the first time in his life how much a bag of flour actually weighed.

He and Keene waited in line while Falcon watched the bread kneading take place. It still fascinated him to see food before it actually became food.

"They're making our prize winning garlic and rosemary loaves."

Falcon looked toward the voice and realized it was Mister Strongbow speaking. They'd reached the front of the line more quickly than Falcon had thought they would. The tall man at the till dwarfed his wife. And though he was slender, his arms looked like they could lift wagonloads of flour.

"Prize winning?" Falcon asked. Did baked goods win prizes?

As if knowing what he was thinking, Mister Strongbow explained, "Yep. Three years running now at the Springhaven Summer Faire."

He puffed out his chest and swept an arm toward the wall where three blue ribbons hung. There were even framed image-stills to go with them, which were expensive and labor intensive to produce. The event must be prestigious indeed.

"Well done." Falcon smiled broadly, happy for the man and his family even though he'd had no idea such a festival even existed until this moment. He glossed over that fact and said, "I've never been, but it sounds grand."

"Never been?" Mister Strongbow guffawed and looked to Keene. "Where've you been keeping this one? Under a rock?"

"A travesty I mean to correct in short order," Keene joked back. He nudged Falcon with his elbow, though gently enough, Falcon noticed, to not potentially aggravate his injuries. "This summer, you and me. I'll show you everything the Faire has to offer."

Falcon's smile curled further up his face, and he got a sensation like birds fluttering around in his stomach. "I'd love that."

When Falcon turned back to Mister Strongbow, the man was opening a low door in the sales counter—the only bit of the setup that wasn't worktables—and he beckoned the housemates through.

Continuing the conversation, Mister Strongbow said, "Those were hard-won competitions, let me tell you. Everyone comes out for them. Everyone wants a piece of the glory."

As Falcon headed behind the counter, which felt strange and somehow not allowed, he asked, "How many bakers come out for it?"

Mister Strongbow laughed again, "Oh, gobs! And it's not just bakers we're competing against. Anyone who can throw together a decent loaf tries their luck."

"There's a lot of camaraderie about it," Keene added. "It's a great chance to get to know your local merchants."

"And a great chance to show who's the best," Mister Strongbow laughed. "Like us."

Keene laughed and slapped Mister Strongbow on the back as the baker led them toward a wide doorway that was only semi-closed off by a pair of swinging shutters.

The door, if indeed it could be called that, led to a massive kitchen with yet more worktables. Atop these waited stacks upon stacks of mixing bowls, huge jars of spices and sugar and other delicious looking things Falcon couldn't identify, and heaping bags of flour that dusted the floor like snow. Massive troughs full of fragrant, yeasty dough in mid-rise lined one side of the wall, while brick bread ovens and the more standard style of ovens Falcon was used to seeing, just much larger, filled the wall on the other side. The kitchen was warm, too warm for Falcon's coat, and he hung it over his free arm as he walked.

Most interesting of all, however, were the people back here. Somewhere between five and seven adolescents between the ages of ten and seventeen kneaded, mixed, measured, and fetched. All had the same dark hair and rosy skin as their parents. Falcon wasn't certain about his count because he kept seeing two or three young girls who all looked the same, save for their various style of hair plaits.

"My brood," Mister Strongbow said proudly. "Wotcha, brood! Say hello to Mister Kohli and Mister Smoke."

"Hello Mister Kohli and Mister Smoke," the children chorused, all out of sync and polite but clearly not interested in whatever the adults were up to.

"Everything's back here for you," Mister Strongbow said.

Through yet another door they went, and Falcon found himself in a cluttered back garden. This clearly didn't get the same attention as the kitchen and shop. A small open-walled shed sat off to one side against the wooden fencing that separated the Strongbow's garden from their neighbor's. Shelves had been built within the shed, and a mix of paint cans, tools, and more heaped upon one another across them. Spare planks of wood leaned against the open sidewall, blocking Falcon's view of some of the mess.

On the other side of the yard was a long but slender garden bed. Seedlings poked up from the recently tilled dirt, and small wooden signs sticking up in front of each row indicated that the Strongbows had planted strawberries, rhubarb, cabbage, spring onions, peas, and herbs. The herbs section had clearly been around a few years and was a bit more haphazard than the rest, as those plants had grown tall and bushy, fighting against each other for space in their little section. One large plant with woody branches and small, flat, bright green leaves towered over the rest, while another with darker, larger, smoother leaves just coming in had grown up spindly, taking any little available space. More woody branches poked through the fence slats from the other side, higher up than even the big bright green one.

Falcon thought he recognized the woody plants and headed over for a closer look. He glanced back over his shoulder as Keene and Mister Strongbow knelt with their backs to Falcon in front of a miniature wooden house, perhaps meant for dolls. He kept one ear open as he furtively pulled from his pocket the sprig he'd found inside his stolen wardrobe at Bits for Bobs.

"She's a good'un, that's for sure," Mister Strongbow was saying. "Cost us a pretty penny, though."

The sprig matched the larger woody plants with the small leaves.

"I imagine it's hard to keep an eye on her with so many other things on your plate," Keene said. Then, in a more playful voice, "You've gotten yourself into some real mischief, haven't you?"

The Strongbows' back garden was open to the alley behind the bakery, and a large cart sat there. Or at least the back end of one, as the rest extended past and was obscured by the fence. The cart looked in better repair than either the fence or the shed, and a wet track across the cobblestones of the alley still glistened in the weak sunlight. Falcon approached the cart, sizing it up. It was certainly big enough to move several pieces of furniture, plus more. An entire household's worth of things if they'd packed it cleverly. He risked another glance at his housemate and the baker. They still had their backs to him, so Falcon strolled over to the cart as casually as he could and peered over the edge to look inside.

The side boards weren't too high for Falcon to reach in and run his hand over the cart's floor. It was sprinkled with a layer of white powder. Falcon rubbed it between his fingers, finding the grain to be very fine. When he sniffed it, it smelled slightly nutty, but only just. He considered tasting it, but ingesting unknown substances wasn't really smart at the best of times. No, it was enough that it seemed to match what he'd seen around his wardrobe's feet earlier that day.

"Managed to find homes for the little ones, but people aren't interested in older models like us." Mister Strongbow chuckled at whatever joke he'd just made, the context for which Falcon had missed.

Falcon wandered around the cart to scrutinize the end he hadn't been able to see from the yard. The apparatus at the front looked like what he was used to seeing for hitching up a horse, but it was currently attached to a strange wooden box on wheels. The box was about half the length and height of a horse, but the same width. The top was open, and Falcon peeked in to see a miniature steam engine of some sort. A partially disassembled steam engine to be more precise. A few wrenches of various sizes hung from metal loops attached to the inside of the wooden casing—specialized tools just for the engine, Falcon assumed. At the back of the box, facing the driver's seat, a mind-boggling number of levers, gauges, and wheels stood ready to... do whatever it was they did.

These sorts of engines weren't common, but those who could afford them and do the fussy upkeep preferred them to horses, given that the only thing you had to feed a motor was coal or oil or other burnable fuel. And that was just when you wanted it to run. Thus, it had the potential to be more economical than a horse.

The clouds above scudded away from the sun, allowing light to pour across the garden like a wash of bright paint. Something glimmering within the cart caught Falcon's eye, and he reached into it again, this time to remove a small fragment of wood. It was barely the size of Falcon's pinkie finger, but the color of the paint across it could have been nothing more than a speck and he'd still have recognized it.

The blue-grey of a peregrine falcon.

His wardrobe had been transported in this cart. He looked it over again, taking in the implications, only to realize he'd left tracks. A puddle of something dark and shiny pooled beneath the engine, and Falcon had partially stepped in it.

"It's a shame there aren't any contraceptives for dogs," Keene said.

"What?" Falcon exclaimed. What on earth were they talking about?

He spun, shoving the chip of wood into his pocket. Keene and Mister Strongbow were standing now. The former held one end of a piece of rope, the other end of which was attached to a small dog. At least, Falcon was fairly certain it was a dog.

The creature that might or might not be a dog consisted mostly of furry cream and tan wrinkles. Short, stubby legs stuck out of the body at all the right doggy places, but the tail was nothing more than a curl resembling punctuation gone wrong. And the face... had it suffered some kind of horrible accident that had left it all squashed like that? The snout, which was black, smushed against itself, barely a bump, and made of yet more wrinkles. Its lower jaw stuck out a touch more than the upper, giving it a mean look. The animal let its tongue loll out, transforming the canine sneer from a moment ago into a soppy, smiling face. Maybe it was actually some kind of mutant pig, for the creature snorted a few times before licking its chops and looking hopefully between the three humans.

"Um..." Falcon said. He almost asked if the possibly-a-dog was alright, but stopped himself just short of it, realizing at the last second that Mister Strongbow might have some attachment and take offense.

No one noticed Falcon's verbal trip, as Mister Strongbow was already saying, "I'm glad to know she's going to a good home."

"Happy to help," Keene said. He then looked back into the shed. "I think I'll have to come back for the house and other bits."

Falcon walked over for a closer look, and the could-it-be-a-long-lost-Old-World-creature smiled again. It stood and snorted, wagging its curly, pig-like tail.

"Feel free to use the wagon," Mister Strongbow replied. "I trust you'll be back soon enough."

"A grand idea! Thank you. I'll have it back toot sweet." Keene laughed, joined by Mister Strongbow. "Falcon, could you hold onto Luffy, please?"

Without waiting for an answer, Keene pressed his end of the rope into Falcon's hand and turned away to help Mister Strongbow.

Falcon didn't mind. He was still fascinated by the cryptid at his feet. He squatted and held out a tentative hand. As far as animals went, he considered himself primarily a horse person, but he knew better than to reach in without warning and take liberties with petting. Luffy, as Keene had called her, ambled over, rocking back and forth like a ship in high waves. She smiled at Falcon, letting her tongue hang out again, and sniffed Falcon's hand for a moment before licking it. Falcon smiled. Yes, it certainly appeared to be a dog. The strangest dog he'd ever seen, but then again, people did breed some odd sorts. One of his mother's friends had one that was almost entirely hairless, save for puffs of long, silky hair on its feet, its head, and the end of its tail. When the thing had died, she'd had the dog stuffed. It now overlooked visitors to the woman's parlor.

Within moments, Keene returned with a small wooden pull wagon in tow, a miniature, engineless version of the big one Falcon had been searching just a few minutes ago. Into it, they loaded the small wooden house, a large bone that looked to have once been attached to a cow or pig, a tough leather ball, and some earthenware bowls.

"We'll take the alley out," Keene said. "Thanks again. Falcon, you ready?"

Falcon nodded, vaguely wondering to whom they were delivering Luffy. His mind was already swinging back to the case, and he gave the herbs in the garden and the big cart one last long look.

~Chapter 12~

Falcon's mind ran over the evidence as he and Keene walked home. Keene was obviously lost in his own world as they went, humming to himself as he pulled the wagon behind him. Luffy had eschewed walking for riding and perched at the front of the wagon like the pudgy captain of her own airship, floating over a footpath-colored ocean.

Meanwhile, Falcon worried over the evidence, which was pretty damning at this point. True, some Bits for Bobs employees could have done it. They, the bakers included, might all secretly be professional thieves. Falcon bit the inside of his cheek, wondering if there might even be a connection to the movers his parents had hired. First Iago often compared Springhaven's criminal underground to ants or termites—they were everywhere, with hideaways in every nook and cranny and a vast connection of agents and accomplices. Falcon didn't like to consider the possibility—he hated the way the Enforcer order taught its members to always assume the worst about people—but the murkiness of this case made him wonder if maybe First Iago was right.

Then again, there was the sprig from the wardrobe. Granted, plants grew everywhere. It didn't automatically mean the Strongbows were involved, but to then also find a wooden chip painted in such a distinctive color in their cart? And the powder on both the cart's floor and the wardrobe's feet. If they were the burglars, how was he going to tell Keene? They had the strength to lift the pieces, and even the manpower to do it quickly, assuming they'd sunk low enough to involve their multitude of children. Keene had obviously already built a relationship with them; he'd be crushed if he learned they'd betrayed him.

And what was Falcon going to do with the knowledge anyway? Their possessions had clearly already been sold. And he'd promised to leave the Enforcers out of it. As a citizen, he had no power, no way of demanding restitution, no cards to play. Ugh, he hated the position the Enforcer order put him in. Follow justice and see the criminals, possibly an entire family of them, locked away forever or don't and let them get away with it. As loath as Falcon was to involve Keene, he needed better ideas. And his housemate was clever. He wouldn't mention the Strongbow's likely involvement yet, though. He wanted to spare Keene's feelings for as long as possible.

When Falcon pulled himself from the mire of his own thoughts, however, he noticed they'd nearly arrived back home. He was really letting his observation skills slide. And Luffy was still seated atop her rolling throne, smiling and occasionally snorting.

"Keene, to whom are we delivering Luffy?" Falcon asked.

Keene threw a teasing look over his shoulder. "You'll see. It's a surprise."

The mischievous twinkling in his housemate's eye pulled a grin from Falcon. He'd never known a man as playful as Keene, and he was finding he deeply enjoyed it. So often, young men were taught to be dignified and proper, which were really just different ways of saying boring. Falcon made a dubious noise back, cocking an eyebrow at Keene, who chuckled before looking away. As they drew closer to the house, however, a new idea entered Falcon's mind. An idea he definitely hadn't signed up for.

"But really, to whom are we delivering her?"

Keene either hadn't heard Falcon or was ignoring him. They came up on Mrs. Spoondawdle's house across the street. That would make sense. A sweet old lady like her could do with a furry little companion. Oh, dash it all! They still needed to have her over. Later, though, because they were passing her house right on by and crossing the road now, skirting around a fresh, dark stain on the cobbles.

"Keene," Falcon said, still trying but mostly failing to keep his voice light, "who's taking Luffy in? Do I know them?"

Keene made a noncommittal sound in his throat that sounded as if he might be stifling a laugh. Thankfully, they passed by the stoop to Falcon and Keene's house and went around the corner. Falcon let his worries go. These last few days were making him nervous, that was all. And then Keene was pushing open their back gate and rolling the wagon across their back garden.

All the concerns Falcon had just released to the wind came gusting back. "You cannot be serious, Keene. We can't have a dog."

Keene still said nothing, and Luffy alighted from the wagon like a bowl full of jelly, more oozing out of it than jumping. Since sense had failed him thus far, Falcon began repeating Keene's name, a trick he'd pulled from his younger sisters' books. Maybe he could annoy the man into answering him.

When they were inside the kitchen, Keene carrying all but the doghouse, which he'd set next to the back door outside, Falcon doubled his efforts, growing louder and more insistent.

"Keene. Keene. Keene. Keene. Keene. Keene."

In a move more akin to a dancer's than anything else, Keene spun back toward Falcon and stopped just short of their noses touching. "I like hearing you say my name. Keep it up." Keene's tone was a low, thrumming challenge.

Falcon suddenly found his mouth dry and voice gone. Butterflies ran riot around his insides, and he bit his lip, unsure what to do with his hands, given that he very badly wanted to reach out and pull his housemate closer.

Keene's eyes fell to Falcon's mouth, watched him bite his lip for a moment before pulling away and calling for Luffy, who'd wandered off.

Falcon forced himself to swallow a few times. Blazes, how did Keene pull off being so smooth? Falcon huffed. No, he would *not* be thrown off his game.

"What possessed you?" he called into the house. He found Keene at the foot of the stairs, watching Luffy investigate the challenging mountain of wood.

Keene looked to Falcon, that same charming smile in place. He held out his arms like this was one big present. "Surprise!"

"Keene!" Falcon pleaded.

Keene waggled his eyebrows at the sound of his name yet

again. And then grew only slightly more serious as he explained, "It works out perfectly. Luffy needs a new home and we need a guard dog."

Luffy's journey up five stairs had apparently worn her out, and she'd settled off to the side of the step for a refreshing mid-climb nap.

Falcon pointed accusingly at her. "*She* couldn't guard a loaf of bread. She'd probably eat it… or think she was looking in a mirror."

"Falcon," Keene scolded, only half playfully now, "you're going to hurt her feelings."

"Are we even sure she's a dog?" He started to think again. "Maybe some kind of tiny, weird, shorn sheep?"

"How dare you?" Keene scooped Luffy up into his arms and made her face Falcon. "Apologize, now. You're being very ugly to our new baby."

Falcon spread his hands before him, trying very hard to not think about the closeness of the words, "ugly" and "baby" in that last sentence. "Sorry! I'm not much of an animal person, except for horses. And she's…" He trailed off as Keene narrowed his eyes at him, followed by Luffy. Though the latter might have just been squinting. Falcon softened, realizing that Keene really was already fairly attached to the odd creature. To try and smooth over hurt feelings, he reached out and scratched Luffy behind the ears with his non-cane-holding hand before putting it on Keene's arm. "Loafy seems like a very sweet girl." Try as he might, he wasn't able to hold back a smile.

Keene tried too, and they ended up laughing together.

"Her name is Luffy," Keene proclaimed, though his grin undermined the gravity of it. "*Luf*-fee."

"Whatever you say," Falcon replied. He wanted to sigh in defeat, to find another argument. There was, of course, the issue of another mouth to feed, but it was a very small mouth. And honestly, there'd been enough heartache and worry the last few days that he couldn't do it. If a fuzzy ball of dough come to life was what it took to lift their spirits, then he'd accept Luffy without further complaint.

In the meantime, given that they'd risen so early, several hours stretched before Falcon until their dinner engagement with the Allens that evening. Keene was, unsurprisingly, back in the kitchen soon after their return home. Falcon, for the moment, had retreated to his bedroom to do his stretches. He was bloody tired of his body aching. And some of what his body aches had led to earlier that morning was frankly confusing. He still felt as if he might have overstepped somehow with Keene, and making his housemate uncomfortable was the last thing Falcon wanted. So he was bloody well taking control of his pain; he'd stop being a victim to it if it killed him. Which felt like a real possibility in his current position.

Falcon had laid one of the more raggedy spare blankets on the floor and was using that as a pad. Next to him was a small collection of papers with typewritten instructions and illustrations of people demonstrating how to do each exercise. He was currently engaged in the one labeled Seat Forward Bend. The simplicity of the name belied the difficulty of the stretch itself, at least for him. He was sitting with his legs straight out before him and had grabbed a spare pair of trousers to assist him. The idea was to bend forward at the hips, bringing one's stomach toward the thighs and, using a couple of tea towels tied together, pull oneself even further down. Falcon had forgotten to grab tea towels from downstairs and couldn't be bothered to trundle back down for them, thus the trousers instead. Doctor Allen had advised him to push himself to the point of being uncomfortable but not in pain. Falcon, however, was having trouble finding that line. He really was going to have to remember to do these more often. Stars, he hated feeling so incapable. He held the position, forcing himself to breathe in time with a slow, steady count.

Four... three... two... one. Yes, done!

Back in a more comfortable position again, Falcon released a breath. He was only halfway through and already perspiring, despite the fact that he'd removed his shirt and undershirt, as well as his socks. He'd have to sponge off in the basin once he was done.

Next came the Cat-Cow stretch, which was blessedly easier, as long as he remembered to give his knees extra padding. He shifted into an all-fours position, hands beneath his shoulders and knees beneath his hips. Then all he had to do was arch like an angry cat, hold, lower to stretch his back the opposite way, hold, and repeat. Falcon closed his eyes, focusing on the feelings inside his body as Doctor Allen had also advised. He breathed deeply, feeling his muscles stretching, tension releasing. He allowed himself a little moan of pleasure, feeling like his body was becoming his again.

When he finished, Falcon opened his eyes to find Keene

standing in the doorway, dark eyes on him and nibbling the corner of his thumb. Still on all fours, Falcon blinked, trying to sort out his feelings.

Keene's gaze was usually clear and present, but right now it was more intense than usual. And the way he was biting his thumb was a fetching look, hesitant but not nervous. Falcon was aware of being naked from the waist up, but that didn't bother him. Propriety among men wasn't nearly the thing it was between them and women, and the Halls of Justice's dressing rooms were nothing more than one big open space with benches and locking cubbies. Another man seeing his bare chest was nothing to Falcon at this point. And he was suddenly more than a little pleased that his physique had come back as much as it had since his coma. It wasn't yet to the point it'd been pre-Halls of Justice attack, but it wasn't anything to sneeze at either. Falcon blushed, however, when he realized *Keene* might be uncomfortable with his state of dress. They shared a room now, yes, but Keene had still been using his own to change clothes.

"Apologies." He sat back on his heels and began reaching for his undershirt. "I should have closed the door."

Keene was already waving his worry away, though, and Falcon stopped, secretly grateful. He didn't really want to replace the garment just yet, not given how sticky with sweat he was.

"No, no. I'm not fussed. It's nice." Falcon wondered at the comment, but Keene quickly amended, "It's nice that you feel so comfortable. That's what we said we wanted, right?"

It was one of the only times Falcon had heard the man sound even the slightest bit flustered. It was adorable, and Falcon gifted him a big smile.

"This is the infamous physiotherapy then?" Keene went on.

Falcon released a sigh. "This is it."

Behind Keene, Luffy snorted and shuffled her way up onto the landing, rolling over the top step like a lump of semi-soft cheese. She lay there panting but looking very pleased with herself.

"We might have to build her a ramp," Falcon said.

Keene didn't look behind him, eyes still on Falcon, as he replied, "She needs to go on a diet. I bet the Strongbow children were always giving her treats."

Falcon nodded. He too would probably put on a considerable amount of weight if he lived at the Strongbow bakery. His thoughts returned to his suspicions about that family. He still wasn't certain what his next move should be, but it was still too early to tell his housemate too. Not until he had something more concrete.

"Shall I join you?" Keene asked. "Maybe it'll be easier with a friend."

Falcon swept his hand over the bit of floor next to him in a grand gesture of welcome. Keene followed Falcon's example and stripped down to his waist. Falcon tried not to look too much at his housemate, but the definition in the man's arms, chest, and back was impressive. Falcon was certain it came from lifting cast iron pans and kneading bread and all the other strenuous tasks his job demanded of him. Keene's eyes seemed to be on Falcon just as much, though, and neither said a word about it.

Falcon set the physiotherapy pages between them, and Keene grabbed another blanket to serve as a mat for himself. Together, they went through the rest of Falcon's exercises. Though he'd never done them before, Keene was better at every one. Falcon knew he shouldn't feel bad. After all, Keene hadn't been blown from a window and into a tree, or abused by terrified protesters. Nevertheless, he couldn't help but want to get one-up on his housemate. He didn't want to hurt him, of course, but a bit of cheeky japery might be in order. Just something to tease and amuse, not to mention shave the prickly edges off of Falcon's feelings.

Near the end of the stretches, as they were shifting positions between exercises—moving up from prone positions to kneeling—Falcon reached over and pushed Keene's shoulder, shooting him a jaunty grin. Keene caught himself, rocked back the other direction on his knees, and pushed Falcon back. Falcon laughed, but was losing his balance. He wasn't worried; he'd been trained how to fall to prevent injuries—trees in the way notwithstanding—but on the way down, his direction suddenly shifted, *too* suddenly. He was flying in a direction he hadn't expected, and in a flash he was back at the Halls of Justice. The sound of an inside wall exploding outward rang in his ears, terrified screams replaying. He screwed his eyes shut and waited for the impact, for the pain and darkness to overtake him, but it never came.

"Falcon," came a voice through his memories. "Falcon, talk to me. What's wrong?"

Falcon came back to himself, opened his eyes. He wasn't at the Halls of Justice. He was in his room, in his little house, with Keene. Who was, strangely, underneath him. Falcon did a quick mental survey and found that he was lying on top of his housemate, their stomachs and chests pressed together, which rather made him feel more upside down than ever. But at least this wasn't in a terrifying way. This was a warm, albeit new and unknown, cozy sort of way. And a little sticky, given that they were both perspiring.

Keene was stroking Falcon's face with his fingertips, brushing his hair back from his forehead.

"Hey, you alright?" Keene asked. "Your heart is racing."

Falcon was aware of their chests pressed together, his heart crashing against his ribcage, thumping against Keene's. In his ebbing fear, he was entirely honest with himself. He wanted to stay here, to rest his head against Keene's shoulder and be held and not move for a while. To be allowed to recover slowly, peacefully, without the expectations of life pulling at him like they always did. He was concerned his poor housemate might feel crushed beneath his weight, though. Falcon was taller than Keene, and a little broader too, and so settled for sliding off to the side. Keene followed, turning with Falcon, keeping his hand close. The two laid on their sides, not even inches between them, Falcon taking deep, blissful gulps of cool air while Keene gave him time to think and gather himself.

"No," Falcon finally said shakily. He lifted his eyes to Keene's. "No, I'm not alright. But I'm working on it."

Keene nodded and brushed Falcon's hair back again, and he realized Keene was doing the same thing Falcon'd done for Keene when he'd been frightened in the wardrobe. It felt delicious and safe, and Falcon wanted nothing more than to swim in this sweet, gentle space for hours, even days perhaps. He realized then his hand was resting on the fleshy space between Keene's ribs and hips. His housemate's skin was so warm. And soft, softer than Falcon expected it would be as he ran his thumb across it, feeling the bumps of Keene's ribs. Falcon tightened his grasp and wriggled closer. A distant part of his mind warned him against it, that it might make things worse, but Falcon was suddenly exhausted. By fear, by the weight of expectations, by memories and uncertainty. He wanted comfort, and Keene wasn't pulling away.

Quite the opposite.

Keene put his hand on the same spot on Falcon's side and shuffled closer too, not that they could get much closer. Their heads lay so close, Falcon could feel every breath Keene took. The tips of their noses brushed, and when they breathed, their chests pushed against the other.

"What happened?" Keene whispered. His dark eyes were so close and warm, Falcon felt he could have melted into them, like a hot spring. "Where'd you go?"

Falcon didn't have the energy to hide, nor did he want to. But he also didn't feel up to telling the entire story, so he settled on a much shorter version. "I was there when the Halls of Justice were attacked. I was badly hurt, and just now, as we were playing, it all came back."

A faint line between Keene's eyebrows creased into a deep gouge of concern. "Falcon, I'm sorry. I didn't mean to... I only... I saw you were falling and got scared, so I pulled you back. I'm so sorry. I never want to do anything to make you feel afraid." He looked down, causing some locks of his ebony hair to fall across his face. And he tensed like he was getting ready to pull away.

Falcon lifted his hand from Keene's midsection and brushed the backs of his fingers across Keene's brow, pushing the hair from his face and cupping the side of it. The comforting fragrance of Keene's warm spices scent wafted across the close space and invaded Falcon's nostrils, wrapping itself around him. "It's not you, I promise. You're one of the few things in my life going right."

Keene looked back at Falcon, a smile pulling at his lips. Blazes, how Falcon wanted to taste that smile, to nibble at Keene's skin and discover if he tasted as good as he smelled. But a new fear was building in the pit of Falcon's stomach. Fear of what would happen if he took that step, fear of what would happen if he didn't. It left him frozen in place.

In a softer voice than before, Falcon asked, "Why were you afraid for me? When I was falling?"

Keene took a deep breath and released it slowly, chilling Falcon's exposed, drying skin. Falcon shivered, and Keene moved his hand, rubbing warmth back into Falcon's arm, smoothing out the growing goosebumps.

"I wasn't sure you'd be able to catch yourself. That you wouldn't get hurt."

"Ah," Falcon said. Now it was his turn to lower his eyes.

"Hey," Keene whispered. He placed gentle fingers beneath Falcon's chin and tipped his head back up so that he was looking at Keene. "I'm sorry. I don't know your limitations, and I wasn't trying to assume them. I was just worried. I'll tell you what I do know, though." He paused, and Falcon held his gaze, waiting with bated breath. "You. Are *not*. Broken."

Something caught in Falcon's throat. A part of him was loosening, relief pouring in. He didn't understand how this man had managed to pierce his armor and find the blackened spots of pain beneath, but he had. Falcon felt seen for the first time in… he didn't know how long. And not just seen, but Keene wasn't judging him. Keene was holding him close and…

Time slowed. Falcon's hand turned and opened, flattening against Keene's bare chest. His heart beat like a drum against Falcon's palm. Their noses were touching, gazes drinking in one another. Keene's hand moved from Falcon's chin, slid over his naked shoulder, fingertips grazing across his pale skin, excruciatingly slowly and yet with the power of lightning. It burned in an impossibly exquisite way, and Falcon sighed and arched beneath the electrifying touch. In an embrace that Falcon felt he'd been waiting ages for, Keene wrapped his arm fully around Falcon's waist, enveloping him in that intoxicating scent, holding him tight. Falcon closed his eyes, breathed it in deeply, and —

Knock! Knock! Knock!

~Chapter 13~

The sound of the door knocker reverberating through the house sent the world into a spin. Keene was pulling away, and Falcon followed suit without thinking. The moment had been shattered like a soap bubble, yanking Falcon back into the real world with all its yowling demands. Without a word, both men pulled their shirts back on and buttoned them quickly. On his way out, Keene picked up Luffy, who'd fallen asleep where she'd conquered the stairs, and Falcon followed close behind. He was vaguely aware of his body feeling better after its stretching session, but not much else. It felt as if he'd just woken up from a dream and was still coming to grips with reality.

With Luffy tucked against him in one arm, Keene answered the door just as the knocker was starting up another round of banging. Falcon came up just behind as the door opened to reveal none other than Varick Hollow. The visitor's eyes roved over the two men, quickly taking in the state of their shirts. Falcon only then realized his was completely untucked.

"Am I interrupting something?" he asked.

"No," Keene said.

"Of course not," Falcon said at the same time. He turned away for a moment to tuck in the offending shirttails.

"Why would you be?" Keene added unnecessarily.

Varick's eyebrow cocked upward in perfect synchronization with his smirk, but he didn't pursue the subject. Instead he tucked his hands in his pockets and, with an even bigger smirk, said "Well, I'm sorry to spring this on you gents, but I don't see any other way for it."

Falcon and Keene exchanged confused looks, and Falcon found himself grateful for the distraction.

In that brief glance, Falcon looked for signs that Keene felt as dazed as he did. Where did this leave them? Was Falcon completely off-base about what he'd thought had been about to happen? What if it *had* happened? What would have been their next moves after that? He tried reading Keene's body language, searched for a flush in Keene's skin, but everything was happening so fast, and Falcon's brain couldn't focus. Now that the moment with Keene was gone, Falcon needed time to sort through the feelings swimming around inside of him.

Varick gestured toward the door. "Do you mind if we come in?"

"We who?" Falcon asked.

But at the same time, Keene moved aside and swept his free arm toward the parlor. "Please, be our guest."

Just like that, Keene had slid back into his easy, welcoming self. Falcon wondered if that sort of mental flexibility could be learned. If so, he needed to get Keene to tutor him in the shortest order possible. Or maybe Falcon really was completely off-base and what he'd thought had been about to happen had just been wishful thinking. He yet again didn't have time to consider his feelings about that, as events continued to hurtle forward like a steam train running at full bore.

Varick turned back toward the street and beckoned with a hand. "Alright, you lot. Let's get moving."

Then he crossed the threshold with the same confidence of a man who owned the place. Without looking, he pointed at Keene and said, "Your buttons are crooked, by the way."

Looking down, Keene said, "Well, I'll be. So they are. Here, Falcon, hold Luffy."

As Luffy was placed into his free arm, Falcon was looking through the open doorway at a large wagon similar to that which had been used to transport his things when he'd moved in just over a week ago. A team of people was already busy unloading a rack of clothing from the wagon. Next to the racks rose small, tarpaulin-covered mountains, but Falcon hadn't the foggiest as to what could lay beneath their coverings.

"Is that a dog?"

Falcon looked to Varick, who'd been the one asking. He had his head tilted to the side, eyes squinting dubiously.

"Of course she's a dog," Falcon replied, a mite more energetically than he'd meant to. It was one thing for him to make fun of his and Keene's furry little baby; no one else was allowed to.

"Are you sure?" Varick pressed, looking more skeptical than ever.

To try and make himself sound a bit less like an overbearing parent, Falcon replied more evenly, "What else would Luffy be?"

Varick tilted his head in the other direction now, clearly thinking. "Maybe a sentient sandbag?"

"Varick?" Keene broke in, watching four very large, very muscular men carrying the rack of clothing up the stoop and inside. "If you don't mind my asking, what exactly is happening?"

The men carrying the rack looked to Varick, who nodded. "Just set it over there near the fireplace for now. We'll move it if we need to."

"I'm afraid Mister Hollow is being dramatic, as is his usual manner of operating."

Falcon spun at the sound of the voice, a bright smile spreading across his face. "Milly!"

Camilla stood in a doorway, the very picture of reliable calm. Her blonde hair was caught up in a fashionable yet simple bun, and her walking dress—a spring green overskirt against sugar pink and white underneath—complimented the light blue color of her eyes.

Next to her, bouncing slightly on her toes, stood her sister, Lenore. They weren't sisters in the eyes of the law or by blood, but in every way that otherwise mattered. Lenore's dark hair, which was only half up, bounced with her, and her green eyes sparkled with excitement. She wore a rather more modern high-low skirted ensemble with trousers underneath. The style was popular with ladies who'd given up fighting with long skirts that always tried to trip them up—to be fair to Lenore, Camilla had inhuman levels of patience.

Falcon hadn't seen Camilla since last week at the Halls of Justice with the spitball incident, not that could really be counted as a proper visit. And it had been even longer since he'd seen

Lenore. Not since last month after the Enforcer reform bill had passed. Granted, he and Lenore occupied that strange space between more than acquaintances and proper friends, but stars, he really was letting his social calendar slip.

"Sorry we're late," Lenore said. "We got caught behind a milk cart."

Falcon strode over to the ladies standing at his door. "It's so good to see you both. Please, come in. I apologize for the house. It's not…" He verbally stumbled, suddenly realizing he didn't know how to politely describe the situation. "Well, it's not usually like this, you see."

Camilla placed a comforting hand on his arm in the same way he'd seen her do for so many ailing patients. "We heard what happened. Heavens, Falcon, what an ordeal. I'm so sorry."

Lenore pressed her lips together, as if something were fighting to burst out of her. While rocking back and forth on her heels, she flicked her gaze to Varick, to Falcon, to Keene, and back to Falcon.

Finally, though a second had barely passed, she said, "Could we get on with the introductions, please?" That had been a bit abrupt, and she must have known it because she chased the statement with a smile too wide to be demure and gave Falcon big apologetic eyes.

"Oh, goodness, yes," Falcon said. "My apologies." It was unlikely Lenore's abruptness had caused any offense in this set, but Falcon still worked to smooth things over with a joke. He was a gentleman after all. "I should be drawn and quartered for such rudeness." He gestured Keene over, who was looking curiously between Falcon and Camilla. "Keene, allow me to introduce my dear friends, Miss Camilla Hawkins and Ms. Lenore Blackbird-Lee."

Technically, only Camilla was his dear friend, but it seemed both rude and wordy to call one a "dear friend" and the other "her sister who I only know a little, mostly in passing, merely through proximity alone, and it's not anything against her, it's just one of those things."

"And this, ladies, is my housemate, Mister Keene Kohli."

Before Keene could offer to take their hands, Camilla extended hers to shake. Falcon smothered a smile, knowing Camilla, like her mentor Doctor Allen, detested the practice of kissing a lady's hand. Both found it unhygienic. Keene, of course, didn't miss a beat and took it as firmly as he would any business associate's, though for these ladies, he included a smooth, low bow with the exchange. He and Lenore followed the same pattern, and Falcon caught Varick watching them all while he checked over the clothes on the rack. Not that the garments seemed in much danger, given that each one was safely hidden and protected within a simple muslin bag. Meanwhile, his hired muscle had disappeared back outside.

"Grand," Lenore said once the introductions were done. She looked to Camilla and Varick. "Can we tell them now?"

"Tell us why *Mister Hollow* is being dramatic?" Keene asked, winking at Camilla.

Camilla colored prettily and gifted him an approving smile.

"I've told Miss Camilla she can call me Varick." The man in question had nearly reached the end of the rack.

"Mister Hollow will do," Camilla replied, a little crisply. Falcon didn't know what quarrel she might have with the man, but would be sure to ask later.

Not having gotten an answer from either her sister or Varick, Lenore took back the reins of the conversation. "What an awful thing you gents have gone through. So we thought we'd take it upon ourselves to help where we could."

Falcon and Keene exchanged a curious look but politely waited for the forthcoming explanation.

Varick spoke with the tone of a carnival barker as he said, "Hollow Ensembles is proud to present..." With that, he whipped one of the muslin bags away from its clothing within. "New suits!" He pressed a hand to his chest and pulled a dramatically sad face. "To replace those mercilessly and tragically taken too soon."

Keene leaned toward Camilla and murmured from the side of his mouth, "Dramatic is right."

Camilla betrayed a mischievous smile, and Falcon knew from that moment on they would be fast friends.

Meanwhile, Falcon nodded and said, "This is extremely generous, Varick. Thank you." He meant every word, but expected nothing from Varick ever came for free.

"I'm more than happy to help," Varick replied. "Of course, they're a touch out of fashion. These are from last season, you understand. And they aren't tailored to you gents either, but bring them back in and we'll get you all sorted, on the house."

Keene blinked at him. "Goodness, that's—"

"Of course, if anyone asks from where these fine garments

came, you'll be sure to direct them to Hollow Ensembles."

And there's the catch, Falcon thought. *Free promotion.*

"Feel free to throw it into conversation at random, of course, too. Or put little placards on your serving tables, Keene." He outlined the imagined words with his hand. "These fashionable raiments have been generously provided by Hollow Ensembles."

An awkward silence passed, and Falcon suspected not even Keene knew how to respond to the tongue-in-cheek suggestion.

"Varick," Lenore said with a warning tone, but she placed a gentle hand on his arm.

He turned to her, and the two locked eyes with each other in a silent exchange Falcon couldn't translate. Varick's expression softened in the short moment, while Lenore's grew warmer.

Next to him, Keene started slapping Falcon's arm. Thankfully, not the one he was using to hold Luffy, just the one he was using to support himself on his cane.

"Do you see that?" Keene hissed under his breath. "Are those two a couple? They're precious!"

Like a twitterpated cartoon from a newssheet, Keene's eyes seemed to double in size as they watched the moment pass between Varick and Lenore. Falcon was glad Keene hadn't asked for details about the maybe-couple because he honestly wasn't certain what their story was, but what he did know contained some rather sad details.

When Varick looked back to the others, his expression really did look a little contrite. "Apologies, chaps. Some habits die hard."

"The suits aren't the end of it, though," Lenore went on. She started bouncing again.

Wonder and confusion began to topple Falcon—what more could there be? The suits were already beyond generous—and he looked to Camilla for help.

Straight to the point but sensitive as always, she answered his pleading look. "I hope you won't think it's too forward of us, but we've taken steps to restore what you've lost."

"We couldn't do everything, of course," Lenore went on in a far less succinct manner. "And none of it is actually yours. Rather, it wasn't before, but it is now. But, well, we hope it helps." She looked down, wrung her fingers a bit inside of her gloves, and looked back to Keene and Falcon with hurt swimming in her eyes. "I... We can't imagine how you feel after being stolen from, so we wanted to try and make it better."

In a move that bordered on scandalous, Varick wrapped his arm around Lenore's waist, pulled her close, and kissed the top of her head. Keene began slapping Falcon's arm again. And this time, Falcon poked him back with the handle of his cane.

"So," Lenore said suddenly, with the tone of someone trying to shake off bad memories, "shall I take this beautiful beastie while you two tell the gents outside where to put everything? And then we can meet up for dinner together later."

Falcon stood stunned and handed Luffy over without really thinking. Had he really heard correctly? They'd... they'd gathered things to try and replace what had been stolen? Now Luffy-less, he headed over to the door, opened it, and looked out at the cart parked in front of their house. The beefy men had begun to roll back the tarpaulins, revealing a sofa, a few chairs of various shapes and models, and boxes supposedly full of housewares. He turned back to his housemate, who looked as stunned and lost as he felt, and then to their visitors.

"I can't believe... How... Could you really..." Falcon had no idea where he was going with this. He honestly felt like laughing and crying all at once. Never had he expected such generosity.

"It was Lenore's idea," Varick said, a huge grin on his face.

Lenore waved his words away with twiddling fingers. "I just happened to hear about it first. Camilla would have suggested the same thing. And Beatrice jumped on the idea, organizing a sort of mini-drive. She wanted to be here too, but she had a previous engagement attending a premiere or some such. I'm sorry none of the pieces will match."

The information splashed cold water over Falcon's joy. "Did she, um... Does my family know what happened? They're on holiday right now, but you know how fast gossip travels."

Camilla was quick to shake her head. "We thought it would be best to leave them out of it for now. It's already invasive enough that we know. We're keeping the circle tight, and you know Beatrice wouldn't betray your confidence."

That was slightly stretching the truth, and they both knew it, though neither said so aloud. Beatrice was an excellent friend, but for the greater good, she would skirt very close to betraying confidences if necessary. A skill learned from her mother, who was an excellent politician. Still, Falcon had a good feeling that wouldn't be an issue in this particular case.

The warmth of knowing he was cared for came flowing back

in like a wave. He smiled all around him, and his thank-you's had gotten away from him before he even realized he was saying them.

"I guess we'd better get on with it, shouldn't we?" Keene asked, sidling up to Falcon.

He lacked his usual verve, but Falcon guessed the man was simply overcome. After all, he barely knew their guests and here they were throwing furniture, and clothes, and other sundry items at them... not literally, thankfully.

As work was getting underway, Lenore asked, "What's her name?" She held up a smiling Luffy to illustrate.

"Lumpy," Varick put in.

"Luffy," Keene and Falcon said together.

They looked at one another, smiling, but Falcon noticed it only half reached Keene's eyes. And Falcon couldn't help but suspect it was something to do with what had happened between them earlier, though he didn't know what that meant.

~Chapter 14~

The move-in process, for lack of a better term, went easier this time than Falcon's first go-round. Probably because they were dealing with such a blank slate… and no ludicrously huge wardrobes or headboards to contend with. Keene, unsurprisingly, was soon in the kitchen making everyone tea. Lenore played with Luffy on the floor in front of the cupboard under the stairs. And, in between directing Varick's hired crew, Falcon and Camilla caught up, though she was noticeably cagey when he asked about her coldness toward Varick.

"He's not good enough for Lenore."

Falcon quirked a smile, thinking of how he might act whenever his sisters began courting. "Who is, though, really?"

Camilla smiled. "Fair point." Then she sobered and fixed Falcon with a firm yet gentle look. "How are you doing, Falcon? Genuinely?"

He gave a well-practiced smile and shrugged. "Miles better thanks to you and your sister. And also Varick, if he's allowed any credit." Falcon then turned to the movers and directed them where to put a poplar hutch that clashed terribly with the small birch table they'd just brought in.

Camilla granted him a chuckle, but she didn't let him off the hook so easily. "You know we're glad to help, but this isn't about us. It's about you."

Falcon tipped his head, keeping his expression pleasant. An expression that said, "Of course I'm fine. Why wouldn't I be?"

"You can give me that fake smile all you want; I've got one just like it." She took his hand in hers. "Falcon, you've had multiple upheavals in a very short amount of time. That can be trying in the best of circumstances."

Falcon's smile melted into one of wry submission. He placed his other hand over hers. "Doctor Hawkins, thank you for your concern. If I feel on the edge of a breakdown, you'll be the first person I call on."

Camilla smiled at him. "Don't jinx me. My final exams aren't until next year."

"But you're already a doctor in my eyes. You know that."

Camilla gave his hand a playful little squeeze. "At least answer this for me: do you still know where to look for happiness?"

An odd question, to be sure, and it gave Falcon pause. Many men would say their profession gave them happiness, or at least pride. He couldn't say the same, never could really. It was a job, a responsibility, something he *had* to do. He used to find enjoyment at the club, playing card games with other young men he'd known most of his life, though he could no longer afford the dues and hadn't asked his parents if they'd let his membership lapse at New Year. But that wasn't the same thing either. When had he last been properly happy? Felt like he'd found somewhere he fit? He wasn't really certain. That sort of thing was hard to pinpoint, but it had been a long while.

"Ready for tea out here?" Keene popped his head into the parlor, eyes landing on Camilla and Falcon's clasped hands for a moment. That was at least the second time today he'd given them a scrupulous glance.

Blazes, he must wonder if we're a couple. Keene was always looking for love between people. The idea bothered Falcon more than he expected it to, and he immediately started trying to think of ways to subtly indicate the opposite. Though that might be difficult without throwing all his gentlemanly training to the wind. Only once all the furniture had been brought inside and Camilla, Lenore, and Varick had said their farewells—at least until that evening— did Falcon find an opening.

"You have such lovely friends," Keene said.

He and Falcon sat at their new dining table—a rather beat up little thing that only sat four, unless people were comfortable being extraordinarily cozy. Three mismatched chairs surrounded it at the moment. Keene and Falcon sipped at the last dregs of Keene's tea and nibbled biscuit crumbs. Falcon looked to his housemate, who was staring out the front window.

"They really are wonderful," Falcon agreed. When he thought on the events of the afternoon, overwhelming gratitude washed over him again. "You know, I thought Camilla and I might one day become an item."

"Oh?" Keene asked. He didn't look away from the window, but Falcon heard the note of piqued interest in his voice.

"Yes, but I quickly realized she would run circles around me. I could never make her happy, so I left off those ideas."

A small smile crept up Keene's face. "I'm glad you're still close, despite that."

"As am I. She's a top-notch friend."

Keene finally looked back to Falcon, and he was surprised to see tears shining in his housemate's eyes. "Do you know, I was beginning to lose hope in people."

"What?" Falcon asked. The sight of Keene so distressed made Falcon's heart flip and squeeze. He extended his hand, realized what he was doing and that it might not be welcome, and stopped midway between them.

Keene shook his head. "I know I put on a good show of optimism, but this whole palaver—" He swirled his hand in the air to indicate their burgled house. "—has had me more shaken than I let on. I was starting to feel that I needed to be more suspicious of people, more on my guard. And being honest, I hate that sort of feeling. It's exhausting and only makes me more unhappy."

"Keene, I know," Falcon said gently. Perhaps this was a good time to put forth an idea that had been brewing for a few hours now. "It's a terrible thing, always looking over your shoulder, wondering if this person or that might stab you in the back." Falcon often felt that way on the job, both when talking to suspects and witnesses as well as his fellow Enforcers. "But maybe we can chalk this up to a fluke. Now that we have furniture and dishes again, maybe we can put it all behind us, quit the investigation."

A part of Falcon flared with indignation at his own suggestion. It wasn't right that the perpetrators should get off scot-free, but he and Keene had painted themselves into a corner. Without Enforcer authority behind him, there was nothing Falcon could do even if they figured out who those perpetrators were. Perhaps they should simply thank their lucky stars they hadn't stirred up trouble during their investigation and move on with their lives.

Keene looked away again, back to the window, and his expression slowly collapsed, trying to hold back some stronger emotion. Falcon reached a little further toward him but didn't touch, only offering in case he was wanted.

"I'm sorry, I'm not trying to be a coward. I just don't know what else we can do." He motioned a hand to indicate their new belongings. "I know it's not everything, but we'll rebuild your tea ware collection. Slowly but surely. I'll chip in what I can, and soon we'll have teapots with flowers that mean remembrance and marital bliss and healthy babies and sweet-smelling flatulence and all that." That last one was pretty lowbrow, but Keene still wore that same crushed expression, and Falcon wanted nothing more than to wipe it away, whatever it took.

Keene shook his head, voice cracking. "It's not that. I'm the coward."

"What? What do you mean?" Falcon asked, his voice barely above a whisper. When Keene didn't answer, Falcon began to feel desperate. Whatever was going unsaid carved a gulf between them, a gulf Falcon didn't know how to cross. He knew he wasn't entitled to an explanation, but without it, how could he help ease Keene's pain from so far away?

"Where are you?" he asked, remembering what Keene had asked him earlier in their bedroom. "What's wrong?"

Keene looked to the ceiling and took an enormous breath, to steady himself, Falcon assumed. Finally, he looked toward Falcon with fear in his eyes.

His voice, however, was steady when he spoke. "When the thieves broke in, they took something no one can replace. I should have told you, I'm sorry. It's… difficult."

Falcon nodded, saying nothing and waiting patiently. He was a little hurt and frustrated that Keene had hidden something from him, something that might affect their investigation, but his housemate was willing to tell him now, and Falcon was ready to listen.

Keene looked down and began tracing the woodgrain of the table with a finger. "I haven't spoken to my father in close to a year, but I keep in contact with my older brother. My father must have found out because he sent a letter with one of my brother's. I... I've never opened it, but..."

When Keene said nothing more for almost a full minute, continuing to trace the woodgrain in silence, Falcon ventured a question.

"Why don't you and your father speak?" He hoped perhaps it was a similar reason to why Falcon's grandfather had disowned him, why his relationship with his parents was so strained now. And he simultaneously hoped it was nothing like that, because Falcon wouldn't wish his situation on anyone else.

When Keene lifted his gaze to Falcon, more fear than ever shone in it, turning his usual warm brown eyes cold. "Please don't be upset, but I'd rather not share."

"Okay," Falcon conceded immediately. "That's fine. I'm sorry. I didn't mean to pry."

Keene nodded. "I thought one day I might be brave enough to open the letter." He gave a hollow laugh that sounded so different from what Falcon was used to. "I'm such a coward. I should have read it when I had the chance. But now I'll never know what it said."

"You're not a coward," Falcon replied. He tried to be firm but caring, and wasn't certain how he'd done.

Keene's expression crumpled again, and this time, a few tears eked from his eyes. "I thought that maybe, once we'd found where our things went, we'd find the box I kept it in too."

Falcon remembered the moment he'd burst into Keene's room, the afternoon of the robbery, and had found him sitting on the floor crying.

"We're going to find it." Falcon said the words before he was even aware of the thought. A new fear immediately followed: the possibility he wouldn't be able to fulfill his promise.

In his mind, he looked that fear in the eyes and told it, *That won't stop me from trying.* For Keene, for the struggle that wasn't Falcon's but one he could imagine, given his own fraught family situation, Falcon would do everything he could.

He pulled out his little notebook and opened it to the pages where he'd been recording case notes. He realized he was, as he'd been trained to do, leaping straight into the facts. However, Falcon had seen witnesses respond better to a gentle hand. He'd gotten caught up in his desire to fix the situation, but Keene was the key to that, and he was still distressed. Falcon yearned to reach out and wipe the tears from Keene's face, to pull him close and stroke his hair again and tell him it would all be alright. But that seemed too intimate, and after how his housemate had fled when Varick had come to call, Falcon wasn't certain it would be welcome. So, instead, he offered his hand across the table again.

Keene swallowed hard, making his throat bob. He took Falcon's hand and squeezed like a tide might suddenly rip him away. Falcon squeezed back to let him know he wasn't letting go.

"Do you mind if I ask you some questions?" Falcon asked, voice soft. "About the box, I mean." Keene nodded, swallowing again, and, hand in hand, they began to navigate the mire of queries together. "What else can you tell me about it? Where was it stored? What else was in there with the letter? Anything clearly valuable the thieves might want to keep for themselves?"

Keene explained how the box—apparently a small, squat, iron strongbox—had been hidden beneath a false bottom in his steamer trunk. Unfortunately, that didn't really reveal much. Both steamer trunks and false bottoms within them were rather common. The real trick was concealing how to access them. Keene admitted that his trunk was a rather old thing, so the secret compartment's access method wasn't anything like novel. It contained the aforementioned letter, some money, a few other correspondences that Keene wanted to keep close—Falcon only pressed to ask if they contained sensitive information—and some of Keene's most beloved secret recipes.

"I have the key, though," Keene said. He was actually beginning to sound a little hopeful as Falcon took command of the situation. "I keep it on me all the time. And they didn't find where the spare is hidden."

Falcon nodded, looking over his notes. "The fact that the box is iron is a point in our favor. Granted, with enough brute force, they can probably break into it, but they'll really have to try. And they'd have to go someplace where smashing at it won't be heard. Unless the lock… What sort of lock did it have?"

Keene actually straightened up for this answer. "The best in the business, a Hobbs."

That actually brought a smile to Falcon's face. The lock industry was intensely competitive, given that they were essentially selling peace of mind—an easily undermined thing indeed. Competing companies often performed demonstrations for crowds, wherein trained lock-pickers would exhibit their skills and pick rivals' locks and then, conveniently, fail to pick those made by the firm who'd hired them. Hobbs was a firm who famously had yet to fall victim to this tactic, at least insofar as the official adjudicators were concerned. Given that Keene had splashed out on such a good lock, Falcon felt hopeful that the thieves really would be forced to smash open the lockbox, which gave them time.

Now it was just a matter of finding the thing.

The sound of the door knocker rapping pulled both their attention away from the notebook. Keene had stopped crying by now and wiped his face with a handkerchief. Falcon began to rise, but Keene was quicker, motioning that Falcon should stay put.

When his housemate opened the front door, a courier announced the firm he represented and asked for Keene by his full name. Keene accepted a letter from the man and thanked him before closing the door and returning to his seat at the table.

Falcon wondered if the letter might contain some kind of ransom demand for the strongbox. The tactic wasn't unheard of, especially with hard to sell or easily recognized goods. Perhaps an unyielding strongbox would inspire them to make that sort of move. A man could hope anyway.

When Keene's face didn't change in any dramatic way, Falcon asked, "What is it?"

"The Randall family wants to contract my services again. I did their middle daughter's wedding a few months back. Lovely event. Lots of holly. Did you know it represents foresight? Ironic considering the great aunt suspected the bride was expecting. I've already been asked to do the baby shower too."

Falcon smiled as he saw his housemate's usual chattiness coming back, and he didn't dare interrupt, hoping it might help Keene.

"I quite liked that great aunt. She had spunk. And porcelain teeth." Keene looked at Falcon and clacked his teeth together playfully. "I won't lie, I wouldn't mind a set of grinders like that. They could do some serious damage to hot water pastry."

Falcon's smile widened. "Don't underestimate yourself; you have excellent teeth, if your smile is anything to go by."

Keene actually laughed then, and it went straight to Falcon's head, making him giddy with a too-much-bubbly sort of feeling. Before he knew what he was doing, Falcon added, "If you ever want to test them, you're welcome to take a bite out of me."

Why did you say that?! shouted a voice in Falcon's head.

Falcon had to admit that he'd played around the edges of flirting with Keene, but that was an outright invitation. He blushed from the top of his head all the way down to his toes and wished for the floorboards to open up and eat him before Keene could let fly his guaranteed darts of rejection.

Thankfully, blessedly, he seemed not to have heard. Keene's eyes were running across the letter in his hand.

Even so, Falcon thought fast to divert the subject. "So is it another wedding?"

Keene's brows creased. "Sadly no. One of the uncles has died." He put down the letter. "Which means I have to work fast."

"Oh?" Falcon asked, still trying to swim out of his humiliation.

Keene gave him a lopsided smile. "Death is extremely rude about sending his calling card round beforehand. He just shows up, and then you need food for the mourners with naught but mere days to prepare."

"Ah, right, of course."

Keene brushed the letter against his chin, thinking. "I'll need to get some of those suits tailored sooner rather than later." He bit his lip. "I hope the Allens don't take offense to us looking like ragamuffins tonight. That's not the sort of first impression I like to make."

Falcon stood, hiding a smile. Keene's worry touched a chord in Falcon's own heart, though Falcon was usually more concerned with how he appeared before the Cru and other members of the Enforcer order. He lowered his head to look Keene in the eye while the man looked back to his letter, clearly wrapped up in the worries of his career and first impressions. Falcon wanted to unwrap him and find the carefree young man he knew lay beneath.

"Oi, where's that gigglemug I'm so used to?" The tease was a gamble, but he felt he knew Keene well enough by now to try it. And it was far enough from flirting—to Falcon's mind anyway—to be safe. Keene met his eyes, concern still drawing faint lines across his forehead. "The Allens aren't like that. You could arrive wearing a cloth sack and they'd still love you. And you're going to smash that funeral."

That drew a little smile from Keene, but it faded almost as quickly. "Falcon, do you really think we'll find it? My strongbox?"

Falcon didn't want to make any more promises he might not

be able to keep, but he also didn't want to crush Keene's hopes. "We'll try our damndest." And then he took a deep breath, knowing the risk, but also knowing he didn't have a chance if he didn't take this step. "And we'll do it together."

Keene's smile came back in force, and Falcon's heart melted at seeing it.

"Good-o," Keene said, his usual cheer returning, hopefully for good this time. "But first, I should find a new safe place for this." He held up a promissory note included with the letter. The note along the bottom read *Non-Refundable Engagement Fee*.

Together, the housemates went through the ensembles Varick had left. They still hung on their rack but had been moved up to Keene's room. The charity effort, as Falcon was calling it in his head, hadn't been able to procure them a bed at such short notice. Fair dues. Beds were semi-immortal items. Bedclothes were changed season to season, mattresses as needed, but the beds themselves were passed down through families. Thus, the two started joking that they were rich enough for their clothes to have their own room.

Keene wouldn't be able to cash the promissory note until tomorrow, given it was now late afternoon, and so tucked it into a book entitled *The Comprehensive History of Accounting*, which he then placed next to his side of the bed.

Falcon blushed at seeing the book, for he too owned a copy. The title was a misnomer. Instead of dry and detailed chronicles of accounting practices through the ages, as the first few pages suggested, the book was actually full of salacious tales that society would say fine, upstanding people had no business reading. Falcon had found many hours of pleasurable enjoyment following the characters, all of whom were of different persuasions and preferences, including people born as women who identified as men, men who fancied men, and more. It was the sort of book Falcon's grandfather would have wasted no time in setting fire to, but it had always given Falcon a sense of belonging, given his own flexible proclivities. Thus, he'd kept it hidden but always nearby. He wondered if it had given Keene a similar experience, but dared not ask. Not with everything that had transpired that day. Instead, he turned his attention to more business matters.

"Do your clients have to pay you in promissory notes? What about those who don't have accounts with the bank?"

Not everyone trusted banks. Falcon's own parents, for

instance, had a vault with theirs, but also kept some more treasured valuables under lock and key at the family manor. He'd seen other families of his rank outright display their treasures, a move Falcon found both ostentatious and, frankly, foolish. And one had to have considerable funds to even open an account with a reputable banking establishment.

Keene was deciding between an emerald green waistcoat paired with a black jacket for dinner or a more plain red waistcoat with a grey plaid jacket. He didn't look at Falcon when he answered, "They can send me actual money, but they need to go through the proper transfer process."

Falcon blinked silently, and when a moment had passed in this manner, Keene looked back at him.

"I don't know what that means," Falcon confessed. Story of his life.

Keene tipped a smile over his shoulder before he went to stand in front of a tall mirror with a crack in one corner—one of the many mismatched items from the charity effort. Placing each possible ensemble over his body, he explained.

"I've contracted with Barker-Nares's Dispatch Service to handle any physical currency for me. My clients give the money to BNDS and watch them place it in my designated strongbox. Then BNDS uses a special form to keep track of everywhere it goes and everyone who touches it. When it's delivered to me, I have to give them my custom security phrase before they'll give me the box. And, of course, I have to sign for it on their special form. It's a pretty fool-proof method; lots of merchants use it." Keene switched to the red and grey ensemble. "Beatrice helped me with the initial setup. She even wrote up my various contracts for me. She's a real ace with that sort of thing."

Falcon nodded, though his mind was elsewhere. Something in Keene's story rang a bell for Falcon, and he pulled out his little notebook. He didn't need to flip through it for more than a second before finding what he wanted. "Did you have your security passphrase written down anywhere?"

Keene slowed his comparison of the two outfits, looking down as he thought. "I might have? I've never worried about forgetting it, but I might have at some point written it somewhere." He raised worried eyes back to Falcon. "I honestly don't remember."

Falcon took a deep breath, thinking. "I think the first thing to do is talk to BNDS about your possible security breach."

Keene nodded, though he looked a little lost. "Okay, right, yes. That would be good."

"Wear the green. It looks nice with your complexion." Falcon waited, hoping his comment brought Keene back around to himself. It didn't; Keene was still looking away from him, as if searching for answers. Blast, Falcon was going to need to hit him with something more powerful. "Not that you need the help. You'd be just as handsome covered in strawberry frosting."

Now Keene's eyes flitted to Falcon. By his voice, he was still a little distracted, but he was at least halfway back to the here and now. Better that than being pulled under by the riptide of fear Falcon knew all too well. Keene's brow wiggled ever so slightly in Falcon's direction. "Lemon would be tastier."

Falcon had a sudden, intense vision of licking fluffy, tangy, yellow frosting from Keene's warm, brown skin, but he dismissed it almost immediately. *He* couldn't let himself get distracted either. "Certainly, lemon then. But wear the green. Then we'll swing by the nearest branch office on our way to dinner. Sound good?"

"Right."

Falcon turned to leave. He wanted to give Keene privacy for changing, but before he was out the door, his housemate called after him.

"Falcon?" Keene's voice was a gentle beckoning. "Thank you."

"For what?" Falcon asked, uncertain as to what Keene was referring to.

Keene smiled at him, warm as mulled wine. "For taking care of me."

Falcon wasn't certain if he was referring to the details of the investigation or something else, but the answer was the same in either case. "Of course. I'm happy to."

~Chapter 15~

The closest branch office for BNDS was small but pleasant, with stanchions and velvet ropes winding back and forth to keep traffic flowing at a brisk but orderly pace. A highly polished wooden counter divided the customer area and BNDS' workspace, within which couriers whizzed back and forth, picking up new loads and dropping off empty messenger bags. Noise not unlike that of a very large buzzing beehive resounded from behind the back wall, and Falcon guessed yet more of the operation was happening back there. The clerks at the counter took money and order details before enclosing each item, even if it was just a letter, into a box with its accompanying work order attached. The boxes were then placed onto a conveyor belt, which took the parcels into the mysterious, buzzing back room.

Only once while he and Keene stood in line did Falcon see someone with a strongbox, and those, he noticed, had to be handled by a clerk with the words "Security Specialist" embroidered onto their uniform. He had to admit, Barker-Nares Dispatch Service really did have a pretty smooth little operation going. Despite having had to join the queue just outside the front door with probably two-dozen people ahead of them, Falcon and Keene reached the counter within minutes.

The clerk—whose name was Sydney, according to the badge

pinned to his uniform anyway—took in the two lads and noticed they carried neither letter nor parcel but instead a squidgy pile of dog. Luffy was currently snoring in Keene's arms.

"We don't transport animals, I'm afraid," Sydney said politely. He smiled pleasantly but apologetically. "I'm very sorry."

When Keene had insisted they couldn't leave Luffy all alone in a strange new place and therefore *had to* bring her along to dinner, Falcon had wanted to argue. For one, Luffy seemed perfectly content in the house already and had staked a prime position in a corner of the new, gently used sofa. But the time for their dinner engagement was drawing near, so he'd decided to leave it without any more than a faltering objection. The Allens were an eccentric set amongst the upper class, and one extra guest, even a wrinkled, furry one, wouldn't bother them a jot. Not that Falcon's own gentlemanly sensibilities didn't still rankle. But here they were now, with Luffy in arm.

"Not her," Keene said, flashing his winning smile. He slid a large, silver, embossed coin—clearly not actual currency—across the counter. "I need to change my strongbox passphrase, please."

Falcon had not seen this before, but he got a quick glance of Keene's name stamped into the coin before Sydney picked it up and looked at it.

"I'm very sorry, Mister Kohli," Sydney began in the same exact tone as before, "but I'm afraid you'll have to go to the central hub in the Copper quarter for that. Do you need the address?"

Falcon's heart sank, and he saw the same reflected in his housemate. Keene's smile wilted like a flower ripped up by the roots, and Luffy seemed to grow heavy in his arms.

"Are they open throughout the night like this branch?" Keene asked, though his voice lacked hope.

A large sign outside, which Falcon had caught a glimpse of on the way in, had listed the address and operating hours for each of BNDS' locations. All the branch offices were open round the clock, in case someone's messages absolutely couldn't wait. He distinctly remembered seeing that the central hub had not had the same hours listed, and the disappointing answer that came next was no surprise.

"I'm afraid not." Sydney's tone, once again, had that same, evenness, and the automaton-like nature of it was beginning to grate against Falcon's nerves. "I'm very sorry, but you'll have to wait until tomorrow morning."

Are you sorry, though? Really? Falcon sniped to himself.

He didn't dare challenge the clerk aloud, not wanting to make life harder for Keene, who was starting to look properly worried. Luffy, however, opened one eye and made an unhappy groan-growl noise at Sydney and licked Keene's arm.

Falcon gave her a scratch behind the ears. *Good girl. You tell him.*

Keene took a deep breath and summoned another pleasant smile, though this one wasn't nearly as bright. "My account may have been compromised. Is there anything you can do from here?"

As if she'd been summoned by name, the nearest Security Specialist zipped over so fast she might have well materialized. Her name badge read Priscilla, and she towered over all three of them.

Priscilla had bright red hair and a frame that looked big enough to challenge Springhaven's most famous pugilists.

"I'm very sorry," she barked in a way that didn't sound sorry in the least. Rather, she sounded as if Falcon and Keene should be the ones apologizing. "If your account has been compromised, I'm afraid we'll have to freeze it."

"Wait, no, I…" Keene began.

Priscilla's hand enveloped Sydney's, the one holding Keene's silver coin, much like a snake swallowing a rat, and took the coin from him.

"Don't worry, Mister Kohli," she said in the least comforting tone possible. "Any correspondence addressed to you will be kept safely within our custody until we get this matter sorted out."

"But wait," Keene insisted. "I have clients. I have things underway. I can't just stop it all."

"I'm afraid you'll have to," Priscilla said. "The Security Specialists at our main hub will be able to assist you. I'm very sorry. This is for our protection as well as yours."

That seemed to slam a coffin lid down on the conversation. Falcon had been trying to think of other options, but he knew too little of this process. And Priscilla was hardly someone he could try bullying, even if he'd been dressed in his Enforcer uniform.

Sydney had apparently been busy at work while Falcon and Keene's attention had been detained. He handed Keene a slip of pink paper—the third in a triplicate stack.

"Your receipt, Mister Kohli. Thank you for choosing Barker-Nares Dispatch Service." He turned to the queue behind Falcon and Keene. "Next in line, please."

Priscilla folded her arms over her chest and, with a single glare, ushered the housemates away. Resignedly, Keene and Falcon followed the velvet-rope-lined path out the exit doors.

)(

Keene was all smiles the moment he and Falcon knocked on the door to the Allens's manor, despite having chewed his lip nearly to oblivion on the tram ride and then on the long walk the rest of the way over.

Much of the upper class cloistered themselves in grand manors within the Rose district. Tram stops were mostly located around its perimeter—people who had to ride the tram weren't usually the sort who mixed with those who lived within Rose. Falcon was gladder than ever that he'd done his exercises that day; the benefit was still holding true, though by the time he and Keene were making their way up the Allens' carriageway, his knees were beginning to make noise again.

After watching Keene gnaw at his lip for a good ten minutes, Falcon had finally nudged him.

"It'll be alright," Falcon had said. He felt bad saying it because he honestly wasn't sure it would be, but it seemed heartless to do nothing.

Keene nodded, and Falcon could see the effort it took for him to push a smile back into place. "Yes, I believe it will. It'll all be sorted soon. How much can go wrong between now and tomorrow morning?"

Falcon didn't bother to answer that, afraid he might jinx his housemate. Instead, he took the opportunity to brief Keene on their soon-to-be-hosts.

The Allens had, by Rose district standards anyway, a rather modest abode. Of course that meant it was by no means small. Falcon knew Camilla and Lenore each had their own rooms, and that there were still a few guest rooms to spare besides. Not to mention a dining room large enough to comfortably seat a dozen and a half.

Esther, the Allens' sweet, elderly housekeeper answered the door and greeted the housemates with all the warmth of a grandmother welcoming her favorite grandchildren. She was squat with silver-white hair gathered into a low, neat bun.

"Let me take your coats, gents," she said, bustling around the two like a mother hen. "Then get yourself in front of the fire to warm up. I'll bring out some nice hot toddies in just a bit."

"None for me, thank you," Keene said with a gracious smile. "I appreciate it, but I don't often imbibe."

"Of course, Mister Kohli. Some lovely hot apple cider for you then? And maybe a leftover bone for your little friend?" She gave Luffy a scratch behind the ears, to which Luffy returned a happy doggy smile.

"That sounds marvelous, thank you." Keene gave Esther a little bow.

She chuckled and led the two into the parlor next to the receiving hall.

The parlor was, as so many Falcon had seen throughout his life, designed for hosting both large and small parties of people. The furniture, however, though still of excellent make, wasn't anything like as ostentatious as that usually favored by the upper class. It was attractive but sensible. Given the late hour and the chill it brought on, tonight's set gathered in a quartet of armchairs around the fireplace, which chattered merrily behind its grate. Across the room, Falcon thought he caught a gleam of something beneath a long sofa, but before he could confirm it, introductions diverted his attention.

Doctor Allen was here, of course, given that she'd been the one to extend the invitation. She apologized on Camilla and Lenore's behalf, saying that the two had gotten held up with some errands and would be along later. Neal, Doctor Allen's husband, was here too. Neal's proper titles included Engineer, due to his position at the Springhaven Museum of History and Nature, and Lord since he was a member of the Magistrate Council. When the man had told Falcon to call him by his first name, Falcon hadn't had nearly the trouble with it that he did with calling Doctor Allen by hers. Truth be told, Neal didn't intimidate Falcon the way Doctor Allen did. It was during introductions, however, that Falcon became very much the odd man out.

"Please, call me Mina," she said upon meeting Keene. "Any friend of Falcon's is a friend of ours."

Not wanting to be the only person calling her by her title, Falcon began practicing using her first name in his head.

While they waited for the drinks Esther had promised, Luffy spent her time feeling out these new, interesting people—did they perhaps have food to share with her? Amongst the humans, most of the conversation focused on getting to know Keene. "What do you do?" came up first, of course. According to the rules of polite society, Keene was then obliged to ask Doctor Allen—*erm,* Mina, Falcon reminded himself again—and Neal about their professions. Falcon was glad to be the unifying link between them, as that meant none of them had to discuss his line of work. And yet…

"Has Falcon told you about the work the Crisis Response Unit is doing?" Neal asked. The man wore a tweed jacket in olive green, the elbow patches of which matched his medium brown skin perfectly. "Rather, that they will be doing?"

"We've discussed it now and again," Keene said. He was being generous. Falcon had used every conversational trick he knew to avoid talking about his work.

Given that none of the humans seemed keen to share any goodies, Luffy had moved onto searching around the perimeter of the room. Watching her from the corner of his eye, Falcon suspected she'd move onto the rest of the house if she came up empty, and he made a mental note to collect her if it came to that. The Allens were very generous hosts, but his furry, little charge would observe at least some rules of propriety and refrain from making the entire manor her stomping ground. It looked as if Luffy might have lucked out when she reached the sofa because she started sniffing so hard it turned into grunting. Neal was just launching into something or other Cru related, but Falcon's eyes were on the gleam from under the sofa. It had returned, two small glowing spots.

As Falcon watched, his brain began to question what he was seeing. A creature emerged from beneath the long sofa, unfolding itself on sleek black legs that went on for far longer than they ought to. The body was a bright coppery red, very much like a fox, but it was so much taller. A thick ruff of fur around its neck made the shoulders look bulky and imposing, which it rather was as it towered over Luffy.

Distantly, Falcon realized the conversation around him had stopped, but his attention was entirely absorbed by watching Luffy face off, or rather face *up*, against the lanky creature before her.

"Not to worry," Mina was saying. "That's just Majesty, Lenore's regal wolf. She's really very gentle."

Falcon wasn't so sure. Mina might claim that Majesty was gentle, but she looked capable of ripping an arm off… or swallowing Luffy in just a few bites.

The little dog, on the other hand… paw?… was staring up at the creature in awe. What must it be like to see a member of your family, distantly related though it was, so opposite from yourself? Majesty was slender and powerful and tall, with fur so thick and luxurious-looking that Falcon fancied he'd lose himself up to the wrist if he pet her. And then there was Luffy, whose doughy body looked as if she'd been squished from every angle. In typical Luffy fashion, she then smiled up at her distant cousin, tongue lolling out. She barked once, adding a little, "I'm so happy to meet you!" hop in with it.

Majesty, who'd turned to look at Falcon and Keene, actually did a double take. The tiny thing before her had made a noise like a dog, but surely it didn't look right.

"She's beautiful," Keene said, gazing at Majesty like a work of art. Then he looked at Neal and Mina with bald confusion. "How did you come to have a wolf?"

Neal chuckled and leaned forward in his seat. Before he could launch into his story, however, Esther scurried into the parlor carrying a tray of drinks.

"So sorry for the delay, my dears. The oven is playing up, and I'm quarreling with it about finishing dinner. It'll be later than promised, but I'm making some other nibbles for you all in the meantime."

"Playing up, eh?" Keene asked. "Mind if I have a look at it? I've battled my fair share of kitchen equipment."

Esther waved her arms in protest. "Oh no, dear, I couldn't ask that."

"I'll come too," Neal said, ignoring her. "Perhaps between our two skill sets, we'll have this sorted all the sooner." When he passed Esther, he hugged her around the shoulders. "Now don't fuss." Which she was definitely doing. "You always take such good care of us."

Keene was grinning as he followed them back to the kitchen. As they went, Falcon listened to the last remnants of their conversation.

"Oh my, Mister Kohli, I'll have to slap up something nice for you to take home. Something to say thank you."

"Well, then I'll be forced to send over something to thank *you* for such a nice gift. Perhaps a treacle tart."

"I'll see your treacle tart, Mister Kohli, and raise you—"

Falcon didn't hear what Esther would raise him because just then he spotted the two canines trotting after the little group. Majesty had lived here long enough to know Esther was the source of all food, and Luffy was apparently smart enough to follow.

"Luffy? Luffy, no," Falcon called.

"Let them go," Mina said, just before taking a sip of her hot toddy. "They're in good hands."

Falcon swallowed hard. This was exactly the sort of situation he'd hoped to avoid by inviting Keene along.

"You know, I think I could be of assistance too," he said, beginning to rise. He had to struggle to make that complete and utter pile of bull droppings sound like he really believed it.

"Actually," Mina said, her voice like the dropping of an axe, "if you'd be so good as to stay, I'd like a word."

"Of course." Falcon lowered himself back into his chair and considered whether it would be better to face this conversation with a clear head or if he should get a little liquid courage into him. He decided on the latter. Drinking might give him extra time to form responses, and so he lifted his cup before him like a shield.

Mina began, succinct as ever. "The Crisis Response Unit, where would you like to see it go?"

Falcon blinked at her. The question was strange because they'd discussed the subject many times. And thus he already had an answer ready, no dawdling required. "The same as ever. I'd like us to break away from the Enforcer order, leave behind our old responsibilities, and focus solely on community assistance—basic triage and ambulatory services for emergency medical cases, disaster response and recovery, perhaps even some public education."

The plans were still foggy, but they'd identified the biggest need-gaps at least. There were only so many doctors in Springhaven, and many of them didn't operate late at night. Falcon had read about the city infirmaries in Bone Port, the city-state located on the southernmost tip of the continent. He thought a few of those could benefit Springhaven, and it would give the Cru centralized locations to deliver patients to. That was a far-distant goal, however. For now, Springhaven needed a quick, efficient team to stabilize patients while doctors were roused from their beds.

And, of course, the city needed people who could rush in and help when disasters struck. A good example was an accident involving black powder at the museum last year. The Enforcers who'd shown up at the scene of the explosion had been ignorant of how to help. They were all living truncheons, whereas Falcon wanted the Cru to be salves and splits and bandages for Springhaven.

"Grand." Mina took another sip of her drink. "I'm so glad we're still on the same page."

"Me too," Falcon agreed, though his tone wasn't nearly as confident as Mina's. Then again, whose ever was?

"Because I have drawn up a solid plan to move the Crisis Response Unit in that very direction. It's a bit like extracting a sick appendix, however. You must cut the connections carefully. Of course in this case, the appendix will go on to serve a beneficial purpose."

"Good?" Falcon replied. He still wasn't certain where this conversation was going, nor was he sure how he felt about the Cru being compared to a pointless internal organ. What did that make him?

"Yes, except that the body containing the appendix refuses to listen to me." When Falcon only looked at her blankly, she explained. "First Iago is the body in this metaphor. Do you remember that I had a meeting with him last week?"

Falcon nodded, though it felt like that conversation had happened months ago instead of just last week.

"I showed him my plans, but he dismissed the idea almost immediately."

Falcon sat up straighter in his chair. "Did he say why?"

Mina flapped an irritated hand through the air. "He blathered on about it not being the right time and some other rot about resources being tight, but you and I both know the Enforcers have more funding now than they ever have. I suspect the fact that I happen to have been born with a uterus has a lot to do with it, but I am also an outsider. There are multiple reasons for him to dislike me and therefore any plan I propose."

Falcon felt his face positively ignite at the mention of "uterus", and he wondered if he might burn to ashes right then and there. It seemed a perfectly legitimate strategy for getting out of this conversation. If Mina noticed his embarrassment, however, she didn't show it. And he suspected she might not care either. She was, after all, quite outspoken against female-specific body parts and issues being treated as taboo subjects.

"Thus, I need to ask for your help," she went on. "I need you to take my plan to First Iago and convince him to adopt it. Stephen, one of my assistants, has already agreed to handle the administrative aspects—paperwork and ticking off boxes and the like. He's good with that sort of thing. But you would also need to manage the process."

"Manage it?" Falcon asked. "What does that mean exactly?"

"You would be the person keeping us on track. I don't trust First Iago to let go of the Crisis Response Unit so easily. For one thing, it would mean losing the one faction of his order that's actually making them look good. For another, it would require him to let go, which is as good as defeat in his eyes."

Falcon took another fortifying sip of his toddy. Mina was right, but as for his part, that sounded far too much like putting himself back in the spotlight.

"Can't Neal or Lady Holmes..." he began, but Mina was already waving away the suggestion.

"They've got their hands full overhauling our justice system. And besides, while Neal might have been the first to suggest the Crisis Response Unit, the brunt of the responsibility has passed onto you and me. And sadly, in the eyes of those with power, I don't rate as worthy. I had to fight tooth and nail with First Iago's secretary just to get that meeting in the first place, and what good did it do me?"

Mina was growing animated, moving her hands more than usual, her voice harder than it had been. Falcon gulped, knowing he needed to choose his next words carefully. He tapped a fingernail against the warm glass of his cup, weighing his options.

"With all due respect, Doctor Al... I mean, Mina, I don't know why First Iago would listen to me any more than he would you."

Mina's eyes narrowed, and Falcon knew he'd said something very, very wrong. She began listing things off on her fingers. "Not only are you one of *them* as an Enforcer, but you have your list of accomplishments achieved under that banner. You have your rank both inside and outside of work. You have your lineage as the grandson of an Enforcer Second, disgraced now though he may be. And let us not forget, you have the distinct and severe advantage of being a man."

Falcon stared down into his drink, feeling about two inches high. The Allens were good people, far braver than he. He knew he'd already lost respect in Mina's eyes, and was probably about to lose more, but she was one of the most sensible people he'd ever met. He just desperately hoped she might understand if he explained himself.

"Mina," he began slowly. "Calling my grandfather out on his crimes was the hardest thing I've ever had to do. He disinherited me, and I had to leave the home I've known my whole life because my actions wrecked my family relationships. I know I did the right thing, but that doesn't change the fact that the Smoke name is now tarnished, perhaps forever, because of me. And I can't stay at the Enforcer barracks because, well, tattletales aren't exactly popular. So I'd rather keep my head low for the moment. I'm sorry if that makes me selfish, but I just don't know how much more misfortune I can take on right now."

Falcon stared into the fire while a long pause ensued. Confession hadn't felt cleansing; he felt worse than ever. He hadn't needed to say that the shame sticking to his family like coal soot never touched him. He was the Enforcer's golden boy, and both he and Mina knew it. He really was a coward. And whatever Mina felt about that would make itself apparent soon enough. When she finally responded, her voice was even again.

"I can't pretend to understand what you've been through lately. I've never had to do what you did. And I appreciate how difficult defaming your grandfather must have been, how difficult it's made things for you and your family. But, Falcon, we are still upon the edge of a knife. It's very possible the Crisis Response Unit will be absorbed entirely back into the rest of the order and nothing will change. And you are best positioned to prevent that." She paused. "Just think on it, won't you? I'm working on getting another meeting with First Iago."

Finally, Falcon looked back at her. "You are? But why? He might just ignore you again."

"Oh, yes, I expect that very thing." Mina almost sounded bright now, but it was the brightness of metal unsheathing from metal. "But I don't give up that easily. I wouldn't be where I am today if I did."

Falcon gave a sad smile. Stars, how he wished he had that same sort of mettle about him. Did Mina, like him, ever feel as if the world was trying to swallow her whole? He wished he had the same well of strength she drew upon to bite back.

Mina stood. "I think that's enough of dark matters for now, don't you? Unless you have more to say on the subject."

"No, thank you," Falcon replied, feeling as empty as his voice.

"Right. Shall we join the rest of our companions in the kitchen then? I'm feeling rather peckish."

Falcon wanted to lighten the mood, to shake off the weights of failure and disappointment, so he made a weak joke. "Careful. If you say that around Esther, she'll bury you in pastries."

Mina chuckled. "That's not the worst way to go."

She gifted him a warm, sincere smile, and Falcon breathed a sigh of relief even as he felt unworthy of it.

When they entered the kitchen, Falcon's eyes went straight to the furry head looming over the edge of a worktable. Majesty. And her muzzle was covered in deep purple stickiness. A jar of preserves laid on its side nearby. Majesty's face was an unconvincing mask of canine innocence. Nearby, Falcon noticed, beyond Majesty's immediate reach sat some small cakes of some kind.

Esther stood with her back to the animal, hands on her hips, while Neal and Keene laid on the floor beneath the oven. It was a wonder they both fit. Not that either were particularly large men, but the legs on which the oven stood weren't particularly tall. From beneath it, Falcon heard Keene and Neal conversing about petrolsene lines and safety measures. And Luffy was sniffing around their legs, looking ready to assist but completely clueless.

At the sound of approaching footsteps, Esther turned. Her eyes caught onto Majesty.

"No, ma'am!" Esther scolded. "You know better."

Majesty abandoned her innocent act and went for the preserves again. Falcon wasn't about to throw himself between a regal wolf and food, and so just watched as she began furiously licking the inside of the jar before Esther could reach her. Through the glass, Falcon saw Majesty's lips pulled back from her teeth, her eyes wide and desperate. The sight, made bulbous and magnified by the angle of the glass, looked so absurd, Falcon burst out laughing.

"Is that my handsome housemate I hear?" came Keene's muffled query from under the stove.

"That was for dessert," Esther was scolding Majesty.

Esther hadn't shared Falcon's fear and had snatched the preserves jar away. The regal wolf hung her head, but the way she kept licking her chops rather ruined the effect of contrite remorse. The preserves had stained her fur, and the look of it tickled something in Falcon's brain.

"And my wonderful wife?" Neal added to Keene's question.

Mina made some light response to that, but Falcon wasn't really listening. The tickle in his brain had found its mark.

The fabric scrap from the gate. It had been a rusty brown sort of color that nearly hid the material's black pinstripes. Was it possible it had been dyed?

~Chapter 16~

Keene and Falcon returned home late that night, stuffed and happy. And in Falcon's case, more than a little tipsy. Keene, as he'd mentioned, had not imbibed, but Falcon had. And he was feeling very pleased indeed. The difficult conversation with Mina had retreated to the recesses of his brain while he, Keene, and the Allens had played parlor games together. Lenore and Camilla had eventually arrived, late and full of apologies, but they'd brought a brand new tea set for Keene. Choosing a design had been what had taken so long, and he was overjoyed with their choice of a hawthorn motif.

Once Neal and Keene's tinkering help had gotten Esther back on track with dinner, she'd kept popping in and out for a spot of conversation and to make sure everyone's drinks were topped up. Thus why Falcon wasn't quite as stable on his feet now as he might have been otherwise. The Allens had been kind enough to pay for a hansom cab to take them home, and now Keene had his arm around Falcon to make sure the man didn't trip up the stairs on their way inside their shared house. Falcon suspected that might have something to do with the fact that he was also holding Luffy. The dog was buttoned up inside his jacket, as she'd begun shivering on the ride home. Now, her head stuck out the top of the collar, right beneath Falcon's chin.

The contact with Keene made Falcon feel as warm as the drinks had, and he leaned into Keene while his housemate unlocked the door.

"Alright, one more step," Keene said. He pushed open the door, and they trundled inside together.

"Liar," Falcon teased. "There's still all the steps upstairs to go."

"Unless you want to sleep on the couch." Keene smiled. "Because we have a couch again! Stars, it feels good to say that."

"But we still need to find your letter," Falcon said. "Just because I'm a little tippled, doesn't mean I've forgotten."

Keene risked letting Falcon go and locked the door behind them. Falcon leaned against it, thinking again of the scrap of fabric. He wanted to have another look at it. Then again, bed was calling. Nice warm bed with brand new blankets. Brand new to them anyway.

"You are more than a *little* tippled, my friend," Keene laughed. He removed Luffy from inside Falcon's coat and set her on the floor to go about her business. "So what shall it be? The couch or up the stairs?"

"I can handle the stairs just fine," Falcon said. "They're just up-ways floors." He pushed off the door, swayed only a little, and headed for the stairway. Somehow, his cane wasn't being nearly as helpful right now as it usually was.

He had enough sense to hang onto the handrail, but the stairway was dark, and he didn't remember the stairs being quite so tall. He stumbled once, but Keene was suddenly there, behind him in the dark. He steadied Falcon, but at first Keene's hands accidentally caught his rear end rather than his middle. They swiftly moved into their intended positions.

"Sorry, mate," came Keene's voice through the dark. "I can barely see you."

Falcon let go of the handrail and waved it dismissively before realizing Keene probably couldn't see that either. So he patted his housemate's hand around his middle instead.

"Not to worry. I trust you implicitly with my bum."

And then Falcon laughed so hard he snorted. Which only made him laugh harder. Keene laughed too, though without the snort.

As they topped the stairs, Falcon asked. "How are you always so smooth?"

"Am I?" Keene said. He sounded genuinely surprised. "How so?"

"Oh, don't give me that." Falcon slurred the words a little. "You know how you are."

Weak petrolsene light from outside seeped into the bedroom just enough to cover the room in a film of ghostly pale light. While Keene headed over to light an oil lamp next to the bed, Falcon leaned against the wall and managed to discard his waistcoat, tie, shoes, and socks before deciding that was good enough and flopping onto his side of the bed.

"You're always so charming. Everyone loves you."

Keene, meanwhile, was untying his tie and hanging it across the top of a squat, new dresser. Falcon rather fancied the idea of using the tie for some of the acts described in *A Comprehensive History of Accounting*, but Keene's voice distracted him before he could dwell on it and get himself in a tizzy.

"Do you really think I'm charming?" he asked.

"Oh yes." The answer came quicker and more confidently than perhaps Falcon had ever answered anything else in his life.

"Would you like to hear a secret?"

"Of course. Is it juicy?" Falcon tried shimmying his shoulders, but it turned into more of a fishy flopping since he was lying down.

"Sometimes, it's all just an act. Sometimes, I just have to fake it til I make it, you know?"

"Act or no, you talk like butter and move like sugar."

Keene laughed louder this time. "You silly gooseberry! What does that even mean?"

"It means you endear yourself to everyone you meet."

After what felt like only a second, Falcon felt Keene climbing into bed next to him, and he opened his eyes. He must have dozed off because Keene was dressed in his pajamas now. Falcon slid a hand across the mattress and traced the stripes racing down one of Keene's sleeves.

"Would you say I've endeared myself to you then?" Keene asked softly.

However long Falcon had dozed, Keene clearly remembered where the conversation had left off. It took Falcon a moment to recall it, but as soon as the memory arrived, so did the answer.

"Absolutely."

Keene searched Falcon's face. Blazes, how Falcon wanted to kiss him. To show him how very endeared he was. After a moment, though, Keene turned over and lowered the oil lamp's wick until the flame went out.

"You're very sweet, Falcon. Thank you. Good night."

Falcon snuggled down into his pillow. Any thoughts he might have had about the exchange were already floating away.

"Keene?"

"Hm?"

"My feet are cold."

Keene chuckled. "Well, you did take off your socks."

"Yes, I did." A pause. "Can I put them against you?"

This time, Keene laughed hard enough to shake the mattress. "Yes, you can."

"You're a pip," Falcon chirped. With his feet, he pushed the legs of Keene's pajamas up to his knees and Falcon snuggled his toes against the back of them. Keene made a happy little noise as Falcon flexed his toes against the spot.

"You know that, don't you?" Falcon asked. Keene didn't answer at first, so Falcon said, "Keene, you know you're a pip right?"

"You are too, Falcon."

Falcon kneaded with his toes again, already feeling warmer, and fell quickly to sleep.

)(

The next morning, Falcon awoke early as usual, but slowly. He could hear Keene puttering around downstairs. Falcon rolled over in bed, feeling a touch muzzy-headed but otherwise not very worse for wear from his indulgence the night before. Checking his fob watch, which sat next to the bed, he confirmed that shops wouldn't even be open for another couple of hours. Good. He and Keene had things to accomplish today. Down near Falcon's feet, something weighed on the blanket. Something lightly snoring. Falcon peered to the end of the bed and saw Luffy asleep there, sounding not unlike a tiny version of himself… or so Falcon had been told. According to his family, Falcon had a terrible snoring habit. He suddenly wondered if he'd snored with Keene in the bed, if Keene had heard him, and what he thought about it. And then Falcon smiled because he realized, even if Keene had heard him snoring, Keene was so easygoing he probably wasn't too fussed by it. If he was, Keene probably would have said so, but kindly. And the confidence in their openness gave Falcon comfort.

Falcon dragged himself from bed and began his exercises. Yesterday was the first time in a while he'd had an extended period of the day without pain, and he grinned wryly as he remembered what Mina had said to him during their chat at the Halls of Justice:

Do the physiotherapy exercises, please. Every morning and evening. You'll be glad you did.

They took a solid half hour, so he rather understood why he'd avoided them in the past. When life got fraught, self-care was the first to go out the window, but he certainly felt bloody good when he took the time. Now, if he could just figure out what to do about the good doctor's latest request, as well as find Keene's lost letter, everything would be right as rain. And that was when he found himself tempted to leave off the stretches and jump into the evidence again.

No, he told himself. *Finish this first.*

So Falcon did his best to put aside the rest of the day's problems and focus on himself for a little while. Breathing and stretching, that was all he needed to think about right now. When he was done, his mind felt clearer, as if someone had released a steam valve in his skull and released some of the pressure.

He then collected his notebook and the little box of evidence he'd compiled and headed downstairs to the sitting room.

It was warm with heat from a low fire, which Falcon hoped had been used to make breakfast. He knew he should probably attend to eating before work, but the problem was mercilessly tugging at his brain now that he had the box of evidence in his hands. He called a vague good morning to Keene before setting himself down at the table and spreading the evidence out before him.

The scrap of fabric was the first thing to examine. There was no reason to expect it had been dyed, but it was within the realm of possibility. And he had to keep all probabilities in mind until they'd been soundly eliminated. The fabric's color had always seemed a strange choice to him. The black stripes were so thin they all but disappeared against the rich cinnamon brown of the rest of the material. Why bother with the stripes at all then?

"Keene?" he called into the kitchen.

"Hm?"

"Do you know how to remove stains from fabric?"

"Why? Are you planning a murder?"

Falcon laughed. "I'd be the last person they'd expect."

Keene leaned around the doorframe and into the parlor, giving Falcon a dramatically dastardly look. In a put-on gravelly voice, he proclaimed, "The perfect crime!" They both had a good laugh at that, after which Keene asked, "What kind of stain?"

"Um," Falcon said. "I don't know." He held up the scrap of fabric. "But I think this might not be the original color."

Keene came over to have a closer look and began thinking aloud to himself. "Beetroot for the red tint? No, that would probably end up being more pink."

"Is this something you actually know about?" It wouldn't have surprised Falcon to learn that his housemate had yet another incredible talent.

Keene waggled a noncommittal hand. "A bit. There's a whole slew of food scraps you can use to dye fabric. I've never done it myself. White's a good base for any event. And it doesn't always produce consistent color, like what's happened with this."

He pointed to a spot in the corner of the scrap, and Falcon drew close. He couldn't make out what Keene meant and took the material over to one of the parlor windows. There! Illuminated by the bright, early morning sun, Falcon saw now that the rusty brown color wasn't consistent across the scrap. It was... splotchy, several shades lighter in the corner than the rest. But it still didn't explain *why* anyone would want to change the fabric's original color? Assuming that this wasn't, in fact, simply a spot that had faded lighter than the original color. Still, it was a new possibility, and Falcon made some notes in his book. Keene looked over his shoulder, and Falcon didn't try to hide the pages like he would have done before.

"You're brilliant," Falcon said as he wrote. "You know that, don't you?"

Keene shrugged, and it brushed against Falcon's shoulder. "I do my best. Maybe walnut shells? Anyway, if you can figure out the tinting agent, we might be able to undo some of it."

Falcon nodded and turned the fabric over in his hands a few more times before setting it aside. He'd figure something out. For now, he moved onto the sheet of paper with the bootprint, and Keene returned to the kitchen.

The print itself was nothing extraordinary. A similar tread pattern adorned Falcon's Enforcer boots. It was a common, knobbly style for those with physically demanding jobs, to grip and avoid slipping and provide maneuverability. But maybe the size would reveal something.

Too often, Falcon's comrades focused on finding *someone* to pin for a crime rather than *the right person*, but Falcon would rather let a criminal go free than imprison an innocent. And while the Enforcers had protocols for collecting evidence, they were cursory and therefore ineffective. He'd rarely ever seen any of his workmates use their provided tape measures, for instance, but he had, and the list of information he'd gathered with it bolstered his spirits.

Falcon had measured the bootprints outside as soon as he'd discovered them. Unsurprisingly, their size matched the length of the bootprint captured on paper. Conclusions tried to form in his mind. It was big, two inches bigger than his own shoe size, which was pretty average. Mister Strongbow was a big man; it could easily be his. Falcon had to stop himself there. This was where so many of his fellow Enforcers went wrong. They'd get so caught up in trying to make a crime fit a certain suspect, they'd overlook other details. A cold chill washed over Falcon as he realized he'd begun to do that very thing. No. He shook his head.

He'd follow the evidence. All of it. To wherever it led him.

As he'd done countless times already, Falcon leafed through the other papers in the box. He'd collected loads of it just in case he might find something else. He suddenly wondered if the letter from Keene's father might be hidden in this jumble, previously overlooked because Falcon hadn't known then to search for it. Doubtful, but his heart leapt anyway as he leafed through the pages. Of course, if that was the case, he might be able to see what was written in the letter. Why Keene and his father didn't speak, and if it was similar to his own situation.

No, Falcon mentally scolded himself. It wasn't his business. And besides that, Keene had implicitly asked him not to pry. So Falcon would only read as much as he needed to confirm each sheet wasn't the letter before examining them more closely.

Sadly, all the pages that had been written upon seemed to be either accounting records or recipes. Falcon scanned each one, front and back, before moving onto the next. Shapes loomed off the surface of many of them. Partial versions of the same boot prints mostly. Falcon set these aside until he came to one with a complete shape along one side. It was not knobbly like most of the others. It was solid, the liver color of melded dust and dirt. And it was small, just over two inches across at its widest point, rounded on one side and squared on the other. Could it be from another shoe?

Falcon quickly flitted through other options in his head. Perhaps the foot of a piece of furniture? But would it have colored the paper in that same shade then?

Falcon picked up the sheet with the complete boot print and held the two side by side. Yes! The two prints were exactly the same color. Perhaps this was a bit of a stretch, but some similar markings, like the perfect circles on one sheet he'd already looked at were far paler and more grey. Using the lesson from before with the fabric, Falcon brought the mysteriously marked sheet over to the window and looked at it more closely.

Wait, there was another shape there too. Lighter, but it had the same liver coloration to it. A sort of rounded-off trapezoid. It was larger than the first shape, close to four inches before it faded into nothing. Perhaps this was a print from a lady's boot. The smaller shape could easily be the heel, the empty space where the boot didn't touch the ground, and then the larger shape where it came back down.

Falcon sifted through the sheets again, looking for anything else. After a good ten minutes, though, nothing new revealed itself. Even so, he sat back down at the table and recorded his thoughts into his notebook.

A cup of steaming hot tea appeared next to him. Falcon was studying the other information now, puzzling over whether any of it was a clue. He felt confident now that the culprits were a man and a woman.

A hip nudged against his shoulder.

This could easily be Mister and Mrs. Strongbow, but it wasn't a guarantee. Not by a long shot. Still, what evidence Falcon had all seemed to point to them. Or it could still have been a professional job. Twigs could be behind the robbery. Their things had been brought, one way or another, to his shop. Or perhaps it had even been Mrs. Spoondawdle. She seemed to know everyone around here. What stopped her from orchestrating the entire thing?

Falcon rubbed his face. Too many possibilities, not enough evidence.

Something rested on his shoulder and gave it a squeeze. "Earth to Falcon. Keene calling."

Falcon looked up at Keene, letting his head flop back. It came to rest against Keene's stomach, though Keene didn't seem bothered. And Falcon was suddenly too tired to worry beyond that point; if Keene didn't mind the contact, then neither did Falcon.

"I'm trying, mate. I really am."

"I know you are," Keene said, smiling sadly, "but don't force it."

Keene's other hand found Falcon's other shoulder, and he began to massage. Falcon closed his eyes as Keene's fingers began to loosen the muscles that had knotted themselves across his neck and shoulders.

"Just relax," Keene crooned. "You'll get there. Let it come as slowly as it needs to."

Falcon inhaled deeply, though his mouth quirked up in a mischievous smile. Sometimes, he heard such strong double meanings in Keene's words, he almost wondered if his housemate wasn't playing with him. Mmm, how fun it would be to play with Keene.

"Falcon, where are you?"

Keene's voice came back to Falcon like a song. He'd been floating through the feeling of Keene's hands slowly working his muscles. He chuckled, opened his eyes again, and found Keene looking down at him with a grin.

"Sorry." He wasn't sure what else to say, not wanting to explain himself.

"Don't be," Keene said. He pulled away, and Falcon sat up straight again. "Come into the kitchen. I have a treat for you to try."

Falcon didn't need to be told twice and was right on Keene's tail, tea in hand, as they made their way past the stairs to the kitchen.

~Chapter 17~

On the kitchen worktable spread a whole mess of items: sugar; butter; small, round, soft biscuity looking things; eggs; and lemons. This last surprised Falcon, as lemons, and indeed most citrus, usually had to be imported from the south, as Springhaven's climate was a touch too cold for it. He'd heard of people growing them in greenhouses, but that required a good deal of space and money.

Keene beckoned Falcon over to the worktable where he'd apparently assembled the ingredients into… well, Falcon wasn't quite certain what it was. On one of the round things that looked too small, soft, and thick to be a biscuit sat a slice of lemon. It glistened as if glacéed and shimmered with a fresh dusting of sugar crystals. Atop that was a small snowy white meringue no bigger than a grape. Falcon approached, wondering just what Keene had created.

Lifting the not-quite-a-biscuit piled with ingredients, Keene instructed, "Here, taste this."

And before Falcon could even begin reaching for the thing, just as he'd opened his mouth to ask a question, Keene popped the treat right in. Flavor burst onto Falcon's tongue. He'd spent his life eating in some of Springhaven's finest restaurants, and none of them had taken his senses on the trip this tiny canapé did. Tartness from the lemon and sweet from the sugar met rich cream and butter in the biscuit, melding into a perfect melange of sumptuous yet balanced experiences. The flavors did not compete with one another but rather played nicely with each of their companions. The meringue added airiness to the chewy lemon and spongy biscuit thing. Even if Falcon hadn't been busy chewing—not to mention too well-raised to talk with his mouth full—he wouldn't have been able to say anything. The experience had thoroughly gobsmacked him, and he thought of nothing else while he let the flavors have their way with his palate.

That is, until Keene spoke again.

"Whoops, you've got a little something there."

And then, with all the familiarity they'd been developing between them, Keene reached with his thumb up to Falcon's mouth and wiped away a dab of the lemony-sugary sauce that had oozed across the biscuit. Falcon was acutely aware of every millisecond Keene's thumb dragged across his skin, his lips. He froze, uncertain where this was going but silently open to the possibilities. Even more unbelievably, Keene offered the offending smear to Falcon, who might be shocked but was not stupid. He wrapped his lips around the end of Keene's thumb and sucked away the sweet and tart glistening sauce.

The moment was so intimate, yet it felt entirely warm and comfortable. He met Keene's eyes while his mouth was attached to his housemate's thumb, and the two exchanged a smile. Keene wiped one last smear from Falcon's face and then licked it from his thumb himself. And his eyes never broke Falcon's gaze. Falcon's stomach swirled and gamboled inside of him.

He had an urge to pull Keene close and feed him one of his own treats, slowly, sensually, like one of the characters in *A Comprehensive History of Accounting* might have done.

Of course, Falcon wasn't nearly so bold. Instead, he finished chewing, swallowed, and then lifted his teacup for a sip. Keene's eyes lingered on him for a moment more, searching. Searching for what exactly, Falcon didn't know. Finally, disappointingly, Keene looked back to his creations.

"Hm," he mused. "It could maybe use a touch more lemon. This is my take on a pond pudding. Such fussy things. This has all the panache without all the work. What do you think?"

Falcon thought his trousers were getting a bit tight, truth be told. Thankfully, men's garments were designed to hide such reactions—propriety and all that. But he also thought he'd made the right choice in not making a move on Keene.

He's just a playful sort of chap, Falcon told himself, *not actually interested in me.*

And Falcon didn't want to ruin what they had. Not that he could say any of that. He stared at Keene, searching for other responses, which all seemed to have vacated his head.

A tiny crease appeared between Keene's eyebrows, and Falcon wanted nothing more than to smooth it away.

"Do you think there's too much lemon?" Keene went on. "Did I overdo it?"

Falcon's wits finally rallied round again. He needed to give an answer. Not that he cared much about lemons at the moment, but Keene did. Very much indeed. So Falcon swallowed, missing the food almost instantly, and found his voice.

"It's perfect."

Keene looked up at him with those dark eyes, which were, surprisingly, filled with concern. "Are you sure? You're not just saying that to be nice? Because believe you me, clients will *not* be nice."

"No, no," Falcon insisted. "Truly, it's spectacular." He assessed the worktable, which contained a good dozen more of the hors d'oeuvres. "Can I have another?"

Keene's concern mostly melted back into its usual warm ease, though a hint of hesitation still lingered there. "I suppose, but I'm taking the rest around to the neighbors for opinions. I still think you might be treating me too gently."

Falcon grinned. "How dare you suggest such a thing. I can be rough with you if that's what you want." Then he blanched, realizing just how suggestive he'd sounded.

Keene was turning away, and Falcon's heart shrank back in humiliation. But the sound that came back was warm, and even a little encouraging.

"Hmm, I'll have to remember that."

Falcon blushed and snatched up another pond pudding canapé, shoving it into his mouth before something even more embarrassing could come out. Keene, thankfully, was already moving on, preparing the treats for transport. Falcon enjoyed his second no less than the first and tried to focus on that instead of teasing himself with *ideas*. Ideas that he was certain only he was having.

Nothing like a crime to take his mind off things. And Falcon retreated back to the sitting room with his tea, being sure to thank Keene. He might be uncertain about everything else, but Falcon knew his manners.

"It really was splendid," Falcon said. "If there are extras, I'll be happy to take them off your hands."

"We'll see," Keene said with a cheeky grin.

Well, that smile certainly wasn't helping Falcon focus. And with the appropriate gratitude shown, he made his escape.

~Chapter 18~

Falcon walked toward the little square of shops that was quickly becoming so familiar. Behind him, he pulled the Strongbow's miniature wagon. With Keene's new event to get ready for, there was a lot to do in a short amount of time. Falcon had volunteered to help, and while Keene had been hesitant, he'd also admitted he needed the assistance. So they'd cashed the promissory note before Keene headed clear across to the other end of Springhaven, to the Copper quarter where BNDS' main hub was located. There, he'd sort his passphrase issue while Falcon took the money and did some event shopping. Keene hadn't liked leaving such an important task to anyone but himself.

"No offense," he'd said to Falcon, "but details are everything."

There just wasn't enough time, though. And so Falcon had strict instructions on where to go, who to trust, and things to watch out for.

Truth be told, Falcon didn't at all feel up to the task. But he'd do his best to help Keene, and he'd written down everything his housemate had told him so he wouldn't risk forgetting anything.

"Ah, good morning, Mister Smoke," Mister Snodgrass, the candlemaker, called as soon as Falcon walked through the door. The bell above was still tinkling.

Falcon tipped his top hat. "Morning, sir."

Mister Snodgrass was a thin man, tall, with no hair on his head and a set of spectacles on his smiling face. When he asked if he could help with anything, Falcon happily gave over Keene's list of requirements. While Mister Snodgrass went to work, the two men made smalltalk. Mister Snodgrass was a bachelor. Good manners dictated Falcon should ask after the man's family, but he couldn't remember if Mister Snodgrass had any other family. The next best thing would be to ask after his neighbors, and the man proved keen for a chinwag.

"Mister Halpern's mare, Maizy's, gone lame." Mister Snodgrass shook his head sadly.

Falcon reached back in his mind for what he knew about the man in question. Across the square, in a lot larger than any of the others, was the blacksmith, though Falcon hadn't realized he had his own horses.

Mister Snodgrass carefully packed bayberry tapers into a box, wrapping each one in a layer of thin paper before placing the next one inside. "Real shame. She's a lovely animal. Does most of our hauling."

"Mister Halpern lends you his horse?" Falcon asked. Horses were expensive animals, not something to just pass around thoughtlessly.

"He lends them to all of us for deliveries and the like. I just hope that finicky engine contraption the Strongbows have starts being a bit more reliable."

Mister Snodgrass reached up to grab another box of candles off a shelf. Keene had asked for quite a few; apparently the family of the deceased followed the "spare no expense for the dead, despite the fact that they're dead" line of thinking. This was one of the things Keene had given Falcon notes about. Bayberry candles were often burned at New Year's. A superstitious tradition held over from the Old World decreed that burning a brand new bayberry candle on New Year's night would bring prosperity. Thus, Mister Snodgrass might not have many left. Or, hopefully, he'd have a surplus and they'd be on sale. Falcon and Keene had even practiced several different possible conversations so that Falcon could be sure to get the best price.

The box Mister Snodgrass reached for sat back on the shelf, just inches from his fingers. Falcon reached up with his cane and tipped it closer so the candlemaker could grab it.

"Many thanks, sir," Mister Snodgrass said. "We've all got to help each other out where we can, don't we?"

Falcon smiled. "Of course."

Mister Snodgrass shook his head again. "It'll be hard with one of Mister Halpern's big ol' beasts out of commission. He's still got Pegs, but she's built more for speed than power, you know."

Falcon nodded even though he didn't know, having never laid eyes on the animal.

"Mister Halpern's looking at getting one of those leg support devices made for Maizy. You know the ones, all springs and rods and whatnot. Fits over the whole leg so the poor creature can heal, but it's not cheap. Mister Strongbow's putting together a collection for him to try and help out."

The candlemaker suggestively tipped an open tea tin sitting on the counter toward Falcon. Feeling the weight of social expectation press down on him, Falcon forced himself to not only drop a few precious coins into it, but to smile while he did so.

It's for a good cause, he reminded himself, which helped... a little.

Mister Snodgrass nodded appreciatively, but he seemed done with his tale for now.

Falcon chewed over the information while the candlemaker continued to gather Keene's supplies. The bell over the door rang, and Falcon observed in his periphery as another customer, a fellow about his height but possibly a few years older, got behind him in the queue.

"How long has Maizy been lame?" he asked. He didn't need to feign concern; the loss of such a useful animal used by so many had to really pinch the community.

"Oh just a few days now, but it's slowed us all up. Mister Strongbow does what he can with his engine, but it's as fussy as they come. I think we're all wishing Maizy a speedy recovery."

A few days. That fit. If Maizy was used to pull more than she was able, like for a cart full of heavy furniture, that could have caused her to go lame. Mister Halpern might have even been the one responsible. Falcon had briefly met the man the other day. He had arms like pistons; a little heavy lifting wouldn't have been a problem for him. Falcon's anger burned. He might not be an animal person, per se, but an innocent horse might have to get put down because of the thieves' negligence.

Then again, if everyone had to start using the Strongbows' cart *and* engine for their deliveries...

Falcon couldn't keep the ire from his voice as he said, "And I suppose since he's organizing it, Mister Strongbow doesn't feel the need to contribute?"

"Oh, not at all, sir." Mister Snodgrass looked positively stricken at the accusation. "He started us off by offering up an impressive sum."

"Oh." Falcon's anger rushed back out like a tide, leaving confusion and contrition behind like so much flotsam and jetsam. "That's very kind of him."

Mister Snodgrass laid the final layer of paper over the candles. "The Strongbows do very well for themselves."

Falcon's mind went to work again. "Even with all those children?"

Mister Snodgrass nodded. "They've got people lined up all day." He chuckled. "Can't blame'em. Best bread in the city if you ask me. Will there be anything else for you today?"

The bell over the door tinkled again, followed closely by a far less melodic, "Hullo! You gibfaced flapdoodle!"

Falcon turned to see a third gent join the queue. He was a big lad, slapping the second on the back.

The insult might have offended his gentle born sensibilities if he'd not been hardened by years of hearing various forms of it, and worse, amongst the Enforcer ranks.

"Ethan," Mister Snodgrass said sternly, with a meaningful look toward Falcon. "Language."

Only then did the two newcomers seem to notice Falcon, who tipped his hat at them.

"Apologies, Mister Snodgrass," said the third, Ethan apparently. Even still wearing a smile, he looked sincerely repentant. He then looked to Falcon. "Pay us no mind. We've known each other forever."

Falcon smiled and nodded. He appreciated that sort of friendship. When he'd been younger, he'd had a few like it—though he'd never have dared to call anyone a gibfaced flapdoodle. Much of the fraternal joviality had faded once he'd become an Enforcer, however.

"You're that Steward of the Sage chappie, aren't you?" said the second man in line. A small lump under his lip made Falcon suspect he held a wad of chewing tobacco there.

Oh, heavens, Falcon thought. He didn't know where this was going, but he had a feeling he wasn't going to like it.

Straightening up, he replied, "I am. Falcon Smoke, at your service."

"Perfect," said the man. "Because I have a crime to report."

Falcon's entire body tensed.

The man's face grew serious. "I'm a murderer." A heavy moment passed, and he pointed at his friend. "I positively killed this jolterheaded cove at cards last night!"

He and Ethan burst into laughter again while Falcon's insides curled in on themselves. He didn't want people to fear the Enforcers; he didn't want them to have to. But he also didn't want people like these two throwing out willy-nilly accusations like that. If they pulled that with the wrong Enforcer, they might find themselves in a world of unnecessary trouble. He hardly wanted to tell them that, though. That would be tantamount to bad-mouthing the order to the very people meant to have faith in them.

"Aiden," warned Mister Snodgrass. "I think Mister Smoke should be able to go about his business without having to listen to foolish prattle like that, don't you?"

In the old candlemaker's eyes, Falcon could see the very fear he was afraid of instilling.

"Not to worry," Falcon said, trying to play it casual, "I'm on leave at the moment." He turned a tongue-in-cheek look of warning onto Aiden. "You got lucky this time. Don't try that with any of the others."

Oh stars, he hoped he was getting his point across. He held out a hand to show there were no hard feelings. Aiden moved his chewing tobacco to the other side of his mouth and returned an enthusiastic handshake.

"See, Mister Snodgrass," he said, slapping Falcon on the back. "This one gets us. We're happy to have you in the neighborhood, Steward Smoke."

"Thank you. I'm happy to be here." Falcon felt a bloom of warmth in his chest as he realized he meant it.

"I'm at the greengrocer's," Aiden said. "Come on by anytime. Ethan here is the local farrier."

Falcon shook hands with Ethan as well, paid Mister Snodgrass for the candles, stored them in the little pull-wagon, and thanked the group once more.

"I'm about to hit a winning streak," Ethan was saying as he left. "I can feel it. You'll see tonight."

"I'll *hazard* a guess you won't." Aiden then laughed at his own joke. "You'll be on the books again before you know it."

Back outside, Falcon took a moment to write down what he'd learned. If the Strongbows weren't in dire financial straits, then why would they have robbed him and Keene? And that still didn't explain how the chip of wood from Falcon's wardrobe got into the bakery cart, nor the flour around its feet at Bits for Bobs. He had yet to investigate Mister Halpern, the blacksmith, as well. But he'd met Ethan now. Ethan had been hired recently, but not *too* recently, if memory served. Falcon might be able to get some information out of him. He just needed to figure out how to go about it without arousing suspicion.

Falcon mused on the problem while he went to the florist next. Keene's intended flower arrangements for the funeral included spruce for farewell, marigold for grief, rosemary for remembrance, and snowdrop for hope. Keene had already identified the sprig Falcon had found as rosemary, but he'd also said it grew like weeds around here, so it might mean nothing. Falcon hadn't really believed that. *He* hadn't seen any. Albeit, he hadn't really known to look until recently, but as he scanned the path to the florist, pulling the borrowed cart behind him, he still didn't see any random rosemary plants waving their twiggy branches at him. In his mind, this confirmed that there must be something to the clue.

Inside the florist's shop was wall to wall plants, some living, some cut, and lots hanging dried from the ceiling. Falcon's notes included what he'd likely have to obtain from this third category, since not everything would be available fresh. Ms. Begonia Perez, who owned the shop, zipped like a dragonfly here and there collecting what Falcon asked for and chattering just as quickly. She too mentioned the fund for the blacksmith and his ailing Maizy and gushed over just how kind it was of Mister and Mrs. Strongbow to lead the charge to help him.

"It'll be terrible if he does have to put Maizy down," Ms. Perez said. "She's such a sweet horse. And where would that leave our little community?" Falcon didn't have time to answer before she went on. "It's not like new horses are cheap." She clucked her tongue. "It's just such a shame all around. Oh no, Mister Smoke. Not those. That's the bayberry for Mister Snodgrass."

Falcon had been reaching for a pile of branches he thought were spruce. Ms. Perez snatched them up and set them aside.

Falcon might have been embarrassed for not knowing a spruce bough from bayberry, but his attention was already focused elsewhere. "Bayberry? Like for his candles?"

"Of course." She said it like it was the most obvious thing in the world before diving for a wooden bucket in which to store the plants. "I get a deal on bayberry, which I pass onto Mister Snodgrass for his candles. Mister and Mrs. Bellows do the same with the tallow they get from their animals. And Mister Snodgrass gives us discounts in exchange. The Strongbows lend us their wagon, and Mr. Halpern shares his horses and their manure. We look out for each other, Mister Smoke."

A new idea struck Falcon just then, one that shook him to his bones. Was it possible they were *all* in on it? The sound of Ms. Perez laughing to herself brought his attention back round.

"Is something funny, ma'am?" he asked. He tried to keep the mistrust from his voice and wasn't certain how successful he'd been.

Ms. Perez didn't seem to have noticed. She trilled, "I've just realized, perhaps it was right for you to reach for that bayberry like you did." Falcon said nothing, not getting the joke. She laughed to herself again. "Bayberry represents instruction, you know. Well, you've learned the difference now I trust."

Falcon hadn't known, but he gave a courtesy chuckle anyway. Again, he handed over money as his little cart—or rather, the Strongbows' little cart—was piled with more goods.

"You can just take whatever rosemary you need from around back," Ms. Perez said with a wave. "It's trying to take over. Don't forget, I've got clippers back there if you need them."

Falcon caught her double meaning this time—rosemary for remembrance—and tipped his hat to her. Outside, he made a few more notes in his notebook and then followed a thin alley that snaked its way between the buildings and around to the yards behind the shops.

Ms. Perez's back garden was as full of plants as her shop. These were all in neatly organized beds with small, painted stones for labels. Collapsible miniature greenhouses covered several of the beds, keeping the plants within safe from the cold. A few beds also laid empty, covered in old newssheets. Falcon suspected by the smell that some fresh manure lay beneath them. He may not know much about plants and gardening, but he knew what fertilizer was. As he parked his pull-cart in the back alley that served the Strongbow's wagon, which he could see two lots down, Falcon found the rosemary. It hadn't been difficult; the plants created a waist-high hedge all along the back of the garden.

Ms. Perez hadn't been kidding when she'd said it was trying to take over. They were currently working to fill the gap that served as a path in and out of the yard and, near the fence, a rosebush was losing the fight for space. Their twiggy branches stuck through the fence's slats, but from both sides, which seemed odd. Falcon walked properly into the alley to see the aromatic hedgerow continued along the rear of the Bellowses' back garden and into the one belonging to the Strongbows, growing shorter and shorter as it went. He remembered it ended in the Strongbows' herb garden, and Falcon's heart sank. Keene had been right; the sprig Falcon had found in his wardrobe pointed to nothing. It could have come from any one of these people. Falcon sighed but made himself straighten up. He was going to have to start pressing people harder, doing a better job of getting them to talk. He hated to consider it, but he might even need to throw his Enforcer weight around. But first, he needed the rosemary Keene had requested.

Falcon had no idea how much his housemate wanted. And Ms. Perez had said to take whatever he needed, so Falcon grabbed a nearby set of the promised clippers and hacked away at the base of the plant nearest to the rosebush, giving it a new fighting chance against the herbaceous takeover. Keene could cut the rosemary bush apart later to whatever size he needed. When Falcon was done, all that was left was some twiggy stubs sticking out of the ground.

He scanned the garden again, wondering if this was something like what Keene wanted for their yard. He'd already requested chickens after all. And Falcon wasn't opposed to the idea. Learning to grow his own food had a wholesome, useful air about it. It'd be nice to be more useful. Something in the nearest newssheet-covered bed caught his eye, something sticking out slightly. It was lighter in color than the darker hickory-brown manure around it, and more reddish. The same shade as something he'd spent quite a lot of time staring at lately.

Falcon looked around. Whatever the thing was, he didn't want to risk damaging it. But he also *really* didn't want to go rooting through dung with his bare hands. Thank the stars! A pair of gardening gloves hung near where he'd found the clippers stored, and he blessed Ms. Perez for her organizational skills. After donning the gloves, he looked around once more to ensure no one was about, carefully folded back the newssheet layer, and began to sweep away the manure with his fingertips. He had suspected this but hadn't dared hope for it. Terribly stained but recognizable nonetheless, the same fabric he had a scrap of back at his and Keene's house lay before him, just much more of it. The thin stripes were the same, the cinnamon shade too. It was a dress, a work dress, and, after a bit of careful shuffling to ensure he didn't damage the garment, he found the most important detail. A tear. No, not just a tear. A hole. A hole where a piece of the fabric had come away from the rest. Now Falcon just needed to remember if he'd seen anyone wearing a dress like this.

Falcon sat back on his heels and almost placed a thoughtful hand against his chin before he caught himself, remembering what he'd just been digging through. He considered removing the dress and bringing it back to the house, but... ew. And also, if he removed it, how could he prove he'd taken it from here in the first place? No, he would leave it for now, and he took care to put everything back the way he'd found it.

Falcon's mind spun. He was getting close! *Someone* had tried to hide this evidence here. He looked back to the flower shop. Ms. Perez, perhaps? He hadn't considered her before, but what motive did she have?

He really needed to talk to Keene. Falcon's housemate knew so much more than he did about, well, so many things. Keene might be able to help him puzzle together the pieces they'd collected.

~Chapter 19~

Back at the house, Keene wasn't home yet. Energy buzzed through Falcon. He needed to *do* something until he could discuss his discoveries with his housemate. He'd already put all his purchases away just how Keene had told him he should, and Falcon decided he ought to put his efforts toward contributing to the household for once. Heavens knew Keene took on far more than his fair share. Falcon may not be able to cook or fix things, but cleaning was easy enough. At least, sweeping and wiping things down and whatnot anyway. And he could build up the fire, nice and toasty for when Keene came home. Falcon thanked the stars for that one domestic skill of his. Luffy, who they'd let stay home while each did their respective errands, moved from her spot on the couch when Falcon got to work in the kitchen. It hadn't taken her long to learn where food came from around here.

As Falcon gathered his cleaning supplies—it took him a little searching since he'd never used them before—a small, indignant noise erupted from around his feet.

Bark!

Falcon's gaze snapped down onto Luffy, who was wagging her corkscrew tail and looking up at him like he'd just promised her a turkey dinner.

"I beg your pardon?" Falcon said. She barked again, and

Falcon replied, "It's not time for your dinner yet."

Bark! Bark!

As if dogs could tell time, he pulled out his fob watch to show her. "See, we've still got… oh, I guess it is about that time."

Luffy gave a satisfied little snort and wandered over to where her disgracefully *empty* food bowl was tucked behind one of the oven's legs. With a chunky paw, she scrabbled the thing out from underneath the black, cast-iron appliance and looked back to Falcon expectantly.

"This sort of demanding behavior is unacceptable, young lady," he said. Nevertheless, he headed over to the icebox. "You're lucky your other father already made up your food for the week. Otherwise you would be tragically out of luck. I have no idea what goes into this mess."

The "this mess" Falcon referred to lived in a large bowl in the icebox and smelled rather nice, if he was being honest, even if it did look egregiously like something one saw after a night of far too much drinking. After spooning out the proper dosage, which Keene had prescribed to get Luffy's weight back under control, Falcon returned to his work, starting with the fire. Behind him, he was serenaded by the sound of Luffy's happy grunting while she tried to both breathe and bury her face in her food. Apparently, she'd never been fed her whole life and was desperate for sustenance.

Not long after, just as he was finishing up with the fire, he could hear Luffy's happy grunts turn to frustrated scrabbling. Despite her purported starvation, she didn't take care to avoid making a mess as she ate, and Falcon turned to help her. Luffy was attempting to squeeze her chunky body beneath the oven. This model, unlike the one at the Allens' manor, barely rose off the floor enough for her food bowl to fit beneath.

"Give me a moment," Falcon said, gently pulling her back.

He couldn't see any dog food bits from here, and he laid down on the floor for a better angle. There they were, just beyond Luffy's reach. Further back, something glinted in the fresh firelight. Something small and more silvery and shiny than the stove. Falcon swept Luffy's wayward food remnants out to her— she'd been trying her best to "help" but really only getting in the way—and reached back toward the mysterious, gleaming thing. No luck. He was too far away. A moment later and he had the fire poker he'd been using not minutes before underneath the oven and reaching.

It was a ring, though he couldn't tell much from either the size or the design. A simple scrollwork pattern set in pewter stared up at him. Falcon also found a thin leather cord near where the ring had lain. Had the ring hung from it around someone's neck or was the cord unrelated? Falcon had the sudden idea that the ring was Keene's. And not only that, but that he'd kept it hidden because it had come from some secret sweetheart.

No, that was stupid. If Keene was seeing someone, he would have said so. Unless… unless he sensed Falcon's attraction and was trying to spare his feelings. Because of course Keene didn't feel the same. Why would he? Talented, clever, funny, graceful, handsome Keene. A horrible, twisted feeling began to burrow up from Falcon's belly and into his chest.

As Falcon examined the ring, trying to ignore his spiraling thoughts, he spied tiny characters swirling along the inside of the band. He refused to think about what kind of invasion of privacy he was committing against his housemate as he went to his Enforcer kit. Falcon forced himself to remain numb to everything as he pulled out his magnifying glass and examined the characters more closely.

I can never lose when I have my lucky dice.

Odd. Keene didn't gamble. He'd once said he didn't see the point when there were so many other things far more fun to spend his money on. It went along with that struggle between spending money on clothes versus tableware. The drilling feeling attacking Falcon's innards eased, and he allowed himself to think again. It might hold some other sentimental value for Keene, and Falcon tucked both the ring and cord safely into his pocket for later. The same worry from before tried to claw at him, but Falcon shooed it away, starting again on his cleaning work.

I have no right to be jealous, Falcon told himself. *Keene isn't beholden to me, nor will he be, so it doesn't matter.*

By the time the front door opening and closing sounded over an hour later, Falcon had shoved all thoughts of the ring, as well as all associated feelings, to the back of his mind and had made quite the impact on the house.

"Welcome home," Falcon called. "Did you get everything sorted?"

No answer. Falcon peeked around from the kitchen, through

the corridor, and into the parlor. There, Keene leaned against the wall, slumped and head hanging.

"Keene?" Falcon ventured. He entered the room slowly but didn't come any further than just inside the entryway, in case Keene wanted space. "What happened?"

Keene lifted his head, and the look of shattered disappointment on his housemate's face nearly broke Falcon's heart.

"One day," Keene said softly. "Not even a day. An evening and a morning."

Falcon came closer, past the table, around the sofa, and leaned against its back. "What's going on?"

Keene threw up his hands. "It took all morning, but I managed to get my passphrase situation sorted. Only to then find out two of my clients tried to send me funds for their engagements while my account was locked. They've dumped me, Falcon. They no longer feel confident in my business practices, whatever that's supposed to mean, and they've broken their contracts."

Keene pressed his hands against the wall like it was the only thing holding him up. Falcon wasn't quite sure what to say. He worried if he asked questions, it would only upset Keene more. And even if he knew the first thing about running a business, he wasn't certain Keene was actually looking for solutions right now. Falcon knew that feeling of just wanting someone to listen, as well as the frustration of trying to scoop out his feelings, only for someone to brush them aside and tell him he was wasting time. Or worse, fling them back in his face and tell him everything he was doing wrong. So Falcon said the only other thing he could think of.

"I'm here, Keene. You can talk to me."

It sounded so stupid when it came out of Falcon's mouth. So trite. So... not enough. Falcon wished he could take it back, or disappear, but he wouldn't leave Keene. Not now. Despite how stupid and ineffective Falcon felt the offer had been, Keene let his head fall back against the wall and heaved a sigh that sounded like he was releasing pressure from his chest. He closed his eyes, and Falcon waited.

"It all just feels too much." Keene spoke so softly, Falcon had to strain to hear him. "My father taught us, his children, all sons, to communicate, to not be afraid to speak our feelings. He was warm and understanding. He's involved in trade, you see—a family business for generations. When I told him my truth, that I fancy men, he didn't bat an eyelash. The fact that I won't continue our line in the traditional way meant nothing. He said to me, 'There's lots of ways to pass down a proud legacy like ours.' But when I shared my own career dreams with him, he wouldn't even look at me." A single tear slipped down Keene's cheek. "He told me I'd fail, and then he just walked off like I was dead to him. I packed up my things and left during the night. Rash and cowardly, I know, but I..." Keene took another deep breath. "Anyway, that's why I haven't spoken to him in over a year.

"I had another roommate for a while, before you. I could tell straight off he was the sort of cove I didn't really want to live with, but I'd had to find something quickly, and beggars can't be choosers. Blazes, Falcon, you should hear the way he talks about women." Keene opened his eyes and pulled a face, which transformed to an expression of anger like Falcon had never seen. "He can talk about them as if they're just a piece of furniture to use and abuse and then discard. Yet when I met a nice chap one night and together we decided to go back to mine..." Keene made a disgusted noise in his throat. "Well, my old roomie saw us in bed together, because by the way, closed doors meant nothing to him. Ex-housemate acted as if I'd buggered him without consent. Suffice to say, I had to get out of there." The wind left Keene again then. "And now with the robbery and these clients." He pressed the heel of his hand to his forehead. "My father was right. My business isn't strong enough to handle this sort of hardship. I *am* going to fail."

Falcon's brows tipped. He wanted nothing more than to take Keene in his arms, stroke his back, and let him know it would be okay. But doubt froze Falcon. He didn't dare move for fear of doing it wrong and making things worse.

Which, it turned out, appeared to be the wrong choice anyway because Keene's face screwed up into a mixture of frustration and sadness. His tone, so unlike Falcon's silence, had the air of someone throwing caution to the wind in the wake of their feelings. "And now here I am making a fool of myself in front of you when you've been nothing but lovely and helpful and trying to help hold me up. Only for it to get you this dramatic mess in front of you. And all I want to do is kiss you and forget about everything for a while. And I know I'm probably just messing up everything more by telling you, but, Falcon, I am tired of hiding and pretending and protecting myself." He slumped further against the wall. "I'm sorry. I'm sorry if I just bollocksed this up too."

Falcon stared, gobsmacked, unable to believe what he'd heard.

"You…" he heard himself saying, all disbelief with no emotion. "You want to kiss me?"

"Yes, alright? I won't apologize for being who I am. But I'm sorry for ruining whatever it is we have between us. I just thought… I thought I felt some sweetness between us. I'm sorry. I'll just go—"

In three strides, Falcon was there beside him. In a moment, he was cupping Keene's face, tipping it upward, pressing his lips to Keene's. And in a split second, Keene realized what was happening and kissed Falcon back.

~Chapter 20~

Their tongues met with nary an introduction, yet all felt right and familiar anyway. The sensation of kissing Keene, finally, after so much uncertainty, washed over Falcon like walking from the cold outside and into a room with a roaring fire going. He let out a sigh. Kissing Keene was like a fresh slice of plum crumble on a winter night: warm, spicy, and utterly delicious. Like his tea, it was full of depth and complexity, and Falcon wanted more as soon as he'd had a taste.

Keene seemed to be enjoying himself too. His hands roved over Falcon's back, fingernails scratching up the back of his neck and through his short hair. When Falcon shifted, Keene grabbed Falcon's bottom lip in his teeth and tugged. Falcon let out a little groan and ran his hands along Keene's face, scraping his calloused skin along Keene's five o'clock shadow, tucking a loose ebony lock behind his ear and stroking the sensitive skin there.

I'm here, Falcon said with his kisses. *You're not alone. Let me take you away from your troubles.*

Falcon moved, nibbling a line along Keene's jaw whilst running his hand along the tender skin of Keene's throat. Keene let out a small, soft noise, something between a sigh and a moan.

"Falcon," was all he uttered, but it snapped a tether in Falcon.

To hear Keene utter his name in such a, well, keening tone was like what Falcon had heard about opium. It took him to a new, euphoric place.

"Keene," Falcon whispered back, and he found Keene's mouth again.

Falcon pressed his body against Keene's, pinning him to the wall. He could feel his housemate growing stiff against his leg, and vice versa. He savored the taste of Keene's tongue once more, sliding his own against it as he pulled back, moving his kisses down the man's chin. He nipped at Keene's jaw before diving into the curve between his neck and ear.

Meanwhile, Keene's hands were rubbing down and up across Falcon's ribs now. His fingers pressed across muscle and bone, massaging and claiming possession. He let out a groan as Falcon lapped at the skin beneath his ear. Keene's warm spices scent surrounded Falcon, threatening to drown him. It complimented the salty taste of Keene's skin.

"Blazes, I've wanted to do this for a while," Falcon murmured. It was every bit as delicious as he'd imagined.

Keene's hips ground against Falcon's. His chest pushed hard as Keene's breath quickened. "You're telling me." His voice caught as Falcon nibbled on his ear. "I've fancied you since you blushed over chicken coitus."

Falcon burst out laughing, spluttering against Keene's neck. Thankfully, Keene started laughing too. Falcon lifted his head, lowered his hand to Keene's hip, and brushed his fingers softly against it.

"I'm not really *that* tightly buttoned up. It just caught me off guard." He leaned back in, savoring the feeling of Keene's warm breath on his face. Falcon smirked, and his eyebrows lifted as he said, "*A Comprehensive History of Accounting* is one of my favorite books."

A smile full of naughty possibilities stretched across Keene's face. He took hold of Falcon's cravat, pulled him close, and dragged his fingertips down the column of Falcon's neck.

The words were hot and heavy against his ear as Keene said, "Is it? Tell me about one of your favorite parts."

Falcon swallowed hard, suppressing a groan of pleasure. He'd never done anything like this before, only read about it. Every touch was so intense, like layers of his skin had been peeled away, leaving him sensitive but without pain. He wanted more, and yet he didn't want this to ever end. He searched his mind as Keene trailed the tip of his tongue down Falcon's throat, kissing beneath his jaw. Falcon let his head fall back, gripping Keene's hips for dear life, lest he float away in ecstasy.

His words came in short, breathy starts and stops. "I like the one where... James and John... get snowed in at the empty cabin, and... and they don't have any wood for a fire—"

"Oh, they had wood alright," Keene murmured against Falcon's neck.

Falcon giggled giddily and slid his hands up Keene's sides, along his chest, and up to his face. He pulled back again and cupped Keene's face in his hands before closing in again. He pressed his lips against Keene's. The flavor of his mouth was new and bright and fresh all over again. Falcon's hands ran through Keene's hair, while Keene's were going to work on the top buttons of Falcon's shirt. Once it was open a few inches, Keene moved down again and nibbled along Falcon's clavicle.

Falcon let out a moan of pleasure. His skin beneath Keene's mouth, even his bones, felt as if they were trembling.

"And then what happened?" Keene prompted between kisses.

Falcon's heart was beating as fast as a woodpecker against a tree. The word woodpecker made him chuckle as he thought of it. He wasn't sure where all this would end up, and back behind the swirling, eager heat flowing through him, he was a little nervous about the possibilities, but more than anything, he wanted as much as Keene was willing to share with him.

Falcon's hands drifted lower, searching for Keene's waistcoat between them and began to unbutton it. "They had to make a tent out of their clothes to keep warm."

"Mmhmm?"

That was where Falcon faltered. He knew all too well what happened next, and he knew what Keene was asking. In so many of those stories, the characters said all kinds of saucy things to one another while in the throes of passion. But Falcon, somehow, couldn't bring himself to recount the spiciest details of the story to Keene. He felt too stupid even thinking of trying, expecting he'd only make a mess of it and a fool of himself. He'd ruin this incredible moment, and then what? Would Keene decide he wasn't... assume that he couldn't...

Keene's mouth finding Falcon's led him from the mire of his thoughts, back into warmth and affection. As Falcon kissed him back, more tenderly this time, he felt Keene pour care into each movement. His hands had slowed, one caressing Falcon's face now and the other rubbing broad strokes up and down Falcon's chest, which now lay half bare thanks to Keene's continued work. Falcon's waistcoat was still buttoned and doing most of the work of keeping Falcon's shirt in place at this point.

Falcon groaned as Keene's fingers circled one of his nipples. His back arched, pressing his hips hard against Keene's. Friction zapped against Falcon, sending a thrill from his nether regions and radiating like a sunburst. Keene must have been similarly affected because he moaned and ground back. The sound was delicious, and Falcon immediately wanted to hear it again and again.

So he plucked up his courage and whispered between kisses, "Would you... would you like to reenact that scene? With me? Upstairs?" He chuckled as an idea came upon him. "I think our bed curtains would make an ideal tent."

The split second of waiting was terrifying, though that terror was soothed greatly by Keene continuing to kiss Falcon. His hands were still running over Falcon's chest, still seeming to search for spots that would give Falcon the most pleasure.

"Falcon my darling," Keene purred. "I would love nothing more than to play any game you'd like."

A huge smile broke out across Falcon's face. Keene had called him "my darling." And on top of that, Keene had talked about playing, which he'd made sound very naughty indeed.

The two quickly made their way upstairs, slowed only by their kissing. That, and Keene tripping over the top step before cracking up into splendid, glorious laughter. Minutes later, the bed curtains around Falcon's bed had been drawn closed, save for one slit left open to allow for the soft light of the oil lamp to seep into the lads' little hideaway. The heavy bed curtains trapped sound strangely, so that even just breathing sounded louder and isolated. Only when they'd cloistered themselves away did Falcon realize again how little experience he had. But he wanted to learn, to allow Keene to know him intimately and to know Keene in the same way. And to show Keene how much he cared for him.

The two knelt on the mattress, in one another's arms again, tongues entwined while hands wandered freely, slowly. Keene had shed his waistcoat somewhere along the stairs, and his shirt hung open from his shoulders like the hero in a romantic story. Falcon had not been so swift, but had at least unbuttoned his own waistcoat. Keene was kissing his neck again, running his hands over the planes of Falcon's chest.

Falcon crooned as Keene gently bit the place where Falcon's neck and shoulder met. "Could you lie down? I want to do to you what Lady Cadence did to Mister Rhythm."

Falcon felt silly hiding behind the characters in a book, but he didn't know how else to express what he wanted. Keene, however, seemed pleased by the idea, cocking a libidinous eyebrow. He flopped back onto the pillows, and Falcon couldn't help but chuckle. He lowered himself to Keene's side and kissed him again.

"You are so silly," he said.

"You love it," Keene replied.

"I really do. Now, lie back and let me, for once, treat you."

Keene did an exaggerated little full-body wriggle, making Falcon laugh again. He took his time exploring Keene's body, given that he'd hardly dared thus far. And Keene was patient, not to mention extremely responsive. He shamelessly arched while Falcon peppered kisses across his chest; it was the most elegant and beautiful sight Falcon had ever seen. Every taste was exquisite, like a sun-ripened, sweet fruit that had been out of reach until now. And Keene's giggles and moans were a decadent sauce over the experience.

"Yes, Falcon," he breathed. "That's—" A sigh. "—smashing."

Falcon appreciated the feedback more than he could say. The licentious array of noises that began coming from Keene were thick with pleasure, unrestrained, and bountiful, giving Falcon confidence in himself. Keene also elicited one of the happiest swears Falcon had ever heard as he used his hands to assist in "treating" Keene as he'd promised, lavishing Keene with the affection he'd let build up all this time.

I want to show you how happy you've made me, Falcon thought.

At one point, in the middle of Falcon demonstrating this happiness, Keene panted, "Falcon." His name, almost like a plea, trilled deliciously through Falcon. "Falcon, my darling."

Keene put a hand in Falcon's hair, pulled gently, and Falcon rose from where he'd been kneeling. He would have worried he'd done something wrong if Keene hadn't been smiling down at him. Still, he dropped a kiss against Keene's hip.

"As much..." Keene had to pause to catch his breath as Falcon's fingers traced long, sensual strokes across the backs of Keene's knees. "As much as I'm enjoying what you're doing, could we go back to John and James' story? I'd like to keep you warm like James did for John."

Falcon knew precisely what that meant, and the idea both thrilled him and made him quail a little. That part of the story involved... mechanics. He'd essentially known how to handle Keene a moment ago because it was similar to what Falcon had done for himself many times. This, however, was something else entirely, something with which Falcon had zero experience.

Keene must have seen Falcon's hesitation because he stroked the side of his face with outstretched fingers. "We don't have to, of course. If you don't want to. We don't have to do anything you don't want to, my darling."

"No, no, I definitely *do*." Falcon's voice was soft. He scuttled up the bed and curled against Keene, kissing his shoulder, his neck, behind his ear. "I do. Especially with you." He didn't really want to admit his own inexperience, but he needed to be honest, for both their sakes. If they couldn't be open with each other, then neither of them could feel safe together. And though Falcon believed with all his heart that Keene wouldn't judge him, he couldn't help but lower his eyes as he mumbled, "I've just... I've never."

He cleared his throat, looking for words. Keene placed a warm hand against Falcon's face and pulled his gaze back up to meet Keene's eyes. There was a bit of gentle but serious discussion then, Keene always encouraging Falcon, never pressuring, asking questions. The exchange made Falcon even more excited to try with Keene, knowing he was in such good, caring hands.

"I'll go slow, and I'll be gentle," Keene whispered. "And I'll stop at any point you want. Just tell me. Sound good?"

"Yes, and thank you." An indecent smile curled up Falcon's face then. Voice husky with desire, he added, "I might even try on you after."

Keene pressed his lips against Falcon's again while sliding his hands beneath Falcon's shirt and waistcoat, which he'd *still* failed to shed. Falcon might have berated himself over that too, but he was too occupied with the feeling of Keene's skin setting fires across his own. Keene's palms were running over Falcon's shoulders, pushing the clothes away.

"Maybe," Keene murmured between kisses. "Though I have every intention of leaving you so utterly satisfied, you're not going to want to move for three days."

As he spoke, Keene's fingers traced along Falcon's muscles

Falcon's Favor

and down his ribs. Up to his chest. Each touch was sparkling sugar, warm and melting and seeping beneath the surface to join Falcon's blood and carry its sweet heat to every corner of his body. Falcon groaned as Keene's words added to the mix.

"You certainly have an excellent fitness regimen, though," Keene whispered against Falcon's neck. He squeezed Falcon's bicep to drive home his point. Falcon flexed not a little proudly. Keene hummed approvingly against the hollow of Falcon's throat, sending a thrill down Falcon's spine. "Perhaps you'll bounce back faster than I expect."

Keene's hands continued to travel down in their sugar-heating-to-caramel way, finally reaching Falcon's trousers. Laces came loose beneath Keene's deft fingers and Falcon thought he might come apart right then and there beneath his touch. If things were this intense now, how much more was Falcon in for? He shivered with anticipation at the thought.

"I should do a better job of warming you up," Keene teased, slowly and luxuriously divesting Falcon of the last of his clothing.

"You're doing spectacularly," Falcon replied, just before Keene did something with a fingertip that made him gasp.

Falcon knew what to do from the story, but the two took their time. Keene told Falcon each thing he was about to do before he did so, which had the added benefit of increasing Falcon's anticipation.

"Tell me what you like and what you don't, my darling," Keene reminded him. A purr rolled in his chest. "And I will pour all. My most *tremendous* effort. Into the things you like."

The words raced into Falcon's brain, hitting it like a drug. Falcon dearly wanted to respond with something equally alluring, but the only word that came to his lips was, "Keene."

"I do so love hearing you say my name."

And he made Falcon say it again, moving onto the next step in the process. They could have been there for hours for all Falcon knew. Taking their time to connect, to merge, to come together in ecstasy and care. Falcon had never considered the idea that communication could be erotic. He discovered this fact firsthand while words flowed as freely between the two as their affections did.

Every moment was positively luscious as the two bathed in the light from their little oil lamp, enjoying one another and melding their pleasure. Joy washed over Falcon as Keene showed him brand new experiences, and Falcon greedily drank in the sounds of Keene enjoying himself just as much.

"Bloody blazes, Falcon," swore Keene. He crouched over him and kissed him with fire on his tongue. "You are magnificent, my darling."

Afterward, they lay down together in euphoric afterglow, Keene's head on Falcon's shoulder. Falcon couldn't stop touching him, stroking his hair, tracing the shell of his ear or the lines of his body. They'd both begun to perspire with the enthusiasm of their adoration, and the slickness made Falcon's digits slide as he pretended two of his fingers were an ice skater dancing across Keene's side. Keene, meanwhile, wore a tired but satisfied smile, eyes half drooped as he remained connected to Falcon's heartbeat via a hand against his chest. Falcon examined his lover's hand against him, and he grinned as he thought back to all the provocative things those hands had spent the evening doing. Falcon had taken mental notes and looked forward to trying his own hands at them. As he traced the lines of Keene's fingers, the memory of the ring he'd found earlier pinged dully in Falcon's brain.

"Keene," he said softly.

The man's breathing had steadied into a regular rhythm, and Falcon wasn't certain if he'd fallen asleep.

A moment later, Keene replied with a drowsy but curious, "Hmm?"

"I meant to tell you, I found your ring." Falcon played with a lock of Keene's dark hair as he spoke. "It was underneath the oven."

"S'not mine. Don't like jewelry."

Confusion momentarily pulled Falcon from his dreamy state. "None at all? Not even, say, on a necklace?"

Keene made a sleepy noise to indicate the negative. "None."

~Chapter 21~

The next day, Falcon felt as if he might be walking on air. He, Keene, and Luffy were making their way down the road toward their little square of local shops. He couldn't stop reliving his night with Keene. He still felt as if he had warm caramel running through his veins, which only warmed more as Keene, with his arm linked through Falcon's, pressed himself against Falcon's side. Springtime gusts of wind came at them again and again. Luffy trotted beside the two, grunting as if telling the wind off.

The warm contact did nothing to help Falcon remain focused on what he was *supposed* to be thinking about, which was the ring he'd found yesterday. He'd tried puzzling it out last night, but he'd been too exhausted to stay awake. This morning had been the same. For the first time in a long time, Falcon had slept in, curled against Keene. He hadn't mentioned the ring again, not wanting to remind Keene of his misery from yesterday. They'd get to it, just not now. Their fresh happiness was too precious to ruin.

Falcon's mind slipped again, wondering if there was a plant that represented new growth or some such. Something that would show Keene just how happy he was that they'd opened up to one another. Ms. Perez at the flower shop would be able to help, assuming Falcon could find a chance to slip away. Not that he was keen at the moment, what with Keene cuddling close to him as they walked.

As the two came within sight of the square, Falcon slowed. The warm caramel in his veins turned cold and sharp. The all too familiar grey and blue of an Enforcer transport cart blared against the backdrop of dark beams, dove-colored plaster, and red brick. It was essentially an oversized strongbox on wheels. A pair of horses stood hitched to the front, while an Enforcer Sixth sat in the driver's seat. It was parked right in front of the bakery. The cart's doors stood open, which meant no one had been arrested… *yet*.

Keene had seen it too, and he stared at the odious vehicle like one would a massive, stinking, and somehow venomous bear. Around the cart, giving it a wide berth, a crowd of onlookers had begun to gather.

"Stay here with Luffy," Falcon said, before he broke away and headed straight for the Sixth in the driver's seat.

He looked young enough to have just come of age, about sixteen. Falcon didn't recognize the chap, but that wouldn't be a problem. As soon as he'd caught the Sixth's attention—easily done given the way Falcon was politely but sternly making his way through the small crowd of onlookers—Falcon flashed his wrist, showing his Enforcer number tattoo there.

Below the number in fresher ink was the symbol of the Crisis Response Unit, a shield of three sage leaves. And in yet fresher ink, barely a month old, was Falcon's rank as Steward of the Sage. Recognizing the tattoo, the Sixth saluted.

"Good morning, Steward. Apologies, sir. Didn't recognize you in your civvies."

"At ease, Sixth Jameson." Falcon read the young man's surname from his uniform. "What's happening here?"

"Had a robbery reported, sir. We're here to pick up the perpetrators."

The crowd around them murmured to one another, and Falcon's insides roiled. Just like that, someone's reputation was blemished, if not ruined. People were perpetrators, not suspects, until proven otherwise. Because guilt always came first. Falcon glanced around him, looking for broken shop windows, but neither the bakery nor any of the other shops looked touched.

"Who's the victim?" he asked.

"Local house," Sixth Jameson said. "Round the corner and down the road a bit."

Falcon swallowed what felt like a stone, which hurtled into the pit of his stomach. The thieves had come back. They'd hit some other poor house. And it was all because Falcon hadn't been fast enough, clever enough, to solve the case.

"Ah, Smoke. Didn't expect to see you here."

Falcon spun at the voice he, unfortunately, knew so well. Fifth Jones stood behind him, barely trying to school his smug expression into something more appropriately neutral.

As Falcon rounded on him, Jones' eyes quickly took him in. "Fancy running into you here of all places. Aren't you supposed to be on holiday in Dogwood Lane?"

Jones had to know that Falcon had moved out of his family manor. That he likely wasn't welcome on a family holiday. Bored, rich people loved nothing more than some good gossip. And judging by the cat-with-a-key-to-the-canary's-cage smirk growing on Jones' face, he'd just surmised that this area was the depth to which Falcon had fallen.

Embarrassment, hot and prickling, washed over Falcon. He practically spat the words, "Jones. Sit-rep. Now!"

Fifth Jones, if it was possible, looked even more smug. "Nothing so serious that you need to involve yourself. We got an anonymous tip that these reprobates broke into a house in the neighborhood and cleaned them out. Looks like most of the goods have already been sold off, but we found a few of the smallest items hidden in the back garden. Pretty much an open and shut case. I might even get a promotion out of it."

Fifth Jones hadn't indicated which shop contained the alleged reprobates, but Falcon had a bad feeling he already knew.

Sure enough, a moment later, Mister and Mrs. Strongbow were led from the premises. Mister Strongbow walked tall and unashamed, looking around at his neighbors with a challenging glint in his eye. His wife was struggling to hold back tears, but her shoulders too were unbowed. Their hands were cuffed in standard-issue iron manacles and chained around the waists. A pair of Sixths led them from the shop with their truncheons out—unnecessary since the Strongbows weren't resisting. All the while, a gaggle of Strongbow children watched, silent and horrified, at the window. Only one, the oldest, stood at the door, glaring after the Enforcers.

The crowd around them grew louder, talking animatedly to one another. Some sounded angry, dissident. Others shocked and hurt. A few looked Falcon's way, and his mind whirled, fumbling for options as events careened around him.

"Michael, take care of your siblings," Mrs. Strongbow called back over her shoulder.

A third Sixth pushed past Michael, carrying a teapot. An evidence tag hung from the handle. The teapot had white violets painted on it, and just then Falcon knew who the victims of the robbery had been.

But who had told the Enforcers?

"Wait! Stop right there. That's my teapot. You're making a mistake."

Falcon spun to see Keene pushing through the crowd. Luffy was nowhere to be seen as he made straight for the Sixths leading the Strongbows. One of the Sixths raised his truncheon, warning Keene to stay back, but Keene either hadn't registered the command or was ignoring it. And the closer he came, the readier to strike the Sixth was.

"Stand down, Sixth!" barked Falcon. He was suddenly between them, Keene and the Sixth.

Clang!

The echo of the impact between the incoming truncheon and Falcon's cane seemed to be the only sound as Falcon glared with all the force of his rank down onto the Sixth. Keene was behind Falcon, pressed against his other arm, which Falcon had thrown out behind him to stop his housemate.

"Steward Smoke, what is all this?" Fifth Jones asked, a distinct sneer in his voice now. "Who is this man?"

"Forget him," Falcon replied. "He's no one."

Protect Keene, his brain was saying. *Protect the people.*

The Sixth before him lowered his truncheon and his eyes, but kept a hold of the chains in his other hand. Satisfied that the Sixth before him had been sufficiently cowed, Falcon looked back to Fifth Jones. As expected, Jones was doing a poor job of hiding his displeasure. The man had always been a sore loser.

"I'm taking over this investigation."

Now Fifth Jones outright scowled. "On what grounds?"

The air began buzzing again, this time with interest. Falcon was certain the people gathered would love nothing more than to see a scrap between two Enforcers.

"I've already begun investigating this case on my own."

Jones jabbed his truncheon in Keene's direction. "This man said the teapot was his."

"He's just my housemate, nothing more," Falcon said. "The house burgled was ours."

Stop looking at Keene, he thought. His fingers twitched while Jones' truncheon hung in the air, still pointed at Keene. He wanted to snatch the weapon away from his fellow Enforcer and toss it into the gutter.

A slimy smile slunk up Fifth Jones' face. He lowered his truncheon, and Falcon felt pressure ease off his chest. "Bad luck, mate. You can't investigate a case in which you're the victim."

Bollocks.

Falcon had completely forgotten that. Enforcers weren't supposed to look into crimes committed against themselves, instead entrusting justice to their comrades. Of course, not many people dared to go against an Enforcer so directly. Not that Falcon trusted Fifth Jones to either have his back or keep Falcon's blundered admission a secret. As soon as Jones got back to the Halls of Justice, he was sure to tell the powers-that-be that Falcon had broken regulation. And the Sixths here knew too. There was no hiding it now. Falcon was left standing in the street without recourse while Mister and Mrs. Strongbow were led past him and into the back of the transport cart. The doors gave a hideous, metallic bang as they shut, and the sound of the lock was a set of jaws clicking against each other.

"Enjoy the rest of your time off," Fifth Jones simpered at Falcon before alighting next to the transport cart's driver. "I'll make sure the case file is closed to you so that you can relax properly."

Falcon didn't dignify the jab with a comment and only watched them go, desperately considering what he could do now. He turned back toward the bakery, wondering if more evidence lay inside or if his Enforcer brethren had taken it all. His gaze found Keene. His housemate's usually-warm eyes had darkened nearly to charcoal, cold and sad and betrayed.

"He's no one?" It was a demand, despite how low and soft Keene's voice was. "Just your housemate? *Nothing. More.*"

"Keene, I—" Falcon stopped short as Keene turned on his heel and stormed off.

)(

Falcon was doing his best not to shout. He and Keene were back home now, Falcon having followed his housemate there, all the while trying to get Keene to talk to him. Keene had silently collected Luffy from Mister Halpern, the blacksmith, to whom he'd handed her, and had kept his mouth shut until the door closed behind him and Falcon. At which point everything had come out and pretty much disintegrated. Luffy was peering at them from under the couch, looking as close to tears as a dog conceivably could.

"Am I just a dirty little secret for you?" Keene asked. "A plaything for home that your mates at the Halls of Justice can't know about?"

"I was trying to protect you from those mutton shunters!" Falcon replied. He really, truly was doing his best not to shout and seemed to be losing the battle. "You remember the riots from last spring? They won't hesitate to strike first and ask questions later."

"You're one of those mutton shunters, Falcon!"

Keene's words sent Falcon back a step. He'd seen people shot with small, metal projectiles during the attack on the Halls of Justice, ammunition that ripped through flesh and splintered bone. That was what Keene's words felt like just then. Falcon put a hand to his heart to check that he wasn't bleeding. He swallowed hard. Words stuck in his throat. He wanted to say he wasn't like them. Keene had once said he saw that, but Falcon couldn't bring himself to make the claim. For one thing, what did he have to show for it? He wasn't doing anything to move away from the rest of the Enforcer pack, not for himself or the Cru. And for another, he was too afraid that Keene's answer would have changed, that Keene would tell him he was wrong.

Keene was staring forward, refusing to look at Falcon. "They're going to torture them, the Strongbows. They might even make them a public spectacle."

Falcon was quick to answer this time. "There's talk of doing away with that." The words sounded so hollow.

Talk. Who cared about talk? It was all empty.

Keene seemed not to hear him. "The Strongbows are innocent. They don't deserve this."

"That's not how the evidence looks." Falcon knew the words were a mistake as soon as they were out.

Keene's eyes flicked to him. "What evidence?"

Falcon swallowed hard. Might as well do it fast. "The Enforcers found some of our things in the Strongbow's garden.

You saw it, the teapot. That's all they really need."

"So you automatically believe them? What if someone put it there to frame them? Maybe the same someone who tipped off the Enforcers."

"There's more," Falcon hurried to add. "I found a chip of my wardrobe in their wagon. The same wardrobe in which I also found a sprig of rosemary, which the Strongbows have growing in their garden. There was flour dusted on the wardrobe's feet. A man and a woman's tracks are on my evidence sheets. Mister and Mrs. Strongbow are both strong enough to move our furniture."

"None of that proves it was them. For one thing, rosemary is practically a weed. A delicious weed, but a weed nonetheless. It gets everywhere. For another, they're *bakers*!"

Falcon flung his hands out to the sides. "What on earth does that have to do with anything?"

"Let's face it, bakers are functionally incapable of being evil."

"That's absurd."

"They gave us a dog."

"They saddled us with a sentient yeast colony."

Silence fell between them for a moment.

"I'm sorry," Falcon said. "That was very unkind of me. I shouldn't have insulted Luffy. She's very sweet."

Keene took a deep breath. "Look, maybe we need some time apart."

Falcon nodded, though he didn't want to. The broken connection between them felt like a chasm. Instead of leaving it, possibly to widen, Falcon wanted to fix it. But Keene wanted space, and Falcon cared for him, so he agreed. But he'd try to throw a rope back across too.

"I think I'm going to go out. Should I maybe pick something up for us on the way back? Something for dinner, I mean?"

"No, thank you." Keene wasn't looking at him again.

A piece of Falcon's heart shriveled, but he told it they'd just needed some time. And he'd work on a solution while he was out. Yes, he was locking Keene out of the process again, but that would be forgiven after the fact, after Falcon thought up a way to fix things.

He headed out, down the front steps, and along the footpath. He'd go wherever his feet chose.

As Falcon walked, he tabulated the evidence in his head. The bootprints. The rosemary. The wardrobe chip. The flour. The hidden dress and its torn scrap. And now the evidence in the Strongbow's back garden. That last piece didn't feel right to Falcon. It was too sloppy. The Strongbows didn't seem the greatest criminal masterminds, but they also weren't stupid. If the entire community was in on it, or even just some of them, had one of their own turned on them? But why? Falcon and Keene had kept quiet about the robbery; no one had been under threat. If it wasn't them, who could it be?

Slow down, Falcon told himself. *Eliminate the impossible. Then, whatever's left, however mad it seems, must be possible.*

He mentally began at the end of the square, with Mister Halpern, the blacksmith. His horse Maizy had been made lame. If it had been due to hauling more than she should, he would have known how much that was, wouldn't he? Wouldn't he be able to tell the signs? He must know his animals as well as his own family. And the horses were his livelihood. He wouldn't risk them for one job. No. He didn't seem a likely suspect.

Then there was Ms. Perez, the florist. He had found the dress stashed in her garden. What motive could she possibly have, though?

The greengrocer? To be honest, Falcon knew next to nothing about him. He rather kept himself to himself. So he very well could have been involved. Except that he was so thin. Falcon doubted he could lift anything heavier than a cucumber. The elderly man couldn't have had an easy time getting up the stairs either.

On and on Falcon's musings went. If the Strongbows were guilty, was there something he could do to help them anyway? Either way, they didn't deserve life in the Halls of Justice. He ended up at the docks and watched the waves of Cobalt Bay lap at jetty posts while he thought. He stayed there so long, the sun was beginning to lower itself in the sky. There was just so much uncertainty. When he finally traipsed back toward home, he decided to stop in at a fish and chips shop. Keene had said not to worry about dinner, but he wanted to make an effort. Especially since he was no closer to a solution.

But Keene wasn't at the house when Falcon returned. Nor was Luffy. They must have gone out to clear their heads too. Falcon's heart sank. Fish and chips were only good piping hot, and he didn't want to leave it out for too long. He waited a little while, letting his go cold too, but Keene failed to return home. So Falcon ate his cold fish and chips and stored Keene's in the icebox. When Keene and Luffy hadn't returned home by the time Falcon usually went to bed, he was really beginning to worry. Then again, when he'd first moved in, Keene had sometimes gone out without Falcon. That's probably where he was. Or so Falcon told himself as he crawled into bed. Mister and Mrs. Strongbow would just be processed tonight, but their questioning would start tomorrow.

~Chapter 22~

F alcon stared at the note like it had slapped him.

I've gone to stay with a friend for a bit. Luffy's with me. —K

Who was this friend? Probably a better friend than Falcon was, that was for certain. But for how long was "a bit"? Was he coming back? Was Falcon going to have to look for a new housemate? When had Keene come back last night to leave this note? And possibly most important, what did the bouquet mean?

Keene had left a small bunch of flowers—a tussie-mussie—next to the note. Falcon recognized the petunias, lavender, and daffodil in it, but he didn't know what the one smelling of licorice was, nor the spike of flowers with crimping around the edges of their petals.

A cursory look over Keene's room and possessions told Falcon he hadn't taken much, maybe just a few outfits, but Falcon couldn't be certain how many. Keene only seemed to have taken items from his old room, though, probably to avoid any risk of waking Falcon. Tears pricked at Falcon's eyes. He *needed* to find Keene. To get answers and make things right and know if Keene was really leaving him for good. Just when they'd finally come together. Maybe he was staying close by? With someone in their neighborhood perhaps?

Falcon grabbed his hat and headed out. He was *going* to find his housemate. He didn't know what else to do as he hurried from the house.

"Falcon, my dear, are you alright?"

The voice came from just above him. Falcon had just marched across the street, but he'd apparently left his wits behind. He wasn't certain where exactly he'd been going or even who he'd planned on talking to first. He spun, knowing the crackling old voice wasn't Keene's, but maybe its owner could help.

Mrs. Spoondawdle stood atop her stoop, watering the flower boxes hanging off the side. She looked properly alarmed, and Falcon realized he'd forgotten to brush his hair. He lifted a hand to pull at his collar, only to realize he'd also forgotten to put on any sort of necktie. What a mess he must look.

"You're in a right state," she said, pointing out the obvious. Mrs. Spoondawdle set aside her watering can and hobbled down the stairs. By habit, Falcon approached to offer her a hand. She took his and then gave it a squeeze. "Why you're as cold as ice, love. Where's your coat?"

Blast it, Falcon had forgotten that too.

"You'd best come inside and tell me all about it," Mrs. Spoondawdle went on.

Falcon suddenly felt very tired. All the anchors he'd relied on throughout his life seemed to be losing their heft, leaving him to drift in the choppy waves of life. Keeping his head above water all by himself was exhausting. He wanted to cry, and holding back his tears took all his remaining strength, so he allowed Mrs. Spoondawdle to usher him into her house without argument.

Inside was as warm and cozy as the woman herself. The layout was exactly the same as Keene and Falcon's little house, and the furniture was a modest, neatly matched set. A fire popped gleefully behind the grate, and neatly folded shawls and blankets sat within arm's reach of every spot. As if noticing what Falcon noticed, Mrs. Spoondawdle chuckled.

"When you get to be my age, dear, all anyone ever wants to give you is shawls and blankets. No one ever just gets me a nice bottle of tipple."

The merest whisper of a smile tickled at Falcon's mouth, and he immediately regretted not spending more time with this delightful woman. He hoped he wouldn't have to move again and therefore away from her.

Mrs. Spoondawdle settled him onto the couch and wrapped a blanket around his shoulders. "There now. Nice and toasty. Have you had breakfast yet today?"

Falcon hadn't. He'd awoken alone, gotten dressed, and then went to look for Keene, only to find that terribly unhelpful note and the glowering tussie-mussie. He shook his head.

"Not to worry, love. I've got some pork pies stashed away. I'll just be a moment." True to her word, Mrs. Spoondawdle returned close to a minute later carrying a small plate topped with a pork pie. No fork, though, Falcon noticed. He wasn't used to eating with his hands, but he also wasn't in a state to care much. He took a bite, not really tasting it, not wanting to notice the flavors because then he'd start thinking about how Keene might describe them.

Mrs. Spoondawdle sat in a chair across from him. "I heard about what happened with the Strongbows round the way. Nasty business. Is it true your house was the one that got burgled?"

Falcon nodded.

"Oh my dear, how awful for you," Mrs. Spoondawdle patted his knee affectionately. "I wish you'd have told me. I've got some bits and bobs round here I'll happily give over. What do you lads need?"

The woman's generosity nearly choked Falcon. With difficulty, he swallowed his bite of pork pie and struggled to summon his voice. When he found it, it cracked with emotion.

"We're alright, Mrs. Spoondawdle. I can't ask you to… to…" Heavens, he was tired. It was hard enough to not break down in front of this woman, infinitely kind as she was.

"But you're not asking me to." Mrs. Spoondawdle's voice was gentle. "We're a community, Falcon. We take care of each other." She shook her head. "That's why it makes no sense."

"Why what doesn't make sense?" Falcon asked.

Please focus elsewhere. Anywhere but on the blubbering mess I'm trying not to be.

"It doesn't make sense that the Strongbows would rob you. Or anyone for that matter. Nevermind that you're an Enforcer. No offense meant, my dear."

Falcon couldn't help but chuckle mirthlessly at that. Of course Enforcer could be interpreted as some kind of insult.

She smiled as she said, "Keene was ever so funny when he first told the Strongbows about you. I happened to be in the bakery getting a loaf when he popped in. 'There he is now,' I said to them. This was the day after he and I'd met, you see. Met you that same day as this happened. Anyway, 'Such a handsome new addition to the neighborhood,' I said."

Falcon smiled, remembering their first meeting. "I did say you were an excellent flirt."

At that, Mrs. Spoondawdle burst out in a creaky titter and slapped Falcon's knee. He was sharply reminded that he'd neglected his exercises that morning. "Too right. Well, Keene then says to me, 'My roommate is pretty easy on the eyes too, you know.'" Mrs. Spoondawdle twirled a finger at Falcon. "I reckon Keene might have a fancy for you, Falcon. See if I'm not right."

Falcon's heart plummeted, and he hid behind a big bite of his pork pie.

Mrs. Spoondawdle sighed. "I do so love a good romance. Shame things didn't work out between young Candace and Aiden. I think Mr. Bellows would have been happy to let them stay together, but you know a mother will have designs for her daughter. Ah, well, back to the story anyway. So I said to Keene, 'You'd better be on your best behavior round that one.' And do you know what he said to me? 'Sage advice, Mrs. Spoondawdle. *Sage* advice.' Just like that. And he winked at me! The absolute cheek!" Mrs. Spoondawdle laughed again. "Of course, we had to explain the joke to the Strongbows after that. And Keene had some lovely things to say about you too. Said you were clearly a conscientious young man. That's a ten-silver word, conscientious, but I reckon he's right."

Falcon smiled weakly at her. "So why does that not make sense? You know, regarding the Strongbows and the robbery?"

"Oh! Yes! Well, I said we take care of each other, didn't I? You see, the Strongbows are some of the best about that. They organized the collection fund for Mr. Halpern's horse, Maizy, you know?" Falcon nodded, and she went on. "And they're always willing to lend a hand at the spring faire, even to their competitors. And believe you me, competition at the faire gets mighty fierce. Last year, Mister Snodgrass had forgotten to bring fresh herbs for his entry into the best baked good competition. Presentation matters, of course, but taste is the real tipping point. That pork pie for instance. It came from Mister and Mrs. Bellow's shop. They put herbs into the crust. It's very good, but just not quite up to the level of the Strongbows' garlic and rosemary loaves."

"Fresh herbs?" Falcon prodded. He felt bad for interrupting, but she did tend to get off topic.

"Of course, yes. Listen to me natter on. The Strongbows gave Mister Snodgrass some of their fresh herbs. The Bellowses tried to claim stealing because the rosemary technically came from them, but, if you ask me, it's not really stealing if the plants get it into their heads to start growing on the other side of the fence. Do you know what I mean? And really, they started off in Ms. Perez's garden anyway. Do try her strawberry rhubarb pie if you ever get a chance, my dear. It's never won any prizes, but it is scrummy!"

Falcon nodded. His mind was gaining clarity again, the wheels beginning to turn once more.

"The Strongbows even defended you on that same day." Falcon's ears perked up at that. "Mr. Bellows was there too. I think I forgot to mention that part. He said some rather sideways things about your order—"

"It's probably deserved," Falcon admitted.

Mrs. Spoondawdle made a funny face that practically shouted, *not touching that with a ten-foot pole.* "In any case, he said some unkind things, and the Strongbows... well, I can't say they took the Enforcer side of things, but they defended you. Said we needed to meet you and judge every person based on themselves. Or something to that effect."

The gears in Falcon's mind spun at high speed now. "Mrs. Spoondawdle, did you happen to be at home the day of the robbery?"

"Remind me which day that was, love."

Falcon did—had it really only been five days ago? So much had happened since then—and she tapped a nail against her teeth in thought. Falcon cringed to think what his parents would do if he ever pulled the same move. "I was, in fact. Yes. I saw the Strongbow's cart that day too." She pressed a hand to her chest. "Blimey! Come to think of it, I might have seen the crime itself. Oh dear, I am sorry. If I'd have known."

Falcon pulled out his notebook. "Can you tell me what happened that day? Don't leave anything out. No detail is too small."

Mrs. Spoondawdle's brows tipped. "Very well, Fal... erm, Steward."

Falcon laid a gentle hand on hers. "I'm just Falcon right now, not the Steward of the Sage. This stays between you and me. You have my word as a gentleman."

The crease between her brows lightened, and Mrs. Spoondawdle nodded. "Thank you, Falcon. I know I'm a bit of a gossip, but I wouldn't want my neighbors to think I was a snitch."

And so she launched into her tale, recounting every moment in painstaking detail. The bakery's banner had been hung up on the side of the cart that day, which was strange since that wasn't the day the bakery usually made its deliveries. Mrs. Spoondawdle had just assumed they had extras that needed to go out. Or perhaps someone had needed to reschedule. That had been the day the greengrocer usually used the cart, but Mr. Snodgrass had been suffering a cold recently. She'd seen Mrs. Strongbow on the seat of the cart, white mobcap and brown work dress as usual, though it must have been especially cold that day because Mrs. Strongbow had been hunched up, and the two people with her in the cart had worn hooded cloaks. That probably explained why Mr. Snodgrass hadn't come out; didn't want to make his cold any worse.

"I didn't know any of the Strongbows chewed tobacco," Mrs. Spoondawdle said at one point during her tale. "You think they'd at least have the courtesy not to spit any old where. Nasty habit. And I think they whipped poor Maizy far harder than was necessary before they went around the corner. She gave an awful whinny anyway." And she hadn't seen them again after that. Mrs. Spoondawdle spread her hands in front of her. "I'm afraid that's all I know, Falcon."

By now, Falcon was in his element, the part of being an Enforcer he felt confident in. He reached across the space and gave her hand a squeeze. Being sure to inject calm warmth into his voice, he said, "Not to worry, Mrs. Spoondawdle. You've been very helpful. And, honestly, I've been remiss in not coming to see you sooner. Let me make it up to you later this week. A nice treat at mine? No tittle-tattle necessary." He gave her a mischievous smile. "Maybe some tipple, though."

Mrs. Spoondawdle chuckled. "That sounds lovely, my dear. Thank you. I can't wait."

Falcon didn't know what later this week would look like. He really hoped Keene would be back by then, and not just because Falcon would have nothing but cold fish and chips to offer Mrs. Spoondawdle if he wasn't. On his way back across the street, Falcon's hopes renewed. He stared at a spot on the ground while a puzzle came together in his head. The truth was about to come out.

But first, he needed one more bit of help from Mrs. Spoondawdle.

~Chapter 23~

Falcon's heart banged against the inside of his chest like those poor birds that didn't understand windows and kept trying to get inside his mother's conservatory. It was late afternoon by now, and a crowd gathered before the bakery just like it had yesterday. The atmosphere had sobered; one of their own had been taken. Falcon fought down the urge to fidget. He wasn't going to make the people much happier, but at least things would be set right. Assuming his plan worked anyway.

"Just a few more minutes," he called to the gathered people. "Then this will all make sense."

Falcon pulled out his pocket watch and checked it again. *Where is that git?*

His note to Fifth Jones had been brief but to the point:

Come back to the bakery. You've got the wrong people. I've got a big reveal this afternoon you don't want to miss. Or maybe you no longer care about that promotion?

It was playing dirty, he knew, but he had no doubt that Jones had already ensured that Falcon wouldn't be allowed access to the case file. And there was nothing Falcon could do about that. If he made a stink about it at the Halls of Justice, their C.O.s would ask questions, Falcon's relationship to the case would come out, and he'd have to waste time fighting a battle he might not even win.

That was time the Strongbows needn't endure inside the Halls of Justice.

So spectacle was the only other option. The power of people had worked this past winter to enact change, and Falcon had to hope it would help him now. Just in a slightly different way.

Next to Falcon stood Mrs. Spoondawdle. He'd enlisted her help to gather the neighborhood together again. He had left the method to her, just so long as she didn't say what was *actually* about to happen. Whatever she'd told them, it must have been impressive because it seemed every single person from their community had shown up. Even Mr. Halpern stood in the back with his horse, Pegs, harnessed but with no saddle. And the culprits were here too. Now and again, a hansom cab or a growler passed on the street behind, using the square as a turning point.

"What did you say to them?" Falcon whispered to Mrs. Spoondawdle.

"Just that you were going to fight that scamp from yesterday. Pugilist style. No shirts."

Falcon's face combusted into flames. At least, he was certain it must have, given how quickly it heated. He assumed "that scamp from yesterday" meant Fifth Jones. And while the man was a complete cretin, brawling shirtless in the street certainly wasn't what Falcon had in mind. And while he might be proud of his physique during intimate moments with Keene, showing it off to a crowd of onlookers gave his gentlemanly upbringing a case of the vapors. He rubbed his neck, expecting soot to come away on his fingers with how charred his skin must be from all the fire underneath.

"But I'm not going to…"

He trailed off as Mrs. Spoondawdle smirked, a mischievous glint in her eye. She gave him a reassuring pat on the arm. "Not to worry, my love. No one's really here for violence. They just don't want to risk missing something everyone else'll be yammering about for weeks to come."

Heavens above, this was already a circus. Then again, he'd wanted attention, and now he had it. If only Jones, that little—

"Finally!" Falcon never had a hope of holding back the exclamation. Tension he hadn't realized had been coiled in his chest exploded like a spring. "Where've you bloody been?"

Fifth Jones, dressed in his street clothes, pushed through the crowd without so much as an excuse-me. He scowled down his nose at Falcon. "Some of us are busy working, Steward Smoke."

The crowd around them began to murmur. To them, it must look like the rumored fight really was going to happen, but Falcon was too wound up to care.

"*You're* clearly not," Falcon shot back, motioning at Fifth Jones' attire.

Jones pushed past Mrs. Spoondawdle, earning him a glower from the old woman. Under his breath, he spat. "You might be First Iago's golden boy, Smoke, but I see through your act. You're nothing but a sad, broken puppy looking for attention."

"I am *not* broken," Falcon snapped back. He gripped his cane, wanting to sweep Jones' leg out from under him and introduce his face to the pavement, but this was about the Strongbows. Falcon took a deep, calming breath and looked out at the crowd. "Ladies and gentlemen, I mean to set things right. Mister and Mrs. Strongbow weren't the ones to break into my house."

The general feeling of response was unimpressed. Falcon couldn't tell whether it was because most of the people there already believed that or if they didn't believe him. Nevertheless, he'd seen reputations left in tatters from a wrongful arrest, so he plowed forward, lest he lose their attention.

"I will now—"

This time a collective sound of interest rose all around.

"—reveal my evidence." He finished.

"He's not going to take his shirt off?" someone in the crowd said. "Shame."

Falcon pressed a hand to his face. "Stars." Straightening back up, "Right. I give you Exhibit A." He lifted the sheets of paper with boot prints on them. "Boot prints, which if measured, you will find match the culprits'."

"But you seem to forget, Steward Smoke," Fifth Jones drawled, "lots of people wear the same size shoe."

For the first time in his life, Falcon managed a withering look, which he directed squarely at Fifth Jones. Apparently all it took was a lifetime of putting up with a complete and utter prat.

"I'm building up to something here." He only just barely restrained himself from adding, "So shut it," though it was a close thing.

A titter of amusement thrummed through the crowd.

Fifth Jones rolled his eyes and made a very loud noise of disbelief. He even had the gall to look at some of those gathered with a *what a waste of time* look, as if they might side with him.

To keep himself from doing anything stupid to Fifth Jones, though well-deserved it may be, Falcon went on.

"Exhibit B, a scrap of fabric found attached to my back garden's gate, through which the thieves operated." He held up the cloth fragment.

"And there's no way it could have come from someone just passing by," Fifth Jones muttered.

From the side of his mouth, Falcon retorted, "You mother would say sarcasm is beneath you." But to the crowd, he said, "Fifth Jones makes a good point, but that's unlikely given this scrap was attached to the *inside* of the gate. And now, Exhibit C, a sprig of rosemary."

Someone in the crowd must have thought Jones' little game of poking holes in the case looked like fun, because they called out, "That stuff grows everywhere round here. Practically a weed."

Falcon could feel the self-satisfaction rolling off of Jones. Thankfully, Falcon was ready for just such an objection, which made it easier to ignore the growing miasma of smugness.

"True, but it doesn't generally grow inside of wardrobes, which is where it was found. My wardrobe, to be exact. Which means the perpetrator had it on their person at the time of the burglary." To Jones, he scowled and said, "I'm sure you'll hear more details about that the next time you report in for duty."

The crowd was making noises of agreement now, possibly beginning to draw their own conclusions. Falcon's eye caught movement from one of the culprits. One of them was getting nervous, shifting amongst the crowd and trying to move back into it without making a scene. Difficult, given the size of the person, which was to Falcon's advantage. Still, it was time to make his move.

"Combine that with yet more evidence I will present to Fifth Jones here and the rest of the order—"

A murmur of dissent went up from the people gathered. Fair enough, given that Falcon, an *Enforcer*, could simply work behind the scenes to make any number of things look true and fix it to his own devices.

"Not to worry," he called. "I'll also be sharing everything with all of you." He looked around, meeting the eyes of his little community. "I know how you feel. For too long, the Enforcers have been... well, let's call a spade a spade. Bullies. My goal as the Steward of the Sage is transparency, and it starts with me."

"Yes, but who did it then?" Someone called. "If it wasn't the Strongbows?"

"Of course it wasn't the Strongbows," someone clapped back. "They're *bakers* for goodness sake."

Falcon shook his head. Where did this dogma everyone had about bakers come from anyway?

"I'm sorry to say, it was Candy, Aiden, and Ethan."

The crowd gasped as one before splitting up, some looking at the first, some the second, and others the third.

"Now everyone just hold on." That was Candy, calm and authoritative. Like her mother, she hadn't needed to raise her voice to be commanding, but the grease pencil tucked behind her ear trembled with indignation. Everyone froze, and Falcon tried to take a few mental notes on her technique. She pointed a finger at Falcon. It stretched firm and accusing in the black leather gloves she wore. "How dare you accuse us. We haven't even seen all the evidence. You Enforcers are all alike. Steward of the Sage indeed." She crossed her arms over her chest. "You're just as rotten as the rest of them."

The crowd began to murmur again, but Falcon was ready for this too. Though it gave him no pleasure.

"I'm sorry for what my order has done," he confessed. "For my own part, as leader of the Crisis Response Unit, I'm trying to do better, to be a good example. We're headed in a different direction. But, Candy, I'm afraid my guilt doesn't absolve yours." He held up the ring he'd found in his house. "*I can never lose when I have my lucky dice. His lucky Can-dice.*"

Candy's cheeks bloomed two lovely roses, and her hand went to her neck.

"Everyone's heard about how the Strongbows discovered your relationship with Aiden. They told your parents, who made you break it off. At least your mother did. She wants you to marry one of my sort, or at least a sort she thinks has money. Sorry about that." He looked to the Bellowses. "Believe me, she can do so much better." He looked back at Candy. "So you made a plan to frame the Strongbows. I suppose Aiden helped you because, well, he loves you. And it was good revenge against the people responsible for splitting you two up. Aiden and Ethan have been friends since forever. Plus…" Falcon found Ethan in the crowd. The big lad was leaning back, as if ready to physically dodge the accusation. "You've got gambling debts, don't you Ethan? This was supposed to be an easy way to make some money to pay them off."

He looked back to Candy. "I expect you thought I would report the robbery to the Enforcers. I mean, why wouldn't I? But then no Enforcers showed up to start questioning the neighborhood, so you had to make an anonymous tip. And you planted evidence that would point straight to the Strongbows, didn't you? But you left your own evidence behind too. The rosemary attached to your grease pencil, right there." Falcon began to gesture at each piece of evidence as he named it. "This ring that Aiden gave to you. And you wore a dress dyed to look like the one Mrs. Strongbow always wears, which you tried to hide in Ms. Perez's compost, but you left this little piece behind." Finally, Falcon gestured at her gloves. "Are your hands still stained from the work?"

The roses on Candy's cheeks had spread across her delicate nose, and she balled her fists at her sides. "It isn't fair!"

"No. None of it is," Falcon agreed. "Now, please, come quietly. I'll argue your case with—"

Candy didn't stay to listen. She spun and began slipping past people, bobbing and weaving like a quail. Meanwhile, with far less dexterity, Aiden shoved his way after her. A hansom cab was just passing by, turning around in the square, and Candy popped up from behind the crowd, still like a quail, but flushed from cover now. Aiden was already ahead and leaping into the driver's seat. He shoved the poor driver off the other side. Candy leapt, Aiden barely caught her by the fingers, and for a moment Falcon thought she might not make it. She teetered as her hand pulled out of her glove. It came free and she tipped back. In that split second, Falcon saw what he knew she'd been hiding. Her entire hand was tinted a pale reddish-brown. Aiden thrust his other hand out, caught Candy around the wrist, and pulled her in next to him as if she weighed next to nothing.

"Aiden, wait!" Ethan was calling.

He'd reacted slower and was trying to make his way toward the escaping hansom. He'd been the one getting nervous earlier. And though Ethan had managed to shuffle his way to the back of the crowd, that was where Mister Halpern, his employer, stood. As large as Ethan was, Mister Halpern was bigger and stronger after a lifetime of bending metal to his will. With the one hand not holding onto Pegs' reins, he grabbed hold of Ethan's collar and snatched the lad back.

All of this happened in a matter of seconds. By the time Falcon could react, Candy and Aiden were on their way.

"Mister Halpern!" he shouted. "Horse!"

Falcon's mind was functioning in compartmentalized pieces the way it always did in a crisis. The hansom cab driver was standing, brushing himself off. Right, he was safe. And Falcon put him out of his mind. He wasn't but a few steps toward Mister Halpern when the blacksmith met him. With practiced ease from years of riding, Falcon swung himself up onto Pegs. His joints complained, not having been stretched properly either that morning or the night before, but, as he'd done in the past, Falcon shunted their complaints lower down in the queue of priorities. He'd be fine; he had a horse. With nary a kick, Pegs took off like a loosed crossbow bolt.

Aiden and Candy had a good head start. They hadn't hesitated to urge the horse pulling the cab into a gallop, but Pegs didn't have anything holding her back. The horse's hooves drummed over the cobblestone streets in a mad tattoo.

"Halt!" Falcon called after his quarry. They, of course, completely ignored him. Now and again, he shouted, "Make way!" when it looked like some poor bystander might unwittingly trod into his or the hansom's path.

The wind whipped Falcon's hair back as Pegs ran. He felt a sharp, cold draft against his back as his coattails trailed behind him in what must look like a battle standard. The scent of clean, crisp air drove itself into Falcon's nostrils, and Pegs moved like water beneath him. Ahead, Aiden drove like a twig in a raging river, veering around other cabs in the road and twisting around corners at breakneck speeds.

The race, for all its excitement, ended quickly. Pegs caught up to the cab within minutes, though actually apprehending the targets posed a new challenge. Aiden swiped a punch at Falcon once, but there was a good few feet between them, giving Falcon time to dodge. Falcon pulled up alongside the cab's horse after that. The poor thing was grunting and sweating, its flanks glistening in the setting sun.

"Do something!" Candy shouted at Aiden from behind Falcon.

Falcon looked back to see Candy... was she taking off her shoe? No time to figure out why. He needed to—

Pegs whinnied as the sweating horse pulling the cab barreled into her, squeezing Falcon's leg between them. Falcon grit his teeth as pain shot from his knee, and he swung Pegs off to the side. Right into the path of an oncoming private coach.

"Fffah!!" Falcon nearly swore. Words were difficult when one was avoiding death. He pulled Pegs back the other way, narrowly avoiding a collision. "Are you trying to get us all killed?!" he called to Aiden and Candy.

Someone from the private coach was properly swearing at them, putting Falcon's attempt to shame, but the sound was already fading into the distance as the two parties raced on. Falcon had to stop them, or someone really was going to get hurt. Quite possibly him. He looked down at all the straps and leather cables connecting the poor panting horse to the cab. A series of slender tethers attached to the bands and straps of the horse's rigging had been braided together to make one thick cable, which now dragged on the ground. Falcon would have thought they served as an extra set of reins or something if any of them had been attached to the horse's bit. Wait. The reins. Of course! It was a long shot, but worth a try.

Falcon reached over and grabbed the reins closest to him. He pulled hard and hoped he wasn't hurting the horse. Unfortunately, he'd momentarily forgotten this was the command to make a horse turn. The poor creature swerved again. Its shoulder collided with Pegs, and Falcon was truly frightened that his mount might go toppling. Pegs' speed gave her agility, though, which was their saving grace. She remained upright, but snorted and nipped at the other horse.

"Sorry, sorry, sorry," Falcon said to both horses. That certainly wasn't going to work.

In the next moment, Aiden pulled the cab's steed in the opposite direction, ripping the one rein Falcon held from his hand. Falcon heard cries of distress rise up from the footpath just before Aiden pulled the horse back the other way, trying to ram Falcon yet again. While Falcon dodged this latest attack, indignant exclamations of, "Well, I never," and "How very rude!" followed the distressed cries. Probably no serious injuries then, but it was only a matter of time.

Falcon's sweat turned cold. As he looked over the complex

network of rigging again, the horrible realization that he had no idea what to do washed over him. He was no engineer or stableman. He didn't want to hurt anyone by messing this up, but he couldn't do nothing. Falcon gulped, swallowing his fear down. Right, there was nothing for it then, and he went for what he could.

Something central that wouldn't make the horse turn again seemed a good candidate, and he tugged at the horse's backstrap. No luck; it was securely fastened to the girth band and various other pieces of rigging. Next was one of the slender tethers, which attached to a sort of hitch apparatus lying across the horse's shoulders. With more determination this time, pouring his growing desperation into the move, Falcon yanked the tether as hard as he could. It went taut, pulling a small ring outward from the shoulder apparatus. The pulled ring released some kind of locking mechanism and it came away from the whole, attached to a small but solid metal shaft. This all happened within a second, and Falcon overbalanced as the force of his pull was far greater than was necessary for the quick release pin.

For a moment, as had happened in his and Keene's bedroom when they'd been stretching together, Falcon's mind tried pulling him into the memory of the explosion that had put him into a coma.

"Remember what happened then?" the memory seemed to say. "What if something worse happens this time?"

A chill passed over Falcon. Beneath his hands, though, he felt Pegs' warm fur, her muscles pumping. He'd caught himself on her neck, and the feel of her kept him anchored to the here and now.

This was a stupid idea. Why did he think he could race into danger? He wasn't the man he used to be anymore.

Aiden brought the cab's horse barreling toward Falcon again. Thankfully, muscle memory from years of riding had made certain Falcon was already squeezing his legs against Pegs, who apparently learned fast, because she shied away as the horse came close again.

They were coming up on a sharp corner now, and Aiden was already steering the cab to go around it. Falcon spotted a small figure, a pedestrian, just emerging from behind the side of a building. Aiden was taking the turn too sharply. He was going to cut the corner off and run over the person. Falcon's instincts took over. He urged Pegs forward, grabbed the cab's reins as he had before, and yanked them back toward him. This time, he guided

Pegs as they went, and they easily glided through the maneuver together. The other horse whinnied as it was forced into the sudden course correction. The cab's back wheel clipped the curb, pitching the cab up and sideways before coming back down and fishtailing for a moment. It had missed the pedestrian by mere feet.

This had to stop. And Falcon was best positioned to make that happen. Though he knew all too well what he risked, he reminded himself, "I am *not* broken," and refocused on stopping Aiden and Candy's wild escape.

He looked to the spot where the tether had been attached; he'd dropped it whilst catching himself against Pegs. The tether, its ring, and adjoined pin had disappeared over the other side of the cab's horse. A small hole where the pin had neatly sat moments ago glared empty now. There were more rings like the first all around the horse's harnessing, all attached to more of those slender tethers. It was some kind of failsafe system. He followed their path to where the tethers were braided into one long cable. The one dragging on the ground. On the side opposite him. Falcon sighed. Of course.

He tried reaching first, stretching his arm across the horse's glistening flanks toward where the braid hung off its other side. He gripped Pegs tight with his thighs again as he leaned, the rushing wind pushing against him. Shouts from people as they sped past grew momentarily loud before dimming to nothing moments later. He tightened his abdominal muscles to support the rest of his body while he suspended himself in air. Just a little further…

Wham!

Something hard and sharp connected with Falcon's head. Once against his forehead just above his brow and once against his jaw on the other side. Mercifully, the second hit was softer, but it knocked him off balance nonetheless. Feeling himself falling, Falcon grabbed Pegs' mane with the same hand holding her reins. Her head jerked back, and she stumbled. For a split second, Falcon had a vision of Pegs going down and of himself falling beneath her, being crushed by the animal's massive weight. A second later, Pegs steadied herself and nickered angrily as she fell into a trot. Something warm and wet ran down the side of Falcon's face, but his attention was already back on the cab, which was gaining distance fast. Aiden slapped the cab's reins against his horse's back and shouted at it to go faster. Falcon wasted no time in prodding Pegs back into a gallop.

"Sorry, girl," he said to the horse. "But if we do this, there's a big bucket of carrots in it for you."

Whether or not Pegs understood, Falcon didn't know. In any case, the horse picked up speed again, hooves eating up the renewed distance between Falcon and his targets.

"Give it up!" he cried in a last ditch effort. "You've got nowhere to go!"

Technically, there was a city exit at the north end of the Cobalt district they could escape through. They'd have to blow through the Enforcer checkpoint to do it, but at this speed, it was possible. It was a miracle no one had been hurt yet, and Falcon wasn't about to let that happen, not without a fight.

He came up on the cab again, past the driver's seat, at which point Candy reached for Falcon. Specifically for his neck. With one hand holding the rail atop the cab's box and the other stretched toward him, she reached, fingers curled like bloody claws, given the reddish color of the dye staining her hands. The pewter-grey of her stockinged feet blared against the solid black of the footwell. Only then did Falcon feel the weight hanging around his neck. A quick glance revealed Candy's shoes hung there, tied together by their laces. That's what must have hit him. She must have thrown them like a bolas. Well, now that he had them, he wasn't about to give them back.

Falcon urged Pegs into another burst of speed, pulling away from Candy and her reaching hand. They drew up to the cab's badly misused steed again, and this time, Falcon reached down to his leg holster. In one motion, he drew out his cane and pressed the button to expand it. With victorious clicks, it popped out to its full length, and Falcon reached, using the handle end as a hook. Aiden pulled at the reins again, but the horse was slower to respond this time. The poor thing must be exhausted.

He guided Pegs closer and winced as his knee and leg were squeezed between the horses' bodies, but he kept reaching. Holding his body up while he stretched and bent over the cab's horse, leg locked in place, made his joints cry out in pain. Still Falcon reached. Aiden was now trying to hit Falcon with the cab's reins, whipping them upward. While Falcon ducked his head to try and avoid this new attack, Candy screamed some kind of abuse at him. He flinched as one of the cab's reins caught him on the side of his jaw, but he didn't retreat. So close now. Just a little... There! He hooked the dragging braided strap onto the handle of his cane and pulled it toward him. Meanwhile, his knee, pressed between horse ribs, sent jolts of jagged, cutting pain up and down Falcon's leg.

Later. Later, he told the pain before dismissing it again and again.

He carried the braided strap over to his side, suspended on the cane's handle, and grabbed the thing with his teeth.

"Hang on!" he said, both to himself and Pegs. Though with the strap in his teeth, it sounded more like, "Hng ng!"

Falcon grabbed the strap in the same hand as his cane, wrapped it around both his forearm and the cane's shaft, and then yanked Pegs into an abrupt halt. She neighed and pulled up short. It took everything in Falcon to hang on while Pegs reared, thighs squeezing hard. The hand holding her reins grabbed onto her mane and held on for dear life. The strap wrapped around his other arm helped, as it yanked Falcon upright for a split second before the emergency release pins pulled free. The tether ends whipped here and there with the force of their release, and one snapped back, catching Falcon across the cheek. It left a streak of stinging fire behind, and he grit his teeth against the pain.

The cab's side rails fell away from the horse, freeing the animal, save for the reins still held in Aiden's hands. A horse at speed was no match for mere human grip, however, and the reins ripped from Aiden's grip as easily as if they'd been coated in butter. The horse kept running and disappeared around the next corner, hopefully to a long and happy life. Meanwhile, the cab balanced on its two wheels for a moment before tipping back. The iron framework on the back of the cab skidded along the cobbles, creating a flurry of sparks and an ear-splitting screech. Aiden nearly fell backward from the driver's seat, but Candy, who'd already been holding onto the rail at the top of the cab, reached out and grabbed him before any harm could befall her beloved. It wasn't but a few moments of skidding before the cab really lost speed and then stopped.

Falcon was already there, still atop Pegs, Candy's shoes still hanging around his neck, with what he expected was blood running down his face, and the emergency release strap still wrapped around his arm and cane. What a sight he must be. A crowd of onlookers was already forming. People emerged from every shop and nook and cranny, some having chased the action from streets past. Along with them, a couple of Enforcers appeared too. Falcon showed them his tattoo and unhappily instructed them to arrest Candy and Aiden. He'd be along to process the young couple soon enough. And all the while, Candy and Aiden held each other's hands.

~Chapter 24~

The ensuing day or two was full of sorting things. Pegs needed to be returned to Mister Halpern. The Strongbows needed to be released. Their house and garden, as well as those belonging to the Bellowses, needed to be searched for other items taken from Falcon and Keene's home. Falcon needed to present his evidence to his C.O.s at the Halls of Justice. The shoes Candy had thrown at him matched the prints on Falcon's evidence sheets, as did Aiden's and Ethan's once Falcon got a hold of them. The whole process was made slower by Jones throwing a tantrum about Falcon not following due process and some other rot. The powers-that-be, however, seemed nonplussed by the slight breach in protocol perpetrated by Falcon. In part because he had a far stronger case than Jones. If there was one thing the Enforcer order liked, it was results. And even better, results that came tied up with a neat little bow, not to mention the discovery of a vast fencing and tax fraud operation—when the Enforcers investigated Bits for Bobs, Falcon's wardrobe was, unfortunately, tagged as evidence and would not be returning into his possession for a very long time. He dearly hoped they wouldn't store the dyed dress recovered from Ms. Perez's garden bed inside of it.

It also helped that the newssheets and tabloids had picked up the story. By the morning after, an illustrated retelling of it plastered across the front page of every publication in Springhaven. Some of them made it sound as if the chase had spread across the entire city instead of just one section of the Cobalt district. And one particularly infamous and creative rag even claimed the beloved Steward of the Sage had engaged in full-on fisticuffs atop the speeding cab. The Enforcers' poster boy was famous all over again. And the fact that Falcon had doggedly followed the thieves' trail to its bitter end only helped to improve their image as a whole.

So it was no surprise to Falcon when he received a note at home from First Iago himself requesting a meeting at Falcon's earliest convenience. Falcon knew "earliest convenience" in this case actually meant as close to "right sodding now" as humanly possible, so he'd hailed a hansom cab and headed over to the Halls of Justice... with just a few little detours along the way.

)(

"Steward Smoke, m'lad," greeted First Iago when Falcon walked into his office. He extended his massive arms wide as if he might hug Falcon. Completely out of the question, of course. Enforcers never, ever *hugged*.

First Iago's office somehow managed to be both gaudy and austere. The cream-colored walls and white marble floor streaked with black and grey were the same here as the rest of the Halls of Justice. Not much adorned the room, just a desk and its chair, plus two others for guests. The only decoration was a single painting. Each of these items, however, oozed luxurious opulence. The painting was of First Iago himself, looking severe and determined in his blue and grey and gold dress uniform. He'd been depicted staring off into the distance with Springhaven's skyline behind him, as if he was the city's sole protector. The hand-carved desk and chairs looked to have cost an average family's yearly income. Springhaven's citizens had paid for the items with their tax money, and Falcon briefly wondered what might have happened if that money had been better spent.

He saluted, which First Iago quickly waved away. "Enough of that. We don't need to stand on ceremony."

Odd, Falcon thought wryly to himself. Literally every other time they'd been in the same room together he'd had to. Of course, he knew perfectly well why that had changed.

"How are you, my boy?" First Iago went on. "What can I get you? Whiskey? Gin?"

"Nothing for me, thank you," Falcon said coolly.

Despite First Iago suddenly treating him like a much beloved son, he remained standing. At ease, but still standing. Honestly, Falcon wasn't certain he was even capable of relaxing around the leader of his order. He was pleased his cane had come through his adventure unscathed, though. The ordeal had left Falcon's knee aching, even after he'd done his exercises that morning and the night before. His face and head stung too. He had a plaster over where Candy's shoes had cut his forehead, a bruise on his jaw, and a welt across his cheek from where the flying tether had caught him.

"Very well then, shall we get right to it?" First Iago sat down in the oversized oxblood leather chair behind his equally oversized desk and picked up a glass already full of brown liquid. "You've done it again, Steward Smoke. Made quite a hero of yourself, haven't you?"

"I only did what was necessary, sir," Falcon replied.

First Iago let out a booming guffaw and slapped his desktop. "That's why I like you, lad. You're so bloody humble."

"Thank you, sir."

"Well, son, I'm sure I don't need to tell you that your actions the other day have gotten everyone's attention."

"I've seen some of the reports, yes."

First Iago put his feet up on the desk and motioned at Falcon with his glass. "In particular, some publishers have contacted me. They want to print serials of your adventures."

This didn't surprise Falcon. Those same publishers had contacted him directly as well. Their letters of introduction and offers had been in the same pile as First Iago's summons.

"There are more offers than just that. All manner of them. And all we have to do is name our price." First Iago let out another huge laugh before taking a long sip of his drink. "Riding bareback through the streets after a speeding cab. Balls, I wish I'd been there to see it." Gold coins were practically shining in First Iago's eyes. "That money'll help fund the order a sight better than this bloody city ever has."

"Indeed. To that point, sir…" Falcon took a deep breath. The moment had come. He turned, headed back to the door, and opened it. "If you all would join us, please?"

Falcon looked at the supreme commander of the Enforcers. First Iago betrayed none of the confusion he might be feeling, just watched with hawk-sharp eyes as he took a much smaller sip of his drink. Into the office filed Mina, Mister Strongbow, and Beatrice. First Iago did not stand to greet the ladies. Falcon had to bite back subtle nudges that kept springing to his tongue about how First Iago should immediately rectify his behavior and act like a gentleman, but he knew it wouldn't help his case. He didn't actually want to make the First angry... well, any angrier than what Falcon had planned already would. Beatrice and Mina took the two seats in front of First Iago's desk while Mister Strongbow stood behind them with Falcon.

"What's all this then, Steward?" First Iago asked at last.

"You said we just had to name our price, sir." As Falcon stood straight and solid, hands clasped behind his back, he pressed his heels together and into the floor harder than necessary. It helped him feel grounded for what he was about to do. "I'm naming mine."

First Iago's eyes roved over the newcomers, not even trying to hide the disdain in his gaze. "I see."

Falcon swallowed hard. This felt rather like a tennis match with dire consequences, and now it was Falcon's serve. He had to make it a good one, and he motioned at Mister Strongbow. "I'd like to present Mister Ebenezer Strongbow. You may recall he and his wife were wrongly arrested and imprisoned the other day as the suspected thieves in the case of my home's burglary."

"I do," First Iago said. He set down his drink and folded his hands over his stomach. "But we got all that sorted. The right people are locked away now."

"Yes." Falcon's heart picked up its pace. "That's my first request. Candy, Aiden, and Ethan committed a crime, yes. They made poor choices, but they have the rest of their lives ahead of them. As the victim of that crime, I say they shouldn't be imprisoned for life."

First Iago's shoulders relaxed, and he flapped a dismissive hand at the idea. "These changes Magistrates Allen and Holmes are working on will handle that. Down the road, someone will figure out what should happen to those miscreants."

"Sir, it really would behoove us as an organization not to be on the wrong side of progress." Falcon was pleased at how confident he sounded despite his insides turning to jelly. "I say we begin our own process of judging cases and assigning more fitting punishments. If nothing else, it will make the transition less painful when governmental changes do come round."

First Iago jabbed a finger at Falcon. "That's soft talk, Steward Smoke." He then turned to Mister Strongbow. "You, sir. You suffered at the hands of these criminals. Don't you want to see them suffer in return?"

"No, sir, I don't." Mister Strongbow's voice was calm and measured, but a vein of molten iron ran beneath his words. "I spent one day in your so-called Halls of Justice. It's a disgrace, nothing but a place for cruel boys to get their mean, little jollies. People shouldn't be treated like animals because they did wrong. If someone hurts society, then they should help society in return."

First Iago scowled and swung his feet off of his desk, slamming his boots onto the ground. No one flinched, and Falcon thought he saw a twitch of annoyance in the First's eye. He turned back to Falcon.

"I'll humor you for one minute more. Let's say I agree to this. What should the punishment be for our three newest inmates? A fine? It'd be steep indeed. I'm not sure the family can afford the cost."

"You're right," Falcon said mildly. "Fines wouldn't help anyone, except perhaps our order's coffers. And they'd disproportionately affect everyone but the rich. Which is why I suggest community service instead."

First Iago's face fell. "Community service. What is this rot?"

"Exactly what it says on the tin. Candy, Aiden, and Ethan would be required to serve a prescribed number of hours within the wronged neighborhood to make up for the damage they've caused. For other cases, such as with violent offenders or flight risks, we could assign an Enforcer to watch over them and ensure they don't escape or hurt anyone else. But I don't think that would be necessary in this situation."

First Iago sighed heavily. "Well, that's all very pretty thinking for a fantasy land, but this is the real world, Steward Smoke. And as the person responsible for keeping order in this city, I say no."

Falcon swallowed a stone in his throat. "I'm sorry to hear that, sir. In that case, I'll have to tender my resignation." First Iago froze, and Falcon jumped on the opportunity. "If I see any posters around the city with me on them, I'll be sure to tear them down. Since I'll no longer be a member of the order, I can't represent them. And I'll let the publishers know that any royalties earned for the books of my adventures should be sent in their entirety to me."

First Iago could have been a statue for how still he'd gone. Only a single eyebrow went up, pulling the eye beneath into a squint. His voice was soft and dangerous as he said, "You won't get a copper. You performed your little adventures while under Enforcer employ. I own you, Steward."

"I think you'll find your case only stands if Mister Smoke is depicted as an Enforcer in whatever creative works come from our future negotiations." That was Beatrice, cool and stolid and smiling like a lioness.

First Iago betrayed surprise as he swung his gaze round to her. He'd very likely forgotten she was even there.

She went on. "I believe these publishers, who have contacted Mister Smoke directly, are really more interested in *him*. They can easily paint him under any number of other guises or even other time periods. There are even possibilities for setting them in the Old World before the Enforcer order even existed."

First Iago looked to Falcon but gestured at Beatrice. "What is this strumpet even doing here?"

Falcon's anger flared, and his words left his mouth before he had a chance to check them. "Miss Holmes is my legal advocate, sir, and while I am still prepared to negotiate, you are in very real danger of losing that."

First Iago's face scrunched into a series of angry squiggles. "No need to get your knickers in a twist, Steward. A man like you doesn't need anyone, least of all a woman, handling his affairs."

"Every reason to get my knickers in a twist, sir. I'm man enough to know my strengths and contracts isn't one of them. But more than that, you owe Miss Holmes an apology." He almost threatened, "Right now or I walk," but he caught himself, biting the words back. He couldn't go that far, couldn't risk Candy and Aiden and Ethan's welfare.

"Thank you, Mister Smoke," Beatrice replied easily. "That's very kind, but an apology from First Iago won't be necessary. I know my worth far too well to need such things, so let us not waste our increasingly valuable time."

Falcon nodded. And waited. Tension swirled over the room like a slow-motion typhoon. First Iago glowered openly at each person sitting there. His eyes finally rested on Mina, but again, he looked at Falcon.

"What's she doing here?"

Mina answered, not waiting for Falcon. "I'm here about the Crisis Response Unit. You weren't willing to listen to my development plan for them before, but perhaps you will now."

First Iago's eyes remained on Falcon. "I suppose this is part of your price as well?" Falcon nodded, and First Iago grumbled, "Quite a lot you're asking, Steward Smoke."

"As you say, sir, I've created quite a name for myself. The Enforcers need to change, and if I can use my considerable influence to help, then I think I should."

First Iago sat back in his chair and folded his hands over his stomach again. He let out a sigh that said this was the most tiresome thing he'd ever had to deal with. "Let's hear it then."

And so negotiations commenced. Mina had her plan, comprehensive and detailed. Mister Strongbow had his experience as both an inmate and an involved member of the public, which he paired with Falcon's experience as an Enforcer. And Beatrice had her shrewd intelligence and charm. She even managed to pull a few smiles from the First, but it was hard won. The talks went on so long that dinner had to be called up.

In the end, it was agreed that Candy, Aiden, and Ethan would be released and sentenced to community service. Falcon and a rotation of other Cru members would be assigned to watch and observe the results of this new experiment. Additionally, Falcon would now be in charge of reviewing minor crimes and assigning sentences. When Springhaven's new court system was established and judges elected, they would take over the task for all crimes. The group hadn't been able to negotiate on behalf of violent offenders, and there was still the issue of all those already imprisoned, but it was progress. And Falcon mentally tucked both issues away as undertakings for the near-future.

The Crisis Response Unit would officially break away from the rest of the Enforcer order under Mina's supervision. Falcon would have to split his duties between that and adjudicating minor crimes. It looked like he would need to assign some assistant C.O. roles, as both jobs were likely too much for one person to handle entirely alone. But he would get to choose who filled the positions if it came to that. There was a great deal of work to do, and change would be difficult, but Falcon had faith in his team and even himself. As long as he remembered to lean on others when he needed to.

By the end of the meeting, Beatrice had several pages of notes written down for how the publishing contract would have to break down between Falcon, the Cru, and the Enforcer order. That third one, thankfully, would only be getting a fraction of what the other two would—it had been a carrot to help persuade First Iago. Falcon was deeply grateful not to have to handle that side of things. He made a mental note to buy Beatrice a nice bottle of wine... as soon as he could afford it.

Mister Strongbow offered First Iago his hand as he made to leave. First Iago looked skeptical but shook it anyway. Mister Strongbow wished the man a good day and left it at that, which Falcon thought was a real show of strength on Mister Strongbow's part. Mina and Beatrice began to make their way out after him, and Falcon saluted First Iago before turning to follow.

"A moment, Steward Smoke," First Iago said, voice steady. Falcon turned back to him and waited. "Those young people broke into your house and barely left you with scraps. You really don't want to see them get theirs?"

Falcon's reply was just as steady. "It's a violation, yes. I can't tell how awful it feels to lose that peace of mind about the place that's meant to be a safe haven. But repaying pain with pain only begets more pain. For over a hundred years, that's what we've tried, and it hasn't gotten us anywhere good. It only divides us more. My community rallied together for me, did their best to replace what I'd lost. We need to lean into our communities and strengthen them, not hurt and divide each other."

First Iago scoffed. "You sound as if you really believe all that blather."

"I do, sir. Which is why I've fought so hard for it today."

"Indeed." A long pause ensued. "Stay for a drink, Steward?"

"No, thank you, sir. I need to go find my sweetheart and make up. You see, we quarreled, and I've got to make it right."

"Ah, I didn't know you had yourself a lady. What's her name?"

"*His* name is Keene." And Falcon couldn't help but smile sadly. "He's my lily of the valley, my return to happiness."

And with that, Falcon saluted again and left, leaving First Iago looking utterly flabbergasted.

Outside the office, Beatrice waited with Mister Strongbow and Mina. Goodbyes were exchanged from the latter two, while Beatrice hung back, chatting with First Iago's secretary. Or rather, the secretary was trying very hard to remain cold and taciturn to her charms. After Mina and Mister Strongbow left, Beatrice joined Falcon at his side again, and they began to walk out.

"Falcon, would you like to come back to mine for a celebratory drink?" she asked lightly. "I think we really have rather earned it."

"Thank you, Beatrice, but I told First Iago back there that I need to find Keene and make up with him."

Beatrice's eyes remained forward as they walked. Something new rang in her voice when she replied, "I really think you ought to come back to mine."

Falcon looked at her out of the corner of his eye. "Are you the friend with whom he's staying?"

"The choice is yours, Falcon."

Something twisted in his stomach, a mixture of eagerness and anxiety. With meaning in his voice, he thanked her. She only nodded blithely to that, and they made the long walk back down to the ground level and out to where the Holmes' private coach waited. On the lush velvet seat within, a small, scuffed strongbox sat. Falcon took it into his lap like precious cargo and hoped that it would be enough to start healing what had broken between him and Keene.

~Chapter 25~

The Holmeses' manor was grander than even the Smoke family home where Falcon had grown up. He'd been there enough times to know his way around the tastefully appointed corridors pretty well, but he didn't know where to go today, where Keene might be holed up in that vast place. Thankfully, Beatrice led without needing to say anything beyond mild chatter about nothing particularly important. It was filler, and they both knew it.

Finally, they arrived at a set of doors near Beatrice's private parlor. Falcon surmised they led to a set of apartments—Beatrice wouldn't be caught dead not providing her friends with the very best in her own home. Just inside, he knew there'd be a sitting room with comfortable chairs and couches.

She knocked. "Keene, it's me. May I come in, please?"

"Of course, my dear," came Keene's jovial response from behind the doors. "Let me just..."

Beatrice didn't wait for him and instead threw both of them open herself. She didn't push Falcon through, per se. Rather, she took advantage of his gentlemanly training, hooked her arm through his, and then suddenly he was inside the room.

"I'll just leave you two be, shall I?" she said sweetly.

And without waiting for an answer, she shut the doors behind

Falcon, leaving the two gents staring blankly at one another. Falcon looked back behind him, collecting his wits. When his gaze returned to Keene, baffled words simply dropped from his mouth.

"She is a force of nature."

"She certainly is." Keene was staring at the doorway a touch sadly. "I asked her not to tell you I was here."

"She didn't," Falcon was quick to say. "She really didn't."

Keene sighed. "No, but she probably gave you *a look* or something and sent some silent signal."

Falcon laughed weakly. "Yes, that about sums it up."

Keene shrugged and the sadness seemed to slide back off of him like a too-large jacket. "I know she only did it because she cares about us."

"Yes." Silence invaded the space like a poltergeist after that. Falcon shifted the strongbox in his hands and suddenly remembered his goal. Holding it out to Keene, he said, "This is yours. It looks a little worse for wear, but otherwise intact. Candy said she meant to break into it using some of Mister Halpern's tools but hadn't gotten the chance yet."

"Thank you." Keene stared at the box a little fearfully. His voice lacked conviction as he added, "That's good news."

Slowly, carefully, he took it from Falcon's outstretched hands. Keene looked at it for a long moment before carefully setting it aside and returning his attention to Falcon. Without the strongbox, Falcon's hands no longer had a job, and he shoved them into his pockets, trying not to hunch his shoulders.

When the silence stretched on too long again, he said, "Well, I suppose I should go then… if you'd rather not see me, but I wanted —"

"Please don't—" Keene broke in.

"I just wanted to say I'm sorry," Falcon hurried to say. It was too important not to get out.

"—go."

Both stopped. Both stared at each other, eyes hopeful but faces sad.

"You don't want me to go?" Falcon ventured quietly.

"No," Keene replied. Then, after a pause. "I interrupted you. I'm sorry."

"I want to apologize." Falcon rushed the words again as regret tried to crush his windpipe and block his progress. He wouldn't let fear hold him back anymore, and he pulled a small bouquet from inside of his jacket. "This is for you."

He handed Keene the arrangement, which consisted of a single bloom each of hyacinth to beg forgiveness, rue for regret, honeysuckle for devotion, and bluebell for faithfulness. Keene twirled it slowly between his fingers, examining each flower.

"I know words aren't enough," Falcon said. "I was such a thoughtless heel. I'm so sorry, Keene. I…"

He trailed off as Keene closed the distance between them and placed a finger against Falcon's lips. The feel of Keene so close again, his skin against Falcon's, made the pain Falcon had been holding within melt away.

"I believe you," Keene said. He lowered his hand, resting it against Falcon's chest. "And I'm sorry too. I acted rashly. I should have stayed and talked things out. And I hope you know I wasn't about to leave you with the rent and all. I wouldn't do that to you. I cherish you, Falcon."

Falcon reached up and placed his hands over Keene's. "I know. But I need you to know I'm not embarrassed about us. I don't want to hide you. I want everyone to know how much I adore you. I even told First Iago about you." Falcon's mouth turned up into a crooked little half-smile. "I told him you were my lily of the valley."

A bright, glorious smile bloomed across Keene's face, and he stroked his fingertips over the inside of Falcon's wrist in the most delicious way. Falcon brought his face close. Their lips met, and it was like tea, warm and sweet and smoky and deep.

A soft knock rattled beside them just before Beatrice poked her head back in, through the door the two weren't leaning against. "Oh, here you are." She seemed completely nonplussed by the fact that Falcon and Keene were locked in an intimate embrace. "Keene, my dear, this just came for you." She reached through the partially open doorway holding a large note sealed with purple wax. Keene took it, still holding onto Falcon.

"Thank you, petal," Keene purred.

She smiled at the two and left without another word. Also without a word, Keene took Falcon by the hand and led him over to a long sofa. When Falcon rounded it, he saw Luffy curled up in one corner next to the arm. She opened her eyes and lurched to her feet, curly tail wagging. As Falcon took a seat next to Keene, pressed against his side, he scooped up the little dog and gave her a cuddle while Keene examined his mail. On Keene's other side was the strongbox now.

Also on the couch, Falcon noticed, was a newssheet. A rather dramatic illustration of him graced the front page. In the depiction, as he rode Pegs his hair streamed behind him, at least twice as long as its actual, admittedly short, length. More newssheets and even a few tabloids sat neatly stacked on the nearest console table.

Keene must have caught Falcon looking at them, because he said, "I've read several of the accounts, but that one's my favorite." He pointed at the one with the long-haired illustration and grinned mischievously. "It says you leapt over an entire family who were crossing the road at just the wrong time."

Falcon groaned and shook his head. "I'm never going to live this down."

Keene's smile softened, and he raised a careful hand to Falcon's face, examining the welt across his cheek and then the bandage on his head. "Probably, but I'm glad you lived to not live it down." He kissed both injuries softly before taking Falcon's hand in his and returning to his mail.

"So this is from the museum," he said, curiosity coloring his voice.

"Odd," Falcon agreed. "You don't have any connection with them, do you?"

Keene shook his head and opened the letter. As he looked over the words, his face lit up like a sun. "They want to hire me for a big event they've got coming up. Falcon, this is tremendous! They're expecting close to a thousand people." Keene extracted a smaller sheet of paper, which Falcon recognized as a promissory note.

"Keene, that's brilliant!" Falcon squeezed him around the middle and planted a massive kiss on his cheek. "What's it for?"

"Something to do with a meteor shower. I'll get more details later."

He turned and pressed his lips to Falcon's. Falcon eagerly reciprocated, savoring the taste of Keene's mouth again. Heavens, he hadn't realized how much he'd missed this. Fire passed between them, and Falcon went for the buttons of Keene's shirt almost as quickly as Keene went for his. A moment later, however, just as Falcon had gotten two undone, Keene gently pushed him away.

"Better not," he said breathlessly. "The Holmeses have been very kind in letting me stay here. It wouldn't do for me to tear your clothes off you and use their furniture to…" He left the statement hanging in the air, teasing Falcon.

Falcon groaned as his excitement grew, but his lover was right. There would be plenty of time for that later.

Keene played his fingers across the skin of Falcon's now exposed clavicle. "It's hard, though—"

"I know. I can feel it," Falcon teased.

Keene's hips were turned toward Falcon, his gentleman's area pressed against Falcon's thigh.

Keene ran a hand along Falcon's hips. "Look who's talking."

Falcon kissed him again, short and sweet, and said, "We need something to calm us down." In unison, they looked over to the strongbox. After a moment, Falcon asked gently. "Do you feel ready?"

Keene disentangled himself from Falcon. "After everything that's happened, I bloody well ought to be."

As Keene pulled the strongbox into his lap, Falcon stretched an arm out behind him, resting his hand on Keene's shoulder.

"I'm here," Falcon whispered into Keene's ear before tenderly kissing it.

Keene twisted his head and kissed Falcon's nose. "I know. Thank you."

From his pocket, Keene drew a key and inserted it into the lock. It opened with a click, and Keene slowly lifted the lid. Various papers and a few bits and bobs littered the inside, but Keene knew right where to go. A letter sealed with green wax sat at the bottom. It simply bore Keene's name in bold, straight handwriting. Falcon gave his sweetheart another kiss against his temple for strength, and Keene took a deep breath. He popped open the seal and lifted the top flap. Falcon caught the words, "To Keene, my beloved son," written at the top before looking away. This wasn't his business; Keene would share with him if he wished.

Side by side, pressed close, they sat while Keene read the letter from his father, written months ago. Only when a small sob escaped Keene's throat did Falcon look back. Keene covered his mouth with a hand, eyes brimming with tears. Falcon asked for nothing, only kissed Keene again.

"He's not angry," Keene whispered at last. "He says he loves me and that he's sorry for what he said. He was hurt. He felt like, by rejecting the family legacy, I was rejecting *him*. But he says he knows that's not true. And he's frightened for me, striking out on my own." Keene looked back to Falcon. "But he says he loves me, and that he believes I'll do spectacularly."

Tears pricked at Falcon's eyes too. He smiled so hard his face hurt. "That's splendid! I'm so happy for you."

Keene pressed his lips against Falcon's before looking back down at the letter in wonder. "I've got to write him back. I've got to apologize for waiting so long. Oh, Falcon, I have so much time to make up for."

Falcon kissed him again. "It's alright. You will." Another kiss. "He'll understand." A third kiss. "And, if you want, I'll be there with you."

Keene wrapped his arms around Falcon, who pulled him into his lap. Luffy came bounding up, and Falcon and Keene both spared a hand to pet her. They kissed again, tears slipping down their faces. Falcon could feel Keene's joy streaming from every touch. It energized Falcon, and a lifetime of possibilities with Keene stretched out before him in his mind's eye.

"I will stand behind you no matter what, my sweet, sweet return to happiness."

~*~

If you enjoyed this book, please consider leaving a review on Goodreads and/or Amazon. Even a single line is massively helpful. Thank you in advance for taking the time to share your thoughts.

To get more goodies from Dana, consider joining her Patreon at https://www.patreon.com/wordsbydana

You can also sign up for early updates, cover reveals, and exclusive content by joining her VIP newsletter. You can sign up for that on her website: https://www.wordsbydana.com/

Otherwise, read on for more from the Broken Gears universe.

Dana Fraedrich

~An Excerpt from Out of the Shadows~

She wasn't going down without a fight. Maybe by some miracle she'd catch a break and get free again. Lenore drove both elbows back as hard as she could, which may have just worked if it weren't for the fact that she and her captor were already falling backwards. She landed on something soft in complete darkness and was on her feet again in less than a second. There was that complete darkness thing, though. When she had been running a moment ago, her path had been lit by the soft glow of petrolsene lights and the moon. Where was she now? Lenore backed up until she hit a wall and remained ready to fight. She began inching her way to the side, thinking there might be a door somewhere. The sound of heavy boots running approached and then faded, followed a few moments later by a single match light. The match light became an oil lamp, and the area all around Lenore was suddenly bathed in a warm, yellow glow. She saw the man first, gingerly holding his arm across his abdomen. She was about to cry out, "You!" but a delicate hand clamped itself over her mouth with a determination that belied its delicacy.

"Shhhh!" a female voice hissed in her ear. "Do you want to get us all caught?"

Lenore did not try to speak, but shook her head earnestly. Of course she didn't, but what did her would-be accusers have to worry about?

"I'm going to let go of you now, but you must stay silent. Understand?" the woman said firmly.

Lenore nodded this time and was released. The woman joined the man and began to poke and prod him in a way that looked more like a medical examination than anything else. The man made no move to stop her, and Lenore watched them both warily. Finally, when the woman seemed satisfied, she kissed the man on the cheek and turned her attention back to Lenore. She glanced at what Lenore could now see as a cellar door and motioned for her to follow. Lenore had no desire to do any such thing, but couldn't think of a better idea. There were Enforcers outside looking for her, but these two could just be planning to turn her in later. That logic didn't really make sense, though. If they had any kind of sense, they wouldn't waste time that the Enforcers could use to accuse them of helping Lenore. Besides, there were no Enforcers inside…as far as Lenore knew, anyway. That being the case, she followed, but at a distance that kept her safe from the couple's reaching arms in case they tried to grab her again.

The three walked up a narrow staircase and up into a large kitchen replete with a potbelly stove large enough to cook an entire lamb in. From the kitchen they walked through a butler's closet—*closet my eye,* Lenore thought—and into a grand dining room. The woman motioned for Lenore to sit, which she refused to do with a defiant glare.

"Suit yourself," said the woman with a very unladylike shrug.

She then sat while the man stood behind her and put his hands on her shoulders.

"First of all," the man said kindly, "let me apologize. I am deeply, deeply sorry for drawing attention to you. We did not mean for you to be discovered."

Lenore was very confused and intrigued by this, but still said nothing.

"Allow me to make the introductions," the man continued. "I am Sir Gwenael Allen and this is my lovely wife, Philomena."

"Mina will do just fine," the woman interjected suddenly, giving her husband's hand a squeeze.

He smiled and added, "You may call me Neal."

Lenore didn't call either of them anything. She simply remained silent, wondering whether or not she could make it out the cellar without being caught.

"We're not going to turn you in," Mina said after several moments.

"Why not?" were the first words Lenore said to the couple.

The two shared a smile that seemed to hold a great meaning for them and then turned back to Lenore.

"We do not…agree with the severity with which criminal punishment is exacted," Neal explained.

"Don't think that means we condone criminal behavior either, however," Mina added firmly, giving Lenore a hard glare.

"Well, I appreciate you hiding me and all. Trust me, I really do," Lenore said defensively, "but, seeing as how my criminal behavior is going to continue, I'll just be on my way."

Lenore turned to leave, but Mina spoke again with such force that Lenore stopped in her tracks.

"And just what is so important for you to get back to?"

Lenore narrowed her eyes at the woman there who was now standing tall and ramrod straight. She didn't like the woman. Who was this stuck up peacock to think she had any business asking Lenore such personal questions?

"Thank you both again," Lenore snipped. "Good night." With that she turned on her heel and left the way she came.

)(

Bitsy was waiting for Lenore back at the attic when she arrived just before dawn. It wasn't really an attic so much as dead space between the attics of her parent's old house and the one attached next door. It grew almost unbearably hot in the summer and bone achingly cold in the winter, as simple wooden walls were all that separated Lenore from the outside. She'd discovered the space when she was little, having accidentally found the hidden latch to the small door and crawling through. She'd found a similar entrance on the neighbor's side and jammed the handle with some scrap metal. Thankfully, no one on the other side seemed to know about the space. At least, Lenore had never heard anyone try to get in. If they did, she didn't know what she'd do or where she would go.

Lenore had to move in her cramped little space carefully, always being as silent and stealthy as fog creeping over the earth, lest the neighbors or new occupants of her parent's old house heard her. She only ever came and went when it was properly dark outside, sneaking out via a window in the attic and the large tree growing just outside.

As for Bitsy, Lenore never worried about her little companion; it was easy for him to disappear when necessary. He was sitting on a rafter when she came in and leapt down to greet her ecstatically. The little creature nuzzled her neck and wrapped his long bushy tail around it as he chattered happily.

"I'm glad to see you too," Lenore sighed. "That was a close one tonight. Glad I caught a break for once…"

Lenore's mind drifted back to the couple that had saved her from certain torture. They were certainly different, odd maybe, but they had been kind, and Lenore had not experienced real kindness in a long time. Oh well, it was done now. Lenore took just enough time to fill her stomach with some stale bread and dodgy-looking cheese before falling asleep to the sounds of a waking city.

)(

Ninth Year of the New Age, Second Day of the Earth
Official report submitted by Fifths Campbell and Ellis:

We were alerted and gave chase to a thief this evening. The thief was preying on citizens visiting the gardens. Cries from the latest victims—a Mister Malachite Nichols and Miss Temperance Hester—alerted us to the trouble just after a quarter past twelve as we patrolled our usual route. Mister Nichols reported a prized piece of Old World Jade as stolen. See the end of this report for a record of the eyewitnesses' descriptions of the thief*. As we began pursuit, the perpetrator made for the Rose quarter of the city. Visual contact was difficult to maintain through the alleys she took between the manors. She disappeared completely somewhere between the Chicory Lane and Anemone Green. We recommend working with local shopkeepers and residents to put up barriers and fences to block these types of escape paths.

Eyewitness Description Report: Female, small, probably about fourteen years of age. Most likely a vagrant, judging by the clothing, which was black, made for a boy, and very shabby. Very dark eyes and long, dark hair. Light skin.

*We understand there were two other eyewitnesses, but they disappeared before we arrived, and neither Mister Nichols nor Miss Hester could name them or remember anything about them.

Dana Fraedrich

~Acknowledgements~

This book is lovingly dedicated to all of those who have helped me find where I fit in the world and welcomed me as I moved to fill that spot.

I wrote this book during lockdown in 2020. During that time, I not only wanted happy, safe, cozy fiction to escape into, but I found it was the only thing I could write as well. Writing is hard at the best of times. When all the uncertainty of a global pandemic is breathing down your neck 24/7, not to mention all the other garbage happening in the world... Well, I want to thank those authors who came before me with warm, silly, fun stories to remind me how much comfort books can bring—Terry Pratchett, Gail Carriger, Ellie Alexander, Mackenzi Lee, and P.G. Wodehouse, just to name a few.

And, as I've said many times before, though writing is a very solitary career, there are so many people who contributed to this book becoming a reality. In no particular order...

Thank you to my incredible editor, Rachel Oestreich of The Wallflower Editing. I was really nervous about hiring a new editor, but working with you was a true delight. Editing is never easy for me, but your suggestions were so on point and well explained. This book is miles better for you having worked on it with me.

To Sally, who understands me through and through, as well as the awkward nuances of relationships with people who we, "only know in passing, merely through proximity alone."

To all my Patreon patrons for their wonderful, continued support: Shannon Lee, Alison Sky Richards, Murky Master, Rebecca Williams, Arbor Winter Barrow, and DJ Gray. And, in addition, especially to Doug Peterson for the myriad research resources he's sent me.

To Nicole Jones, for the outstanding audio editing work and for gifting me the book, *Floriography* by Jessica Roux. It was referenced many, many times in the writing of this book.

My husband, Mike, for all the hard work you do and are continuing to do for the both of us. In all the ways that means. I love you and I'm so glad I'm married to you.

Scout Underhill, I count you among my dearest friends and I don't think I'd be the person I am today without you. Thank you so much for all the support and encouragement and love you've always shown. Also, friends, Scout is an amazing graphic novelist. You should check out their web comic, DnDoggos, and their forthcoming DnDoggos graphic novels. Dogs playing TTRPGs. What's not to love?

I want to shout out Stacey Rourke of The Blurb Doctor. Y'all, I hate writing blurbs. Hate. It! What a relief it was, as I was typing up the information for this book, to know someone who's way better at blurbs than me (and probably doesn't despise it) would be wrangling that task. What an even bigger relief when it came back and it was so, so good! Blurb writers, y'all. Magic.

Thank you to Heather, who's always willing to hear me whinge about writing problems, even when she has no context for what I'm banging on about. Sorry no one died in this one, though. ;)

Thank you to my parents, who imparted skills and experiences to me that have helped shape who I am today. From my mom introducing me to tea at a young age to my dad always opening his bookshelf to me. Thank you for being wonderful parents.

A.E. Gill, who is also a fantastic author, is everything I could ever ask for in both a critique partner and a friend. I've learned so much from you. Thank you for always being willing to hear about ideas and struggles and all the writing things and for always encouraging me. I look forward to our weekly chats so very much.

Megan, thank you for being such an amazing reader. You have no idea how much your love for my books means to me.

Brandon, thank you for bringing the audiobook to life with your incredible voice work and dedication.

A huge, huge thank you to all my ARC readers. Reviews are such a vital piece of the book publishing process. Even just a single line makes such an impact.

Paul Hollywood, thank you for making a GBBO technical challenge so infuriatingly unfair that I felt the need to put it in a book.

And last, but certainly not least, thank you, dear reader, for picking up this book, for buying it, and giving it your valuable time and attention. Thank you also to those who have pushed this book onto a friend. I know the weight a good friend's book recommendation carries, so thank you for using your influence to support me. And thank you to the friends who had this book pushed onto them. I also know the trust that can require, and I appreciate you taking a chance on me on nothing more than the word of your friend.

A great many thanks to all of you. I wish each and every one of you nothing but the best for your lives.

~About the Author~

Dana Fraedrich is a dog lover, self-professed geek, and author of the steampunk fantasy series Broken Gears, which includes the Amazon bestseller, *Out of the Shadows*. Dana's books are full of secrets and colorful characters that examine the many shades of grey that paint the world. When she isn't busy writing or attending book shows and author conferences, she can be found playing video games and frolicking among the Bookstagram community (the bookish corner of Instagram).

Even from a young age, she enjoyed writing down the stories that she imagined in her mind. Born and raised in Virginia, she earned her BFA from Roanoke College and is now carving out her own happily ever after in Nashville, TN with her husband and two dogs. Dana is always writing; more books are on the way!

If you enjoyed reading this book, please leave a review. Even it's just one line to say you liked it, that really helps independent authors like Dana continue to create kick-awesome things for you!

Find Dana online at www.wordsbydana.com
Facebook: https://www.facebook.com/wordsbydana/
@danafraedrich on Twitter, TikTok, and Instagram
Follow Dana on Goodreads or her Amazon Author page
Or you can support her on Patreon and Ko-fi
Sign up for exclusive access to Dana's VIP Newsletter, short stories, and giveaways on her website

Thanks!

www.ingramcontent.com/pod-product-compliance
Lightning Source LLC
LaVergne TN
LVHW041700060526
838201LV00043B/502